Praise for *Birth of Our Power*

"Nothing in it has dated. . . . It is less an autobiography than a sustained, incandescent lyric (half-pantheist, half-surrealist) of rebellion and battle."
—*Times Literary Supplement*

"Surely one of the most moving accounts of revolutionary experience ever written."
—Neal Ascherson, *New York Review of Books*

"Probably the most remarkable of his novels. . . . Of all the European writers who have taken revolution as their theme, Serge is second only to Conrad. . . . Here is a writer with a magnificent eye for the panoramic sweep of historical events and an unsparingly precise moral insight."
—Francis King, *Sunday Telegraph*

"Intense, vivid, glowing with energy and power . . . A wonderful picture of revolution and revolutionaries. . . . The power of the novel is in its portrayal of the men who are involved."
—*Manchester Evening News*

"*Birth of Our Power* is one of the finest romances of revolution ever written, and confirms Serge as an outstanding chronicler of his turbulent era. . . . As an epic, *Birth of Our Power* has lost none of its strength."
—Lawrence M. Bensky, *New York Times*

Birth of Our Power

Editor: Sasha Lilley

Spectre is a series of penetrating and indispensable works of, and about, radical political economy. Spectre lays bare the dark underbelly of politics and economics, publishing outstanding and contrarian perspectives on the maelstrom of capital—and emancipatory alternatives—in crisis. The companion Spectre Classics imprint unearths essential works of radical history, political economy, theory and practice, to illuminate the present with brilliant, yet unjustly neglected, ideas from the past.

Spectre

Greg Albo, Sam Gindin, and Leo Panitch, *In and Out of Crisis: The Global Financial Meltdown and Left Alternatives*

David McNally, *Global Slump: The Economics and Politics of Crisis and Resistance*

Sasha Lilley, *Capital and Its Discontents: Conversations with Radical Thinkers in a Time of Tumult*

Sasha Lilley, David McNally, Eddie Yuen, and James Davis, *Catastrophism: The Apocalyptic Politics of Collapse and Rebirth*

Peter Linebaugh, *Stop, Thief! The Commons, Enclosures, and Resistance*

Spectre Classics

E.P. Thompson, *William Morris: Romantic to Revolutionary*

Victor Serge, *Men in Prison*

Victor Serge, *Birth of Our Power*

Birth of Our Power

Victor Serge

Translated and introduced by Richard Greeman

SPECTRE
CLASSICS

Birth of Our Power
Victor Serge. Translated by Richard Greeman
Copyright © Victor Serge Foundation
Translation, introduction, and postface © 2014 Richard Greeman
This edition © 2014 PM Press
First published as *Naissance de notre force*. Paris: Les Editions Rieder, 1931.

ISBN: 978–1–62963–030–4

Library of Congress Control Number: 2014908064

Cover by John Yates / Stealworks
Interior design by briandesign

10 9 8 7 6 5 4 3 2 1

PM Press
PO Box 23912
Oakland, CA 94623
www.pmpress.org

Printed in the USA by the Employee Owners of Thomson-Shore in Dexter, Michigan. www.thomsonshore.com

Contents

Introduction

by Richard Greeman

Birth of Our Power is an epic novel set in Spain, France, and Russia during the heady revolutionary years 1917–1919. It was composed a decade later in Leningrad by a remarkable witness-participant, the Franco-Russian writer and revolutionary Victor Serge (1890–1947).[1] Serge's tale begins in the spring of 1917, in the third year of insane mass slaughter in the blood- and rain-soaked trenches of World War I, when the flames of revolution suddenly erupt in Russia and Spain. Europe is "burning at both ends." In February, the Russian people overthrow the Czar, while in neutral Spain militant anarcho-syndicalist workers allied with middle-class Catalan nationalists rise up in mass strikes aimed at taking power. Although the Spanish uprising eventually fizzles, in Russia the workers, peasants, and common soldiers are able to take power and hold it. *Birth of Our Power* chronicles that double movement.

Serge's novel follows an anonymous narrator's odyssey from Barcelona to Petrograd,[2] from one red city to the other, from the romanticism of radicalized workers awakening to their own power in a sun-drenched Spanish metropolis to the grim reality of workers clinging to power in Russia's dark, frozen revolutionary outpost. Where Dickens constructed his *Tale of Two Cities* around the opposition between conservative London ('white') and revolutionary Paris ('red') Serge's novel is based on the opposition of two cites, both red: Barcelona, the city 'we' could not take, and Petrograd—the starving capital of the Russian Revolution, besieged by counterrevolutionary whites.

Like Homer's Odysseus and Virgil's Aeneas, Serge's nameless narrator is fated to pass through the Underworld on his two-year odyssey from the defeated revolution to the victorious one. He spends over a

---

[1]   Please see the postface in this volume, "Victor Serge, Writer and Revolutionary," for an overview of his life and works.

[2]   The once and future 'St. Petersburg.' In Soviet times, 'Leningrad.'

year in French World War I concentration camps for subversives. The novel ends in Petrograd with something of an anti-climax: The city of victorious revolution, the city where 'we' have taken power, is revealed not as a vast tumultuous forum, but as a grim, half-empty metropolis, "not at all dead, but savagely turned in on itself, in the terrible cold, the silence, the hate, the will to live, the will to conquer."

Whereas the defeat in Barcelona is partially transformed into a victory by the heroic exaltation of the masses newly awakened to a sense of their own power, in Petrograd, the original question of "Can we take power?" is superseded by an even more difficult one: "Can we survive and learn to use that power?" The novel thus plays on the ironic themes of 'victory-in-defeat' (Barcelona) and 'defeat-in-victory' (Petrograd).

Autobiography into Fiction
Serge lived it all. The novel follows its author's own two-year itinerary across war-torn Europe from an aborted revolt in Spain to the promise of a victorious revolution in Russia, but strange to say, the novel is not really autobiographical. Serge's anonymous narrator is little more than a 'camera eye' giving multiple perspectives on the action. He has no personal life. He never gets to speak a line, only to observe and narrate. Indeed, the pronoun 'I' appears only once or twice per chapter. The fraternal 'we,' the first-person plural, is Serge's preferred part of speech, beginning with the very first sentence, indeed with the title.

> I feel an aversion to using "I" as a vain affirmation of the self, containing a good dose of illusion and another of vanity or arrogance. Whenever possible, that is to say whenever I am not feeling isolated, when my experience highlights in some way or other that of people with whom I feel linked, I prefer to employ the pronoun "we," which is truer and more general. We never live only by our own efforts, we never live only for ourselves; our most intimate, our most personal thinking is connected by a thousand links with that of the world."[3]

Serge's novel presents these events in a kaleidoscoping series of tableaux studded with 'epiphanies'—realistic incidents that unveil transcendent social truths. Given *Birth of Our Power*'s somewhat disjointed, cinematographic style—no doubt influenced by such modernist

---

3   *Memoirs of a Revolutionary* (New York: NYRB Classics, 2012), 53.

masterpieces as Andrei Biely's *St. Petersburg*, Boris Pilnyak's *Naked Year*, and John Dos Passos's *USA*—readers are often at a loss as to how to contextualize the novel's rapid succession of impressionistic scenes in terms of real-world politics and history.

The opening pages of *Birth of Our Power* are steeped in symbolism and poetic beauty, but they may prove exasperating for the reader who does not share the author's intimacy with Spanish revolutionary history. Indeed, Serge never refers to Barcelona by name, only as 'this city.' And it is only through passing references to the War in Europe that we are able to place the events there historically.

For most readers, the phrase 'Spanish Revolution' brings to mind the 1936–39 Civil War. But in fact the Spanish revolutionary tradition, with all its passion and brutality, goes back much further, to Napoleonic times (think of Goya's *Disasters of War*). Throughout the nineteenth century, repeated attempts to establish liberal government in Spain resulted only in bloody fusillades and paper reforms. Spain entered the twentieth century, after its stunning defeat by the United States in 1898, as a backward, corrupt, priest-and-soldier-ridden monarchy. The anarchism of the Russian Bakunin caught the imagination of the peasants and of the workers in the new industrial centers like Barcelona, and their revolt took the form of *jacqueries* and individual terrorism—a situation similar to that in even more backward Czarist Russia.

The monarchy's response to social unrest was the establishment of a new Inquisition responsible for wholesale arrests and executions and for the brutal torture of anyone even remotely connected with the revolutionary movement. The judicial murder at Montjuich, the craggy mountain fortress that overlooks the city in Serge's opening pages, of Francisco Ferrer, the progressive educationalist, blamed for the 1909 general strike, raised a worldwide storm of protest, including street battles in Paris, in which nineteen-year-old Serge took part. In *Birth of Our Power*, the citadel of Montjuich, where many rebels had been tortured and shot, becomes the symbol both of the revolutionary past and the oppressive power of the present.

The immediate cause of the uprisings of the summer of 1917 in Barcelona was the increased confidence of both the bourgeoisie and the working class of Catalonia during the World War I industrial boom. Neutral Spain was making money hand over fist selling to both sides. The bourgeois nationalists of the Lliga Regionalista were in the forefront of the fight against the autocracy, and for them the fight was for increased regional autonomy and a democracy. The Lliga fixed the date of July 19, 1917, for the calling of an assembly. The anarcho-syndicalists of the CNT (National Labor Confederation) criticized this movement as a nationalist diversion by the bourgeoisie in order to sidetrack the imminent and inevitable worker's revolution, but supported it nonetheless. The workers hoped that Catalan bourgeoisie would assist them in carrying out a Spanish version of Russia's February Revolution. Serge's *Memoirs* recount that "three months after the news of the Russian Revolution, the Comité Obrero began to prepare a revolutionary general strike, entered negotiations for a political alliance with the Catalan liberal bourgeoisie, and calmly planned the overthrow of the monarchy."[4] What is remarkable in these forgotten pages of history is the extent to which the Spanish workers were inspired by the February Revolution in distant Russia. According to Serge, "the demands of the Workers' Committee, established in June 1917 and published by *Solidaridad Obrero* ('Workers' Solidarity') anticipated the accomplishments of Soviet Russia." On the basis of this historical coincidence, Serge's novel develops his theme of power in complex counterpoint.

Serge arrived in Barcelona in February 1917, fresh out of a French penitentiary[5]—expelled to Spain after serving five years straight time for his implication in the notorious 1913 trial of the Tragic Bandits of French anarchism. It was in Barcelona, in April 1917, that Victor Kibalchich, heretofore best known by his anarcho-individualist *nom de guerre* 'The Maverick' (Le Rétif), first began signing his articles 'Victor Serge.' Significantly, the subject was the fall of the Czar, and the name-change symbolized Victor's simultaneous political rebirth and return to his Russian roots.[6]

Victor soon found a job working as a printer at the firm of Auber i Pla, earning poverty wages of four pesetas (about eighty American cents) for a nearly twelve-hour working day and joined the small, thirty-member printers' union there. Within a few weeks, he and his workmates were swept up in the growing wave of social unrest. Soon

---

4   *Memoirs of a Revolutionary*, 63.
5   The setting for his first novel, *Men in Prison* (Oakland: PM Press, 2014).
6   Victor Serge, "Un zar cae," *Tierra y libertad*, Barcelona, April 4, 1917, 1.

accepted by the local revolutionaries, Victor became an intimate of their outstanding leader, Salvador Seguí, affectionately known as *Nay del Sucre* ('Sugarplum'), the inspiration for the character of Dario in *Birth of Our Power*. Here is how Serge recalled Seguí in his *Memoirs*, where he is introduced as "Barcelona's hero of the hour, the quickening spirit, the uncrowned leader, the fearless man of politics who distrusted politicians."

> A worker, and usually dressed like a worker coming home from the job, cloth cap squashed down on his skull, shirt collar unbuttoned under his cheap tie; tall, strapping, round-headed, his features rough, his eyes big, shrewd, and sly under heavy lids, of an ordinary degree of ugliness, but intensely charming to meet and with his whole self displaying an energy that was lithe and dogged, practical, intelligent, and without the slightest affectation. To the Spanish working-class movement he brought a new role: that of the superb organizer. He was no anarchist, but rather a libertarian, quick to scoff at resolutions on "harmonious life under the sun of liberty," "the blossoming of the self," or "the future society"; he posed instead the immediate problems of wages, organization, rents, and revolutionary power. And that was his tragedy: he could not allow himself to raise aloud this central problem, that of power. I think we were the only ones to discuss it in private. . . . Together with Seguí, I followed the negotiations between the Catalan liberal bourgeoisie and the Comité Obrero. It was a dubious alliance, in which the partners feared, justifiably mistrusted, and subtly outmaneuvered one another. Seguí summed up the position: "They would like to use us and then do us down. For the moment, we are useful in their game of political blackmail. Without us they can do nothing: we have the streets, the shock troops, the brave hearts among the people. We know this, but we need them. They stand for money, trade, possible legality (at the beginning, anyway), the press, public opinion, etc."[7]

Serge recalled having been pessimistic about the possibilities of victory in such a poorly prepared fight, allied with a class whose interests the workers didn't share. "Unless there's a complete victory, which I don't believe in, they're ready to abandon us at the first difficulty. We're

---

7   *Memoirs of a Revolutionary*, 64–65.

betrayed in advance." The Workers' Committee, entirely too Bakuninist, failed to fully analyze the situation and prepare for all eventualities. They were certain of taking Barcelona, but what about Madrid? And the rest of Spain? Would they overthrow the monarchy?

Power. This, Victor saw, was the problem, the only one that counted. And no one in Barcelona seemed to be posing it besides him and Seguí. Once the city was taken, then what? How was it to be governed? "We had no other example before our eyes but that of the Paris Commune of 1871, and seen from up close it wasn't encouraging: lack of determination, division, needless blather, competition between men lacking in eminence." What was lacking was a head. "Masses overflowing with energy, impelled by a great, inchoate idealism, many good rank and file militants, and no head." And all these lacks could be laid at the feet of the anarchists who didn't want to hear about the seizure of power. "They refused to see that the Workers' Committee, once victorious, would be Catalonia's government of tomorrow."

The February Revolution in Russia was also headless, and as Serge had accurately seen from Barcelona, it was soon co-opted by socialist lawyers who continued to send the poor peasants into the trenches while denying them the land reform for which they had made the revolution. But the Russian Revolution did not remain headless for long, and with the return of exiled revolutionaries like Trotsky and Lenin in April 1917 it found its leaders: organized professional revolutionaries who were not afraid of taking power. Serge's lifelong admiration for these leaders, despite his reservations and criticisms, is rooted in this fact. On the other hand, political power, even in the hands of the purest revolutionaries, is a double-edged sword, ready to turn against the revolution itself. This irony of 'defeat in victory' in Petrograd becomes palpable in the final chapters of *Birth of Our Power* and is the central theme of Serge's next novel, the ironically titled *Conquered City* (1932).

In an imaginary dialogue with Dario, the narrator of *Birth of Our Power* sums up his feelings about the June 1917 Barcelona uprising and its predictable defeat titled 'Meditation on Victory':

> Tomorrow is full of greatness. We will not have brought this victory to ripeness in vain. This city will be taken, if not by our hands, at least by others like ours, but stronger. Stronger perhaps for having been better hardened, thanks to our very weakness. If we are beaten, other men, infinitely different from us, infinitely like

us, will walk, on a similar evening, in ten years, in twenty years (how long is really without importance) down this *rambla*, meditating on the same victory. Perhaps they will think about our blood. Even now I think I see them and I am thinking about their blood, which will flow too. But they will take the city.

These lines, penned in Leningrad in 1930, turned out to be prophetic. Five years later, in 1936–1937, the Barcelona workers were 'in the saddle,' to use Orwell's classic expression. By then, Serge's friend Seguí had been murdered by the bosses' *pistoleros*, but a new generation of Barcelona revolutionaries had replaced them. These included Serge's friends among Spanish workers' leaders like Angel Pestana the anarcho-syndicalist and Andrés Nin of the independent Marxist POUM, who briefly shared power in Barcelona during the early days of the Spanish Civil War, only to be betrayed and assassinated by the Stalinists. Serge's 1930 meditation, set on the eve of a doubtful July 1917 insurrection, has thus acquired new layers of historical irony.

Meanwhile, back in July 1917, Victor Kibalchich's personal Odyssey took a new departure. When the Barcelona uprising fizzled, he heeded the call of Revolutionary Russia, the land of his exiled Russian revolutionary parents, the land where in February the 'we' of *Birth of Our Power* succeeded in overthrowing the Czar and are now contesting for power under the pro-Allied Provisional Government. The road to Russia led through wartime Paris, where, in order to be repatriated to revolutionary Russia, Victor tried to join the Russian forces still fighting on the Western Front. There, he found his former French anarchist comrades mostly demoralized and was soon arrested and thrown into a French detention camp for 'undesirables.'

Précigné (depicted in the novel as 'Crécy') was one of seventy officially nominated 'concentration camps' set up during World War I into which the French Republic threw anarchists, pacifists, refugees from German-occupied Belgian and dozens of other countries, Gypsies, prostitutes, and even an odd American ambulance driver (the poet E.E. Cummings, whose *Enormous Room* is often compared to this section of Serge's novel). At the end of the war, after sixteen months of captivity, Victor was released as part of an exchange of alleged 'Bolsheviks' (including children!) imprisoned in France for an equal number French officers held hostage by the Soviets. Accompanied by a group of returning revolutionary exiles, Serge-Kibalchich debarked in Red Petrograd and joined the Revolution on the side of the Bolsheviks at the darkest moment of the Civil War.

Serge's Literary 'Restraint'

In a review of *Birth of Our Power* published in Paris in 1931, Marcel Martinet, Serge's literary mentor, praised his style for its 'restraint' (*pudeur*) and its total absence of exhibitionism. However, Martinet also wondered aloud if these virtues were not "defects" in a novel. Comparing Serge to Jules Vallès, the revered revolutionary novelist of the Paris Commune, Martinet demanded of him more emotional expressiveness (*pathétique*).[8]

From Leningrad, Serge replied to his mentor, explaining apologetically that his years in prison had hardened him and made him incapable of that kind of romantic literary emotional expressiveness. On the other hand, subtly defending his post-romantic twentieth-century modernist aesthetic, Serge pointed out that his style was appropriate to the modern age: "I wonder if Vallès' emotional temperament would be able to withstand the singular power of the telephone in an age of terror. The formidable killing machines invented and put in place since 1914 have succeeded in obliterating some of man's essential instincts."

Such is Serge's restraint that the reader of his 'semiautobiographical' *Birth of Our Power* would have no idea that 1917–1919 was a critical time in the personal and political life of its author. Serge's narrator functions as a camera-eye, presenting the reader with a series of jump-cut scenes, sharing his political reflections but nothing of his personal life. Through the narrator's eye, we see Barcelona as a vibrant, joyful, sun-washed city, but in fact Serge's *Memoirs* tell us that prison was still hanging heavily over his head and that he was obsessed with guilt at having escaped the common fate of his generation: participation in the great slaughter that was World War I. He also went through a political crisis. It was in Barcelona that Kibaltchich settled his score with French anarcho-individualism, was drawn to syndicalism under the influence of the charismatic workers' leader Salvador Seguí (Dario in the novel), returned to the orbit of his Russian forebears, and metamorphosed himself into "Victor Serge."

---

8 Review of *Birth of Our Power* by Marcel Martinet, the poet and theoretician of of proletarian culture in France, Comptes rendus, *Europe* 105, no. 15 (September 1931): 122–23.

Nor do Serge's mainly political *Memoirs* divulge that their author also went through a sentimental crisis during this period. Victor had been in love with Rirette Maitrejean, his coeditor of the Paris journal *l'anarchie* since 1910. It was partly to shield her that he took the rap in the 1913 'anarchist bandit' trial that landed him in the penitentiary for five years. Rirette, who was a great beauty and took 'free love' literally, joined her lover in Barcelona after his release from prison, but she did not stay long, and her departure left him desolate. Nor did Serge ever talk about the serious emotional crisis he passed through during the year he spent in the French concentration camp at Fleury-en-Bière (Cummings's *Enormous Room*) before being transferred to Précigné ('Trécy' in the novel).

Liberated a month after the Armistice, Victor fell in love again in 1919, on the ship taking him to Red Russia through mine- and iceberg-infested waters, and for once his personal, sentimental interest is reflected in the novel. He bonded with another returning Francophone revolutionary exile, Alexander Russakov, a Russian-Jewish tailor and idealistic anarchist, the father of five children (and the model for 'Old Levine' in the novel). Victor fell in love with Alexander's oldest daughter, Liouba Russakova, the 'child woman' whose haunting portrait illuminated by firelight appears in "The Laws Are Burning," in the climactic scene that ends the novel. In Petrograd Victor lived in a collective apartment with the Russakovs, forming a Franco-Russian household, and a year later Liouba give birth to their son, Vladimir Kibalchich.[9] It was in this collective apartment, now invaded by a resident GPU informer, that Serge, now an outcast, wrote *Birth of Our Power* during 1929–1930.

Nonetheless, there is almost nothing 'confessional' in *Birth of Our Power*, Serge's most autobiographical novel (or for that matter in his so-called *Memoirs*).[10] Indeed, the novel tells us next to nothing about the narrator's (or Serge's) personal life. The true subject of the novel is not Serge's personal rebirth but the rebirth and coming to consciousness of the worldwide workers' movement after its collapse into the fratricidal nationalisms of World War I. Although the 'plot' follows the narrator's

---

9   See his website at http://www.vlady.org. 'Vlady' (as he signed himself) grew up as Serge's companion in deportation and exile, one of the 'comrades.' In Mexico, where his father died in 1947, he became a well-known painter and muralist. Part of his work is dedicated to his father, and in the course of many conversations over the years, helped me to understand Serge's life and works.

10 The title *Memoirs of a Revolutionary* was invented by the publisher.

somewhat picaresque wanderings, his near-anonymity shifts the reader's focus to the true 'hero' of Serge's novel, which is not an 'I' but a 'we.'

Serge's Collective Hero

Underlying *Birth of Our Power*, indeed running through all of Serge's novels, there is a permanent and collective protagonist, a revolutionary subject, identified the 'comrades,' the 'we' of *Birth of Our Power*, the permanent revolutionaries of all lands and epochs, the invisible international. Behind this self-identified cohort stand the masses themselves—the workers, the poor farmers, the youth, the downtrodden and dispossessed—who are ever present in Serge's novels. In this vision, individual rebels may be obliterated, but "the comrades" will always exist, gagged, exiled, jailed, or storming the heavens on the wave of revolution. So too the masses, in victory or in defeat, ensuring that no defeat will be permanent.[11]

Serge's concept of 'we' as collective subject flows directly from his spiritual heritage as a child of exiled members of Russia's unique revolutionary intelligentsia for whom the meaning of life was to understand, to participate, to consciously integrate oneself into the process of history. He also spoke out of a long experience of European worker militancy and a lifelong identification with the international revolutionary movement. He saw himself as one of its 'bards.'

As an organic intellectual of the working class, Serge's 'Marxism' was as integral to his vision of his narrator's epic journey as Dante's Christianity to his narrator's road from *Inferno* to *Paradiso*. Serge conceived literature as "a means of expressing to men what most of them live inwardly without being able to express, as a means of communion, a testimony to the vast flow of life through us, whose essential aspects we must try to fix for the benefit of those who will come after us." He concluded, "I was thus in the main line of Russian writers."[12]

Serge believed that fiction, what he called 'truthful' fiction, could communicate aspects of the revolution better than history or theory. Although definitely a writer with a 'message,' his technique was to bring experience to life on the page in all its multiplicity, using the modernist

---

11 By the end of Serge's life, most of the comrades in Europe and Russia whom he had immortalized as a collective hero had been exterminated by Hitler's Gestapo and Stalin's GPU. Serge's posthumous novel, *Unforgiving Years*, depicts the fate of a few survivors of this hecatomb.

12 Serge, *Memoirs of a Revolutionary*, 346.

device of stream-of-consciousness to multiply perspectives on a single action. For example, in the splendid bullfight scene in Barcelona on the eve of the uprising, we see the action simultaneously from a kaleidoscope of viewpoints: wealthy spectators seated on the shady side of the ring, armed workers in the bleachers opposite, the Killer down in the ring and facing him . . . the bull! The whole spectacle becomes symbolic of the class confrontation that will take place on the morrow, and the masses identify both with the powerful, angry, tormented beast and with the agile, skilled Killer—who is, after all, one of *them*, a poor cowboy risking death for money.

In *Birth of Our Power*, more than anywhere else, it is Serge's collective hero, the "comrades," the first-person plural pronoun of the title, who supply the underlying unity to the novel. It is "we" who awaken to power in Barcelona, "we" who suffer the frustrations of confinement in France, "we" who must face the problem of power in Petrograd. The collective hero is introduced in the first chapter of *Birth of Our Power*, significantly titled "This City and Us." How does Serge characterize this "we"? Neither as an ideological abstraction nor through any blurring sentimentality, but quite matter-of-factly:

> There were at least forty or fifty of us, coming from every corner of the world—even a Japanese, the wealthiest of us all, a student at the university—and a few thousand in the factories and shops of that city: comrades, that is to say more than brothers by blood or law, brothers by a common bond of thought, habit, language, and mutual aid. . . . No organization held us together, but none has ever had as much real and authentic solidarity as our fraternity of fights without leaders, without rules, and without ties.

Dario, El Chorro, Zilz, Jurien, José Miro, Lejeune, Ribas, and the other comrades whom Serge introduces here are not idealized; indeed, some turn out to be actual betrayers. But, although each is a perfectly individualized type (Serge excelled in the ability to create a sharp, living portrait with a few rapid strokes), they are at the same time representative of thousands of others: the rebels of every time and place.

Later, in the center section of the novel, after Serge has introduced us to the world of the concentration camp (another microcosm, with its deportees from every land, its criminals, its capitalists, its idealists and madmen) we meet another group of comrades. This time it is the organized group of Russian revolutionary prisoners, for whom

solidarity is not just a word but the only means of survival against star-
vation, epidemics, and the psychological ravages of life in the camp.
There is Krafft, the doctrinaire Bolshevik who strangely refuses to return
to Russia when he has the chance; Fomine, the white-maned old rebel
who is too worn out to face the long-awaited revolution when it finally
comes; Sonnenschein, the Jew who can settle any political argument
with a folk tale that reminds you of Sholom Aleichem; Karl and Gregor,
sailors from an American battleship, two silent giants who more and
more incarnate the power of the revolution as they move closer and
closer to their goal; Sam, "Uncle Sam," the ironic paradoxical character who is the most devoted revolutionary and yet—a double-agent.
The chapter title is "Us."

> We formed a world apart within this city. It sufficed for one of
> us to call the others together with that magic word "Comrades,"
> and we would feel united, brothers without even needing to say
> it, sure of understanding each other even in our misunderstand-
> ings. We had a quiet little room with four cots, the walls papered
> with maps, a table loaded with books. There were always a few of
> us there, poring over the endlessly annotated, commented, sum-
> marized texts. There Saint-Just, Robespierre, Jacque Roux, Babeuf,
> Blanqui, Bakunin were spoken of as if they had just come down
> to take a stroll under the trees. . . .
>
> When there are six of us around a table, we have the expe-
> rience of all the continents, all the oceans, all the pain and the
> revolt of men: the Labor parties of New South Wales, the vain
> apostleship of Theodor Herzl, the Mooney trail, the struggles of
> the Magón brothers in California, Pancho Villa, Zapata, syndical-
> ism, anarchism, Malatesta's exemplary life, anarcho individual-
> ism and the death of those bandits who wanted to be "new men,"
> Hervéism, social democracy, the work of Lenin—as yet unknown
> to the world—all the prisons.

Here, the meaning of "the comrades" is extended not only across
oceans and continents but backwards in time, with Robespierre and the
others, and forward into the future with Karl and Gregor, with Lenin.
However, if like Malraux's "virile fraternity," Serge's "comrades" were
held together only by a common heroism or by a subjective feeling, the
novels might be moving, but they would not have the solid foundation nor the biting realism they do in fact exhibit. But the basis here is

not sentiment but necessity, objective social truth, as Serge shows in a characteristic scene of "epiphany" or unveiling, where realistic detail is used to reveal a social reality, in the chapter titled "The Essential Thing."

At last the small band of revolutionary exiles reach the famous Finland station in Petrograd, the scene of Lenin's triumphant return. Serge creates a scene of anti-climax. As the narrator listens to the official welcoming speech, his eyes wander over the freezing musicians standing the cold in their shabby, mismatched uniforms. The trombone player had put on a pair of "magnificent green gloves. Others had red hands, stiffened by the cold. Some wore old gloves, of leather or cloth and full of holes." Their appearance expresses nothing but "hunger and fatigue." The narrator reflects:

> Never could the idea come to anyone to rush forward toward them with outstretched hand saying Brothers! for they belonged entirely to a world where words, feelings, fine sentiments, shed their prestige immediately on contact with primordial realities. . . . I stared intensely at these silent men, standing there in such great distress. I thanked them for teaching me already about true fraternity, which is neither in sentiments nor in words, but in shared pain and shared bread. If I had no bread to share with them, I must keep silent and take my place at their side: and we would go off somewhere to fight or to fall together, and would thus be brothers, without saying so and perhaps without even loving each other. Loving each other? What for? Staying alive, that's what counts.

Rarely has the true heroism of the revolution been presented in a grimmer, more realistic light. The ragged, starving musicians are not pathetic. They are just there, a fact. They are there because necessity has put them there. They are comrades, not out of love, but because the revolution has given them a common social destiny—or a common death. And Serge, in this scene, has managed to epitomize a whole world and the individual's relation to it, in the outlandish green gloves of a shivering trombone player.

"The Laws Are Burning"
The final chapter in Birth of Our Power, titled "The Laws Are Burning," is based on an actual incident that took place in February 1919 when, soon after their arrival in Petrograd, the Soviet authorities moved Victor and the Russakov family into a vast empty apartment formerly occupied by

a senator. This assignment was no privilege. The reason there were so many palaces vacant is that it was impossible to heat them, and floor-boards were quickly consumed. How to cope with this problem? The climactic passage of Serge's novel reveals the practical solution and in so doing transforms essentially anecdotal material into a concretely significant symbolic structure, what Serge's contemporary Joyce, applying a religious notion to literature, termed an 'epiphany.'

> The Levines had gathered in the smallest of the rooms, probably a nursery, furnished with two iron bedsteads with gilded balls on which only the mattresses remained . . . (one of them appeared stained with blood). This candle-lit room was like a corner in steerage on an immigrant ship. The children had fallen asleep on the baggage, rolled up in blankets. The mother was resting in a low armchair. The young woman, like a solemn child, with large limpid eyes which seemed by turns distended by fear and then victorious over the fleeting shadows, was dreaming before the open stove, the reddish glow of which illuminated from below her graceful hands, her thin neck, and her fine features. Old Levine's footsteps echoed on the floor of the grand salon, plunged in darkness. He entered, his arms loaded with heavy green-covered books which he dropped softly next to the stove. Silent laughter illuminated his ruddy face.
> "The laws are burning!" he said.
> The friendly warmth in front of which the young woman was stretching out her hands came from the flames which were devouring Tome XXVII of the COLLECTION OF THE LAWS OF THE EMPIRE. For fun, I pulled out a half-burned page, edged with incandescent lace. The flames revealed these words forming a chapter heading: CONCERNING LANDED PROPERTY . . . and, further down: ". . . the rights of collateral heirs . . ."

The anecdote of "The Laws Are Burning" is an example of the *petit fait vrai*, the commonplace observation which Stendhal prized so highly for its undeniable authenticity and consequent ability to authenticate a whole idea, description, or emotional effect. Serge has dramatized it and given it symbolic significance by turning it into 'Jewish humor.' Old Levine's exclamation is the punchline of an elaborately prepared visual pun, albeit a pun which could only be understood in a precise historical situation. Like any pun, this one is based on a verbal ambiguity—the basis of much of the power of poetry as well. Since laws cannot "burn" in any material sense, the effect created by "The laws are burning!" explodes like a Surrealist poem or an anarchist slogan; a powerful image of the violence and destructive energy of revolution.

Yet, as the text unfolds, the same destructive energy of the flames which "devour" Tome XXVII of the *Laws* is revealed as the "friendly warmth" toward which the young girl stretches out her hands, while the final image, that of *"Landed Property"* and *"the rights of collateral heirs"* framed in the "incandescent lace" of the flames suggests yet another possibility: that the social class represented by the Levine family, merely in order to survive, to keep warm, has been obliged to obliterate the society based on property and all its heirs (the class represented by the senator's family) in the course of its struggle for existence.

The passage evokes a whole complex of interconnected social, political, and historical relationships of individuals and classes which can be understood only in terms of an actual historical event *outside of* the text (the transfer of power of 1917)—an event which is in turn illuminated and made comprehensible for the reader with greater force and with more complexity through this purely "literary" text than it could be through any amount of abstract historical analysis. It is within this context that the passage's climax (beginning with the exclamation "The laws are burning!") acquires a richness and symbolism that goes far beyond its purely "realistic" function as an authenticating *petit fait vrai*.

Victor's achingly romantic vision of his beloved Liouba as she must have appeared in 1919 comes through in this climactic passage, which must, for the author, have already been tinged with nostalgia. For by 1930, when Serge penned this touching portrait of a fearful child-woman, Liouba had already been diagnosed as insane, essentially driven mad by the persecutions to which she and her family had been subject as a result of her husband's refusal to renounce his principled opposition to Stalinism. This is as close as Serge gets to confessional in this 'autobiographical' novel, whose principle literary quality is its 'restraint.'

Serge thus brings his final chapter to a climax on a note of ironic lyricism, but it is not the traditionally triumphal lyricism of Red Armies marching into the sunset. The vision is rather one of a necessary but ambiguous victory, of a new class placed precariously and uneasily in the seat of power, beset by internal and external threats and ironically conscious that the power which has been sought for so long and at such great cost will present greater problems in the future than any the powerless have ever dreamed of. Here Serge brings the stamp of authenticity to his literary text and then moves beyond the mimesis of reality to a realm of vision which includes history and poetry as its poles and where the text can be said to 'authenticate' history as much as history authenticates the text.

Thus concludes Serge's epic tale of two cities, his fictional Odyssey from Barcelona, where 'we' could not take power, to Petrograd, where holding onto 'our power' turns out to be problematical. The hopeful Barcelona theme of 'victory-in-defeat' is superseded by the ironic Petrograd theme of 'defeat-in-victory.' And the problem of revolutionary power posed by Serge's fiction remains an open one in our internet age of international revolution (think 'Arab Spring') and globalized counterrevolution.

Historical Note

The opening pages of *Birth of Our Power* are steeped in symbolism and poetic beauty, but they may prove exasperating for the reader who does not share the author's intimacy with Spain and Spanish revolutionary history. To point up the universality of his story, for instance, Serge never refers to Barcelona, the setting for the first half of the novel, by name, only as "this city." And it is only through passing references to World War I that the reader is able to place the events in the early chapters historically.

For most of us, the phrase "Spanish Revolution" brings to mind the 1936–39 Civil War. But in fact the Spanish revolutionary tradition, with all its passion and brutality, goes back much further, to Napoleonic times (cf. Goya's "Disasters of War"). Throughout the nineteenth century, repeated attempts to establish liberal government in Spain resulted only in bloody fusillades and paper reforms. Spain entered the twentieth century, after its stunning defeat by the United States in 1898, as a backward, corrupt, priest- and soldier-ridden monarchy. The anarchism of the Russian Bakunin caught the imagination of the peasants and of the workers in the new industrial centers like Barcelona, and their revolt took the form of *jacqueries* and individual terrorism (a situation quite similar to that in Czarist Russia). The government's response to social unrest was the establishment of a new Spanish Inquisition that was responsible for wholesale arrests and executions, and for the brutal torture of anyone even remotely connected with the revolutionary movement. The judicial murder at Montjuich of Francisco Ferrer, the progressive educationalist, after the 1909 general strike, raised a worldwide storm of protest. Spain was again a land of martyrs.

In *Birth of Our Power*, the citadel of Montjuich, where many rebels had been tortured and shot, becomes the symbol both of the revolutionary past and the oppressive power of the present. Under the shadow of

Montjuich, the masses, led by a handful of anarchists, awaken to their power and prepare to do battle for a better life. Many of the characters are real personages; Dario, Serge's hero, was modeled on the syndicalist leader, Salvador Seguí, who was murdered by government scabs in 1922. The events are all historically true. The confused day of street fighting, described in Chapter 9, took place on July 19, 1917. It was followed by a full-scale insurrection in August.

Neutral Spain had been trading profitably with both sides in World War I, but the ancient political forms had not kept pace with the rapidly developing economy. Both the liberal parliamentarians and the anarchistic workers felt that the time had come to put forward their demands. The revolt failed because the liberals abandoned their alliance with the workers at the last minute, leaving them to face the government alone, and because the Barcelona workers were so poorly organized. The workers had failed to co-ordinate their movement with groups in other parts of Spain, and were (with the possible exception of Seguí) so anarchistic that they had no idea what they would do if they actually managed to win.

What is most remarkable in these half-forgotten pages of history is the extent to which the Spanish workers were inspired by the February Revolution in distant Russia, and the fact that the demands of the *Comité Obrero* in Barcelona actually prefigured those of the Soviets in October 1917. On the basis of this historical "coincidence," Serge develops his theme of power in complex counterpoint. The two cities, Barcelona and Petrograd (the setting for the last part of the novel), at opposite ends of Europe, complement one another. In the first, "that city that we could not take," the accent is on the revolution in expectation, and on the sudden discovery by the masses that they possess power—a victory that transpires the actual defeat of the insurrection. In Petrograd, the theme of power takes on an entirely new, and terrifying, aspect; the question implicit in the Barcelona chapters—"Can we seize power?"—is replaced by another, truly awesome question—"What will we become when we do take power?"

The collective "we" of these questions brings up another important facet of Serge's work. "The word 'I,'" wrote Serge, "is repellent to me as a vain affirmation of the self which contains a large measure of illusion and another of vanity or unjustified pride. Whenever it is possible, that is to say when I am able not to feel myself isolated, when my experience illuminates in some manner that of the men to whom I feel tied,

I prefer to use the word 'we,' which is more general and more true." The word "Our" in Serge's title reveals this preoccupation. And it is the opposition of "them" and "us," of "their city" and "ours," that in fact forms the basic framework for, and gives a consistent point of view to, *Birth of Our Power*. "We"—the collective hero of Serge's novel—are the men to whom the narrator is tied, the poor, the exploited, the down-trodden, the rebels of all places and all times; "they" are the exploiters and the complacent. However, the former are never idealized, and the latter are often treated with great delicacy. Moreover, the basic opposition becomes richly ironic in the final section of the novel when "we" have at last taken power in Russia, and the narrator discovers that "the danger is within us."

With *Birth of Our Power*, Serge created both a compelling portrait of modem revolution and a probing examination of the problems that attend it. The novel captures in a lyrical, yet powerfully direct, manner the enormous vigor and excitement of the revolutionary spirit of our century, and it is at the same time an historically valuable study of humanity at the crucial moment of upheaval and social change—a study that speaks with the eloquence of deeply felt experience and is full of important implications for our times. For Victor Serge, the revolution did not end with the defeat of the revolution of 1917 or of 1936 in Spain (or with the transformation of the Russia of 1917 into its opposite); in *Birth of Our Power* he wrote, "Nothing is ever lost. . . . Tomorrow is full of greatness. We will not have brought this victory to ripeness in vain. This city will be taken, if not by our hands, at least by others like ours, but stronger. Stronger perhaps for having been better hardened, thanks to our very weakness. If we are beaten, other men, infinitely different from us, infinitely like us, will walk, on a similar evening, in ten years, in twenty years (how long is really without importance) down this *rambla*, meditating on the same victory. Perhaps they will think about our blood. Even now I think I see them and I am thinking about their blood, which will flow too. But they will take the city."

Let us hope that, after years of exile, Serge's works find the audience they deserve: those "other men, infinitely different from us, infinitely like us" who are carrying on the struggle today.

Richard Greeman
New York, 1966

ONE

This City and Us

A CRAGGY MASS OF SHEER ROCK—SHATTERING THE MOST BEAUTIFUL OF HORI-
zons—towers over this city. Crowned by an eccentric star of jagged
masonry cut centuries ago into the brown stone, it now conceals secret
constructions under the innocence of grassy knolls. The secret citadel underneath lends an evil aspect to the rock, which, between the
limpid blue of the sky, the deeper blue of the sea, the green meadows
of the Llobregat and the city, resembles a strange primordial gem . . .
Hard, powerful, upheaval arrested in stone, affirmed since the beginning of time . . . stubborn plants gripping, hugging the granite, and
rooting into its crevices . . . trees whose obdurate roots have inexora-
bly-cracked the stone and, having split it, now serve to bind it . . . sharp
angles dominating the mountain, set in relief or faceted by the play of
sunlight . . . We would have loved this rock—which seems at times to
protect the city, rising up in the evening, a promontory over the sea
(like an outpost of Europe stretching toward tropical lands bathed in
oceans one imagines as implacably blue)—this rock from which one
can see to infinity . . . We would have loved it had it not been for those
hidden ramparts, those old cannons with their carriages trained low on
the city, that mast with its mocking flag, those silent sentries with their
olive-drab masks posted at every corner. The mountain was a prison—
subjugating, intimidating the city, blocking off its horizon with its dark
mass under the most beautiful of suns.

We often climbed the paths which led upward toward the fortress,
leaving below the scorched boulevards, the old narrow streets gray and
wrinkled like the faces of hags, the odor of dust, cooking oil, oranges,
and of humanity in the slums. The horizon becomes visible little by
little, with each step, spiraling upward around the rock. Suddenly the
harbor appears around a bend: the clean, straight line of the jetty, the
white flower of a yacht club, floating in the basin like an incredible giant

21

water lily. In the distance, heaps of oranges—like enormous sunflowers dropped on the border of a gray city—piled up on the docks . . . And the ships. Two large German vessels: immobile. Under quarantine for several years now, they catch the eye. A six-master, under full sail, glittering in the sun, sails slowly into the harbor from the ends of the sea. Her prow, fringed with dazzling foam, cuts serenely through the amazing blue of liquid silk. She opens horizons even more remote, horizons which I can suddenly see, and which by closing my eyes I see more perfectly: Egypt, the Azores, Brazil, Uruguay, Havana, Mexico, Florida . . . From what other corners of the earth did these golden sails come? Perhaps only from Majorca. The ship probably bears the name of an old galleon, the name of a woman or a virgin as sonorous as a line of poetry: *Santa Maria de Los Dolores* . . . Christopher Columbus on his column is now visible above the harbor. Looking out from the city over the sea, the bronze explorer welcomes the sailing ship as she moves in toward him from a past as moving, as mysterious, and as promising as the future.

The city is most attractive in the evening, when its avenues and its plaza light up: soft glowing coals, more brilliant than pearls, earthly stars shining more brightly than the stars of the heavens. By day, it looks too much like any European city: spires of cathedrals above the ancient streets, domes of academies and theaters, barracks, palaces, boxlike buildings pierced by countless windows—A compartmentalized ant heap where each existence has its own narrow cubicle of whitewashed or papered walls. From the very first, a city imparts a sense of poverty. One *sees*, in the sea of roofs compressed into motionless waves, how they shrivel up and crush numberless lives.

It is from the height that one discovers the splendors of the earth. The view plunges down to the left into the harbor, the gulf lined with beaches, the port, the city. And the blue-shadowed mountains, far from shutting off the distances, open them up. The vast sea laughs at our feet in foamy frills on the pebbles and sand. Plains, orchards, fields marked as sharply as on a surveyor's map, roads lined with small trees, a carpet of every shade of green stretches out to the right on the other side of the rock down to the gently sloping valley, which seems a garden from that height. Mountains on which, when the air is clear, pale snow crystals can be seen at the peak—where earth meets sky—extending our horizons toward eternity.

But our eyes, scanning the faraway snowcap at leisure, or following a sail on the surface of the sea, would always light on the muzzle of a cannon, across the thicketed embankment. Our voices would suddenly drop off, when, at a bend in the path, the stark, grass-covered corner of the citadel's ramparts loomed up before us. The name of a man who had been shot was on all our lips.[1] We used to stop at certain places from which we could see the narrow confines of the dungeons. Somewhere within these fortifications, men like us, with whom each of us at one time or another identified ourselves, men whose names we no longer remembered, had undergone torture not long ago. What kind of torture? We did not know precisely, and the very lack of exact pictures, the namelessness of the victims, the years (twenty) that had passed, stripped the memory bare: nothing remained but a searing, confused feeling for the indignities suffered in the cause of justice. I sometimes used to think that we remembered the pain those men suffered as one remembers something one has suffered oneself, after many years and after many experiences. And, from that notion, I had an even greater sense of the communion between their lives and ours.

Like them—and those ships we saw coming into the harbor—we came from every corner of the world. El Chorro, more yellow-skinned than a Chinese, but with straight eyes, flat temples, and fleshy lips, El Chorro, with his noiseless laugh, who was probably Mexican (if anything): at any rate he used to speak at times familiarly and with admiration of the legendary Emiliano Zapata, who founded a social republic in the Morelos mountains with his rebellious farmers—descendants of ancient bronze-skinned peoples.

"The first in modern times!" El Chorro would proclaim proudly, his hands outstretched. At which point you noticed that he was missing his thumb and index finger, sacrificed in some obscure battle for the first social republic of modern times.

"A little more," he'd say, "and I would have lost my balls as well. A stinking half-breed from Chihuahua nearly snatched them from me with his teeth . . ."

"*Si hombre!*" he would add, breaking into loud and resonant laughter, for the joy of that victory still vibrated through his body.

He made his living selling phony jewelry over in the Paralelo. With a friendly touch and an insinuating laugh, he'd fasten the huge silver loops on the ears of girls from the neighboring towns, sending shivers

---

1   Probably a reference to Francisco Ferrer, a libertarian-educator executed at Montjuich in 1909. See note, page 47.—Tr.

down their spines as if he had just kissed them on the neck. They all knew him well: from a crowd they would look at him with long, smoldering stares, from beneath lowered eyelids.

Zilz, a French deserter, pretended to be Swiss: Heinrich Zilz, citizen of the canton of Neuchâtel, who taught languages—*los idiomas*—with childlike earnestness, lived on oatmeal, noodles, and fruit, spoke little but well, dressed carefully, went to bed every night at ten-thirty, went to bed once a week with a five-peseta girl (a good price), and held people in quiet contempt. "It will take centuries to reform them, and life is short. I have enough of a problem with myself, trying to live a little better than an animal, and that's plenty for me."

Jurien and Couet (the one blond, the other chestnut-haired, but whom you would have taken for brothers from their identical Parisian speech, their little toothbrush mustaches, their jaunty walk), had both fled the war, one from the trenches of Le Mort Homme,[2] the other from the Vosges, by way of the Pyrenees. Now they both worked in factories for the benefit of those who still persisted in getting killed, Jurien nailing boots and Couet loading grenades for export to France. They lived happily, from day to day, in the satisfaction of being spared from the fiery hell.

Oskar Lange, a slender muscular lad with reddish hair, bloodshot eyes, thought to be a deserter from a German submarine, was their closest companion. They made him read Kropotkin and Stirner, in that order. And the sailor who had thought only of escaping the fate of rotting in a steel coffin discovered a new source of strength and pride in what he had thought to be his cowardice—thanks to them. We smiled to hear him pronounce the word "Comrade"—somewhat awkwardly—for the first time.

There was also an athletic and intelligent Russian, Lejeune, elegant, handsome, graying at the temples, who had been known for a long time in his youth as Levieux. He lived with Maud, worn-out yet ageless, who had the body of a nervous gamin, a Gothic profile, brown curls, and sudden, catlike movements. And Tibio—*el cartero*, the postman—with his broad Roman countenance, wide forehead, and noble carriage, who studied the art of living and wrote commentaries on Nietzsche after systematically distributing letters to offices in the business district. Then

2   Le Mort Homme, or Hill 295, one of the Verdun defenses, captured by the Germans in 1916 and retaken by the French 1917.

there were Mathieu the Belgian, Ricotti the Italian, the photographer Daniel, and the Spaniards Dario, Bregat, Andrés, José Miro, Eusebio, Portez, Ribas, Santiago . . .

There were at least forty or fifty of us, coming from every corner of the world—even a Japanese, the wealthiest of us all, a student at the university—and a few thousand in the factories and shops of that city: comrades, that is to say, more than brothers by blood or law, brothers by a common bond of thought, habit, language, and mutual help. No profession was foreign to us. We came from every conceivable background. Among us, we knew practically every country in the world, beginning with the capitals of hard work and hunger, and with the prisons. There were among us those who no longer believed in anything but themselves. The majority were moved by ardent faith; some were rotten—but intelligent enough not to break the law of solidarity too openly. We could recognize each other by the way we pronounced certain words, and by the way we had of tossing the ringing coin of ideas into any conversation. Without any written law, we comrades owed each other (even the most recent newcomer) a meal, a place to sleep, a hideout, the peseta that will save you in a dark hour, the *douro* (a hundred sous) when you're broke (but after that, it's your own lookout!). No organization held us together, but none has ever had as much real and authentic solidarity as our fraternity of fighters without leaders, without rules, and without ties.

TWO

Sentry Thoughts

I HAD LEARNED IN THAT CITY THAT IT IS NOT ENOUGH TO FILL YOUR LIFE with the certainty of not being killed by the end of the day—a prospect dreamed of in those days as the supreme happiness by thirty million men on the soil of Europe. It often happened, during my strolls on the Montjuich rock, that I had the sensation of being at one of the earth's extremities, which resulted in a strange despondency. There, facing the horizon, or during night walks through the happy city, this feeling—usually indistinct within me, attained a somber clarity. The peace we were enjoying was unique, and that city, despite the struggles, the pain, the filth hidden away in her hunger-ridden slums and her indescribably squalid *callejitas*, was more than happy just to be alive. We were, nonetheless, only a hundred miles from the Pyrenees: on the other side, the other universe, ruled over by the cannon. Not a single young man in the villages. On every train, you encountered the leathery faces of soldiers on leave looking out from under their helmets with probing, weary glances. And the farther north you went, the more the face of the countryside—aggrieved, impoverished, anguished—changed. The feverish but static image of Paris: brilliant lights extinguished in the evening, dark streets in the outlying districts where the garbage piled up, lines of women waiting in front of the local town halls, dense crowds on the streets where countless uniforms mingled, less diverse, no doubt, than the hands and faces of the Canadians, Australians, Serbs, Belgians, Russians, New Zealanders, Hindus, Senegalese . . . In war the blood of all men is brewed together in the trenches. The same desire to live and to possess a woman made soldiers on furlough of every race, marked for every conceivable kind of death, wander the streets. The maimed and the gassed, green-faced, encounter those as yet vigorous and whole, bronze skinned, the maimed and the gassed of tomorrow. Some of tomorrow's corpses were laughing raucously. Paris in darkness, the drawn faces of women in the poorer quarters during the bitter February cold, the feverish exhaustion of streets endlessly bearing the burden of an immense disbanded army, the sickly intimacy of certain homes where the war entered with the air you breathed, like a slow asphyxiating gas—remained implanted in my very nerves. And, still farther north—I knew then, Jurien, only a little farther—those trenches of Le Mort Homme which you described to me under the palms of the Plaza de Cataluña on those evenings, cooled by the sea breeze, so magical that the joy of living quickened every light, every silhouette, the hoarse breathing of the vagabond who slept, every muscle deliciously relaxed, on the next bench—those trenches you described, with their odor of putrefaction and excrement. A shellburst knocked you flat, bitter sentry, into a ditch. You saw, your blood (your last, you thought) run into the filth.

("And I didn't give a shit, you understand? I didn't give a shit," you said. "To die here or elsewhere, like this or in any other way—it was all the same to me. All equally stupid . . . But that stench was choking me.")

Then the ruined villages, the demolished towns, the leveled forests—hazy memories of news photos. And more corrosive, more intoxicating than anything—gnawing, abrasive—the language of the maps. Since childhood, maps had given me a kind of vertigo. I used to study them. I learned them by heart at the age of twelve, with a desperate and obstinate desire to know every country, every ocean, every jungle, every city. Desperate because I knew in the back of my mind that I would never go to Ceylon, never go up the Orinoco in a dugout canoe, or the Mekong in a gunboat: this desire filled me with a dull ache. Now the serene voices of the maps spoke a terrifying language. Artillery barrages on the Yser and on the Vardar, on the Piave and on the Euphrates; Zeppelins over London, Gothas over Venice. Blood on the Carpathians and blood on the Vosges. The defense of Verdun, that incredible mass grave, the crushing of Rumania, the battle of the Falkland Islands, the Cameroon campaign. Every ocean—where the child's hand had traced the shipping lanes—was a watery grave.

How then to live in this city, stretched out along the gulf, adorned in the evening with a million lights, like an odalisque asleep on the beach; how to live here with the acute awareness of the absurd torture Europe was undergoing? I don't know why, perhaps because of Jurien (who no longer thought of it himself), I was obsessed by thoughts of the sentries in the trenches, of silent soldiers dug into their holes—taking up as little room in the earth as the dead—with only their eyes alive, watching a mournful horizon of mud and barbwire (and, of course, a fleshless, rotting hand sticking out of the ground) in that narrow band of earth that belongs to no one, except to Death: no man's land. Identical in their silence, on both sides of the trenches, under helmets scarcely different, dented by the same explosions, protecting the same gray cells of the human animal at bay . . . Sentries, brother sentries, stalking each other, stalked by Death, standing watch night and day on the boundaries of life itself, and here *I* was, strolling in comfortable sandals under the palms of the plaza, my eyes dazzled by the festive Mediterranean sunlight; *I*, climbing the paths of Montjuich; *I*, pausing before the goldsmiths' windows of the *calle* Fernando, flooded by light in the evening as if by a motionless fountain of huge diamonds; *I*, following the Miramar path cut into the rock above the sea; *I*, living as that city lived, without fear, invincible, sure of not having my flesh ripped open tomorrow. *I* possessed these streets—these *ramblas*—loaded to excess with flowers, birds, women, and warm masculine voices. *I* had my books; *I* had my comrades. How was this possible? Wasn't this somehow horribly unjust, incredibly absurd?

It was mostly after nightfall, when the city abandoned herself to the pleasures of life—her cafés crowded, certain of her narrow streets transformed into rivers of light, streets where men and women pair off, leading each other on endlessly, couple after couple so closely intertwined that their walk seems an impudent, delicious prelude to clinches in stuffy rooms along streets haunted by sighs until dawn; when we strolled up and down the *ramblas* in groups, our heads held high, filled with the music of ideas—it was then that I was tortured by the remorse of not being a sentry myself, of being, in spite of myself, so careful of my own blood, of taking no part in the immeasurable suffering of the masses driven to the slaughter . . . a feeling sharpened by a revulsion against the blithe felicity of this city.

We suffocated, about thirty of us, from seven in the morning to six-thirty at night, in the Gaubert y Pia print shop. Skinny kids, naked under their loose smocks, went back and forth across the shop carrying heavy frames, their thin brown arms standing out like cables of flesh. At the back of the shop, the women were folding away—sweating, lips moist, looking at you with dark-eyed glances that seemed almost to caress you as you passed by—repeating the same motions seven thousand times a day to the rumbling of the machines. The movement of the machines was absorbed in their very muscles. I set up type on the composing stick, fatigue mounting in my body, overpowering from three o'clock on, in the hottest time of the day. Toward four o'clock, mechanical concentration falters, and like one in prison, I am assailed by fantasies originating from the secret folds of the brain. To no avail, I cross the shop floor to get a drink of water from the *canti*—the leather flask you hold in both hands above the head, so that a hard stream squirts into your mouth like a fountain. The corrugated iron roof gives us little protection from the implacable sun.

It was at those times of day, when the boss, el Señor Gaubert, had turned to face a visitor in his glass-enclosed office, that my neighbor Porfirio would tap me on the shoulder with a finger hard as a stick:

"*Hé, Ruso!*" (Russian)

Tall, brittle, with nothing on under his blue overalls, Porfirio had the broad, dark, pock-marked face, the face of an intelligent ape. His black mouth was lined by horrible yellow teeth that seem broken, but his grimacing smile, spreading from ear to ear, was fraternal. In actual fact, he wasn't really a comrade, not even a union member (only two of us were union men out of thirty printers and typographers at Gaubert y Pia's, but the others had as much solidarity as we did—we knew it as well as they); bull-fighting was his only interest. His eyes were black as charcoal.

"*Hé! Ruso! Que dices de la revolución?*" ("What have you to say about the revolution?")

The dispatches from the newspapers came one after another, offering a welter of surprising details about the great Petrograd days. I can still see Porfirio, intoxicated as if by drink, with the *Vanguardia* spread out in front of him tinder a lamppost, rereading aloud in a delirious voice an article relating how, at the call of a non-com named Astakhov (almost completely unknown in Russia) the first regiment went over to the insurgent masses in a Petrograd street . . . "Magnificent!" said Porfirio in a voice made hoarse by emotion; and with a gesture he called our shop mates together as they emerged from the factory. The folders Trini, Quima, Mercédès, Ursula joined our group, their shoulders suddenly thrown back, their faces suddenly serious as if stiffened by a chill, bracing wind.

Through him I learned what inordinate hopes were rising in the poor neighborhoods of the city. It was during the noon break at work. I was walking along a deserted street without a patch of shade and thinking vaguely how life could be as searing, as naked and as empty: Sahara. Porfirio caught up with me. I could tell immediately from the bounce in his step, the lively animation of his features, that he had something extraordinary to tell me.

"D'you know?" he said. "The strikers in Sabadell have won their fight."

He turned on his heels, stopped short, and faced me, his hard hands on my shoulders.

"You know, *Ruso*, it's our turn next! We're going to win too—in another battle. You'll see, *amigo mio*, you'll see!"

He wouldn't say more: probably because he didn't know any more. It was then nothing but a confused rumor, a vague readiness in the factories and shops. Roughly, Porfirio yanked a hunk of bread out of his pocket and took a hefty bite out of it with the side of his mouth. He was too poor to eat in restaurants, but would grab a few bites in the street before taking a refreshing twenty-minute nap on a bench in a nearby park.

I continued along my way with a quickened step, my heart pounding. I entered the little Ventura restaurant (where a few of us ate under the sharp, cordial eye of the fat *patrón*, an old anarchist, who had once "done" five years in the presidio) with a burdensome guilt lifted from my shoulders: I too awakened to high hopes. Sentries! Sentries! In this city we will accomplish our mission, a better one than yours!

THREE

Lejeune

FROM THEN ON WE LOOKED AT THE CITY THROUGH NEW EYES.
Nothing was changed in appearance; but the workers' power surged through the city like new blood injected into the arteries of an old organism. Only those in the know could detect the feeling of excitement in the faces, movements, voices, pace of the city. Voices strayed from their normal patterns: sudden outbursts would follow murmurings among the groups seated at the Café Español. This enormous room was extended indefinitely by mirrors framed in heavy gilt and by terraces animated with voices crackling like the wind over dry grass: it opened onto a street flood-lit by little theaters, night clubs, dance halls, and big working class bars. Some side streets, covered with a reddish dust, wind their way up toward the citadel; others, uniformly gray, cool and dank with the eerie dankness of disease, bathed in the light of naked bulbs at the end of dark corridors—where tired women and avid males copulated endlessly and at random year in and year out.

The café, crowded at every hour of the day, has tables which are—in a manner of speaking—reserved. The anarchists occupy one section of the terrace and a double row of tables inside, under the dazzling mirrors. The police informers, recognizable by their phony veneer of workers or clerks with time to kill; by their leaden, indolent, shifty hands made for playing dominoes, fastening handcuffs, or noiselessly wielding a blackjack; the police informers, with straining ears and prying eyes, form a familiar circle—not far off—at a round table. (We have an old trick we play every few weeks—of all pretending to sit down for a long evening together, and then having the waiter, a comrade, serve them burning hot coffee. As soon as the steaming cups of coffee are placed before them, we gulp down our drinks and hotfoot it out of there. Only El Chorro remains, laughing silently at the spectacle of the crestfallen faces of those "sons of bitches" who are forced to choose

between losing the coffee they've paid for, or losing their "clients.")
The "ego-anarchist" corner is full of foreigners. If an overly elegant
bull-necked gentleman, one of those habitués of swank bars who traf-
fic in white slavery, happen to find his way into our group, the unlikely
attention of the police informers and the forbidding indifference of the
workers scare him off immediately. He recovers his aplomb on the terrace, at the sight of some French girls sipping orangeade through long
straws. A calliope fills the hall with arias from operas and love songs.
Through the din of the mechanical brass band, we are able to discuss
things among ourselves without worrying too much about being over-
heard by the informers.

Five of us were there, late one afternoon. Eusebio, a plasterer with
the handsome, regular features of a Roman legionary, a bristling mustache, large, soft, brown eyes—luminous, primeval, accustomed to
bright colors (but not nuances). Andrés, an editor of the Confederation
paper, a thin, swarthy Argentinean with sharp, squarish features, a
pointed chin, and a querulous look, held a pointed cigarette between
purple lips. Lolita, Eusebio's "wife" (and someone else's), a pale, skinny
factory girl with hair so dark it seems blue-tinted, sunken eyes concealing a lusterless gaze (like an indifferent caress), pale nostrils, a double
fold of pursed lips as red as the inside of a pomegranate. Heinrich Zilz,
his necktie carefully knotted, his face slightly flushed (for he has a yen
for Lolita) was smoking with a smile on his face.

Eusebio leaned toward us over the white marble table, his eyes shining. He opened his thick muscular hands and said:

"How many of us will fall tomorrow! How many! But what's the
difference? What's the difference!"

He repeated the same words twice over, at a loss for others. He
cracked the joints of his fingers. How to find the words to express the
power, the joy, the earnestness, the faith in tomorrow?

Hardly moving his lips, Andrés said:

"The people over in Manresa have promised some grenades. Sans,
Tarrasa, and Granollérs are ready. Our pals in Tarrasa already have a
hundred and forty Brownings. The Committee is negotiating with a
junta of infantrymen. But what cowards these republicans are!"

"So you're really itching to get yourselves chopped down, eh?" Zilz
broke in, lighting another cigarette.

"What? What?" Eusebio cried. "What are you saying?" He heard well
enough, but the hostile notion took a moment to sink in.

"I said," Zilz continued, "you can count me out. My skin is worth more than any republic, even a workers' republic."

A heavy silence fell over us. Then Lolita got up stiffly. Her mouth, a bleeding pomegranate, narrows: eyes now nothing but two shadows under the horizontal ivory of her forehead.

"Let's go."

A few feet away I heard a shuffling of chairs at the table of informers.

"Good-by, then," Zilz said. "I'm staying."

We went out. Lolita, in front of us, moved rapidly through the crowd, silent, her head—with its stubborn rebel forehead—high. Andrés said what we were all thinking.

"The ego-anarchist poison. People like that, you see, don't risk their necks any more except for money."

Lejeune's clothes were cut from British cloth; he wore silk shirts and underwear, and Mitchell felt hats, black or gray according to the season. The air of a well-established businessman, a frequenter of fine restaurants. Thickset in the face, through the shoulders and waist; graying at the temples and in his thick mustache; his eyes a colorless gray as if fatigued, yet alert, never lax. Discreetly, their attentive gaze, without flame or color, scanned every face in a group, every shape around him in a crowd. Lejeune usually sat in cafés in such a way as to take advantage of all the mirrors' treacherous possibilities while presenting to others only the view of his well-shaved neck. He preferred establishments that had a back exit, and there, certain corners where you could almost disappear from sight, back well into a wall, behind an open newspaper. His insignificant name was known only to a few of us; his past to no one. Certain comrades remembered having called him "Levieux" fifteen years earlier in Paris and London. Then he disappeared. Had he been mixed up with the legendary Jacob of Amiens?[3] Had he been a counterfeiter? A convict who had "done" eight years? That's what people said: he said nothing himself. Insurance broker (doubtless a "front"), owner of a traveling circus, wholesaler of "Parisian goods," he lived extremely

---

3 (1879–1954) The "Robin Hood" of French anarchy, who stole only from the Church, the Military, and the wealthy, and gave most of the proceeds of his daring exploits to anarchist welfare funds. His specialty was to make monkeys out of magistrates and to escape from prisons (including Devil's Island). He furnished the model for Maurice Leblanc's famous character, Arsène Lupin. —Tr.

well. The rare guests to his bachelor apartment used to wonder at a testimonial signed by the queen, for philanthropic services to the Red Cross. ("That's a prize! It really impresses my respectable visitors. It cost me three hundred pesetas; and I came out five hundred ahead of the game by setting up a lottery. And if the wounded in Morocco are being robbed, it's those señoras who are to blame!) We ran into him once in the cafés accompanied by an incredible little Andalusian, ageless, olive-skinned, skeletal, dressed like a footman in distress. "My secretary," said Lejeune. (A pause.) "He can neither read nor write, but he's marvelous at looking after horses." Jovial, without being vulgar, he enjoyed reading good books.

We left the Liceo together: the enchantment of the Russian ballets was totally in keeping with the magic of the nights in this city. In a blue *paseo* (boulevard) overlooking the glowing hearth of the city and the deep blue of the harbor—somewhere, suspended between sea and sky, the narrow linear beacon of a lighthouse scanning the horizon at regular intervals—we took leave of two charming, perfumed young ladies who know nothing of our real identities and would not have understood our language. Bourgeois china dolls—Mercédès the blonde, Concepción the brunette—with tiny graceful hands designed for the piano, tiny souls suited for prattle, tiny bodies (in time lascivious) made for the leisure of villas. These graceful creatures of another human species, strangely confined, imprisoned by money as are so many of our people by poverty, amuse us like figures in a ballet; we can anticipate their gestures, their speech, even their inner moods, like the movements of a dance . . . They let us hold their hands, and sometimes their waists; they possess, these delicious mannequins, the suppleness of the human animal in its first bloom of youth, and firm breasts sheathed in white silk. When we were alone we returned to our real faces; our real thoughts returned to us.

Lejeune came to a halt on a street corner. Shiny automobiles slid along the asphalt, leaving a phosphorescent trail behind them—in our eyes.

"I'll hit the banks," he said. "There are bound to be a few days of disorder, you see. So, I'll hit the banks. *My* revolution will be over quickly. I don't believe in *theirs*. Monarchies, republics, unions—I don't give a damn; you understand? Get myself killed for a bunch of sanctimonious, honest, syphilitic *homo sapiens*? I'm not so dumb. You only live once. If you shoot the Jesuits and the generals, I won't be distressed; but I won't go out of my way just to watch. I'd much prefer, you see, to walk that exquisite, brainless little Mercédès home again. If you take a beating, a few bastards who escape the firing squads will always find enough at my place to get themselves over the mountains or across the ocean; I'll write you in at the head of the list. Of course, that won't stop you from saying afterwards that I'm a coward. But don't worry about it. Just don't ask me for more. *Nada más!* That's it, old boy."

The night dragged on; yet we weren't the least bit tired. He continued his soliloquy.

"You see, nothing is real except you for yourself. Me for myself. I am alone, just like you. Close your eyes: the stars disappear. You might love a woman to the point of wanting to kill yourself for her: but you still wouldn't feel anything when she had a toothache. Alone. Alone. We are all alone. It's awful when you think of it! And life goes on, old boy, life goes on . . . I'm getting gray. I've got high blood pressure. What do I have to look forward to? Ten years? Fifteen? Not even that many. See, I might almost envy Concepción or Mercédès—or that twenty-year-old bruiser."

(A brawny soldier passed by along the street.)

"Death is nothing; it is life that is ineffable. How extraordinary to be here, to breathe in this coolness, to feel yourself moving, desiring, thinking, and to discover the world all around you! For the past fifteen years I've never been separated from this little toy (he opened his palm wide, uncovering a triangular object of blue-black steel). "Seven bullets ready at any time. The last one for me. With that certainty, no one is freer than I. When that decision has been made once and for all, you become strong. And wise. I love life, my friend. And I have only my own life. I only risk it to save it. I only fight for myself.

"I have three forms of wealth: women, animals, and plants. My happiness is to walk in a garden where the plants are hardy, the flowers opulent. I crave plants that cry out, that bleed, that sing. And palm trees. Have you ever thought what a palm leaf is? It's strong, supple and firm, full of sap, calm like the stars. There's life. My happiness is to stroke a horse. You put your hand on his muzzle, pat him gently on the chest, and he looks at you like a friend. You'll never have a better friend. (Have you ever noticed how the flesh of animals is charged with electricity?) My happiness is women, all women: I don't even know which give me more pleasure, those I look at or those I take . . . What do you want me to risk all of that for? Go ahead and fight: I'll hit the banks and then it's off to Brazil!"

FOUR

Arming

I HAD NO ANSWER FOR HIM. FAITH, CERTITUDE, ABSURDITY—THEY DON'T need an answer. "All the old poisons of Paris flow through your veins, my friend. Good night." . . . Sometimes, under a light gray sky, the Seine brings strangely opulent iridescences to the slick surface of her still, green waters: pearl-gray, purple, rainbow-hued, opalescent blotches that poison her. More than anyone else—since I had seen them kill off the strongest of the strong—I was conscious of certain imponderable poisons, synthetic products which combine bourgeois temptations with a natural love of life, intelligence and energy with rebellion and poverty . . . Oh happy counterfeiters, carrying your bundles of "merchandise" stuffed in your left pants' pockets, your right hands resting casually on your Brownings! You surely would never have been willing to fight for the *Comité Obrero* (Workers' Committee). But cornered in a dead end with prison the only way out, you died— valiantly—shot down by the cops. That ending was, for you, inevitable . . . after the squalid fights . . . the unspeakable anguish under the eye of the shopkeeper whose sharp looks peel the gold off the phony coin . . . the unavowable murders on the outskirts of town . . . the double crosses you perpetrated against each other—free men, outsiders, proud of being "neither masters or slaves," of living according to reason in the cold, clear light of "conscious egotism" . . . Gangs of rebels, born to adventure, the gray autos carried you off to the guillotine—five thousand francs sewn in your pants' lining, three clips of ammunition (twenty-one bullets, nicely pointed and explicit), and: "We're nobody's fool any more."—"We no longer believe in anything."—"We will carve out a new life for ourselves." But one of the boys, who didn't believe in anything either, found it even more convenient to make blood money on you and sold you out to fat policemen—cash on the line.

No, I much preferred the very different truths held by El Chorro, Eusebio, and a few thousand other comrades who, at every hour, were crossing and recrossing the teeming city, running secret errands.

"Come along," the Mexican said to me, late one afternoon under a reddening sky. You're going to have a good laugh."

The muscles of his massive, square-chinned face were twitching with imperceptible laughter. In a cloud of red dust, we crossed the Gracia quarter: houses, white or red, doors half-opened onto the extraordinary cool, blue shade inside. Not a soul in sight. In the middle of a sweltering, deserted market place the murmur of a fountain mingled with a monotonous female voice: "A-a-a-i-o . . ." A young gypsy was squatting in a narrow triangle of shade, rocking her child to sleep. Red earth, shimmering with heat, dull buzzing of glittering green flies around the squatting young woman, copper flesh of a ripe breast, and the heavy sky where great fiery waves were unfolding invisibly.

Merciful shade gave us back the power of speech. We were climbing a hill.

"You know what's really great?" El Chorro said, "is waking up with the birds in the early morning out on the sierra. The mountains are purple, and the night has fled across the forest. You recognize the birds' songs. You hear the movements of the animals going to drink. The dew sprinkled on the leaves like diamonds. The sun appears and warms without burning . . ."

"Will we take the city, El Chorro?"

"No sé! coño!" ("I haven't the foggiest notion!"—followed by the foulest obscenity). "What we need is a man, a real man. Five thousand men, ten thousand men without one man, and all is lost. One they will follow and obey; one they can love. One leader, and I'd answer: 'Yes.'"

We arrived. "You'll have a good laugh!" El Chorro cried out once more. He led me toward a tumbledown shack built right against the rock on the side of a hill. Our only vista a vegetable patch down below. My companion slapped his thigh joyfully and, pushing open the swinging door, we entered. A young woman seated before a second door rose to meet us. Through a hole the roof, a wide ray of orange sunlight fell across her skinny brown shoulders. She smiled. We passed through that ray of red gold, that smile, the shadow, another swinging door . . .

At first I had trouble making out several squatting forms hovering around a curious low-slung machine. Factory girls. Then I recognized

Jurien, lying with his elbows on the ground, a cigarette between his lips. *"Salut!—Salut!—Salut!"* A huge laugh spread silently across El Chorro's face in the shadows. He pointed to the young women, workers from a nearby factory (just, by chance, next door to an army barracks) and to the curious machine whose familiar mechanism Jurien was checking: *"Madre de Dios!* Those foxy bitches have stolen a machine gun!"

"That's what I was telling you," he added, his voice dropping. "All we need now is one man."

I marveled at the Castilian language, which by calling a man *un hombre* enabled me to hear *une ombre*.[4]

A taxi stops in a narrow backstreet, in front of an ordinary-looking shop window: Café Valenciano. Two gentlemen in traveling clothes get out, carrying heavy suitcases. A young man wearing a cap is smoking not far off. The driver pulls away slowly.

A few moments later the door of the little café opens, letting in four workmen in sandals, caps, overalls. "How are you, Vincent?" says one of them to the owner, who is leaning on the bar.

"Fine, go on in."

One by one, they pass into the back room. Andrés greets them, notebook in hand.

"The San Luis factory," says the first. "Twenty-seven. Then the *Canadiense*: eighteen."

"Very good."

The man from the San Luis factory turns back toward the café and calls out, "Gregorio!"

Gregorio comes in. In a corner of the room, under a window with muslin curtains, José Miro, tall and wiry, his resolute face set off by black eyebrows and metallic eyes, brusquely opens a suitcase resting on a table and full of the blue-black reflections of somber metal. José's pale hand plunges into that heap of black steel and pulls out a Browning. He counts out three clips.

"Take it."

Gregorio takes the gun and the three clips from the edge of the table. His chest is constricted with emotion. He can't think what to say. *"Gracias,"* he finally murmurs. Andrés, José, and the man from

---

4 A shadow, in French —Tr.

the San Luis factory look at him attentively. But already, the next man is being called in.

"Benavente! . . ."

At times José Miro walks up to a young man, looks him in the eyes, and says: "Every bullet belongs to the Confederation . . ."

One man from the *Canadiense* is missing. Andrés and Miro stare at each other. The leader of the group, suddenly worried, searches his memory.

"Eighteen, you said."

"*Si, si*. Eighteen."

One didn't show up. One got lost on the way. The street, however, was still safe. The *patrón* vouched for it. But one weapon remained, useless, at the bottom of an empty suitcase, its bluish reflection mirroring the anxiety on three faces. The specter, as yet unacknowledged, of betrayal was already in the air . . .

"My God!" cries the delegate from the *Canadiense*. "Quiroja didn't come. His wife is having a baby."

"Then give him this," says Miro, "for the baptism."

The empty suitcase clicks shut. The specter disappears. The *patrón* brings in several glass *porros* (decanters) filled with a red wine so thick it is almost black . . .

Workers stream out through the dazzling city toward their homes in the poor quarters, their steps lightened, shoulders thrown back with a new feeling of power. Their hands never tire of caressing the weapons' black steel. And waves of pride and strength flow from that steel into their muscular arms, through the spinal column to those precincts of the brain where; by a mysterious chemistry, that essential life force we call the Will is distilled. A man carrying a weapon (especially if he has been disarmed for a long time, and especially in a modern city where possessing a weapon, secret and dangerous, always assumes near-tragic implications) is boosted by the dual awareness of the danger he is carrying and the danger he is running. The gun, restoring his primordial right, places him outside the written law (the law of others). In the busy crowd along the main arteries these workers, who had always felt degraded by the contrast between their sloppy old suits or overalls and bourgeois dress, pass expensive restaurants they never enter, luxurious cafés from which strains of music emanate, shop windows with astonishing displays of objects so beyond their means as to be not even tempting: leathers, silks, chrome, gold, pearls. Here they encounter the women of that other race, sheathed in precious fabrics, their complexions colored by good health and luxury as by a soft inner light. Here they encounter well-fed men with relaxed faces, haughty, superior looks under broad felt hats. The workers caress their Brownings and move about, already like lean wolves creeping unseen into a fat and peaceful flock, contemplating the boldest of assaults.

Once they enter the slum streets where they feel at home, their exuberance brings them together in talkative groups. Now and then the weapons glisten in the palms of their powerful hands as they feel the virile heft of sleek metal or hold them out nervously at arm's length. It becomes a kind of game to load and unload them: that is how Juan Bregat of the mechanics' union killed himself.

They don't have much reason to ponder over the value of their lives, these people. Never will they escape from these shacks (which stink from cooking oil and bedbugs), from the factories (where their bodies and brains are drained each day), from the stifling slums, from the swarms of kinds with their dirty, matted, lice-infested hair. Never will the young charms of the *novias* (fiancées) survive the effects of hunger, the hospital, the dirty wash, the warmed-over meals, the oppression of whitewashed walls. Never, never, never. Only by force will they break out of the closed circle of their fate. And tough luck for those who fall by the wayside (losing nothing of importance anyway). The others, the victors, would open the way of the future. What kind of future? The more thoughtful quote Reclus, Kropotkin, Malatesta, Anselmo Lorenzo with feverish enthusiasm. But what need is there to think so much? Any future would be better than the present.

FIVE

Allies

A SILENT BACK STREET IN THREE CLASHING COLORS: FAÇADES WHITE, PAVE-
ments of reddish clay, a high stone wall casting blue shadows. The wall
(the color of dead leaves) is pierced at intervals by narrow windows
with ornate wrought-iron bars. Behind that ironwork flowers lie imprisoned under the cool shadow of a soldiers' barracks. The white faces of
women with fat chins and calm gluttonous lips can sometimes be seen
there. Peacefully, they gaze into the street with large, black velvet eyes
where life seems to stagnate as in a still pond. Next to a low door over
which a double escutcheon has been carved into the stone, a soldier
stands watch like a living statue, his hands folded across the barrel of
his short rifle. A black, three-cornered hat, a black cape, yellow leather
straps crisscrossing his chest: he too, motionless, oppresses the lifeless
street with his stagnant gaze. At times, when we stare at him, a stubborn black hatred is aroused in his eyes—a tiny white spark that glows
and sinks into dark pools. A rough, square-cut beard hardens his features. These *guardia civils*, recruited in the old-fashioned, backward
provinces, well-housed, well-fed, are perhaps the only soldiers in the
city loyal to the king. On the highways they escort the convoys of prisoners traveling to the presidios. They surround the scaffold while the
executioner slowly tightens the garrote around the neck of a man who
is already nothing more than a gasping, terrified rag of a man. During
military ceremonies they surround the Señor Governor, whose career
might be shortened by a bomb—if it weren't for the bulwark of their
black and yellow bodies.

Two men walking along the narrow sidewalk across the street from
the sentry turn around suddenly and face him. One is thin, hard, wiry
with a dark metallic look; the other, rough-hewn, dressed in a shabby
gray suit, collarless, his cap pushed down on the back of his neck, slightly
aslant, as certain dock workers wear them. The sentry stares at them.

A nervous impulse electrifies his limbs; his hands, already prepared for quick action, tremble on the rifle. The two men across the way, apparently peaceful, exchange glances, each has his right hand in his pocket. The situation is clear. Behind the wrought-iron grill of the nearby window, where cool clinging vines hang drowsily, a woman is looking out, her elbows on the sill. But now her lips turn pale and her pupils darken with awful premonition.

"He's recognized you," the thin than says to his companion. "He's going to set off the alarm. The bell is right behind him. Don't move a muscle. I'll let him have it."

The second answers quickly and quietly behind a false smile like an ill-fitting mask:

"Don't do anything stupid, José! What are you, crazy?"

The flat tone of his voice is decisive. The mask adjusts; the false smile is now real. Slowly the man in gray draws out of his right-hand pants' pocket (the sentry's hands tighten on the rifle barrel, and two pairs of fascinated eyes follow his movement with horrified interest) a silver-plated cigarette case, and opens it:

"Got your lighter, José?"

José brings out his right hand too. Relaxed, they exchange glances, a tiny white spark still burning deep in their eyes. Having lighted their cigarettes, they move on without turning around. The sentry's hands relax their grip on the rifle barrel, the plump woman heaves a long sigh from behind her high grilled window. What happened? Nothing. Why nothing of course. But what heat! Jesus, it's hot.

The perfume of flowers mingles at moments with the salt smell of the nearby sea. The two men plunge into the noisy crowd on the avenue. They enter a quiet street lined with pretentious bourgeois residences, their façades white, pink, blue, green, parti-colored, some overloaded with gilt decorations and lined up, like wealthy matrons wearing all their jewels, along the route of procession. They ring at number 12. White apron, white cap, a vague, pleasant smile tinged with curiosity, the little maid ushers them into the cool shade of the vestibule. They can imagine what they must look like: one a moving man or a contractor inspecting the water mains, the other a suspicious intruder. The taller of the two shakes off their embarrassment with an expansive shrug of the shoulders: an old habit from his days as a dock worker—shaking off the invisible load forever weighing down on his shoulders. He darts a knowing look at the lady's maid, making him uglier than he is, with his round nose, too small for his massive rubbery face, and his sparkling goggle eyes that are a little too far apart (like the eyes of a mischievous fish, I used to think).

"My adorable child, your master is expecting us at four o'clock."

The girl blushes a little, her lips pursed. "Enter, señor." They find themselves in a small gray room furnished with Cordovan leather chairs and a black marble table on which there are some magazines. Out of an ebony frame, an El Greco portrait of an emaciated old man stares down at them, as if through a window, with unfathomed sadness.

"I was right not to shoot," murmured José, surprised at the sound of his own voice, even though it was almost inaudible.

Then they notice another portrait, hung in bizarre apposition to the first, and framed in heavy gold leaf. Huge curved mustaches, enormous blue eyes, rimless glasses and ruffled hair speckled with gray: the leader of the Republican party gives the impression of seeing nothing.

"The son of a bitch," whispers José through clenched teeth.

Just then, as if that were the magic word, a door opens noiselessly between the two portraits and His Honor, the Señor Deputy Domenico y Masses (a fine name—with a hexameter resonance) appears, both hands outstretched, a smile beaming from his eyes, his sensual mouth, his well-tailored frock coat and even, it seems, from his glistening patent leather shoes. The two visitors might have thought they were his intimate friends, he seems so overjoyed by their presence. In his study, bathed in the green light of a rose-studded garden, a pink marble Aphrodite with raised arms stands over the desk. There is also the portrait of a young boy, like one of Van Dyck's little English princes. From the depths of a red leather armchair a bald man, freshly shaven, rather stout with bushy white eyebrows, half rises and bows ceremoniously to the visitors. A double chain of gold is strung across his white polka-dotted vest. José Miro smiles, imagining himself as amiable, but only succeeds in uncovering a set of teeth that makes him look like a young wolf.

"Here is the government of tomorrow," Señor Domenico is saying, his palms outstretched, "or most of it."

They talk, for an hour, resorting at times to euphemisms and circumlocutions, interrupting themselves at just the right moment to light a cigar (Señor Domenico surprised them by opening a little safe hidden behind a tapestry, and, smiling resplendently, bringing out his most precious Havanas). A map is spread out at Aphrodite's feet; the ex-stevedore outlines a wide semicircle around the city with his thumb. A heavy envelope with a number in four figures in the corner is swallowed in the pocket of the gray-jacketed visitor. Dates are worked out.

Señor Domenico personally shows his guests to the door. The other man had hardly budged from his armchair. At the age of fifty-six Don Ramon Valls would say, not with out pride: "I got my start at the age of twenty-three with two hundred thousand pesetas; I'm worth a couple of million today. O.K.! By the time I'm sixty, I'll have doubled my capital." He exports oil from Tortosa, wood from Galicia, ore from the Asturias, books from Madrid. His character combines a certain American touch with the good-natured simplicity of a former ship owner who has no objections to mixing business with pleasure so long as he is able, as the evening wears on and the air grows thick with off-color stories, to innocently strike the most telling and treacherous blows against his antagonist with admirably feigned cordiality. This "old hog," as he was cruelly nicknamed by some young businessmen (whom he cheated while leaving them the satisfaction of thinking they were much smarter than he) was able to pick up 30 per cent of his seemingly reasonable profits off the carpets of drawing rooms and private studies. His forte was his ability to judge men, and to bring off a big copper deal, paying less attention to the probable fluctuations of the market than to the temperament of the prospective buyer.

Now, left alone, he raises his eyebrows (with him a sign of the greatest perplexity), and his eyes, the eyes of a great, melancholy dog. Dealing with men unlike any he had ever known has left him angry with himself. "Smalltime hoodlums," he thinks. On the other hand, that self-assurance, that clearheadedness, that grip on something bigger— bigger, actually, than any juicy deal in the millions . . . As the deputy returns, the exporter grumbles:

"Formidable allies. Are you sure we're not better off with our enemies?"

"Don Ramon, it's people like that who make revolutions. The riffraff begin the job, the parliaments finish it."

". . . by finishing off the riffraff," said Don Ramon in that toneless voice he uses for dubious transactions.

The two visitors move off, out of place on that street lined with stately houses.

"Will they go along with us?" José asks brusquely.

The ex-stevedore shifts the invisible load on his shoulders.

"They need us."

"If they do go along, Dario, so much the worse for them."

"Don't say that, my boy. There are things that those foxes can over-hear at a distance, through the thickest walls. Their ears are made that way."

And if they don't go along," José continues, "so much the worse for them!"

"And so much the worse for us. [Dario whistles.] Eh, *Chico*, I think that this time we're being tailed for real . . ."

They are. Two gentlemen, wearing Panama hats and carrying canes, are walking resolutely down the street twenty paces behind them.

Dario represses an uneasy feeling. How the streets seem to narrow at times like this! The Committee's money weighs heavily in his jacket. Fortunately a car pulls up. He hops in. José Miro turns on his heels—hard and straight like a steel mannequin—at the curb.

The plain-clothesmen, now uneasy themselves, approach him. They slow their pace. When they get to where Miro is standing, glaring hard at them, they begin talking loudly about a certain Conchita and look away. Miro follows them. The hunters feel hunted now. That very day an informer had been found, in the center of town, with a hole clean through his head. Icy shivers run up their spines as Miro's measured step falls in with theirs. That night, Miro described that chase to us, laughing like a mischievous child.

"In the end I swear to you they were dying to take to their heels like rabbits. Every five yards they would turn around. I was making a horri-ble face, so as to keep from laughing, you see. One goes into a cigar store. The other stops outside the window. I do likewise. We peer at each other out of the corner of the eye. He gets brave: 'Mister . . .'—'What?'—'Mister, you shouldn't hold it against us . . .' (Oh, that hangdog look on his paunchy face. It's true, I didn't hold it against him any more.) 'Ours is a dirty job. But I have three children. Three daughters, mister: Maria, Concha, Luisa' (He told me the names and I remember them, how do you like that?), 'seven, eight, and nine years old. And a bullet in my leg, mister, brought back from the Riff. And no trade to work at. But I'm a sympathizer' (he said 'sympathizer!') 'believe me. And if your plans work out, remember my name. You have a friend in the 2d Brigade: Jacinto Palomas, Pa-lo-mas. Tell Señor Dario that we all admire him. He's a re-mark-a-ble orator!'"

SIX

Dario

DARIO'S DAYS BEGAN AT SIX IN THE MORNING, WITH THE EARLIEST STARTING factories. He swallowed his coffee in the open air at one of the street-corner stands where workers grab a bite on the run. At an hour when the police informers were still rubbing their eyes, he would burst into a little print shop with a freshly washed window, give a friendly tap on the behind to the apprentice who was sweeping up, and bend down between two piles of posters depicting blue-and-yellow acrobats swinging from white trapezes (THE LAURENCE BROTHERS INIMITABLE ECCENTRIC in dazzling letters straddling the paper) and a huge woman's face, half-yellow, half-purple: GRACIOSA LA MISTERIOSA. Farther down, Dario's hand was attracted by stacks of little yellow papers covered with fine print, nesting between the posters. As he read, his head cocked to one side, his mischievous eye saw a host of things through that wretched yellow paper. "Soldiers! Brothers!" . . . How much art it had taken to draft this appeal in terms both moving and familiar, to put in the words that fire the imagination, "barricades," and "to arms"; to mention the great man who was shot in 1909,[5] to recall the Moroccan campaign; and all of this without inflaming the cautious bourgeois of the Regionalist League, all without displeasing the comrades of the Confederation, without incurring the anarchists' veto. "Sons of the people, be with the people! For justice and for liberty! For the bread of the workers!" Everybody would find whatever he was looking for in one or another of these ambiguous words.

Noon. A strident whistle blast suddenly called forth a crowd in blue coveralls, near a factory in Sans, a neighborhood of cheap working-class

---

5   Francisco Ferrer, executed October 13, 1909, at Montjuich. A libertarian teacher, he happened to be in Barcelona during the general strike which had forced the government to flee. Accused—without the slightest evidence—of fomenting the whole rebellion, his trial and execution sparked a worldwide protest movement similar to the Sacco-Vanzetti movement a generation later. —Tr.

hash houses. Dario, perched on top of a chair, smiled as he watched a terrified policeman being chased by some kids throwing stones on the other side of the square. "Run, you old beggar, run; you'll have to do lots more running!" And so Dario began his speech in the midst of side-splitting laughter, power and confidence already awakened among the three hundred men crowding around him, surrounding him with an odor of male perspiration, machine oil, metal dust, and tar. Dario found the right words to reach these men. An open mouth, a damp forehead, a flushed glance revealed to him that his words had struck home, his efforts were rewarded. The Moroccan dead, the war dead, the bombed-out cities, the fortunes made "in blood, in excrement, and in mud," the red flags flying over Russia, the famine invading Europe, the Jesuits, the degenerate King—"*el rey cretino* with his slack mouth like a slit in a piggy bank and his chin all unscrewed" (laughter almost broke out, relaxing the tension in the crowd; but the orator's voice climbed up an octave and—like an athlete who recovers his balance on the bar—recovered possession of three hundred souls suspended on the brink of laughter and brought them all violently under the spell of his awesome words), "the miserable King who shot our great Ferrer . . ."

Then, to temper the heat of that just hatred, Dario threw out some facts and figures with cold precision: Eight hours of work. Minimum wage. Fifteen per cent increase. Moratorium on rents. Lower rents. Repeal of administrative sanctions . . . Each listener, brought back to reality, measured the calculated realism of these demands against his daily pain and poverty. It was now time for the final appeal, spewed out in symbolic words, vague and boundless, carrying everything with it: solidarity, justice, the republic, labor, the future . . . Dario plunged into the crowd which surged around him, hugging, kissing, questioning, and arguing with him. A bare-chested giant whispered in his ear, in a cloud of garlic and wine: "We're twenty Brownings short." Warm voices vibrated through the air. Comrades surrounded Dario all the way to a courtyard with two exits where he jumped onto his bike and rushed off to carry the word to a place twenty minutes away, just a few moments before the whistle blast which called the men back to work. The echo of his words continued to electrify their minds long afterward. And, sensing this wake of energy trailing behind him, he shrugged his burden of fatigue higher up on his shoulders and slept, exhausted, for two hours on a friend's cot (near the window a young woman was noiselessly doing her wash, immersed in a soft bluish halo against the white wall: the orator's eyes closed over that calm and serene image. He awoke to the refreshing sight of children's clothing decked out like flags across the room). Around four o'clock he entered the *Comité Obrero* without knocking.

This was perhaps the most tiring hour of the day. For here he would find Porter, the cement worker, ceaselessly demanding explanations, setting limits, criticizing errors, warning of dangers, stuffing his speeches full of complex allusions with triple meanings—incomprehensible at first—or declaring brutally, both fists square on the table, hair in angry disarray: "Any comrades who see themselves as future ministers . . . any dictators-in-embryo, whatever service they may have performed, will have to be crushed!" And he would look straight in front of him into the emptiness of a dirty mirror. If there were any angry outbursts, he would say dryly: "I'm not pointing at any individuals. History is there, comrades, to show us the danger." He listened to Dario with a sort of ostentatious deference. And his question fell, like a stone in deep water, radiating countless ripples:

"Will we take power, yes or no?"

Dario was forced to explain himself: We are not power seekers. We are libertarians. But we have to take practical necessities into account. We will accept full responsibility for the consequences of our acts. The Committee would be a temporary revolutionary organ expressing the will of the Confederation, and not a government." Dario was well aware that he was becoming entangled, that he was playing with words, not daring to come to the point or to call things by their right name. A dull desire fermented within him to smash his fist down on the table, releasing all his pent-up brutality, and to cry out: "We'll do whatever must be done, *Madre de Dios de Madre de Dios!* and our sacrosanct principles won't be any the worse for it!" But that would have been a victory for calm, collected Portez, who would immediately have quoted Kropotkin, the bylaws of the Confederation, its conventions, Spartacus, Baboeuf, Anselmo Lorenzo, and carried the majority on a vote of no confidence. At moments like this, Dario became ugly, his large body slackened, his relatively small head hung awkwardly on a wrinkled, vaguely grayish neck, his eyes turned colorless. His words and gestures—evasively acquiescent—were delivered with half-hearted cunning. Portez pushed home his advantage by proposing the creation of a Control Commission authorized to relieve members of the Committee of their authority if they overstepped their mandates . . . Dario voted "for" with indifference.

"Back to the agenda," murmured old Ribas, the chairman, without raising his white head.

Now it was Dario's turn to take the offensive. He was never one for arguing on general principles . . . "The men at Granollérs haven't yet received any weapons. What's going on? . . . Sans is twenty Brownings short . . . Perez Vidal of the barbers' is an *agent provocateur*: this has been known for several days and he is still alive . . . Why has the Committee's envoy to Paris not left yet? . . . Things will never be ready for the nineteenth."

Heated voices rose to answer him. The room was, filled with hubbub. A young woman wearing a gold-colored scarf on her head appeared in the doorway and whispered, smiling:

"Comrades, you can be heard outside in the courtyard!" That golden smile, that voice—like a fresh-water stream among their voices—calmed the men.

"Let's get back to the question of rents," said Ribas.

I would meet Dario sometimes in the evenings, in a tiny lodging which was dark and cool. The air and the noise of the street wafted in through the balcony. On extremely hot days, the gray shadow of the high wall of a medieval convent lent shade to that house, our refuge in the evening. There was wine in big glasses on the unvarnished wooden table. Some tomatoes, red peppers, and onions lying nearby in a dish where everybody took what he wanted made it even more like a room in an inn. Dario would gulp down his wine. His narrow greenish eyes were now relaxed; the faint ugliness of his features seemed to disappear; he spoke about the coming insurrection with an infectious confidence. "Oh, sure, all those readers of *La Conquête du pain* don't really believe we can win. Hold out one week for history's sake, that's the main thing as far as they're concerned. Afterward—they all hope to escape to Argentina; for they have a vocation for collective martyrdom and an individual love of self-preservation. But it doesn't make any difference. The main thing is to begin. Action has its own laws. Once things get started, when it's no longer possible to turn back, they'll do—we'll all do—what must be done . . . What will it be? I haven't any idea, Comrade. But certainly a whole lot of things we don't even suspect . . ."

"You have to burn your boats. If Cortes hadn't burned his, his conquistadores would have re-embarked like cowards. Burn your boats . . ."

"In 1902 we held the city for seven days. In 1909 we held out for three days, without, moreover, finding anything better to do than burn a few churches. There were no leaders, no plans, no guiding ideas. Now, all we need are a couple of weeks to make us practically invincible."

Indeed? Obviously Dario wasn't saying everything he was thinking. Had he really thought it out himself? He made us explain the Russian events to him while he wrinkled his brows like a schoolboy having trouble following the lesson. Then, suddenly erect, joyful:

"I've got a feeling we're going to catch up with the Russians! That would be beautiful, Europe burning at both ends!"

Dario often slept in that dwelling, after secret meetings that might last until the hour when the city of pleasure lighted its lamps: a fiery glow mounting above the gloomy convent from the brightly lit streets. Couples entwined along the street, standing motionless in front of the old doors with their wrought-iron knockers. From his balcony, Dario would lean out over them for a few moments, breathing in the throbbing freshness of the night, stretching his great arms (capable of carrying two-hundred-pound loads), mouthing a cry of power and fatigue which had to be repressed. He would totter back into the room where a shade-less oil lamp was burning on the table among the wine glasses and the remains of supper. With the indolent step of a tired cat he crossed through that feeble yellowish light and entered a sort of dark closet built under the stairway, where there was just enough room for a chair and a bedstead. It was there that he lay down, without a light, cramped as if in a dungeon, a Browning at his bedside.

But sometimes a mouse like noise made him stretch out his hand and draw open the bolt. Then Lolita would slip in next to him, naked under her red-and-blue striped Indian mantle (the colors invisible in the dark), svelte and cool, yet burning. She pressed herself close to him without speaking a word. He sought her face and found only her ardent lips. "Let me look at you," he said. He struck a phosphorus match against the wall. A sputtering blue star, hissing and spidery, burst into flame at his fingertips: her delicate, soft-toned face—with its huge dark eyes, each now lighted by a spark, shining from out of their deep-set, dusky orbits—was nestled in the hollow of his arm, with a poor, gentle, worried smile. Dario gazed at it until the ephemeral light singeing his fingers went out. They made love in total darkness—in silence, for he was hurried and tired, and she always felt on the verge of losing him.

SEVEN

The Trap, Power, the King

AT THAT PRECISE MOMENT A TELEPHONE RANG IN THE LARGE, QUIET OFFICES of the Deputy Commissioner of the Security Police, a stubborn old civil servant with the smooth, hairless face of an actor. Don Felipe Sarria put down his cigarette in a nickel ashtray. "Hello? Ah, it's you. Very good." At the other end of the line, a constrained voice was battling against the fa-la-las of an orchestra. Hard little heels hammering rhythmically on the boards made a din like thick hail beating down on that prudent voice. The man was evidently calling from the wings of a dance hall. The Deputy Commissioner listened with great attention. "Himself! Well, well. At Lloria's? *Calle* Jeronima, number 26? Just a minute . . . On the second floor, you say? The room is on the right, under the stairs, at the end of the hall. The nearest window is on the courtyard? That's it?—Good-by." The insidious voice fell silent over the receiver. The Deputy Commissioner turned a switch and the room was flooded with light. The full-dress portrait of the King appeared, set off by a massive gilt frame, between the safe and a strongbox containing the informers' dossiers: a feeble smile and a sidewise glance hanging in the air behind the policeman. Don Felipe looked through a big file: "*Lloria*, married to Sarda, Maria (Lolita), aged 27 . . ." From another file containing the plans of houses occupied by the activists ("extremely dangerous") entered on list #A-2, Don Felipe withdrew a more interesting card: the doors, the heights of the windows, the turnings of the corridors, everything fell clearly into place before his eyes, and this perfect layout, carefully drawn up by a prize student of the School of Art and Design, became the blueprint for a trap . . . With the point of his pencil, Don Felipe, pensive, slowly traced a circle on the plan, in the room where Dario was sleeping. Then, still completely absorbed, he put in three little dots—the tiny, schematic representation of a face.

"Of course. Of course."

The pencil point mechanically traced another circle, sketching another head, somewhat smaller, hugging the first one: a slightly heavier line representing the mouth. Only then did the policeman come out of his dream: Two men in the courtyard. Two men in the street. Three to make the arrest. No exit. A perfect trap. Very good. Don Felipe rubbed his hands together. He was about to ring, to close this trap with a mere push of the finger in the shadows. The King approved silently from his shining frame and purple velvet backdrop above. But, but . . .

But the anger of those thousands of workers, tomorrow, in the back streets, the cold fury of all those men in File #A ("dangerous") would haunt the city, invisible, controlled, vehement yet ready to explode in an outcry or, worse still, in the dry crackle of pistol-shots. Two or three officers would be dead by nightfall, without any doubt. Don Felipe peered into the future. And after that?—After that was the great unknown of the masses' anger.

And then this man, asleep in the rectangle now marked by two circles . . . "Hmmm," thought Don Felipe in spite of himself (one thought crossing another en route from the depths where the light never penetrates), "two heads, one against the other . . ." The Regionalist League feared him more than anybody. Arrest him? Enrage the workers, calm the regionalists. Self-interest added its ounce of gold to the dark nugget of fear on the invisible scales.

The next day we buried Juan Bregat. He killed himself accidentally while handling a Browning with a child's delight and clumsiness. Some comrades had left his body in an empty bystreet, and most people believed it had been a crime of the police. We knew better. The bullet made a hole in his forehead above the left eyebrow: and this hole, black at the edges, plugged with a cotton wad, gave him the look of a young victim of the firing squad. The totally tragic character of his death was apparent in the attenuated sharpness of his features, the greenish tint of his skin, the stale odor given off by that livid flesh—virile only yesterday—in the insistent buzzing of the flies over that darkened mouth; apparent, too, in a different manner—transformed into living, suffering flesh—in that dark form standing at the bedside, straight but broken, showing the pallor beneath the veil and two shriveled hands clasped one over the other (whose rigidity made me think of the frozen hands of the women in mourning one finds among the stone figures of cathedrals). Standing around the dead man in the small, white hospital room, the comrades were saying, "The first blood." They passed gravely by him, murmuring almost aloud, as if he could have heard them, "Adieu! Adieu!" They stood around the corridor and in the courtyard with its barred windows, discussing this perhaps senseless death on which their faith had now conferred a higher sense. For the light of humanity to be suddenly snuffed out within an ardent young brain, what absurdity!—no matter how it happens. But to die from a clumsy gesture while loading your weapon on the eve of the battle or to die from a stray bullet during the shooting, what difference is there? Somehow it seems even more absurd to be the first one killed in the insurrection or the last one killed in the mutiny, and yet it is the nature of things that we must cry for these two. Or to fall, judged and vanquished, after the combat, under twelve bullets from twelve miserable soldiers whom you hate with all your soul in that awful moment but whom you nonetheless forgive, shouting; "Brothers!" You don't choose your time. This first blood was the purest, the blood of a young worker with his vision firmly attached to life, loved by a wife and a child—and by us—spilled in vain (but again, can one ever know which is vain and which is fruitful? And wasn't it the fertility of your blood, poor Juan, that gave us that feeling of strength when, several thousand strong, we addressed you our soldiers' farewell?).

There was no singing, no music, no speeches. The coffin, nailed shut over that energetic brow, was lifted by anonymous hands, in a silence so profound I thought I could hear the beating of hearts. The coffin floated above our heads, carried, one might have said, on the wave of a blue tide, for practically all these men were dressed as usual in their blue overalls, sandals, and caps. Not many women had come, because of the vague apprehension that hovered over us. The workers' wives pressed close to their men. The red ribbons of the wreaths clung like glowing cinders to the bare, black hearse which bore no cross. The black horses cut through the crowd, their tall plumes bobbing. We were that crowd, first a few hundred, then a few thousand, then waves of people flooding the street . . . We who preceded, who surrounded, who followed that solemn rig, bathed in an extraordinary silence: the tramp of countless feet, the murmur of voices, and, set above it all, concentrated around that body with the hole in its brow, an oppressive expectation, unexpressed, inexpressible: as if a song were held suspended over all those silent lips, ready to fly up—a song or a shout—a shout

or a sob—a sob—no, no; a cry, an outburst . . . The estuaries of the
streets opened to that procession like the future to deeds; and little by
little our mass formed into a column, set off from the passive and ill-
assorted people who watched us pass from the sidewalks, by its work
clothes (punctuated by an occasional soldier's uniform) and by its air of
tension. We followed the tall black plumes through a wealthy quarter.
Our unexpressed outburst—the song on our silent lips—carried us along
more than we carried it. There was defiance in our step, in our looks,
in the stiffening of our necks, in the squaring of our shoulders. The
opulent houses watched us parade by, silent too, like faces with closed
eyes. Frightened faces, some with wide-open eyes, fixed us with dogged,
fearful stares through half-parted curtains. We turned onto the bleak
highways that lead out of town. Buildings became scarcer. No more
crowds—only, at long intervals, some groups of people at doorsteps.
Old women or little girls asked, "Who died?"—surprised to hear the
name of an unknown man and to see thousands of men accompanying
that unknown man to the cemetery, moving forward with firm steps as
if marching to meeting the living. By that point we had formed a long
column, almost uniformly blue and gray, moving rhythmically. As we
approached, the police disappeared. The column was composed mainly
of young men whose heavy weapons could be seen bulging under their
light clothing and at times carried openly. Their eyes answered any per-
sistent stare by suddenly unsheathing hard, sullen looks. We were no
longer a dead man's companions, but a group of shock troops on the
march with tense souls and ready hands.

Dario, who was also hiding behind curtains, watched us pass, meas-
uring our spirit in his mind and reflecting that Juan Bregat's blood
(poor lad!) had at last solidified the workers' strength. No one knew
that Dario was standing at that window, indistinguishable from all the
others. No one, except Señor Felipe Sarria (the only one who shouldn't
have known it) and who, knowing just about everything, was by now
almost unable to do anything.

That afternoon had been cool; the evening was sweltering. Heavy clouds
carried by hot winds came toward the city from the sunbaked plateaus
of Castille and probably from even farther off, from the African desert.
The crowds on the boulevards strolled more slowly than usual. Their
bodies were damp, the lights were glaring, the shadows opaque. And

suddenly a current began to pass from person to person, keying up the nerves of all those people who, a moment before, had been walking nonchalantly under heavy, overhanging trees. Those who were walking up toward the heights turned around, as if hypnotized, and descended toward the harbor. Human rivulets flowed from all sides toward the dense and murmuring crowd which had gathered suddenly near a café where huge perpendicular letters of fire burned out: BRAZIL. A gleaming automobile, like an extraordinary dark beetle, greenly iridescent, stopped there; white sheets of paper were being tossed out in sprays around it, and snapped up by hands and eyes more eagerly than flowers during the Festival of Flowers. And when two men appeared, standing up on the seat, erect above the dark and moving crowd, sharply illuminated by the fiery letters (BRAZIL), the murmur of the human tide changed into a crackling of hands, a long ovation, then a clamorous outcry. The acclamation, dying off and rising up anew, was mingled with distant rolls of thunder. Señor Domenico y Massés greeted the crowd with bows and more bows, from his handsome beard, his outstretched hands, and the smile of his gleaming teeth. He begged for silence so that the leader of the Regionalist League, more massive and rude, with the square face of a Flemish squire, might speak . . . The latter's peremptory voice snapped like a flag in the wind.

The comrades stood out in that perfumed crowd whose exhilaration they did not share. If Señor Domenico had felt the weight of their defiant looks on him, his triumphant smile would certainly have faded like the light of a candle, a candle which makes huge shadows dance in the night but which vanishes under the clear light of day . . . "*Salut*, Lejeune!"—"*Salut!*"—"They say that the infantry *juntas* . . ."—"Yes."— "And informer was killed this morning, at San Andrés . . ."—"So you're still going along with those jokers?"—"Come and drink an orangeade."

At the same time as on the previous evening, the same call on the telephone obliged Don Felipe to put down his cigarette in the nickel ashtray. This time a queer, hollow voice was trembling at the other end of the wire. Don Felipe was obliged to catch it on the wing to hold it. "Hello, hello! Yes, of course . . . I can't hear you . . . What do you say? Killed? Where? At home? Perez Vidal? . . ." ("Already!" thought Don Felipe. In fact, the stabbing came at a convenient time. A considerable sum of money had been saved: once Perez Vidal had been "uncovered," it would have been necessary to pay his way to Buenos Aires.) "You think you've been spotted? Of course . . . Count on me. But if you're not completely sure of it, try to wait it out a few days. Come now, you are probably under considerable emotional strain because of this unfortunate inci- dent . . ." The hollow voice on the other end of the line thrashed about like a fish in a creel: Let me have some money: some money and then the fastest train to Madrid! Wait it out? . . . The man who was speaking felt a vague nervous ache at the point on his chest where Perez Vidal had had his flesh pierced by a thin, *triangular* blade. "Count on me!" repeated Don Felipe, but he reflected that in three or four days the men in file #A-2 might perhaps save him some more money.

Nonetheless he sighed at the thought of that big hairy devil now doubtless stretched out on the black marble table of the morgue. (The larynx distends the skin around their throats in a strange manner, as if a knot had been tied underneath; their toes, rimmed with shapeless toe- nails, look miserable and tragic.) A good spy, Perez Vidal. Better than this one . . . Not as cowardly. He dared to write. Imprudent. Not a liar, though, nor a scatterbrain . . . Too bad. Don Felipe turned the switch. A white light rippled across the room. The light made him feel better. Between the safe and the strongbox containing the secret agents' dos- siers ("the stoolies' box") the King's feeble smile stood out against its purple background reflecting the heavy gilt of the frame. The King, all decked out, gave the impression of emerging from some place of ill repute, his flesh emptied, his jaw elongated by a flabby complacency. Don Felipe took a few steps. Walking on a thick carpet always gave him a feeling of security. A strong odor of jasmine penetrated through the Gothic arch of the window. The thin trickle of a fountain was hissing out there on the tiny patio. Don Felipe turned his ear to that soft sound whose wordless melody turned the night from black to blue and peopled the growing silence with reassuring voices. But now the noisy shout- ing of a crowd, slow and powerful like the tide, came from the patio through the window frame, filled the brightly lit room and broke in an inexorable wave around the happy King. The clamor died and built up again, a little closer, a little louder.

Don Felipe moved back into the interior of the room. The King seemed to be smiling into space at the thought of some low pleasures he had just left behind the purple hangings in the background. For the first time in his life, Don Felipe looked at the august portrait with a kind of hatred which even he was surprised to feel. A poor portrait. A stupid smile. (He shrugged his shoulders . . .) "It is true, he does look as if he's thinking dirty thoughts." The thunder was still rolling along the boulevards. Don Felipe caught himself saying out loud:

"As for me, Your Majesty, I'm heading over the Pyrenees!"

And, as in former times back in school when, as soon as the teacher turned his back, little Felipe would stick out his tongue in a complicated grimace which was his greatest secret and his most powerful weapon, now the Deputy Commissioner of the Security Police, fifty years old, balding and overweight, stuck out his tongue at the King.

EIGHT

Meditation on Victory

NIGHTS. OUR FOOTSTEPS IN THE NIGHT. OUR VOICES, THOSE MEDITERRANEAN voices ringing like cymbals . . . "This is the land of lotteries," cried Eusebio. "Who wouldn't play his life on the lottery of the barricades? Double or nothing!" We were certainly neither Germanophiles nor Alliadophiles (another term coined by the newspapers). But with each faraway upheaval of the shell-torn soil on the Somme, the Artois, Champagne, or the Meuse, we were better able to hear the foundations of the world cracking. "What a great Paris Commune there will be after the defeat!" Deserters embroidered on the stories of the April mutinies among the immensely weary horizon-blue armies. "There will be a German revolution," asserted others, who seemed more daring. Germany and Austria were subsisting on chemically prepared foodstuffs, the newspapers proclaimed daily. A French Commune, a German Commune—after the Russian Commune—we could already make out the red flags waving proudly through the haze of the future. They were necessary to reason, to that vague confidence in the universe without which life becomes unthinkable to anyone with his eyes open. And what if the circle of absurdity were not broken? If, after this war, these millions of dead, this disemboweled Europe, we were to know once again the peace of times past with the old, multicolored flags flying over the bone heaps? This city, this country condemned the war from the depths of its soul. The newspapers kept it quiet, for they all lied (and the propaganda bureaus of the belligerents gave them new reasons for lying on the first of every month), but everyone said it. We lived in expectation of a catastrophe which would be at the same time a retribution and a renascence, a rehabilitation of human energies and a new reason for believing in men. The Russian Revolution, the first sign, had revived that universal expectation.

Couet sometimes wore a pair of heavy infantryman's boots which marked him out on the streetcars as a deserter. People would stare at him. Once someone asked him: "Deserter? . . ." He nodded yes, out of defiance. "Ali, you are quite right, young man," said a well-dressed old man, putting his arm around his shoulder. Another smiled his approval . . . When, in order to avoid an unnecessary conversation I gave the same answer (falsely, as it happened) to the butcher while he was cutting meat, he immediately wiped his hand clean and held it out to me, cordially . . . In the factories, the workers were willing to work short weeks in order to keep management from laying off the deserters: those fugitives who, by withdrawing their own lives from the tempest of the Front, seemed to be defending life itself.

And this city, this country, peaceful, vigorous, happy, voluptuous, laid out along the edge of the brilliant blue sea, listened to the dulled echoes of the artillery barrages, listened to the beating of the exhausted heart of a wounded Europe, and lived on spilled blood—a profitable pasture! We were all working for the war. We were, in the factories, all of us more or less war workers. Clothes, hides, shoes, canned goods, grenades, machine parts, everything, even fruit—the sweet-smelling Valencia oranges—everything that our hands made, worked, manipulated, embellished" was drained off by the war. The faraway war caused factories to be built in this peaceful country, and filled them with workers who often came from the burning fields of Andalusia, the mountains of Galicia, the barren plains of Castille. The war raised salaries. The war unloosed that fever to live and laugh, to maul women on shabby back-room couches, to see the *bailarinas* flitting about, with their naked breasts, in the cabarets; for after the pressure of work it was necessary, in that constant fever of death and madness, *to feel yourself living*. The avidity of men in shirt sleeves turned loose by the factories in the evening, miserable but muscular, without a place to stay Worth sitting under a lamp in, but with a peseta in their pocket to buy an evening of painted pleasure—without confidence in the future, or rather with no other hope than that of their simmering revolt.

Every city contains many cities. This was ours. We did not penetrate into the others. There was the city of the calculating businessmen who gorged themselves in the best restaurants and who spent their nights undressing the expensive creatures whom we glimpsed passing in limousines. There was the city of the priests, the monks, the Jesuits in their monasteries surrounded by vast gardens like fortified cities. The city of power—held in contempt—with its decorated generals, its policemen bought for a *douro*, its jailers, its informers. The city of writers, professors, journalists—a city of paid phrases, of poisoned words and ideas, of lucrative alchemies. The city of spies, labyrinth of mines and countermines, of secret rendezvous, of multiple treacheries like equations with several unknowns: military intelligence, consulates, Herr Werner, financial dealings through Amsterdam, Mata Hari carrying an address in her handbag (another equation—the exact equivalent of that last bullet, the *coup de grâce*, that would crash through her skull within a few months at the foot of the stake in Vincennes).

Prowling spies sometimes crossed our paths, ready to strip our power bare like the vermin who strip corpses on the battlefields. They offered their money and they asked for nothing in return: the last word in subtlety! The careers of secret agents would be made or broken by the general strike, the possible ruin of the industries working for the Entente. A whole stinking underground mob, drooling over the limbs of a proletarian giant ready to leap forward, imagined they were making it move at their will, like a puppet. That made us laugh. "What a rude awakening they'll have, those s.o.b.s, if things work out! . . ." In those cities the blood of Europe and the labor of three hundred thousand workers had brought forth a strange spring of wealth, spurting into a network of golden rivulets. And we knew it. It was in the order of things! Dario would explain: "*They* can no longer put up with the rule of the bureaucrats in Madrid and the political bosses in the provinces. Neither their wealth nor their businesses will be safe as long as the old court camarillas and their personnel of pious, lazy, corrupt scribblers whose bribes start at twenty-five centimes are in power. They are choking, and money is suffocating them." Dario laughed. "And they need us to pull their chestnuts out of the fire. We need them to shake up the old edifice. Afterwards, we'll see . . ." Yes, we'll see. We know the old story. With the monarchists overthrown and the Jesuits in flight, three to six months later, the republics establish order by machine-gunning the workers. An old tradition. Whoever lives will see. We won't always be the weaker. With what is brewing on the other side of the Pyrenees . . ." We'll twist the neck of tradition, right?"—"We're the power, the only power."—"In '73 Alcoy and Cartagena held out for months. We have our Communes, which will be remembered. Wait a bit. *Hombre!* this will be something beautiful!"

It is already something beautiful to be carrying that victory within us. I have doubts, but it is because I am a newcomer in this city: I cannot, as you do, Dario, feel the strength of this people mounting in my very veins. In spite of myself, I often see you with the skeptical eyes of a foreigner: and I see your inexperience, your embryonic organization, your boldly delineated ideas, shedding great light here and there, but incapable of organizing themselves, of becoming precise, disciplined, implacable and self-critical in order to transform the world . . . Only a few thousand union members among three hundred thousand proletarians. Tiny unions that are in reality more or less anarchist discussion groups. Doctrines that border on dreams, burning dreams ready to become acts because men of energy live by them (and because at bottom they are no more than simple truths raised to the level of myths by minds too richly primitive to operate on theories). It is true that at the call of a union of about a hundred comrades, thousands, perhaps tens of thousands of workers would be there, in the street, at our side. It is true that, for more than ten years, the government has not succeeded in building a new prison in this city. The boys in the building trades don't go in for that kind of work. When the government tried to bring in workers from the provinces it only took a few explanations and a few bloody noses to inculcate the feeling of proletarian duty in them.

Dario, I don't know whether we will win. I don't know if we will do any better than they did at Cartagena or Alcoy. It is perfectly possible, Dario, that we will all be shot at the end of this business. I am uncertain of today and I am uncertain of ourselves. Only yesterday you were carrying loads in the harbor yourself. Bent under your burden, your elastic step carried you over the rickety planks laid out from the *quai* to the loading deck of a freighter. The dark oily waters sent you back the reflected image of a giant slave, hideous from the front, your face encrusted with bitter grime, bowed under an Atlas' burden. Your dripping body was ablaze in a flash of sunlight. I, myself, was wearing chains. A literary expression, Dario, for only numbers are worn nowadays, but they are just as heavy to bear. Our old Ribas from the Committee was selling detachable collars in Valencia. Portez spent his time grinding up stones in mechanical molds or drilling holes in steel cogwheels. Miro, with his feline agility and rippling muscles, what was he doing? Oiling machines in a cellar in Gracia. The truth is that we are slaves. Will we take this city? Just look at it, this splendid city, look at these lights, these flames, listen to these magnificent noises—automobiles, streetcars, music, voices, bird songs, and footsteps, footsteps and the indiscernible rustle of silks and satins—to take this city with these hands, our hands, is it possible?

You would certainly laugh, Dario, if I spoke to you aloud like this. I would read in your crafty eye an ironical thought which you would not voice. You distrust intellectuals, especially those who have tasted the poisons of Paris. And you are right to do so. You would say, opening your broad hairy-backed hands, so fraternal and steady: "As for me, I feel able to take everything. Everything." Thus we feel we are immortal until the moment when we no longer feel anything. And life goes on after our little droplet has returned to the ocean. Here my confidence meets yours. Tomorrow is full of greatness. We will not have brought this victory to ripeness in vain. This city will be taken, if not by our hands, at least by others like ours, but stronger. Stronger perhaps for having been better hardened, thanks to our very weakness. If we are beaten, other men, infinitely different from us, infinitely like us, will walk, on a similar evening, in ten years, in twenty years (how long is really without importance) down this *rambla*, meditating on the same victory. Perhaps they will think about our blood. Even now I think I see them and I am thinking about their blood, which will flow too. But they will take the city.

"The citadel," said Dario . . . "We will take the citadel from within."

NINE

The Killer

IT HAPPENED THAT AN APPARENTLY TRIFLING EVENT CROSSED OUR PATH AND stirred up the human tide of the city in a very different manner. Fervent multitudes stood night and day in the boulevard in front of the windows of the hotel where Benito was staying. His appearances on the balcony were greeted with joyful ovations. His automobile was constantly blocked by a dense crowd that threw flowers and would have torn his clothes to pieces each time had he not been protected by some husky sports whose friendly shoves were like punches. "Benito, *Olé! Olé!*" Waves of shouting pursued the retreating red automobile from which a sharp, swarthy profile with a hawk nose and large white teeth was smiling beneath a broad felt hat, looking for all the world like an Indian warrior in a detachable collar. A precious Sunday was lost because Benito had to kill his bull that day. The thin sword in the hand of this ex-cowherd from Andalusia seemed to by parrying the death blow aimed at the monarchy. Everything was forgotten; only the matador existed. "He kills like an angel," wrote the newspapers. "Let's go watch Benito!" cried Eusebio, "we'll fight better afterwards!" When Benito entered the ring a hushed whisper went through the stands. Ten thousand pairs of eyes were riveted to this athlete in silk stockings—narrow in the hips, broad through the shoulders in his gold-embroidered maroon jerkin— as he saluted the other city with his sword: the *capitán general*, a fat old man with a chest full of ribbons; the governor (white sideburns, black paunch); the important citizens in their loge draped with garnet-colored velvet; the ladies, leaning out over floating, arabesque-covered tapestries resembling fantastic flowers from a distance, black lace mantillas over tall hairdos, the ivory of faces and bare arms, the play of fans. The bravos and the shrill applause came across to us from the enemy city which occupied the shady side of the arena. Next, more discreetly, with a slight bowing of his head and his sword, Benito greeted the people, the masses of ardent faces on which the sun was burning harshly. *"Olé! Olé! Olé!"* Benito met this tumultuous outcry with a starry smile.

The bull charged, his gallop heavy and emphatic (but muffled like the beating of some great heart) toward this flamboyant man, admired by the multitude, on whom the living light of ten thousand pairs of eyes and the ill-contained passion of ten thousand men were concentrated, surrounding him with a sort of magnetic field in the sudden silence. The beast was a thoroughbred with such a powerful head that his legs seemed short by comparison. The yellow, green, and orange *banderillas* stuck into his neck lay flat over his back; his flanks were striped with thin streams of red. Dazzled and furious, made drunk by the noise, the sun, the colors, the warm blood, the beast had struggled alone, for ten eternal minutes, against glittering shadows. Every time he thought he had finally caught one of those agile phantoms on the end of his horn, his huge and baffled fury ended up in the tantalizing folds of a flashing cape. Blazing colors such as are never seen in the sierras or on the plains of Andalusia, or even in blood itself—the purples burning like black flames, the reds redder than blood, the blinding blues, the emerald greens at once liquid and hard—appeared like lightning flashes; and the man, the gilded shadow, appeared again farther off, elusive. The animal was gathering speed again, his muzzle flecked with foam, his back steaming—in his glassy, bloodshot eye there was a glow of intelligence, a tiny flame at the bottom of a well, struggling against bewilderment and rage in order to take aim at the new enemy who seemed to be waiting, without a cape, a huge grotesque insect with gilded wings. The *banderillero* twists his body deftly, escaping the black horn which would have torn his innards had his muscles slipped five or ten centimeters. He straightens up again, elegantly, on the toes of his dancing slippers, have planted another dart—carrying the royal colors—painful arrow of fire in the brute's neck. The beast turns and thrashes about on the golden sand in the middle of a circle like a living crater, tormented by man, multiple and false, agile, winged with purple, with blue, with motley laughter, man dancing around him in a cleverly cruel game. The beast turns about and the city turns around him, savage, with ten thousand fixed stares, all alike: those of the ragged beggars, the sweating proletarians, the well-dressed gentlemen, the charming señoras; of the elegant dandies, the officers in stiff corsets, the heavy businessmen, the overweight doctors; alike on the shady side and the sunny side— perfumes and perspiration, great furies simmering under momentary forgetfulness and carelessness with pretty white teeth, soft sensual looks, leaders whose calculations are as precise as the mechanism of machine guns—all turns around under the implacable umbrella of a blue marble sky, around the maddened bull who wants to kill and who will be killed.

"Eusebio?"

"What?"

Heads, bodies, hands are growing all around us like tropical vegetation; a powerful odor of warm and vibrant flesh—the smell of masses of men and of sunlight—makes our nostrils throb. I also breathe in the acid smell of the oranges being eaten greedily by a young girl of whom I can see only a head of luxurious black hair (giving off a vague aroma of almonds) and the sunburned line of a neck which makes me think, for a fraction of a second, of enormous flower stems, of the thrust of tall palm trees, then of the whole outline of a sunburned body, terribly thin, hard, and hot.

"What will happen tomorrow, Eusebio?"

That square Roman legionary's brow, damp now, those pupils enlarged like cats' in the darkness, their flood of reflections, that grimace of a smile which looks sculpted into rough old wood by a barbarian hand: Eusebio, hardly glanced at me in reply.

For below in the pit the bull brandishes a horse and a man at the end of his wide horns, a gutted horse and a terrified man. A pinkish foam rings the horse's nostrils. We can hear his panting breath and it is horrible *that he cannot cry out*, that there is nothing but this breathing. The bull lashes his warm, entrails, brandishing the picador—a misplaced puppet with eyes searching wildly for a place to fall—three yards above the ground . . . Man and beast thrown down, greenish steaming intestines unwound like snakes on the sand—now everything is crumbling. Ah! you hold him at last, bull, your enemy; you conquer, you drive on, you live.

But no! The lure of a purple cape leads you on already, a victorious beast being toyed with, toward the killer.

(What fog is this blurring your eyes, Lolita, in their deep orbits? Thus a snowflake melts, all at once, in one's hand. That snow, your look, Lolita.)

Benito moves into the center of the ring with measured step. Eusebio's arm grips my shoulder, hard and knotty like an old vine. "Look! Look!" The killer and the beast observe each other. Benito, in the face of that driving violence gathering speed with each bound, presents the calmest restraint, a few tight movements, a simple twist of the torso, which the red horns seem to graze, the leap of a dancer, motionless a moment later on his high heels; and his fingers gracefully touch the tip of the horn. Thus his skill mocks that huge black power . . . At last he presents himself to the danger, calm, powerful, cruel, the short brilliance of steel in his hand, his shrewd eye seeking out the vital point where the precise sword must strike. Man and beast turn slowly around each other—aiming, aimed at, clearheaded, maddened, coupled by the necessity of combat. Around them silence reigns. Expectation. I see Lolita hunched over from her heels to her narrow brows, her lips pressed together like a scar—and I seem to feel the being who is there within her, under that appearance of carnal immobility, like a bent bow whose string already quivers imperceptibly on the verge of shooting its arrow into the clouds, yes, into that abyss where vision fails.

A double climax, rapid to the point of imperceptibility, below; it takes a long fraction of a second for us to grasp that the sword has glittered, thrust by the killer with an almost rectilinear movement of his arm, at the precise moment—one thousandth of a second before the beast would have completed his final, deadly charge. The bull collapses with all his weight. His mouth is dripping bloody foam.

"*Olé! Olé!*"

The city is on its feet. The whole city. Ten thousand heads are lifted in joyful, riotous clamor, mingled with whistles, guttural cries and the rumble of stamping feet. Countless hands emerge over this human ocean, handkerchiefs waving like flowers of foam. *Olé! Olé!* The tide is mad, the whole city is shouting for joy, and the triumph carries everything along with it.—Triumph of man over beast, triumph of the beast over man?—Benito raises a proud forehead toward the reviewing stand, his short red cape over his arm, his thin, shining sword (a dress sword, senora) in his hand, saluting the ladies while treading on flowers . . . They throw everything at him, even jewels, watches, parasols. They yearn to throw down their half-parted lips, their half-closed eyes, and other eyes, as wide as the horizon, open hands that would fall like chrysanthemums, pearly breasts and even the warm secret treasures hidden in the sacred folds of their flesh. And that is the only thing of which he is aware in this moment: what marvelous booty.

"Tomorrow!" Eusebio shouts in my ear.

All doubts are swept away by this breath of conquering joy. Over the heads of the crowd, over the head of the victor, Eusebio's eyes seek out, in the governor's loge, the heads that will have to be removed. (I can't hear what he is shouting at them, his clenched fist outstretched. His voice is lost in the torrent.) Those smiling faces contemplate at length the pit in which we are a boiling lava. "Tomorrow will bring us other feasts . . ." His Excellency the *Capitán general* is perhaps dreaming that a well-placed row of machine guns is—against the huge, ten-thousand-headed wild beast that we are—a weapon as sure as the matador's sword. Everything is in the precision of the aim. If this damned little Andalusian cowherd (to think that only three years ago he was looking after cows in the Sierra de Yeguas!) had made a half-inch's error in the marvelous intuitive calculation of his sword point, he would probably have been killed, certainly vanquished. Choose the right time, and strike home.

It was Eusebio who thought out loud:

"Choose the right time, and strike home."

We leave. Lolita draws her shawl over her shivering shoulders. The inner bow has relaxed, the arrow has been shot. A great emptiness remains. "At times I'm scared," she says.

TEN

Flood Tide

NOTHING UNUSUAL HAS HAPPENED, BUT THE EVENT IS THERE, GRANDIOSE, on the verge of bursting forth. In such a manner do heavy clouds gather imperceptibly over a calm summer landscape; a gust of wind will carry them in a few instants from the blue horizon to these orchards, these prairies, these peaceful lands where children are returning from school toward white houses. A tragic shadow is extending over this corner of earth. Every living thing feels the approach of the hurricane; the heavy calm that precedes the first black rumblings will already be full of the storm.

Patrols had made their appearance in the streets on the previous day, toward evening. Their paths crossed with ours. And the animation which had been until then indefinable and uneasy, bore the strong stamp of their passing. The *guardia civils* went forth on horseback, in rectangular formations, black on black horses, shoulders square under their black capes, towering over the crowd with their tricornered hats and their stiff heads, as impassable as painted wooden figures. Their vigilant eyes searched into the corners of alleys, into dark doorways, into tightly pressed groups, into anything that might hide deadly aggression, bullet or bomb, the sudden great stride of death over frightened heads toward the tense horsemen riding toward their fate. Theirs, ours! Our patrols moved otherwise, opening the streets with the firm step of a dozen resolute workers, moving through the crowds along the boulevards without disappearing within them: caps, overalls, Brownings, hard faces, glances smoldering with fire. Here they come! In the heavy silence the men turn in on themselves: you had to turn the threat you felt outwards; to threaten others. "We belong to the race of those who have always been crushed by authority, don't we, Joaquin? It's hard for us to believe that we are the stronger."—"Shut up . . . What swine they are! How I'd love to take a good shot at them! You know, those vultures are cowards, you'd see them take off . . ." Thin, cut in sharp angular lines, Joaquin the weaver (twenty-seven years old, tubercular, six months of preventive prison, two children, three pesetas a day) has his mouth twisted in an expression of hatred; the contours of his cheekbones sharpen; the scar at the base of his nose reddens. The blood mounts to his face. The other patrol notices us. What is time? An instant, an infinitesimal fraction of time passes in which, here and over there, hearts beat a little faster, various actions are planned, co-ordinated, sketched out and put aside inside these heads, the heads on one side straight by obedience, that iron bar on the mind, those on the other held high by rebellion, that flame. The governor's order posted this morning: "Suspicious groups will be searched on the spot and individuals discovered with arms on their persons will be placed under arrest. "Go ahead and try it! Come on!" Passers-by, strangely uneasy, feel the looks of defiance being exchanged over their heads. The two patrols graze each other. A swarthy sergeant, his three-cornered hat low on his forehead, opens the way. His horse steps elegantly, as if on parade, in a clatter of iron on the pavement. "So you've read the governor's order? Huh, eunuch?" Joaquin grumbles between clenched teeth, "Come and search us then!" The Committee's order: Under no circumstances allow yourselves to be disarmed. (Yesterday some of the boys had let themselves be searched by the police, who had good-naturedly, frisked their pockets at street corners, found their weapons immediately, and said softly to the humiliated men: "Beat it.") But now they pass on. They are afraid! Afraid! In a single pulse the blood climbs from heart to brow, unfurling between the temples in joyful scarlet banners; proud smiles tremble on lips: "Did you see those yellow bastards? You could have knocked them over with a feather." They move away like huge wooden soldiers, useless scarecrows. So it really is true, true that we are the power. Joy glows red.

This morning the police came to seize the Committee's newssheet, *Solidaridad Obrera* (Workers' Solidarity) at the print shop. Some courteous officers took away one hundred and fifty copies, left there for them out of a kind of politeness. The forbidden sheet is now being distributed in the streets. The factories got it as early as noon. The white sheets carrying the appeal are seen in people's hands by passing patrols. The indifferent *guardia civils* circle about quietly under the trees. Teams go about posting the sheets on walls. People gather. WORKERS!—PROGRAM OF THE WORKERS' COMMITTEE.—*We demand: 1st—2d—3d* . . .

An elderly gentleman reads these things with astonishment; reads them again without comprehending, stares at his neighbors with an anxious eye. "Organ of the National Confederation of Labor . . ."—"A republican government and guarantees of workers' rights . . ." These words are grotesque. The King? The Señor Governor? The old gentleman has the impression of a sort of earthquake. Is he dreaming? The street is as always. Politely, he asks his neighbor on the left, a respectable, well-dressed man: "What is happening, señor? Please be so kind as to explain it to me for . . ." For his voice is trembling. His outdated politeness exhumes thirty years of existence marinated in an old country manor in the provinces. The well-dressed neighbor answers sedately: "The Assembly of Parliamentarians, tomorrow, you understand?" No, he doesn't understand. "A thousand thanks, señor. But my dear señor, and the King, the King?" A dreadful voice explodes at that instant: "The King, you old fool, can shove it up his ass!"—Laughter breaks out, and everyone, even the well-dressed neighbor, fifty years old, an estimable man, of good sense moreover, is laughing too. The old gentleman, astounded, collapses, without even feeling the affront, finding these things all so extraordinary, and moves away from the gathering, gesticulating to himself. Not until then do people notice that he is wearing a coat of long-outmoded cut, shiny at the neck, and a faded gray felt hat, and that he walks as if hopping along, leaning on a cane with a carved silver handle.—"Old bug! Sparrow head!" taunts an urchin nonsensically.

Someone has entered the gathering and calmly torn up the poster. Altercation. The tumult, at first imprecise, seems to concentrate around the imaginary point of intersection of three human forms, by turns separated and brought together by words and gestures like projectiles. A tall young man, elegantly dressed, disentangles himself from the surrounding group, shrugging his shoulders. His silence is emphasized by an expression of disdain. He stops at the edge of the sidewalk, turning his back on those who challenge him. One must remain calm; calm at any price. This abominable rabble doesn't even deserve a word or a blow. Nothing but pure scorn, even to the exclusion of anger, and the firmness of steel, like St. George's sword striking down the dragon . . . From the depth of his memory, at a distance of ten years, this image comes to the surface like an astonishing anemone: a blond, frank-eyed, St. George victorious over the hideous and terrible beast. "The strength of the saint is in his faith, my child," Father Xavier used to say in those days (that lock of white hair over his temple, that otherworldly voice, low—a whisper—and penetrating . . .) "not in the armor, the lance and the sword, which are nothing without faith." The quivering of his lips has subsided. What clarity in his soul! Strength and faith. Light. A smile is about to come to his lips.—"*Soli! Solidaridad Obrera!*" cries the shrill voice of an apprentice. The young man takes the copy offered him and, without unfolding it, calmly tears it in four pieces. The white scraps fall at his feet in the gutter . . . "A pretty girl"—or so he tries to think with carefree ease as he watches a heavily made-up girl crossing the street toward him—bold glance, swinging hips. He often likes to look at such creatures but avoids their mysteriously impure, secretly tempting contact. He is about to turn away his eyes when, firmly planted in front of him as if she were saying to him: "Want to come with me?" she gives him two hard slaps, echoed by bursts of laughter, and walks away. Twenty steps away, two purely decorative policemen turn their backs on the incident; you can see their fat fingers moving slowly in white gloves. The one who has been slapped, like a wronged child, can feel the tears, undoing his rash scorn for "that rabble," and putting out his frail inner light," sees, out of the corner of his eye, the approach of a shabbily dressed tough swinging a pair of fists like meat axes. The street snickers, turns on its axis, and fades away. The sky, washing away everything, suddenly spreads out its immense white coolness. Salt taste of blood in his mouth. Nothingness.

The operator of the shoeshine stand, on the corner of the *calle* Mercader watches the patrols pass by with his one eye; and the brushes go back and forth under his agile hands; making the thick English leather glow. Sanche *el Tuerto*, ("One-eye") usually, sees men only from the knees down. He can classify feet at a glance; at a distance of fifteen paces he is able to predict which pair of stylish shoes will stop in front of him while a ringing voice from above says: "Make it quick, boy!" Certain shoes, of indefinite shape, pursued by a mournful fate, never stop; others, disgusting to shine, cracked, worn out, still resist, still ask to be shined—"as if you were a big shot, eh fuss-budget! I'll bet you did without lunch today, Señor Bare-backside." One-eye doesn't like poor customers; he even saves for them a particular inferior wax that gnaws the leather. "When your toes come through, you won't be so fussy;

instead of having your clodhoppers shined, you'll be shining 'em like me, you'll see! Do I make a fuss?" He has respect for rope-soled sandals, stylish pumps, and bare feet, covered with a good layer of hardened dirt that protects as well as suede leather. Having finished shining a pair of yellow shoes, without seeing the man—probably a sailor, for the shoe is foreign, well cared-for, new, but not fresh—and put away his brushes, One-eye picks up *Soli*. He rarely reads, and when he does he puts the words together with difficulty after dividing them into syllables. ("I could read better when I had both eyes.") Does he understand, this time, what he is reading? A sort of smile twists his mouth. He wouldn't be able to repeat or to explain what he is reading, but a great contentment flows into the marrow of his bones.

A rich French shoe has come to rest on the stand in front of him. "Hey!" says the customer, tapping his foot nervously. One-eye breaks off spelling out a long sentence with a distant meaning (". . . equal rights for foreign workers . . ." He is from the province of Murcia, but what, exactly, are "rights"?), notices the edge of a blue silk stocking, a very expensive shoe, and grumbles, without raising his head:

"No time."

The customer would have thought he hadn't heard correctly if it hadn't been so clear. He goes away with the understanding that something is happening in the world.

This "No time" of One-eye's worries and enlightens him immeasurably more than the two events of the previous night; spread all over the newspapers: the torpedoing of a Brazilian steamer, sunk with all hands, by a German U-boat off the Azores, and the bombardment of London by Zeppelins—sixty casualties.

One-eye finishes reading, jumbling the lines together, going back to the same ones as many as three times, skipping others. The magic words, whirling around in his brain, bring with them a strange warmth—like a goblet of wine or sunlight—mingled joy and strength flow through his limbs. Ah, *Madre de Dios!* One-eye, looking up, sees people, discovers the whole street, the city, the black three-cornered hats bobbing above the sea of heads. Two little girls pass by arm in arm, talking excitedly; black tresses falling all the way to their waists; adorable, well-formed legs.

Now One-eye placards his copy of *Soli* on the wall with care. This improvised poster covers up another, a gray one faded by the rains, on which you can still read in large official lettering: SUSPENSION OF CONSTITUTIONAL GUARANTEES. *We, by the Grace of God . . .* —The next line cries out: "WORKERS!" . . . But what is this empty space forming around Sanche? No one on the right, no one on the left. Farther on, the two little girls have turned around, all white. Horses' nostrils breathe a warm dampness down his meek. Suddenly he sees the black capes, the tall tricornes, and an olive face, bearded and grimacing, a bare saber circling above him. He feels terribly alone, choked by wild anger, like that faraway time when, as a sixteen-year-old farm boy, his master threw him out, blinded in one eye, for a theft he hadn't committed: it had been necessary to put out his eye to make him bow before the injustice; as on that other time when his wife ran off with a policeman. The saber scrapes off the magic words. The street snickers, turns on its axis, and, fades away, knocked about from all sides by giant horsemen making frantic gestures on their rearing mounts.

The sky, washing away everything, suddenly spreads out its immense white coolness. Salt taste of blood in his mouth. Nothingness.

ELEVEN

Ebb Tide

THE 19TH. *TODAY.* FOUR O'CLOCK. A SURPRISING CALM PREVAILS OVER THE uproar. The heedless mutiny is dying out slowly in the back streets. What is it then? Brawls are joined and unjoined like human knots at the points where the lines of the soldiers and the waves of the crowd intersect. I ran into Eusebio, calm and tense, in an excited group. Eyes wide open, hands in his pockets, seemingly motionless in the middle of a sort of senseless circus, Eusebio let out a guttural laugh: "It's all over, over, ha! ha!" Some running men cut us off. They were carrying someone: we might have said something. A squad of cavalry charged, by in a whirlwind and vanished around a street corner where gilded letters danced out: CERVEZERIA LOPEZ HIJOS. The moment was broken into two strangely juxtapositioned blocks: one of silence, here, in the sudden emptiness—the other of shouting and clashing, over there, behind the closed blinds of the *Cervecería*.

The *guardia civil*, in closing off the boulevard, pushed us slowly backward. We were easily five or six times as numerous as that double line of spaced-out mannequins marching on us with lowered rifles and stiff, hardwood heads coifed with great black tricornes. Every step they took toward us was pushed on by fear, opening an enticing void before them. Between us and them there remained a moving space of about ten yards where some exasperated, clumsy fool was always hanging back, gesticulating absurdly.

A young man planted himself there, poised like a statue, a package wrapped in newspaper at the end of his arm. The two lines, theirs and ours, wavered without moving; then the void grew larger around the man who had appeared. He cried out:

"Gang of cowards! Dogs of the King!"

As fear lowered the rifles toward his chest, he raised up a round object wrapped in an illustrated page of the *A.B.C.* We crossed the intervening distance—springboard for death's leap—just in time, and dragged him off. His heart was beating so hard that its throbbing rhythm could be felt just by holding his arm. His muscles were hard with anger.

Flanked by a cavalry charge preceded by a band of fleeing men rolling the breath of panic before them, our group breaks up instantaneously, in the manner of unexpected events. A handful of us—men, women, a child, an agitated pregnant mother—are forced back into the blue-and-white stairway of a small hotel. A rifle under a tricorne cuts us off from the street. Trapped. The hands of the *guardia civils* are trembling— fear or fury. His eyes, black marbles, staring, search us out; and accompanying them, a third black spot, steadier, empty but with an incredibly deep darkness: the muzzle of the rifle. Whom to shoot, Virgin of Segovia? He makes his choice.

First movement: pull your head into your shoulders, pull in your shoulders, shrink up, flatten out, crouch down behind the people in front—your comrades, your brothers—make a shield of them, for you've got the good spot, way in the back, one of the last . . .

Second movement: Ah, no you don't, you filthy beast. A little dignity! Hold up your head, your body, stand up all the way, slowly, above the bent backs while fear turns into defiance, and cry out with your eyes to that swine: Shoot, go ahead and shoot, you murderous bastard— long live the revolution!

The explosion tears through the silence like the gale ripping a sail at sea, and throws us forward onto that murderous mannequin animated by a new panic fury. Bewildered flights and cores of resistance collide everywhere in the street. Some of the boys turn over a kiosk. Farther on a cart is burning under a column of black smoke. A tearful woman's voice is crying, "Angel, Angel." An unhorsed *guardia civil* runs after his mount, hobbling. The even line of mannequins with tricornes reappears, inexorable . . .

We break out, all at once, into the Plaza Real as into an oasis of silence and peace. The gray arcades that surround the square are filled with a peaceful half-light. The warm shade of heavy palm trees, the benches dear to lovers in the evening and to vagabonds at night;

squatting Gypsies are waiting for our storm to pass in that refuge. Joaquin holds us back with an imperious gesture that makes us all smile, for at that moment we realize that he has only one sleeve left on his coat. As we emerge from the riot, we see two heads, close together, in the shadow of a pillar: of the man, the back of the neck and shoulders; of the woman, the face, upturned, eyes closed, radiating happiness, covered by his kisses . . . We check our steps, we hold back our voices. Our footsteps leave a red trail behind us on the flagstones.

The closest meeting room of the Committee was in a little café near the cathedral. A few old women were coming down from the porch; you could feel the calm weighing on the city. An ordinary street—and even the song of a guitar:

". . . Monde, monde, vaste monde . . ."

Five o'clock. Only an hour has passed since we began to understand that today is a defeat. In the back room of the café, Ribas is presiding, as usual, without looking at anyone. His face, haloed by white hair, emanates serenity tinged with sadness. Dario seems crushed under the lash of Portez' sarcasm . . .

"Misled by the apostles of coalition with the bourgeoisie, yes. Betrayed, no. You had to be naive, like some people, to think that they would really go along . . ."

Under the crushing blow of defeat Dario had turned inward in meditation. Visual images troubled his train of thought: black automobiles carrying off irresolute parliamentarians through the police lines in front of the city hall; Señor Domenico bursting into the little notarial study hung in pearl-gray silk where Dario is waiting for him; shaking both his hands, reassuring, exalted, feverish: "Dear friend, you must understand. We have to make use of all the political possibilities. We are gaining two weeks of preparation, dear friend. Please tell that to the Committee. We will never retreat, never, never. You do understand, dear friend? Never!"—holding up his hand as if swearing an oath. Dario, overcome by a brutal desire to laugh, had replied in a hollow voice, "Too bad for you if we have to fight alone."

Now the allusion to "some people who are too naive" fell on him like a whiplash; he made a disdainful face and threw his own barb out into the void, aiming at "the worst danger at this moment, the terroristic hysteria of those who take a setback for a defeat, a diversion for a catastrophe, hesitations for a betrayal . . . that state of mind which the back rooms of certain espionage bureaus are perhaps trying to foster . . ."

"Nothing is lost," said Ribas softly. "We can only be defeated today by discord. I'm moving on to the second point on the agenda."

Around midnight, in a street which the moonlight divided into vast shadowy patches, half-blue, half-black, José Miro, who was wandering about, a cigarette in his lips, meets Lejeune, taciturn, his eyes lowered. They shake hands distractedly. "What's the news?" A hard smile lights up Miro's sharp features. He puts his arm affectionately around the shoulder of his companion: "You look out of sorts, old man, what's happened to you?"

They walk along for a moment without speaking. The shadow of an octagonal tower envelopes them. "Maud has left me," Lejeune says finally, and his low voice reveals a great defeat.

(Maud: a nervous tomboy's worn-out body, an ageless, Gothic profile, brown curls, sudden catlike movements, faded gray eyes under lowered lids, mouth faded at the fold of the lips, but such a mobile face, such lively eyes, full of questioning mingled with worry, laughter, deceit, greed, sadness, and God knows what else . . . Maud: her narrow hips—Maud.

This gray-haired man was holding back the desire to cry like a baby. He had been walking for hours, an extinguished cigar between his fingers; repeating her name under his breath: Maud; having but one idea, which at times was only a word, in his devastated brain—"left me"—in his eyes only her Gothic profile, her gray eyes, her narrow hips, Maud.)

"You understand," he says, "the 'other man' is Paris . . . But you couldn't understand. You're too young."

"Only a woman," thinks Miro, who also has been walking for hours that evening, overcome by a feeling of terrible pain, a savage sorrow repressed by a feeling of powerful joy; consuming one cigarette after another, saddened to the point of tears one minute, humming along the next; filling the deserted streets with the sound of his springy step . . .

"Angel is dead," he answers abruptly. "You know, little Angel of the machinists'. A bullet in his stomach. It took him two hours to die, from five to seven. We had three dead."

"Yes, three dead," Lejeune repeats mechanically. (Maud has left, left, left, left.)

"*They* had at least one that I know of," continues Miro, his eyes shining. "Angel never regained consciousness. I was at the hospital, at his bedside. His dying gasps drove into my head like nails. My head was full of burning nails when I walked out of there. I left . . ."

(. . . left.)

". . . without knowing where I was going. At nine o'clock, imagine, with that headache, that gasp, those nails in my head, I leaned against a wall exhausted. I heard someone shouting at me: 'Move on.' I roused myself: I was standing in front of the *guardia civil* barracks. The sentry was watching me; all I could see of him was a black shape. I went over to him, I said: 'Do you know Angel? He was a little Andalusian with a beard.' He thought I was drunk and repeated: 'Move on.' I fired through the pocket of my jacket: it's burned, look, in three places. He didn't fall right away; he stuck to the wall, then he slid along the wall sighing. I leaned over him; his eyes were still alive. I saw them glowing, the sky was reflected in them. I said to him: '*Angel, you killed him . . .*' They must have fired at least twenty rifle shots from all sides into the night. I walked calmly away, my head as cool as if I had rinsed my brain in ice water. But you couldn't understand, no, you couldn't understand how good I feel this evening . . ."

TWELVE

The End of a Day

RIBAS PACES, CAGED, IN A CELL OF THE MODEL PRISON. DARIO AND PORTEZ are in hiding. Lejeune and Miro spend their days together, in a small boat off the coast, taking turns rowing, then resting while the gentle waves rock them. Lejeune smokes, dressed in a white piqué shirt. José, naked to the waist, hard and burned like a Malayan, sings at the top of his voice; sometimes revolutionary songs:

> *Pour leurs entrailles, ô grain de blé!*
> *O grain de blé, fais-toi mitraille!*
> (For their entrails, o kernel of wheat!
> O kernel of wheat, turn yourself into grapeshot!)

or ballads:

> *Ta candeur de visage*
> *Ton coeur de gitane . . .*
> (The frankness of your face,
> Your gypsy's heart . . .)

The blue waters mirror a pure sky in their shimmering silk folds. Invisible strings tremble on the burning air like the flight of bee swarms. The light hums. In the distance are white sails. Flights of seagulls describe curves of whiteness which fade like a light caress in the crystal blue air. The rocks of Montjuich are tinted with amber.

In the evening José speaks at meetings of metalworkers, construction workers, and men from the *Canadiense* works. Lejeune, on a back street where the rare passers-by avoid each other's glances, raises the knocker of a door with a barred peephole. An extremely old woman with gray lips leads him into the purple darkness of a corridor where the sound of feet is smothered by carpets. Three naked women lie on animal skins in a long, low room, waiting for the call of a stranger's lust; reading over and over, in cards reeking of cosmetics, the fired mysteries of the Jack of Hearts and the letter that will come from across the sea (but a dark-haired woman is on his path . . .)—Inès, Viorica, Dolorès. One has a child—Marquita, who is growing up in a garden in Granada; another a lover—Evelio, who is in prison; the third has the clap, gray eyes with long ashy lashes, no eyebrows, a bony face as pale as alabaster which looks like the face of a dead woman when she closes her eyes, lips as red as a fresh wound. "Play dead!" the men say to her sometimes, and her head, thrown back on the black silk cushion, seems frozen; her eyelids narrow over the bluish globes of her eyes, and her breathless half-open mouth reveals the cold whiteness of her teeth, in a defenseless grin. Some gilded switches are standing in the corner, on a little black Moorish table with white filigree.

At the hour when Lejeune enters there, three other women, at the other end of the city, are getting ready to go to the Sans cemetery. Erect in her old widow's clothing, the mother, already joining her fleshless fingers in prayer, goes to the kitchen door and says, "It's time, Concepción."—"Yes, Mother," gently answers Concepción, whose soft face—still the face of a child—has just aged all at once, under the corrosive blast of an invisible furnace. Concepción throws a black shawl over her sloping shoulders; she takes Teresita by the hand, Teresita who is ten years old and carries flowers. They move in silence, hurried, black; the mother, the wife, the sister—she whose life is finished, she whose life is broken, she whose life is beginning. When the silence becomes too heavy for them, Concepción talks of the factory. "Mother, they say they're going to lay off some girls in the sorting department." The mother doesn't answer; she has gray eyes, no eyebrows, a bony face as pale as alabaster which looks like the face of a dead woman without it being necessary for her to close her eyes. At the cemetery there is a fresh grave, without a cross, where flowers have been planted. The red ribbons on the metallic wreaths are fading in the grass. The mother would have preferred a cross, but Concepción had said no so firmly, her lips trembling (though she, too, would have preferred a cross, but Angel had exclaimed one day, laughing: "It's so stupid, all those crosses and monuments in cemeteries . . ."). The mother prays before that grave where even the consolation of a symbol is missing; but she had forgotten the words of the prayers so long ago that, trying to find them in the dark well of her memory, she becomes tired and forgets herself . . . "Angel," murmurs Concepción. She would speak to him as if to a living person, if she dared. She is still suffering from having annoyed him the other Sunday when he wanted her to wear her shawl with the big red flowers. "Is it possible, señor? Is it possible?" Teresita lays the flowers on the grave and murmurs, very low, fascinated by the comings and goings of the industrious ants from one grave to another, "This is for you, big brother. We haven't forgotten you, Angel. Uncle Tio came over to the house last night, the orange cat had four kittens, I'm keeping one, for you and me . . ." And Teresita, bending over the grave of her big brother, smiles about the orange cat who is giving milk to her kittens at home.

I have returned to my composing stick at the Gaubert y Pia print shop. We set up racing forms and religious works. The metallic clanging of the presses dissolves into a monotonous hum in the ears after a while. The hunchbacked boss looks down on us from his glass-walled office. Porfirio, my neighbor, is a wizard: the black type-characters with their long silver facets seem to leap by themselves into his hands which line them up tirelessly. It's the same in all the shops, in all the factories of the city. Yesterday we were three hundred thousand strong, flowing over the city like waves of lava, ready for anything with so much blood in our veins; today we are back in the shops, the yards, the factories. The machines are turning, twisting, screeching, sawing, crushing, pounding; tools in black hands bite into metal. In the evening we go out, three hundred thousand of us at once, our skulls, stomachs, and muscles empty. Nothing has happened. The city taunts us with its lights, its diamonds and jewels, the violins in its cafés, the displays along its boulevards, the lamentations of its beggars, the printed smiles of its dancing girls, the oily smells of its slums, the sleep of its vagabonds on the back street sidewalks . . .

Etchegoyen, of the carpenters, has run across the border with the union treasury, nine hundred pesetas. Good riddance, the bastard.

Gilles, my former cellmate, writes me from a detainees' labor squad, slaving away somewhere in the Massif Central that he spends stupefying days digging up shells, after target practice. "You are lucky not to be like each of us, a tiny cog in a huge munitions factory . . ." Gilles, old man, one should never deduce another's happiness from one's own misfortune . . . The communiqués lie and contradict each other day after day. The newspapers line up one after the other, on the Allied side or the side of the Central Powers. It is impossible to recognize the same events in the labyrinth of lying phrases . . . Sentries, sentries, where are you now in all of this, dug into the earth stinking of corpses and excrement? Bombardment of Amiens, in the quiet sector of the Vosges. Life goes on like yesterday. Porfirio's intelligent simian eyes are sadder than usual. Twice a week he is absent from the shop in the afternoon in order to go to the San Luis Hospital to bring some oranges to, his little girl who is recovering from typhus. He probably doesn't eat every day. He pretends to be consulting me over the text in 8-point Roman on his composing stick (". . . the blessèd childhood of St. Theresa . . ."):

"Things are going badly too, over there?"

Badly, yes. The papers are full of contradictory dispatches through which it is possible to discern a victory for the old order brought about by the Cossacks; Lenin and Trotsky in flight, arrested, shot, who knows? Bolshevism routed. The Kronstadt sailors are still holding out, it seems. While we were getting ready here, other crowds, over there, were lining up in massive columns behind red flags for an assault similar to ours. "During the entire day of the 17th, the Tauride Palace was besieged by crowds of workers and soldiers demanding the resignation of the 'ten capitalist ministers.' The Social Revolutionary Party leader, Mr. Chernov, was almost slashed to pieces by some sailors." Last night I was reading these prosaic lines from a newspaper correspondent's report and I thought I could hear, echoing our footsteps, the dull rumble of those multitudes on the march, on the march like us; only wearing gray uniforms; only carrying in their heads, their bellies, their fists that nameless anger brought back from the Lithuanian front, the Galician front, the Rumanian front, the Armenian front; only stronger than we for having undergone the ordeal of fire, the ordeal of blood, the ordeal of victory . . . (That evening when I had gone home giddy with joy, repeating the disconcerting words over and over again unable to realize their true meaning for want of precise images and because the news was so great that it was overpowering—newspaper headlines: REVOLUTION IN PETROGRAD. ABDICATION OF THE CZAR. TROOPS GOING OVER TO THE PEOPLE.) . . . stronger than we because they went forth preceded by those who were hanged, those who were shot down before the firing squad, those who were deported, those who were martyred throughout a half-century of tenacious struggle—and were guided by those who had escaped . . . According to the latest news, the treason of the Bolshevik leaders is a proven fact: German agents. We know what that means: formulas of this type are as necessary as ammunition for the twelve rifles of the firing squad. If they did take money from Germany, well they were damn smart to do it, for they must have needed it, and the Germans are wasting their money. "Taking money," says Dario, "being incorruptible . . . What is the point of being incorruptible if you don't take money?"

Ten hours of work in the shop are on our backs; it weighs you down. I have lifted eight thousand characters. Ten hours standing on our feet. At the age of forty, most typographers have varicose veins. El Capillo, that yellow-toothed swine, has put us on piecework, the dirtiest job imaginable. Now we are on our way downtown in the soft cool of the evening—the poets' "mauve hour." What we would really like is to take a bath or to punch someone in the nose.

"You'll see," says Porfirio suddenly, still thinking about the foreman, "if I don't smash in his old horse's teeth for him one of these days!"

It's very light out. A lulling transparency attenuates the shapes of things, even to the delicate outlines of the foliage. It is not yet dusk, but the full light of the day has already passed. The turquoise tint of the sky and the straight clear perspective of this avenue which reminds one of a garden call an image into my companion's mind: the image of a half-starved child being eaten up by bugs in the San Luis Hospital. I, too, am thinking of your Paquita. I know that you are going to talk about her. You say, without any transition, as if you knew that I am reading your mind (and perhaps you do):

"The nuns are badgering her because she doesn't want to say her prayers."

Perhaps this is the very moment when the sister noiselessly approaches bed number 35, room IV. The little girl is lying down with her eyes closed pretending to be asleep, but she can hear the ineffable rustling of starched clothing, the slithering of gray heelless slippers along the floorboards. The little girl can feel the stern gaze of the old woman's dismal, petrified face falling on her blue-tinted eyelids.

"Paquita, I know you are not sleeping. Paquita, you are a wicked child. Say your prayers."

This is the awful moment of the blue cold. The blue cold starts in Paquita's kidneys and climbs up, climbs up slowly, squeezing her in a vice, toward her heart, her throat, her brow; it presses in at her temples for an instant, like an icy halo, and vanishes: it's over; she can open her eyes, she is no longer afraid . . . The old woman has gripped Paquita's hands with authority and forces her to join them—the blue cold comes from the touch of those bloodless old hands which would nonetheless like to be good. Paquita obeys, but her terror has already passed. Slowly, with a depthless obstinacy in her powerless glance, Paquita says "No" with her eyes. And the sister goes away, sad and severe.

In his cell at the Model Prison, old Ribas stops abruptly with his back against the door: from this point the whole length of a green branch may be seen in the narrow window, sometimes motionless, sometimes gently waving. Although he is nearsighted, Ribas has never worn glasses; that is the secret of the distant expression we have often noticed in him. He would really like to know what kind of leaves they are; it tortures him and makes him smile at the same time. He is alone, calm, weakened, without fear, confident. He knows that we will win in a month, three months, six months, twelve months. The length of time is of no importance. He knows that there is always the great expedient of dying like Ferrer, in order to live on usefully in the comrades' memories, leaving a kind of dignity to the children, and that it isn't even very difficult any more when you have a long, wearisome life behind you like a gray ribbon, grayer and grayer, almost black. "After all, at my age when one is not very intelligent, it's about the best thing that can happen to you." The day, however, has been a bad one. No letters from home. It is ridiculous, of course, to be worried like this. But what if something had happened to little Tonio? And besides, he only left fifty pesetas in the house.

Dario is talking in the back room of a café on the Tibidabo road. You can hear cars going by, carrying people to supper at the all-night restaurants. He is surrounded by twelve heads, dramatically silhouetted in the reddish shadows. An oil lamp is placed in front of him. His blue pencil traces out straight lines and crosses on a sheet of paper in order that these men should understand exactly what must be done. The lamp sputters darkly.

THIRTEEN

The Other City Is Stronger

HERE AND THERE ACROSS THE BLACK MASSES OF MONTJUICH, THE MOON spreads patches of shiny blue, near-white, lacquer. The houses at the foot of the mountain are blue and black rectangles, stippled with gold dots along the line of the windows. Each of these perforations is a lamp lighting up a home. In each of these homes reigns the repose of the evening, the talk of the evening, the concerns of the evening; when that luminous pinpoint vanishes, the man and the woman will have gone to bed. And tomorrow the luminous dot will be lighted again, and thus each day . . . One is overcome at the thought of the relentless persistence of all these little destinies. In each one of these lighted compartments, men are sitting down at this moment across the table from their lives: lives that still wear the same face of an old, ageless serving-woman, resigned to her cloistered existence. There are some who are happy. The old serving-woman smiles on them; a few little joys, of which some are unclean, swarm over them in the impoverished air.

We are having a discussion on the balcony; behind us, in one of our rooms, there is a lamp burning which, seen from that house over there in the distance, is also nothing but a pinpoint or luminous perforation. The round tower of the fortress, on the summit of Montjuich, is in clear view.

We are at Santiago's house because he has not been under surveillance since he was let out of prison—last year—after that sabotage business in the streetcar yards. He pretends to be discouraged: we suspect a certain amount of sincerity in his role. We can hear him splashing about under the faucet in the kitchen. All the noises of this house come floating around us for a moment; they seem light and transparent to me in the moonlight. The baby, in his crib, is doing a kind of dance in the air with his little legs and purring: "m-mm-mm" or humming "a-aa-aa-aa" on a flat note. The mother is ironing linens on the plain wooden table. We can hear the dull thud of the iron on the cloth. The mother is chatting quietly with a neighbor. The two voices are alike: one could be the slightly amplified echo of the other. Whole sentences mingle with our discussion.

"You're right," says Dario, "that's the real revolution. The real revolution begins when millions of men begin to move, feeling inexorably that it no longer possible to turn back, that all the bridges have been burned behind them. It's a human avalanche rolling on."

Miro and Jurien are smoking. Tibio is quietly plucking his mandolin, dropping chords into the night which glide down to the earth and are lost, amber disks, among the vacant lots.

"*Our* job is to give a good shove to that first big stone that will perhaps bring on the avalanche."

Other voices, inside the house: "Six pesetas, the grocer; two, the baker; three, the sewing machine; eleven . . ."

A barking dog, a banging door drown out this accounting. Then: ". . . how she loved him though, how she loved him! Do you know what she did . . . ?"

We will never know.

A short, dark-haired woman, annoyed by our vain chatter, has gone over to lean on the railing and looks out at the beautiful night horizon— the horizon of her poverty—almost without seeing it. Her sour voice, her tired glances darkened by some vague reproach, her blotchy skin are familiar to me. She is at the age when well-dressed women are still desirable, and the others are already finished. I know what she is thinking: "As if they wouldn't do better to try and earn a little more money."— "It's all right," she was saying a little while ago, "we land on our feet every month, then back into our misery like a cat that some nasty kid throws out the window at regular intervals. It's already something to be able to feed our faces almost every day." Her husband had wanted to be a painter: he's a sign painter. They haven't loved each other for a long time. And why should they love each other, as dull as worn-out coins where the eyes on the effigy of some ideal republic have been rubbed away? Existence—it certainly can't be called life—is too hard.

Dario thinks the movement is soon going to start up again with a good chance of success. He talks about salaries, the employers' association, the artillery juntas that have just sent an insolent appeal to the governor; events and forces seem to take shape under his hands like pieces on a chessboard . . . I answer that the workers' force has not yet become clearly conscious of itself. That there is no organization: sorry number of union members, amorphous groups. No clarity of ideas, no body of doctrine . . .

"Oh, doctrines!" says Dario with an evasive gesture of both open hands. "The fewer there are, the better it goes. A specialty of intellectuals. There will always be time to make theories afterward."

"I mean no lucidity. Vague ideas—some only good for leading us to a dead end. No precedents. The habit of being defeated. We have never yet won. All the communes have been strangled. We are on the verge of discovering some great truth, of finding the key, of learning to win. But the old defeat is still within us."

There comes a time when Dario stubbornly refuses to listen any more. He puts on his mask of weariness and repeats:

"That's all very possible. But if the employers association refuses to agree to the fifteen per cent—and they will refuse—the strike will become generalized; if there is a general strike, the troops won't march against us. If the troops don't march, we will be the masters of the situation . . ."

He shrugs off the invisible load that weighs endlessly on his shoulders and says, jovially:

". . . and one bright morning we will wake up having found the key, as you say, but without having looked for it. While if we waste our time looking for it . . ."

Tibio says, while the fleeting chords escape from his fingers like amber disks:

"The rich lands have all been fertilized by the life and the death of countless organisms. You have to enrich the soil in order to harvest good crops. We will always have been good for something."

I fall silent, finding argument useless since I know that at this moment Dario has nothing to answer me. He is the man of this hour, of this country, of this proletariat which he must lead toward uncertain lights: the future. Sometimes they call him "Comrade Future-minister," and that makes him smile with a mischievous glow in his eyes which seems to say, "Well, why not?" and grudgingly shrug his shoulders. In fact he is much closer to the fortress dungeons or the little anonymous mounds of the cemetery . . . These men are the leaven of a people slow to awaken. Each does his job, performs his task, and passes. We no longer even know the names of those who were tortured in Montjuich and in Alcalá Alcada del Valle, but without them several thousand proletarians of this city would not have this tempered courage, this burning hatred, this exaltation that makes fighters of them in the pain of their daily existence. "We will always have been good for something." But I am unable to cry out to you that it is no longer enough, that it is imperative to turn that page; perhaps to go about it entirely differently.

The other city is stronger.

Stupid Sunday. Sunshine everywhere: yellow streetcars shuttle back and forth. The balconies of the wealthy houses slightly grotesque, are decked out with red cloth; some little stunted trees, raw green, are steaming in the sultry air. All this is raw and colorful; all stupid, stupid, stupid with the incredible satisfaction of being stupidly stupid in the sunshine. A procession is going by between two rows of bored-looking ninnies. And it's hot. Marching in a procession makes you sweat.

Hats off, they watch the procession go by as sluggish as a bored, broken-winded animal. It drags itself out for the length of the avenue, to strains of music which sound sleepy in spite of their din . . .

There's an old priest with the low forehead of a sly animal, mopping his brow with a pitiable air of weariness. "Oh Lord, what drudgery! What heat! And what an exasperating idiot, that fellow over there, carrying his candle at if it were an umbrella!" He is probably saying such things to himself, marching solemnly on the heels of a bald, sanctimonious gentleman with glasses, solemnly carrying a beautiful, brand-new checkered flag, stiff with ennui. Pompous gentlemen, dressed up in their Sunday-best solemnity, carry bulky smoking candles. The Municipal Guards—solemn in their black helmets trailing white plumes, blue shirt fronts, white gloves swinging sleepily back and forth—escort a perspiring group. A plaster Virgin, surrounded by candelabra, glass gewgaws, and artificial flowers, weighs down on the shoulders of eight obese bearers.

The other city is stronger. José's mouth narrows—the sign of something wrong; his face is hardened wax. We cross slowly over to the next street corner, for the crowd is kneeling in front of the Blessed Sacrament. The soldiers bend down on one knee, their rifles at the ready, their heads bowed. We are the only ones standing, held up by a kind of defiance. But their city is stronger, stronger . . .

Wearing a gilded cape, a little old man wrinkled like a mummy (but with big red hands folded over his (stomach) advances under a canopy.

Without those big peasant's hands you might think he had just stepped out of a reliquary, iced over in his golden embroideries. People hold open the folds of his train.

He moves on. The flabby paunches, the skimpy shoulders, the shapes, sharp or buried under layers of fat, all dressed in black, the faces rosy or blue-tinted, close-mouthed, the white-tonsured pates, crudely carved out of dirty wood—file by one after another. A fat sweaty gentleman wearing his high silk hat and carrying his candle stops for a moment and you can see that his fingernails are black. Little girls in white strew flowers in front of all this Sunday ugliness on parade, moving inexorably forward, following tall black horsemen . . . This city will march over our stomachs. First the gendarmerie and then the processions. These same little girls will throw flowers onto the pavement where our blood has been spilled.

But now José, disarmed, is smiling. Two brown-skinned kids are making pee pee under a tree. Huge smiles spread across their gritty faces; they're having a swell time pissing during the procession. "Except ye be converted, and become as little children . . ."

The four towers of the Holy Family, held aloft by intricate scaffolding, extend their apocalyptic ugliness into the blue. They look like monumental factory chimneys, only misshapen, crying out their uselessness. They also make you think of phallic symbols.

Under the watching stars, at the corner of two narrow, dark streets, the fiery furnace blasts forth. Circles of liquid fire flicker ceaselessly around the flamboyant letters, now red now yellow, announcing FIFTY BAILARÍNAS. On both sides of the entrance, repeated six times, Juana the Cuban (more svelte and more ardent on these posters than in real life, a Creole at thirty pesetas a trick)—a white shawl dotted with golden flowers, arms and legs darting like flames, long oblique eyes which seem to laugh out of their shadowed depths like flashing knives.

Poor devils, who can't even go inside—for lack of the price—devour her with their eyes. There are always three or four of them on the sidewalk, looking for an improbable windfall.

The hall is poor, almost bare, cruelly lighted by huge arc lamps. You sit at white marble tables. Drink. Look. Think of nothing. Your day is over. It's not time yet to go to sleep on your cot in your four-pesetas-a-week hole in the wall, where you can hear your neighbor coughing on one side and, on the other, through the paper-thin walls, a panting couple making love after a bitter whispered argument. Here is the fruit of your labor, the climactic moment of your day. Feast your eyes on forms, on colors, on rhythms, on delirium, on laughter, on everything denied you in life. From dusk to dawn fifty women will act out, for you, all the joy they know. Some of them will talk to you without seeing you, the spangles about their waists tingling through your veins; their castanets and their heels will echo in your loins long after; you will drink greedily as soon as they have gone off into the wings, and, this night, for a long while, long before the deep, black sleep of the weary carries you off—you will see before you the white and red smile of their lips, the black and fire of their eyes.

Lucecita, a skinny girl sheathed in black, a purple knot around her hips, glides before your eyes, leaving behind a suggestion of despair: the image of an ash-gray mask, an overpainted mouth and a pointed chin, eyes like raindrops glistening out of shadows under black lines.

El Chorro's hairy fingers beat out the rhythm of the dance on the table. José is preoccupied by his idea: we must shake this city out of its torpor by acting with sudden and terrible boldness. A few men would be enough. He himself—afraid of nothing, no longer able to wait, consumed with a desire for action and sacrifice—would go first. He idolizes the memory of Angiollilo the typographer, gentle yet obstinate like a missionary, who, twenty years ago, followed Cánovas del Castillo (the butcher of Montjuich and Cuba!) patiently from town to town in order to strike him down one day in the name of that future anarchy where human life will be sacred. He refuses to get married: "That's like drowning. No thank you! A true revolutionary can't have a wife or kids. Above all don't imagine *you can live*—or you're good for nothing except wearing a collar." I found him a while ago reading over the trial of Emile Henry.[6] There is a legend that says that Henry faltered at the last minute, three yards from the scaffold. "That's impossible," José grumbled. "It's a filthy lie made up by the newspapers." He was unwilling to understand how that final crisis might yet heighten the dauntlessness of the condemned, the fruit of a difficult victory won over himself. "I tell you he was all of one piece!"

"Benito will kill again on Sunday," José murmurs.

"So?"

"The governor will certainly be in his box."

---

6   A young French anarchist, executed May 21, 1894, for having exploded a bomb at the Café Terminus in Paris. At the trial he took full responsibility for his act and practically demanded to be guillotined. —Tr.

At the next table the woolly-haired, low-browed stokers from an Argentinean freighter are laughing heartily because two women, Asunción the blonde, Pepita the brunette, with saffron scarves wrapped around their waists, are doing the dance of the breasts with convulsive smiles. One girl fair, the other dark; one cool, the other arid as the desert. The fruits of their flesh, set off by coral tips, quiver as they shimmy all over, standing in place. Guitars twang. The heat from their loins mounts to the brain, flushes their faces and clouds their eyes. José alone retains a glacial calm. He barely unclenches his teeth:

"Take a good look at these men, this room! Don't you see you have to shake them up, snap them out of it, out of this place, out of their stupor?"

I see that you are alone, José, with your exalted valor which intoxicates you like wine that is too heady; alone, ready for anything, absurd like heroes who come before their time. Lost. The other city is stronger . . .

On the way out of there, toward midnight, José spies a poor wretch with the look of a dead fish on the edge of the shadows, about to disappear into the night. José takes him by the arm:

"Come on, old fellow. I'll buy you supper. Don't laugh. I'm not drunk. I'm a man. Maybe you don't know what that is."

FOURTEEN

Messages

THE MAJORITY OF THE FRENCHMEN AMONG US ARE OF ZILZ'S OPINION. THE herd of humanity is not worth fighting for; revolutions won't change man's destiny in the least. Let's look out for ourselves. Derelicts marked for prison or death in the trenches, they create this escapee's philosophy for themselves, not unlike that of certain profiteers of the existing order. We were just talking about the Russian Revolution. Zilz struck each of us in turn with his triumphant question:

"Do you like coffee with cream . . . ?"

Next over to the Russian Consulate. A blond smooth-faced clerk had me sign some papers. All I really saw of him was a shirt cuff, some well-manicured pink fingers bearing a signet ring, and shiny hair slicked down over his skull with such perfect care and such heavily scented brilliantine that I was dying to muss it up. In a thin voice he insinuated to me that "today even our ministers don't know how to spell properly." Thus a revolution is envisaged under carefully combed hair.

The *Arriviste* received me in the middle of a white and gold *moderne-style* room. At times he seemed to be gazing lovingly at his well-manicured fingernails; the white handkerchief in his breast pocket was puffed up like whipped cream; even the inflections of his voice were full of nuances and kind attentions; but his eyes, the eyes of a pretty boy accustomed to making a good impression, said—strangely—nothing. What color were they in fact? As with the faces of certain Greek statues the pupils are represented by shallow holes; any shadow, however light, emphasizes the absence of vision, that abstract depth. I understood in the very first minute that he was successful with women, that is to say, with ladies, published free verse in slim volumes with parchment covers, made an effort to read Bergson, add professed at once and the same time an energetic nationalism ("What we need is a Catalan Barrès": that phrase of his was to become famous) and the eloquent republicanism of "our great Pi y Margall . . ." I could see him as he will be in thirty years, a sure fate: heftier, pale-skinned, his eyelids heavier, decorated, no matter what the regime may be—for even the Republics of Labor will have to invent decorations for this kind of precious servant!—ten years from a peaceful death that will utterly obliterate him, all at once, like a newspaper, its charred headline an urgent cry, forgotten without having been heeded, licked by the flames in the hearth. His sympathies tend naturally toward the great cause of the Entente. Naturally because the contrary would have been just as natural. And how could I help but take his part with Letter of Transit #662-491 pressed tightly in my billfold! Already this ticket, *Good for one death like the others*, engulfs me in deceit and print's a hypocritical smile on my face. The *Arriviste* requested some correspondence from me about Russia for a newspaper:

"Via Stockholm (well, you like to travel). Our only rule is: Objectivity, local color."

I know, I know, The little superior air of not taking sides: a maxim of *Realpolitik*, an allusion to sociology (modern journalism being scientific) a digression on the Slavic soul, and some picturesque, some human interest, some exotic words: *muzhik, izba, traktir, chinovnik* . . . This job is at bottom no worse than the other, which consists of spending ten hours a day setting up the names of the Duke of Medina-Coeli's horses in 6-point italic. The one ruins the lungs, the other deadens the brain: both stupefying in the long run.

"Bah, one can always take a pseudonym."

An hour later the mendicants had reconciled me with the tragedy of life. The beggars of this city are magnificent. (Their misery is a slap in the face to wealth, smug self-satisfaction, the blue sky.) You can see them dragging themselves around on the porches of the churches, in the gilded dust of the boulevards, filthy, misshapen, pitiful, with their stumps of limbs and suppurating sores, stares tenacious as leeches from eyes ringed with tainted blood, maniac glances of eyes flecked with white. Detestable vermin multiply in their rags with joyful abandon. Horrible diseases: leprosy, lupus, psoriasis, erysipelas, pullulate in their open sores. They have local color. I know one who plays rasping music on the steps of the jetty. This flabby gray slug glues himself to the stern stone shaft which stands erect, cleaving the very gold, the very azure of the sea. And the shaft transports him. "Blind from birth"—a fake blind man, they say, a fake slug, that slug; but we, we are authentic. At the door of the cathedral a mummy's hand shoots out of a gray stone nook toward a rather plump milky-skinned passer-by who is carrying roses and sweet Williams to her patron saint, doubtless a saint who watches over thrifty widows (HERBALIST'S SHOP: *medicinal teas our specialty* . . .) A cadaverous voice issues from behind that long-dried-out corpse's hand, as august as that of Ramses II: *"Carida por l'amor de Dios, Señora."* (Charity for the love of God, Madam!) The passer-by has passed. Never will that hand fall into dust . . .

A Herculean torso, bearing a huge, ill-connected head, is dragging itself toward us on its belly and its leather-strapped wrists. With each lurch forward of this half-man, the head, jerked to one side by the shock, spits out a long guttural supplication; you would think it was spewing forth inexpiable curses at the world if you didn't hear the words *"Nuestro* Señor" falling heavily like drops of dark blood from those fleshy lips. Voices answer each other. Echo. In the silence of the cathedral, I can hear the same hill mouthed syllables repeated with fervor by a child's voice falling like drops of gold, heavy and brilliant: *"a Nuestro* Señor, *a Nuestro* Señor . . ."

"That man," I say to El Chorro, "makes one think of an earthworm that has been cut in two by the blade of a shovel."

El Chorro throws away his cigarette:

"Very apt! That's old Gusano: the Worm. The whole town calls him that . . . Hi! How are you, Feliz. Here's one of the boys from *Tierra.* What's new, you sanctimonious sans-culotte?"

The stump of a man laughs, exposing strong teeth, greenish at the gums. Ever since a fall of thirty yards from the scaffoldings of a new basilica for the Holy Family diminished him by one-half, Feliz, of the *Tierra y Libertad* (Land and Liberty) Party, has been up to his ears in land, and starving in liberty. Policemen turn away, when they hear him apostrophizing some respectable passer-by: "It was building your house that broke my back! Eh, landlord . . . !" He is still able to be of service. His straw mattress is the last place they would look for Cuban certificates of naturalization, fabricated by . . .

"Gusano," says El Chorro, "this comrade is leaving for Russia tomorrow."

Gusano stops laughing. His big shaven head, browned by a layer of sweat and dust, looks as if it had been severed and placed casually on this ugly, hairy torso rounded off in a shapeless bulb below. We look at each other intensely for a moment, down to the inexpressible depths of our being. I no longer see anything but the half-man's eyes: he has gray-blue irises streaked with brown. A sunset over mountain snows. Warmth and virile vigor.

"He is lucky," Gusano says simply at last.

The harbor is peopled with lights. The lighthouse beacons are coming on. The black hull of the *Ursula* (Montevideo) stands out, steeper than a cliff, a few yards from the dockside. At night the ships lying in the harbor make you think of great prehistoric reptiles. But the lines of human invention are sharper than those of nature. Collins. Small craft carrying signal lights are moving across the water—which is like flat ink, spotted here and there with phosphorescent arcs. A green light blinks at the other end of the basin between two vertical hedges of masts.

Some bales of jute that will be loaded aboard tomorrow shelter us comfortably in the uncertain glimmer of a lantern hanging from the corrugated roof of a nearby warehouse. There are about twenty of us perched on bales between two piles of merchandise covered with waterproof canvas. NO SMOKING: we know only too well what is inside: this is no time to start any trouble. Dockers, seamen, watchmen from the storehouses—all comrades, in any case. A stool pigeon? Probably. But what difference can it make to us, this evening, that there should be one that's false among these valiant souls?

We talked about the fifteen per cent and the general strike. From out of the shadows a voice, grave with forty years of labor clearly analyzed the elements of the bosses' resistance: orders from the Allies, support from the banks in Madrid, competition with certain industries in the Asturias, underhanded dealings of a group in the pay of the Central Powers, discontent created by the customs tariffs, the coming revision of Franco-Spanish agreements . . . And suddenly here I am, not having budged, at the center of this group to which I bear a message. "Objectivity and local color!" the Arriviste told me. That recollection is enough to dispel my scruples at being an informant without information.

There are things which, if they took place on a planet of the constellation Orion, these twenty men would understand at the slightest hint. Like war, which no people wants. The general strike overthrowing a monarchy like a well-placed sock on the jaw puts you out of commission: *knockout.* That it takes time, years, thousands of men, thousands of years in prison, thousands of men hanged, shot, murdered, insurrections put down, assassinations, betrayals, provocations, fresh start after fresh start until, in the end, an old Empire, eaten away by termites, suddenly collapses because some workers' wives have begun to shout "Bread!" in front of the bakeries, because the soldiers fraternize with the mob, because old policemen decorated for zeal are thrown into the icy waters of the canals, because . . . I don't have to teach them, they understand these things perfectly. But someone wants the incredible truth repeated: that it has really happened. Someone demands, his hand outstretched:

"Well, and the Czar? . . ."

"No more Czars."

Like a breeze—the final eddy of a hurricane uprooting oaks on the other side of the ocean—that makes the leaves tremble gently in a wood, the same breath of inspiration makes these men tremble with excitement. And we carry on this dialogue of shadows:

"The army?"

"With the people."

"The police?"

"No more police."

"The prisons?"

"Burned."

"The power?"

"Us."

This extraordinary confidence, this leap into confidence, I owe to you, Gusano. It is your gray-blue eyes streaked with brown that I see before me at this moment. It is you who are speaking within me, you, your sober gaze, that masculine strength underneath, so sure of life *no matter what happens*. We know how to live and to survive, truncated like worms . . .

The voice of the man heavy with forty years of labor asks for some clarifications. We are the power, on condition that we start up the revolution once again. The one just completed is not yet ours. The wealthy classes know only too well how to juggle away revolutions: "Abracadabra!" and one sees nothing but red, the blood of the workers. But the Russians see through this. Their eyes are wide open. It's all right. Take over the land, take over the factories.

"And the war?"

Many of them are worried. A docker says he believes the Germans will win. Germany could strangle the revolution. Phrases clash like crossed swords. The revolution is the daughter of the war. No, the daughter of defeat. The vanquished, whoever they may be, will make it. Long live defeat! The future belongs to the vanquished. But all of Europe is already defeated! Declare peace on the world. Take over Europe . . .

I am leaving tomorrow. I carry with me, as my only provisions for the journey, as my only message, these twenty handshakes. And Gusano's, twenty-*one*.

FIFTEEN

Votive Hand

TUFTS OF STEAM VAPOR CLING TO THE BRANCHES OF LEANING TREES: BIRCHES, fragile greenery with pale silvery reflections, slender leaves green with moisture, green light. And the parched plains. The web of telegraph wires rises and falls. Sparrows—the notes on these dancing staves: the horizon rises and falls with the rolling of a ship. Refreshing breeze of voyage; cinders and dust lashing the face. The burning of noontide on the rust-colored plains. I think avidly of that city, that city which we did not take, of those men, comrades, my comrades. I should like to open my arms, to stretch my whole being out toward them, to say to them—what? I can only find a single word: "Comrades"—richer perhaps in their language: *compañeros*—because of so many warm men's voices united by hope and danger whose echoes are still vibrating in my ears . . .

El Chorro's story this morning on the streetcar still provokes laughter within me, as bracing as a swallow of rum when you are very cold. Not that it was a happy story: but so much liveliness came through the tone and the accent that, lowering my eyelids, I could imagine myself walking along a great enticing highway, in the early morning, with this secure and hardy companion:

"*Hombre*, I became a man by falling off a ladder. You'll see what I mean. I used to be a house painter working for a fat swine of a Huertista[7] not far from Veracruz. One fine day I fall from a height of four yards with a bucket of red paint in my hand only, my boy, right on top of that bastard—as he was passing under my ladder—so that my bucket lands right on his head. I couldn't have done it better if I had been trying. My knee is hurting me, but I begin laughing, laughing so hard that my heart, my stomach, and the rest begin dancing a crazy *jota* inside me.

---

7   Follower of Victoriano Huerta, during the 1915 Mexican Revolution.

My buddies throw a bucket of water in my face, but it's too late. They put me under arrest. 'You a union man?' I didn't even know what that meant. 'No.' They tie my hands up neatly behind my back. A couple of slaps on the puss given by an extraordinary pair of hands, you can believe me, send me flying and pull me back again before I even hit the ground. 'You a union man?' This time I say *yes*. You'd be a union man for less, right? Well, then the guy gets real nice, gives me some cigarettes. 'Do you want a priest? Would you like to spend the night in church, *Chico*? You shouldn't die like a dog. Think of your soul.' I say: 'In church, sure,' in order to gain time. Without that, they would have dispatched me on the spot; they used to slaughter a man without a sound, in three movements, with a nice machete chop under your chin. So I spend twenty hours waiting around like a good Christian, at the local church between two lighted candles, to be bled the next morning, just like a pig, but with the firm promise of Paradise. I spend a poor night crushing spiders with the head of a little silver saint. Well, imagine that at five in the morning the Carranzistas[8] take over the town! They enlist me, naturally, in a red battalion. I begin to understand things. I join the union. Then we go off to fight against Zapata and I go over to the enemy, for he was worth a lot more than we were . . ."

El Chorro was on the station platform. His massive jaw, his square teeth, his big nose, the rusty patina of his fleshy Aztec face.

"*Adios!*"

He raised his mutilated hand: the thumb too short, too wide, the index finger straight out, the sharply cut stumps of three fingers. And that whole hand seemed cut off to me, hanging in space, a votive hand.

What else did I see in those last seconds? A tall, elegant Negro went by, carrying a little leather suitcase with shiny silver buckles.

We sometimes think that life is always the same, because it carries us along with it. False immobility of the swimmer who abandons himself to the current. That moment on the *rambla*, when Angel fell, will never come back. That other moment in the Plaza Real, that couple in the semidarkness under the gray arcade and Joaquin's torn jacket; the shrug of Dario's shoulders; it is finished, all of it. There is nothing left before me but that votive hand, floating, and about to disappear. How to snatch it back?

---

8   Followers of the liberal President, Venustiano Carranza.

A pair of taciturn *guardia civils* are escorting a little music hall *poule* to the border. She pouts at them from time to time. It is at those times that she looks out at the landscape; then she puts on some lipstick and looks sulkily into her pocket mirror. *They* stare into space, straight ahead. I have the feeling that she is about to stand up and smack them with the back of her hand, like Punch slapping the Inspector; and their heads will dandle pitifully right to left, left to right, like the Inspector's head. Some wrinkles around her nostrils cheapen her unpretentious little lady's face. She must have a nasty voice on the high notes, the calculating mind of a housewife who knows all about prices, and a great jealousy of the rich. She is ashamed of wearing misshapen eighteen-franc shoes. Her lover's name is Emile.

"Isn't that so, mademoiselle, his name is Emile?"

She would look up with a start. "Fresh!"—then calmer, feeling me entirely disarmed, would ask without hiding her surprise:

"How did you guess?"

This scene was played between us in the zone of possible events, just before the dark explosion of a tunnel.

We fall for a long time through the darkness: we are about to fall into the bright light.

And the idea which I am trying to get rid of pierces me, like an electric needle, from one temple to the other: Dario will be killed, for that city, for us, for me, for the future. Every morning when he leaves the house where he has slept, every evening when he enters the back rooms of little cafés where fifteen men—including one traitor—are waiting for him, at every moment of his patient agitator's labor, he moves toward that end marked out for him. And one of the many men he is (for we are composites: there exist within us men who sleep, others who dream, others who are waiting for their time, others who vanish, perhaps permanently) knows it. It is the one whose mouth has a little tired line and whose eye wanders at a friendly meeting looking for something in the distance, shelter, refuge, unforeseen exit.

My letter of transit may take me far, too. This thought restores my serenity by reestablishing in some way the balance between our destinies . . .

When the little blond dish goes to the lavatory, a *guardia* waits for her in front of the door, solid as a post, rigid as his orders.

Not far from the railway, an old town comes into view, with rounded towers, crumbling crenellated walls, old slate roofs, a great desolation all around. A town sleeping on the edge of life's highways, Hostalrich.

Another town, laid out along a dried-out *rio*. This stony, sandy river-bed, the color of burnt earth, is as gloomy as a dismal death under the desolation of the devastating and parching sun. Tall sun-baked houses gaze out over the drained river from all their little windows where wash is hanging out to dry. Old houses, old prisons, poor lives floundering on, each in its pigeonhole under crumbling roofs like thoughts under a wrinkled brow. The shadowy gaps of narrow streets led perhaps toward an arcaded square, calmed by the shade of tall plane trees where a good-natured tavern keeper would serve you the sourish local wine. An angular church tower, sharp gray stone, pointed belfry, town clock, looks over the town: and it is the only thing which points upward: an iron cross in the hard sapphire sky.

SIXTEEN

Border

THE ASSISTANT TO THE SPECIAL INSPECTOR OF THE BORDER IS A GENTLEMAN full of good humor with rather short arms, and a rather large and rather red nose. I am certain that he can recognize good vintages infallibly at first taste. His house is white with green shutters; two big rosebushes on either side of the entrance greet him each morning with their wordless song: "How good it is to be alive, Monsieur Comblé! You have slept well, Monsieur Comblé, between clean lavender-scented sheets next to your satin-skinned blonde. You're going to have a good breakfast, Monsieur Comblé, and there is a chance, Monsieur Comblé, that you will get a promotion at the first change of personnel." Monsieur Comblé savors the scent of a hollyhock, Color of My Mistress' Breast ("A horticulturist's success and poet's find") and gaily answers his pet roses in the silence of his happy soul, so comfortably housed in an almost sound body (a little arthritis, alas): "It would be only just, exquisite flowers, that Monsieur Comblé's excellent services should be rewarded. Did I not arrest that little brunette spy with the funny little upturned nose whom my dear Parisian colleagues had allowed to escape this far? And if they are getting her ready for the firing squad at Vincennes, it's thanks to little me, thanks to little me . . ." His files are kept in an exemplary manner, like his little garden. There are ones for suspects, for international thieves, for expelled, wanted, and escaped persons; there is the secret file: a whole invisible flowering of crimes, sufferings, punishments, intrigues, and shadowy struggles shrouds these files. Without trembling, Monsieur Comblé plunges in a fat hand and pulls out an identification card:

"Got her," he says. "Perfect."

A slight, almost imperceptible clicking of the tongue is the sign, with him, of professional satisfaction, akin to gastronomic satisfaction. The blond floozy, accompanied by the two dark gendarmes, makes her way with little hurried steps, with the poor nervous smile of a rabbit being slaughtered, toward two fat horizon-blue gendarmes who exchange a wink when they see her: "Not bad, that little broad . . ."

Monsieur Comblé, having unfolded my letter of transit, looks up at me with a cordial smile, borrowed from Albert Guillaume's pastels. He looks at me with the unrestrained sympathy he usually reserves for his roses (and, after a well-prepared lunch, for tiny Madame Comblé— "Little Dédé"—in their moments of great intimacy).

"What you are doing is a very fine thing, monsieur. Allow me to congratulate you."

I take these congratulations flush in the face, like stepping into something slimy.

"You are returning at a time when so many cowards can think only of crossing the border . . .

Fortunately a broad, black hand holds out a square of cardboard in the air at the height of my shoulder: "Faustin Bâton, landowner at Grande Saline, Republic of Haiti." The nails of that black hand cover a rosy pulp. The edge of a starched cuff exposes the deep brown of the wrist. The elegant Negro I caught a glimpse of while leaving pushes me gently aside. A paper with a consular letterhead informs Monsieur Gamble that Monsieur Faustin Bâton "who has distinguished himself by his generous gifts to the Red Cross is traveling to France in order to contract a voluntary, enlistment in the Foreign Legion there."

"But that is admirable!" says Monsieur Comblé. To leave the Antilles— that must be quite nice, too, owning land at Grande Saline, Haiti—to cross the ocean to come to fight in France, that's really extraordinary, that's amazing. "A swell guy, the Zulu!" Admiration forces Monsieur Comblé to rise; he is on his feet, he is about to say a few heartfelt words to this Negro whose grave immobility has truly moved him . . . But Monsieur Perrache, that sourpuss of a bilious sacristan, has just appeared. Monsieur Perrache has that funny kind of overfriendly look whose meaning is altered by an undefinable hint of irony. "A treacherous look," says Monsieur Comblé at times; "the look of an s.o.b." say the men on duty. Monsieur Comblé's flabby hand disappears within the powerful black hand, its joints lithe and its muscles sinuous, of Faustin Bâton. The white hand is dank; the black, cool. Close to his own face, Monsieur Comblé sees a protruding jaw, thick wine-colored lips, huge eyes of white enamel and burnt agate which seem to be trying to recognize him, but without the warmth of friendship, with even a kind of hostility as if they were saying to him: "What? You? So it's you, then, whom I've been looking for since Gonaïves? It's not possible . . . !" Monsieur Comblé attempts to smile and proffers an *"On les aura!"*

Monsieur Perrache's glance envelops both of them in a strange coldness. A tired old customs inspector wearing the Madagascar medal has just come in; some Spanish workers are waiting outside the door. Faustin Bâton turns toward the door and suddenly feels terribly embarrassed, too well dressed, too tall, too black, too strong, too new, with his little too-bright suitcase, its nickel-plating gleaming like a happy man who has suddenly fallen in among old prisoners.

The hillsides are still green high above: flocks are doubtless grazing over there in the immense calm. The spine of the mountains outlines an ideal border. Hard, sharp, pure, this accessible peak, a majestic granite spire wounding the sky; if I could reach it, it would disclose an even wider expanse of peaks, of new borders to be overcome in order to know the world (or that part of the world which can be encompassed by the eye) . . . From every side the vertical fissures in the rocks fall toward the sea and toward this blue cove—a primitive drinking cup cut out of the coast. A tiny rounded cove with the semblance of a beach, thick gravel, fishermen's boats, nets drying on the pebbles, two cafés where customsmen sit half asleep in front of their *apéritifs* on the terrace—a tiny bay, surrounded by the vast blocks of the mountains with a huge vista opening into the infinite Mediterranean between two abrupt slides of granite. The sharp point of the headland slices into the sea and the sky at the same time; fans of foam break over its near-black stone in shimmering rainbows. Crystal-like laughter runs over the surface of the sea. The air is fair. The water below is so clear that you can see fleeting, shadowy commas of life flitting across a bottom of white and brown pebbles, sometimes green from algae.

My footsteps send lizards scurrying between the rocks. One of them, however, allows me to approach him: his green throat is throbbing, his round eye the eye of a curious old man, his wide thin mouth the mouth of an actor who has outlived all the vanities, his scaly clothes have the cool tint of a young plant dampened by the dew; this is not without its profound reasons. My glance falls from that triangular peak edged with tawny rust over there to this being suspended in flight. This faint tingle in the air, the radiance of these stones, this water, this tiny life stationary in my path, this brilliance which doesn't cause the eyes to blink, this enveloping flame which does not burn, this transparent limpidity, *lucidity*, joy . . . The big white pebbles cause a pleasant burning sensation on your feet. The swimmer's feeling of plenitude, the cool of the water, the soft curves of the waves as you cut through them, mirrorings, breakings, suspensions of crystal and of a liquid dust which capture the rays of the light in mid-air in immaterial jewels. Powerful eddies, warnings from the depths, raise up the insignificant man who no longer has any weight to support but that of his skull: a little gray matter under the frontal carapace and those two minute dark chambers which contain the only image of the universe that exists. You are only able to know yourself, oh world, in our eyes: this lizard on the rock, myself borne on these pure waters, more ancient than these rocks but eternally renewed. Joy. Joy . . . It's more beautiful than cities, more beautiful than rains, more beautiful than nights, more beautiful than dreams. It's . . . I forget to think.—But an idea comes to the surface, the words cut out in striking relief:

"It would be so good: to live . . ."

"Helloo!"

Answer, echo, this ringing cry to my right. Like a dolphin sporting in the waves, Faustin Bâton is swimming with powerful strokes, disappearing completely, rising up to the waist streaming with foam; and I see him smiling. Joy lights up his face, shining with drops of silver.

We swim toward each other, laughing without any cause (but there is only this laughter, our laughter, the reflection of the play of the sea; and, later, I would be unable to imagine this moment without that laughter). We greet each other with our eyes, understanding without thinking that we are united by a friendship, vague, supple, and powerful like the lazy waves which pull us back toward the pebbly beach.

". . . Really feels great!"

"Helloo!"

Like the lizard on the rocks, we dry ourselves in the sun before getting dressed. The light sculpts my companion's outstretched body into hollows and reliefs, shadows and metallic reflections. The dark grain of his skin, rather brown tending toward coppery red, is naturally sharp. The purity of flesh.

Hello, there's somebody, over there. A breach between the rocks suddenly reveals the next beach, an old house, a barrel, a bench, and on the bench, a man. Can he see us? Slumped down rather than seated, his back against the wall, propped up on crutches, skeletal hands: the heel of one frail leg is dug into the fine gravel; the other is cut off well above the knee. A cap flattened out over the side of his head seems ready to fall off; and that face, at this distance, is so colorless that it almost seems to blend in with the wall, already halfway absorbed by the stones, not really pale but the color of flesh returning to the earth. Does this man see us—Célestin Braque, fisherman by trade, twice gassed, right leg amputated, Croix de Guerre with palm-leaf clusters, decorated by order of one army for his exploits in the Haudremont Woods where he may have dealt a fate similar to his to some fisherman from Swinemünde whom I imagine sprawling at this very hour in the same position before the Baltic and its soft, slate-gray reflections? We see him as an accusation.

SEVENTEEN

Faustin and Six Real Soldiers

FAUSTIN BÂTON BELIEVES PRACTICALLY EVERYTHING HE READS. THE UNMIXED heroism of the *poilus*, the historic last words of dying men, the articles of General N—, of M. Gauvain, of M. Bidou, of M. Lavedan, and of all the armchair strategists in editorial rooms who never tire of analyzing communiqués, the claptrap designed to raise morale in the rear, from the story of the German babies being born without hair or nails because the Boches' bodies have already been so badly weakened to the one about the man who was wounded four times crying on his hospital bed in front of the pretty, peroxide-blond nurse because he is not yet able to go back to the front. All this absurd prose makes a great impression on the naïve soul of this great-grandson of slaves who bowed under the master's stick on the plantations before holding it in their turn; grandson of partisans, perhaps grandnephew of some black emperor (Faustin the First: Faustin-Robespierre-Napoléon Soulouque . . .). He believes everything in the way certain drunkards drink any kind of alcohol indiscriminately. And it's not that he's stupid. If he were stupid he wouldn't have this profound capacity for believing, he would be better able to discern the big lie; the clever subtleties would be less effective on him; fewer ideas, fewer words would be interposed between him and reality. Perhaps it would have been enough for him to have opened, one after the other, a pro-German and a pro-Allied American newspaper to have thrown them both in the same garbage can; the same lies, the same sophisms in one as in the other, the same hooey. At times, in my mind, I call him an imbecile, for it is really too much to take the counterfeit coins of so many humbugs for coin of the realm, but I know that I am unjust. He possesses the lively intelligence of simple and vigorous beings who are able to flesh out even false notions. From that point on, an imaginary world made up of a terrible jumble of words rises up solidly between his sharp mind and things as they are. He is a newcomer on our dunes; he walks along them with great strides, accustomed to the solid earth, not seeing that he is being swallowed up. Literal comprehension and an open mind are not sufficient for finding your way in our old labyrinths; you also have to be inured against error, trickery, illusion, the past, desire, other people, and yourself. You must become mistrustful, arm yourself with critical method, arm yourself with doubt and with assurance, become wary of words, learn to burst them like those marvelous soap bubbles which, fallen, are reduced to paltry artificial spittle. "Faustin, my friend," I say, "the art of reading our newspapers is a much more difficult one than that of tracking the fox through our forests . . ." We have become friends; he confessed to me from the very first the great confidence he is ready to offer any man expert in the splendid play of words and ideas. Certainly no swindler could ever have made him take a worn-out horse for a sound one, a low quality bicycle for a good make. Faustin Bâton, landowner at Grande Saline, Haiti, is not one to be bamboozled in that kind of deal, but it is possible with the help of Right, Civilization, History, the Holy War, the War of Liberation, to make him cross the Atlantic, put the latest model grenade in his hand, and send him to his death. I know that he will be the first one to leap out of the trenches, dauntless, held so erect before the danger by his feeling of heroic duty that it will take a few moments for the warrior's instinct of his ancestors, who went into battle hunched over with springy feline steps, to awaken within him . . . And besides, those few seconds will be enough; a magnificent target, he won't go any further.

I could, of course, demolish his ingenuous faith; and at times I am tempted to do so. But to my careful irony (he can't understand irony, especially the kind that talks without smiling) he answers with the disabled looks of a baffled child caught at fault, suddenly doubting the lessons he has learned. And it is a serious matter to destroy a man's faith without replacing it. And then I have my task, my road to take: Letter of Transit #662-491 already surrounds me, wherever I go, with a pernicious atmosphere.

We were traveling together. It was in a little café in a town in the Midi, *Au rendez-vous des Ferblantiers*, that Faustin Bâton made his first real contact with men at war. We had seen some ill-dressed soldiers entering there, home guards and convalescents come to see off a helmeted friend—loaded down with heavy haversacks—whose profile to us seemed austere. "Furlough's over," I remarked. The setting was that of an ugly industrial suburb: rails, a low wall, a wooden shack plastered with torn-up posters: LOAN . . . VICTORY . . . We followed the group into the café. "Willya set up a round, Moko? somebody cried out to my companion. (Why "Moko?") "With great pleasure, gentlemen," he answered, with a broad, serious smile. Then they stared at him; his voice, almost grave, impressed them. "Be so kind as to come over and have a chair," said someone else. The tone had lowered. There were six of them: the helmeted man on furlough whose face was not actually austere, but ravaged, drawn, full of perpendicular lines, with a tuft of red whiskers on his chin; the others seemed a motley crew, yet unified—except for one whom I took to be a schoolteacher—by a common expression and way of talking, local people, workers who would some day like to run a little workshop of their own, shopkeepers who had been workers.

"Traveling?" the fat fellow with the face of a cab driver asked us politely. "We're seeing off Lacoste here. He's leaving on the 10:30 for a quiet sector."

"Perhaps we will meet each other there," said Faustin politely.

He felt himself to be at a great moment in his life. Six real French soldiers were listening to him. He told them, addressing himself in particular to the man on furlough, that he had come from America to fight. That his ancestors had played a part in the French Revolution. That he forgave Napoleon for the imprisonment and death of Toussaint L'Ouverture. That he was ready to die for Civilization, the liberator of the Black people, the liberator of all men. That he admired more than any others the heroic soldiers of the Marne and of Verdun. Lacoste, the soldier on furlough, seemed to be looking at him from far away with gloomy astonishment. When Faustin had finished, the silence came crashing down around our shoulders with all its weight. The innkeeper's wife—beautiful bare arms—had come over to our table, opposite a smiling Alsatian girl who was holding out a square bottle toward us from a chromos on the wall.

"Well!" said Lacoste at last.

He had had a lot to drink, and was consumed by a boundless sadness. He must have understood that he had to find another answer in response to those strange black eyes full of a kind of anguish which burned in that ugly chimpanzee face across the table.

"Well," he said, "then you must be right, if that's the way things are. C'mon. Try on my helmet. Let's see if that kind of headgear will look as good on you as it does on me . . ."

He put his helmet over the kinky hair, loosened and then tightened the chinstrap. He was himself no longer anything but a man prematurely old who hadn't shaved since the previous evening and hadn't slept all night (because his wife had begun to cry at dawn). But Faustin appeared to us under the surprising mask of a true warrior, with a terrible smile and carnivorous teeth. His head looked as if it had been made for the helmet.

"No," cried Lacoste. "It looks better on you than it does on me. You can keep it, y'know! Ah, son of a bitch, how I'd love to change heads with you, Black Beauty! I'd even be willing to sleep only with a Negress for the rest of my life . . . C'mon, let's change heads!"

He seized his own head between both hands, as if to tear it off—and suddenly hid his face in his sleeve on the edge of the table.

A hushed conference convened next to me.

"What a brute! He's trying to make an ass of us, I tellya. It's impossible that anybody could still be such a jerk these days. It might've happened three years ago, I don't say no. I c'n understand, the rest of us, we don't have no choice. And then we've been invaded. But that dopey jerk! With his L'Ouverture and Napoleon! He talks like a newspaper. Myself, I feel like pushing in his face!"

The one who was talking must have been a convalescent. All I could see of him was the back of a hand covered with a large, freshly scarred burn. His neighbor, an old home guard, replied:

"Don't try to be funny. One man's as good as another. When they add it up, all they want is the right count of carcasses and broken arms. If one comes over from America, maybe that saves one of us. I don't have any objection to him gettin' killed instead of me. It ain't right that it's always the same ones gettin' killed. There ought t' be more of 'em comin' from all the countries in the world. At least then they'd be able to leave the old classes behind the lines guarding the railroads. Me, I'm in favor of the Black Army."

He raised his voice:

"Monsieur Bâton, I believe? Monsieur Bâton you're very right. And I hope you'll have the Croix de Guerre before long . . ."

". . . with thirty-six palms," added someone under his breath.

The schoolteacher observed Faustin with cruel fixity.

"Hey, Francois," he said to my neighbor, "I think I understand this fellow. Look at that jaw: it explains everything. I once met a volunteer like that in the Argonne, only white, a poacher from the Vosges for whom the whole war was nothing but a nice man hunting party. He'd shoot your Boche down for you with mean delight. He was a coward, like a bedbug at bottom: the soul of a murderer. I told him once: 'You're not a soldier, you're a gangster.' I wasn't in the least put out when he caught a nice little piece of shrapnel right between the eyes."

Lacoste raised his head. A kind of bewilderment held him between rage and laughter.

"Gimme back my helmet, Black Beauty," he said violently, "since we can't exchange heads. I like mine well enough anyway. Com'on, hup; gimme back!"

He practically tore the helmet out of Faustin's helpless hands. He banged his fist on the table, making the glasses jump.

"To hell with it all boys. All together:
C'est à boire, à boire, à boire
C'est à boire qu'il nous faut ô ô— . . ."

They sing.

Faustin is silent. A grieved smile draws his features. The expression of a man who has made a mistake he would like to be forgiven for, who would like to lie, and understands that it is useless. His sharp ears have picked up bits and pieces of dialogue which he refuses to understand but which he cannot forget. I put my hand on his shoulder.

"Farewell, Faustin."

"What? But I . . ."

"No, you're staying. Faustin, my friend, the truth: the Front begins here. Your place is among these soldiers *who have had enough* . . ."

The words I speak strike home, enlarge the inner wound. He hesitates, bewildered.

"C'mon, Black Beauty," cries the man on furlough with a sudden snarl in his voice, "all together, I tell you:
Le troisième dans l'escarcelle
Ne trouva qu'un écu faux . . .
C'est à boire, à boire, à boire . . ."

EIGHTEEN

A Lodging. A Man

I CONTINUE MY JOURNEY ALONE. THE SOFT GREEN LANDSCAPES SLOWLY DIVIDE in front of the express—and doubtless, come together again behind the long metallic snake as, its old links flaming, it patiently devours the miles. Beauty of the earth in August. The color of the world is golden . . .

"Landscapes give me a pain in the ass!"

The faded eyes of an exhausted man yelled this at me when I smiled vaguely at some russet fields, perhaps thinking how alive the earth is. "Pass me the canteen," he said in a heavy tracked voice.

The trains are full of soldiers. I should like to see this ant swarm around the railroad stations from way up high. A chimerical order reigns there, assigning to each individual precise but incomprehensible routes. Each searches for his life, comes, goes, resists, hesitates, but in the end all these trains unload their human cargo in enormous communal graves . . .

"Reasons give me a pain in the ass!"

The exhausted man stuffs his pipe with rage under the NO SMOKING sign. There is also:

TAISEZ-VOUS, MÉFIEZ-VOUS,

LES OREILLES ENNEMIES VOUS ÉCOUTENT.

(Keep still! Watch out! Enemy ears are listening!)

I am the only civilian in the compartment. I am the right age to be a dead man on active duty; I have the health of a man who has just spent six months living in Catalonia. All these worn faces under their old gray helmets look at me almost as if I were an enemy.

"Enemy? You kidding? You and all the others give me a pain in the ass!"

Their greatcoats are faded and spotted: the horizon-blue of the muds, the rains, the fatigue. Their rucksacks heavy and shapeless. Their helmets dented. Under their harness the torpid men seem emaciated with hard bones and tanned leather, tenacious souls turned in on their useless anger. A convalescent as fresh as a young girl is leaning in the corner. "What didja have?"—"A bullet in the top of my right lung; two months in the hospital."—"A cushy job, eh!" That is all that is said about the war for several hours. And this from a vintner, who had got off at the previous station: "As for us in the Vauquois . . ." At the sound of that name I cocked my ear. But it was only a story about booze, soup, monkey meat and a bastard of a sergeant: "So I says to him . . ." Nothing in this monotonous story about insignificant things (punctuated with "So I says to him's,"—"So he says to me's,"—"So's," and "Then's") came through of the battlefield, where these things had probably really happened, filling a man's life for days and his memory perhaps for years . . . They talk about furloughs, women, wine, the prices.

"The war? It gives me a pain in the ass!" the exhausted man would say. "I'm fighting in it; that's already quite enough."

These men are hard and faded like the stones at the bottom of a waterfall, rolled, polished, broken by countless shocks. Their falling increases the strength of the falls that rolls them along. They are nothing. They kill. They are killed. They live. They are dead. Dead in advance, by anticipation. This one here, puffing on his pipe with dark lips, will have his head blown off in four days, accidentally, on his way back from the latrine. Nothing will be found of his cunning smuggler's head, which is at this moment cooking up some "ideas," some clever, life-saving "system . . ."

Dead in advance without any anticipation; for so many others, identical to them, are actually dead that each of these has his forgotten double somewhere underground.

A bad day. I ran all over Paris, from Montrouge to Bercy, from Levallois to Montparnasse. My addresses are running out, and time is moving on. Despite Letter of Transit #662-491, a feeling of insecurity creeps into my bones along with the fatigue—a dull ache. In a hotel, Letter #662-491 would probably not prevent me from being arrested. Where to find a roof tonight? A few hours under shelter, time to recharge my nervous equipment, and the future is saved. I knocked at Julio's door on a deserted *quai* in Bercy. A fat woman with tired eyes opened up with hesitation. At the name of José Miro her face cleared up: "Julio is

in hiding; we're being watched; the business of the Marseille deserters, you know." I don't know anything, but already this commonplace
room with its rickety sofa oppresses me. Hmmm . . . Someone behind
me on the *quai*. Let's get rid of this doubt in which fear is lurking. *Métro*.
The oar bangs against an iron bridge; the greenish Seine mirrors
the pure sky so well! The odor of dust and asphalt, crowds, soldiers. A
twenty-five-year-old officer, his face divided by a wide black bandage
beneath the eyes—no nose, probably, an artificial jaw—is talking softly
in his murdered-man's voice to his blond *marraine*, who looks as though
she had just stepped out of a page of the rotogravure. This monster
adores you, Mademoiselle; you'd better close your eyes or look into the
distance. At the end of the green avenue the Carpeaux fountain raises
an aerial globe imprisoned by the metal of which it is made:

Rue d'Assas: nobody. "That gentleman left last week . . ." I think
things over on a café terrace. Six o'clock: only one more address. I saw,
a young man in front of me being accosted: "Your papers?" There is a
sort of unseen manhunt going on among the waves of passers-by. I practice trying to spot policemen. The newspapers clamor of war. Noyon,
Soissons, Reims, bombardment. Posters clamor of war. Australians rub
elbows with Serbs. That little brunette at the next table, powdering her
nose, after having judged me at a glance ("Nothing doing"), knows at
the age of twenty how twenty races make love. I can hear her telling
her girl friend that last night, during the alert, she was with a slow, tor-
turous Japanese who didn't care a thing about the alert. "It wouldn't
have been funny to get killed at a moment like that . . . I was thinking
about it, you know. Seems they have gasses that freeze you up right
on the spot . . . What would people have said, the next morning, when
they found us . . ." The idea of that ridiculous death, braved by lewd-
ness and "work," sets off pearly laughter.

Let's go try our last chance at the rue Guénégaud. This Paris
crowded with men is for me still a wasteland. How to recognize ourselves in these multitudes? The comrades have burrowed themselves
into their narrow lives or only come out disguised like everyone else.
If we exist in this city, it is as termites, invisible, gnawing at the high
dike which the waves can't overwhelm. A seventy-six-year-old Jacobin
whose Tatar's head has already acquired the tones and shadows of a
death's-head is muttering into the white bushes of his mustache that
we should declare total war, move the f—ing government to Charenton,
send Caillaux to the firing squad: bring on dictatorship, the mailed fist,

a few more tons of blood to be drawn from this foundering France, *"et nous les aurons!"* (and we'll have them!). Then he is moved to pity over some poor slaughtered buggar in the front lines. His youthful rebellions have soured, and he has turned reactionary. He is full of the obstinate lust for life—he who already has one foot in the grave in this time of mass slaughter—the lust for victory—he, the old man in the rear who knows everything of life for having used it up—while the virile men at the front—their veins empty, who aspire only to keep breathing but know what victories are worth, with what they are paid, and the filthy profiteer's face they wear—would like to send the whole thing packing off to the devil. Bread rationing, anemic children, two hundred thousand women turning out shells in the factories; a million proletarians, pliant human machines imprisoned by steel cogs, working the metals, the gasses, the leathers, the provisions, for the war, the war. Gaunt, impoverished Berbers collect the garbage at dawn. Tubercular Annamites guard the prisons. By means of a marvelous alchemy, one hundred thousand businessmen transform pain, courage, faith, blood, shit, and death into streams of gold, National Defense Bonds, solid issues, de luxe autos, and de luxe whores . . . the rue Guénégaud wears the same face it wore ten years ago, twenty years ago. It's a proper little old lady in a lace bonnet.

. . . If he is not there, what will become of me tonight in this enemy city? A sixth-floor door. I knock sharply in the silence, like someone throwing dice: odd or even—the sudden clarity of chance. No sound—but the door opens wide, all at once, framing the unknown comrade: close-cropped hair, big triangular nose, the double shaggy brush of mustaches—a dour type.

"Monsieur Broux?"

"That's me."

He is wearing a soldier's tunic and an old pair of black corduroy pants. Behind him, in a glassed-in bookcase, yellow and green books are lined up (Alcan collection, science, philosophy). We stare at each other for a moment in the half-light; it is the instant when, somewhere in the depths of a being, that ineffable warmth, confidence, is born—or, that tiny cold blue flame: mistrust. "I'm so-and-so. Here's a note from Marie. And regards from Lejeune as well. I have been mobilized but . . . there are several important *buts*. My papers are only halfway in order, if not less . . ."

"Of course. I suspected as much," says Broux.

And, in spite of the darkness, I can see his dark-brown glance, friendly perhaps, yes, timid: the glance of a man who is a little afraid of men.

"It's all right. You're in luck, my friend, for the place isn't very big. I don't know what we would have done if there were three of us. But my girl friend walked out on me two weeks ago. You'll be all right here. I have an excellent reputation; you can sleep with both eyes shut. Wait a moment while I turn on the light."

We move into the white brilliance of an acetylene lamp hanging above a table covered with white oilcloth. The books speak quietly under their glass. *Les Feuilles d'herbe*, *Le Chemin de velours*, *L'Éthique*: thus contemplation rises up, from a blade of grass to the empyrean. The hum of Paris comes in through the window opening onto a horizon of roofs. Here we are, alone, two comrades among these four million men. Black coffee steams in bowls. We break bread like a couple of good companions, chance-met, sure one of the other, on the side of a road. Life is that road, and the war moves along it pushing gray legions toward the shadows.

Broux, a convalescent, escapes twice a week from the Vincennes camp. He talks about men despairingly: "What a collection of brutes!" and of his soldier's life with a resigned disgust: "The art of living consists in thinking. There are a few good moments: that is when, book in hand, you can lie down in the grass for an hour . . ."

The comrades? The names and faces appear in our memories as on a screen. In prison. That other one in prison too. Vanished, perhaps a deserter. Mobilized. At the Front. Many are at the Front. Several are dead, heroes in spite of themselves, without believing in anything, full of helpless desolation. A few are making it. Some ex-counterfeiters have the Croix de Guerre. "We" no longer exist. Wages are high in the factories; the women are having fun with all the soldiers in the world. Nothing doing. Nothing.

"No kidding, you really thought you could take the city? Honestly? You're not trying to pull my leg a little?"

Here, a few anarchists, a few syndicalists, some humanitarians . . . In Germany a Liebknecht; one Liebknecht out of millions of men, bespectacled, pushing his Sanitation Department wheelbarrow. An Adler in the prisons of Austria, alone in the clink, like Don Quixote, for having tilted at windmills . . .

"And the Russians, what do you make of them? That torrent? Kronstadt in mutiny?"

Broux shakes his head. They will be crushed. How should they not be crushed?

We are smoking, leaning out the window. The night comes in like a cover of blue gas. Suffocating sounds, pointed resistance of lights. Lamps light up under the mansard roofs. Behind some geraniums, a hanging lamp illuminates a family's supper. Kids calmly eat their soup, unaware that the world is in peril. In the sky a star moves out of the constellation of Andromeda and descends slowly toward the horizon, steel cockpit bearing two watchers like ourselves, armed with a machine gun. They see the Seine rolling by, a blue eel with shining scales laid out between rectilinear stoneworks.

Let us wait; let us wait for the future, even if we are not here to witness it. I have come from a country where the flame is smoldering under the ashes and, at moments, flaring up. I am going toward a country in flames: just yesterday it was the land of the greatest passivity. All is not lost, since we are here, you and I, with our certitudes, even when close to despair. Are you really so, sure that those two men, up there, in their star of death, are not nourishing the same hopes as we? Do you know how many men, tonight, in the trenches, confusedly desire the same thing we desire? If, all at once, they could rise up, what a clamor!

NINETEEN

Paris

A LARGE EMPTY RECTANGLE ON THE TAPESTRY OF THIS LEGATION WAITING room betrays the absence of a portrait of the Emperor. I consider for a moment that canvas turned against the wall somewhere in an attic storage room among broken-down umbrellas and faded screens. Two colonels are chatting quietly under the bare tapestry. The voyage of this canvas, by way of the service stairs, may prove rather troublesome to their destiny. Several young officers in high boots greet each other with precise bows and clicking of heels: magnificent suppleness, these vigorous bodies. St. George Crosses, cigarettes held in slender fingers, disdainful glances falling sharply in the direction of our corner. What are we doing there, in fact: me, a printer dressed up in his Sunday best and my neighbor, who introduced himself unceremoniously: "Fleischmann. And you?" More than shabby, Fleischmann: moth-eaten, and, almost, broken down. But, not quite—thanks to the old steel spring he carries somewhere in him in place of a feeling heart. The jacket, four years ago gray and well-tailored, no longer has any shape or form. Both pockets bulge: one round with a half-head of Holland cheese, easily recognizable, the other square with a book containing several bookmarks, themselves marked up in turn in a scrawling hand. His detachable celluloid collar displays a combination of rancid yellows and dubious whites bordering on yellow. A three-day-old shave, a pair of comical pince-nez shored up in the middle with a piece of that black cord (known as gendarme's thread), perched slightly askew above a Galician nose; large eyes, underlined with wrinkles, veiled by the parchment-like lids of an old night owl concealing an extraordinarily preoccupied, mobile and tenacious gaze that sticks to you, strips you bare, insistent, and then suddenly turns away. A penniless Jew, well past forty: twenty years of struggles, of poverty, of lectures in the co-operatives of the rue Mouffetard and the clubs of Whitechapel, of illegal correspondence with the homeland. I am guessing at this past, for our conversation is practical. I am "going home" too. I want to go home in order "to fight," an official formula which fools no one. We will be fighting in any case, but not in the manner in which these old colonels understand the word. So we are in agreement: Let's have them receive us together.

Four paces across the carpet and the décor changes. Décor, for here everything is as in a stage play, from the sober politeness of the officer offering us his leather armchairs with a gesture to our circumspect manner. The officer listens to us amicably, his gaze gliding over my neck-tie and Fleischmann's in turn, which probably remind him of the realistic details in naturalist novels. A handsome chronometer marks the times of his appointments on his wrist. The harmony of style between his silver epaulets and his American-style mustache, trimmed every morning, is obvious. St. George Cross. Harmonious timbre of a charming conversationalist's voice: "Gentlemen, or rather *comrades* . . ." (The mocking tone echoes inside me against El Chorro's rough voice: *compañeros* . . .) Here it is: our case is a difficult one. England, exercising control of the seas, is not overly willing to authorize the return of repatriated people. Fleischmann and I, in these leather armchairs, confront the great power on which the sun never sets. "We have no intention, I say, of forcing Admiral Beatty's lines . . ." The best advice this comrade can give us is to have ourselves inducted into the corps fighting in Champagne: it shouldn't be too difficult. With what prepossessing airs you open the door of the trap for us, Comrade Do-nothing, Comrades-with-handsome-silver-epaulets! Let's stay serious, however. "I'll think about it . . ."

Fleischmann rises, adjusts his pince-nez, pushes back the armchair—so comfortable that it seems to incline the unwary sitter to compromise—and stuffing the half-head of Holland cheese back into his right pocket with an angry fist, goes one notch past the point of absurdity.

In the middle of his tirade, the result of which is that he is going to telegraph to the Executive Committee of the Soviets, this grand phrase stands out:

"But *we* are the revolution, do you understand!"

Fleischmann, me, many others—and millions of unknown mugs. "The Provisional Government *owes*," owes us. We face the officer with the protracted stare of poor relations who have suddenly turned out to be creditors. He shakes his head. Yes. Yes. Of course. He understands very well. He is all acquiescence in principle, but there are practical difficulties. Very great ones. Besides—and "I cannot say whether this is a cordial digression, a diversion, or a veiled recall to order—*he* too (including the epaulets?) belongs totally to the revolution. He bears the name of a barrister who, in 1907, was nearly exiled. Fleischmann's anger dies down, neatly parried. There is no longer any adversary and all of this, from beginning to end, is like a joke.—"Think about it, comrades. Good-by."—"Good-by."

"Wait a minute," murmurs Fleischmann in the corridor, "I know an orderly here . . ." He turns out to be a young *muzhik* from Riazan, wide cheekbones and horizontal eyes. Soft blond fuzz covers his upper lip. His strong peasant's hands hold a silver tray on which, next to the *Echo de Paris*, a glass of tea trembles.

. . . Telegram from Petrograd: REPRESS BY FORCE AFTER ULTIMATUM.

This telegram was received yesterday. If they don't surrender today, the mutineers in the camp at La Courtine will be bombarded tomorrow in the name of the faraway revolution they acclaim.

"Do you think they will give the order to fire?" asks the big blond boy.

And the glass of tea trembles a little more.

Fleischmann points his bristly chin at the door which has just closed behind us.

"Those phony Comrades?"

Obvious conclusion as crushing as the shrapnel which will send fountains of blood spurting forth tomorrow, making rows of corpses of blond soldiers just like this one in the barracks rooms the day after . . .

From a distance of two thousand miles as the crow flies we can sense the sleek, fat vermin of smiling traitors crawling over the revolution. Behind this door, the "Comrade" is adding notes to our dossiers: *suspicious (confidential)*.

Sam confirms the news. He has just come from Champagne; his division is in the second line. They call him Sam because he landed one day from the other side of the Atlantic, tall, thin, hollow-cheeked, with a silky beard and a crooked smile revealing a set of cannibal teeth. Uncle Sam, born of real Cossacks in a village of Little Russia, tempered by the penitentiary at Orel (Great Russia), escaped from Sakhalin (at the far end of the greatest Russia, on the border of the lands of the Rising Sun), transformed by a few years at a good job in the factories of Pittsburgh

(Pa., U.S.A.). The Russian soldier's forest-green tunic hangs loosely over his bony shoulders. His cold look and his large, slightly twisted mouth suggest a mocking attitude. "Let's not be in such a hurry," he says. "We'll arrive just in time to occupy the cells of Kresty or to be shot by the Republic with bullets inherited from the Empire."

We stride along the Paris sidewalk on a sunny afternoon. BOUSSARD ET PIGNOTEL FILS: *Flags, Banners, and Pennants of Every Kind.* Established in 1876, gold medal at expositions . . . Here's what we need, Sam. These "purveyors to H.M. the King of Belgium" can purvey to us in our turn. Turn about is fair play! Ecclesiastical ornaments and multicolored silks fringed with gold fill the window with the sacred emblems of every creed in the universe. The Virgin's banner, the oriflamme of the Sacred Heart of Jesus, the Stars and Stripes, the black, yellow, and red of the lack-land King of Furnes, the red crescent of Tunisia and even the celestial sphere of Brazil on which a white ribbon encompasses the star-studded heavens the better to proclaim that the coffee planters' motto is the very law of the universe: *Ordem e progresso.* Boussard, bald, with round owl eyes red-rimmed from chronic conjunctivitis, greets his customers at the threshold of a shop bathed in the discreet half-light of a sacristy. Some gilded halberds make one look forward to the entrance of a solemn Swiss Guard. Then enters Pignotel the Younger, the most jaded of the patriots of the class of 1919: horn-rimmed glasses and the look of a collegian dulled by nights spent in brothels. Boussard and Pignotel purvey to every fatherland. Men of every race bleed under silks embroidered in their workshops by women on piecework, the prettiest of whom spread their docile slaves' knees to Pignotel the Younger. Sam has come here on behalf of soldiers far from home to look for the emblem of a new fatherland.

"We should like a flag, gentlemen, and as rapidly as possible . . ."

"Russian, no doubt?"

Seen from the side, Sam's polite smile adds a mocking grimace to his Notre-Dame gargoyle's profile.

"Precisely, monsieur."

The white, blue, and red silks are ready. Here are the styles. All prices, like wholesale oils. The firm also prepares special orders. Sam's slender hand pushes the samples disdainfully aside.

"I beg your pardon, monsieur. There is a misunderstanding. We would like, for the Russian 10th Division, a red flag bearing these words in two languages: *Russian Republic* . . . Fringes will not be necessary."

For an instant the nocturnal Boussard and Pignotel the Younger are round-eyed, like fish being pulled out of a fish tank.

We do not know, gentlemen, if we will be able to furnish the article for you. You would be very kind, gentlemen, if you would come by again tomorrow or this evening, this evening between six and seven . . . Gentlemen . . .

The Rear smiles at the war—this lie covering everything, emptier than a Detaille painting—with the smiles of all its Home Front soldiers, of all its profiteers, of all its general staffs, of all its journalists, of all its little chippies so well appreciated by clean warriors from overseas, of all its tipsy men on furlough who don't understand anything (". . . and anyway, it's better not to understand"). Astonishing frivolity of life a hundred miles behind the firing, lines in this age of mass slaughters stage-managed like scenic effects on the stage of the Théâtre du Châtelet: ("Around Verdun, or Eighty Thousand Dead?") Loungers, joy girls, autos, cafés, newspapers. In the distance the towers of the Trocadéro rise up over the Seine against a pink sky imperceptibly tinged with hazy blue, horizon-blue. Paris abandons herself to life under a Watteau sky. Our people are being fired on at La Courtine. A camp, somewhere in Creuse, surrounded by cannon in the middle of peaceful farmland. A shred of the revolutionary throng snatched from our revolution: peasants from Perm, workers from Tula, fishermen from arctic shores . . .

"There were too many men," said a drunkard whose gestures seemed to be sending lyric message to the stars in a dark street yesterday. "There was no room left on the earth. Can you feel how well off we are in the Rear? We're really living now that the war has made some room for us . . ."

Scientists could prove it better, with the help of graphs. "They're firing on our people at La Courtine, do you hear, Sam?"

"No," says Sam seriously, "I don't hear anything, unless it's the noise of the bus and the voices of two Canadians talking about rugby."

A soldier's voice:

"What's the big fuss about? They're lucky if you ask me. They still won't be as bad off as we are where come from, over near Berry-au-Bac."

One gentleman's opinion:

"Discipline is the law of armies. Besides, monsieur [this is not spoken aloud, for decorum's sake, but addressed to me in an aside which I can hear quite clearly], I find your indignation most displeasing. What are you doing here anyway? The Rear must be purged."

It is being purged. Denunciations, suspicions, that peculiar second sight that spots the spy, that marvelous, sharp hearing which can hear—through hotel room walls—defeatist talk mingled with the sighs and groans—send police sleuths scurrying out on countless leads. Men in dinner clothes, soon to be tied to posts at Vincennes, are holding forth in salons. A rare gourmet with a triple chin and greasy neck, who collects erotic etchings in the evening, demands the establishment of a Patriotic Inquisition every morning in his newspaper. Someone enters furtively into a prison cell where a strange sick man with enormous Creole eyes dreams distractedly, speaks softly to him, raises his curly head, passes a noose around his neck with lulling gestures, and tightens . . . tightens. "More arrests are imminent." The beauty of Paris smiles on implacably like summer.

TWENTY

Meditation During an Air Raid

WHEN THE SIRENS, ANNOUNCING THE APPROACH OF ENEMY SQUADRONS, BEGIN to shriek into the night, and footsteps hurry down the stairway under the furtive glow of candles, we sit down at the window. Broux carefully hides the bowl of his pipe under his hand, and I'm not entirely certain that it's in jest. "You ought to go down," he told me the first time. "Personally I'd just as soon not bother. All those half-dressed people in the cellar are not exactly pretty. You'll see the little old lady from the fourth floor in her bathrobe and curlers hugging a horrible poodle with an almost human expression in her witch's arms; you'll see my pretty neighbor, with hardly any clothes on, fresh from her bed but wearing lipstick, her nose powdered. Perhaps you will dream of how in forty years her desirable arms will be as fleshless as those of the witch with the poodle. What finer theme for meditation, down at sewer level, during an air raid?" He talks this way sometimes, in an even voice, and the words of his sentences fall into place with a muffled rhythm. I can see that he must be capable of writing beautiful letters in which round phrases fall nicely into place and where the ideas rise up with a serenity mingled with irony and finesse. "I only went down there once, and then only to climb back up four steps at a time at the end of the alert. You see I feel so good here, among my books, that even for being killed in the place would not be a bad one . . ."

There are only two portraits, side by side, between the bookcase and the bed—two fraternal old men: the great Walt, white and hoary, of *Sands at Seventy*; Elisée Reclus, high brow crowned with white ash, stern look like a fine ray of light penetrating from across vast spaces. Broux says:

"If by chance a bomb were to destroy all this"—with a wave of his hand he designates the books squeezed into their bookcase, the two portraits, a pile of notebooks bound in black oilcloth over in one corner—"frankly, I'd just as soon not outlive it. This is all I have in the world. It is my refuge. I am attached to it. Whereas life . . ."

We philosophize. The sirens have stopped wailing. The night—like other nights. Gray clouds move slowly across a background of stars. Explosions crackle on endlessly. We see nothing out of the ordinary. Yet somewhere, up there above these clouds, among the phosphorescent shadows crossed by fresh gusts from distant continents, men dressed in leather are trying to fix this city in their bombsights. And explosive blossoms, forming concentric circles in the middle of the sky, search for them—hunters made prey—in turn. This game lasts about thirty minutes.

Broux is talking about his former shopmates (he is a cabinet-maker); about the duties, totally ridiculous duties, which he performs at Vincennes; about the manifesto, *To Mothers*, published by a few comrades who have just been arrested, a rather mediocre piece of work. "As if the mothers could do something about it!" And, suddenly uncovering the glowing bowl of his pipe, he concludes:

"It is impossible to escape."

A prison, this city, this country, the war, Europe.

"And America, Japan, New Zealand, Mozambique, Borneo! A prison—the universe. Even in the brush, in the untamed jungle, they count out money, bend men's backs under the rod, obey orders, go about their dirty jobs. Everywhere it is necessary to undergo fourteen hours of pain, of servitude, or of degradation each day, depending on the circumstances, in order to reach the fifteenth, which may be spent with the great Walt or old Elisée. And yet I'm one of the lucky ones," says Broux, "for the intensity of the work is less crushing in the workshops than in the factories. I am not totally brutalized in the evening. Those who work in factories, on the line, come out exhausted in the evening, good for the movies, old boy . . . And all washed up at the age of forty: good for the little café . . ."

He who tries to save his life will lose it. A handful, out of thousands, get rich, discover the other side of the world through the windows of sleeping cars. The money costs them dearly, and there is always the risk of never making it. To step over the bodies of a hundred others in order to become one of those thickheaded scum, the *nouveau-riche?* To grab up sous, then francs, then gold louis out of the misery of other men and then to say that the world is well made, when everyone who fills his lungs with the fresh air of the beach is followed by an invisible train of

men and women bent under their tasks, imprisoned by the machines
as in a vise, imprisoned by hunger, by love, by the wish to live, for the
wheels are grinding perfectly when all a man's desires fall back on him
with the weight of chains?

Civilization reaches its high point in this senseless combat above
the Louvre, which bombs that are in no sense "strays" may very well
be destroying at this very moment. The bombing plane closes the cycle
that began with the victory at Samothrace. Masterpieces of ingenuity,
summing up the work of all races in all times—millions of men suffering, striving, daring—seek each other out, with the greatest human
lucidity, in order to destroy each other; yet it's only an artillery duel.
And the essential business of this city consists in turning out shells.

"It's a question to ask ourselves if we're not mad. But who are the
madmen, in God's name? Those who wonder about it, or the others? If
we ever began to speak out loud, what would they do with us, tell me?"

Broux has stopped believing in rebellion since he saw rebels gouging
their money out of the blood of old landladies and then being pushed
off to the guillotine like the monsters who strangle little girls.[9] "There
are stray forces, like your friend from Haiti, the landowner at Grande
Saline. They are wasted forces. It's mathematical: either they adjust or
they will be cut down. Your Negro was born to leave his skull, more
or less full of holes, among a whole pile of other skulls, under a monument to be erected by the cannon makers later on . . ."

The working class does every kind of job, except its own, without,
when all is said and done, being aware of its own existence. How can you
expect it to emerge from this nullity when every morning they measure
out the fodder for its belly and the fodder for its mind: so much bread
and meat on the ration card, so much poison for the mind. Tell me, do
you remember the myth of the general strike? A real myth, right? And
of the "insurrection against the war?" Those who used to demand it
are now demanding that they bomb Munich to wreak vengeance on
the Pinacothek for the risks run by the Louvre, about which they don't
give a damn anyway. The Kaffir warrior who lay sleeping within their
souls has awakened: "An eye for an eye . . ." We will all end up blind,
for they will put out our eyes too.

---

9   Allusion to the "Bonnot Gang" or "Tragic Bandits" of French anarchy whose fate
    deeply affected the young Victor Serge (see translator's biographical note Victor
    Serge, page 220).

Somewhere I read a report about the *Quinze-Vingts* Hospital. There are several badly wounded men living there who have, no more arms or legs, and who are blind.

Haven't you ever been grazed by a bus in the street and secretly wished for an accident? When you go home after having done some dirty job for a hundred sous. When you have cheated a comrade for fifty francs, because it was the last thing you could think of before throwing yourself into the Seine or cutting the throat of an old gentlemen going home late at night? Haven't you ever looked at things and told yourself coldly that you would rather not be there any more? I can tell you how refreshing it is. If you are passing through the war in order to get to the revolution, then do your filthy soldier's job as well as you can and don't weigh yourself down with scruples; that's my advice. After Factory Man, halfway between Shantytown Man and Barroom Man, Trench Man is still a fine specimen of humanity. Just tell yourself that life—after what they've made of it—is not such a great good that it is a crime to take it or an evil to lose it.

The bombardment dies in the distance and disappears. We do not know that a house has just been split in two and that a nestful of crushed children is struggling under the wreckage. The silence has nearly the perfection of infinitude. We do not know that a Gotha is flaming in the fields ten miles from here; that two human forms, instantaneously emptied of human content, are being thrown up, cradled, rolled, and cast down there by the sumptuous flames. Eyes which were full of this night, of these stars, of that anxiety of battle when, an hour ago, you pointed out to me with your hand the two fraternal portraits hanging behind us, have seen the world come to an end in a blaze of fire like a collision of stars. It is nothing; exactly nothing. Newspapers: "Last night's Gotha raid was not marked by any notable incidents. The damage was insignificant."

"In short," says Broux, "impossible to live. I withdraw into my corner and I read. I try to live a little anyway, but unnoticed, in order to be forgiven for that. What is to be done? the impossible?"

The revolution? Who will make it? Cannon, machines, poison gas, money, the masses. Masses of men like you, yanked bodily out of their submissiveness in the end, without at first understanding anything about it—by cannon, machines, poison gas, money. Don't you see, Broux, your two great old men, Walt and Elisée, are not good masters. I could almost hate them, I who love them. Their fault is in being admirable. They arouse us to the impossible; they almost make it possible. It is not for us to be admirable! We must be precise, clear-sighted, strong, unyielding, armed: like machines, you see. To set up a vast enterprise for demolition and to throw ourselves into it with our whole being because we know that we cannot live as long as the world has not been made over. We need technicians, not great men or admirable men. Technicians specialized in the liberation of the masses, licensed demolition experts who will have scorn for the idea of personal escapism because their work will be their life. To learn to take the mechanism of history apart; to know how to slide in that extra little nut or bolt somewhere—as among the parts of a motor—which will blow the whole thing up. There it is. And it will cost whatever it costs.

TWENTY-ONE

Fugitives Cast Two Shadows

"WHAT? YOU, HERE?" EXCLAIMED PHILBERT, STANDING ON THE EDGE OF THE
sidewalk of the rue de Buci, a newspaper in his hand. "Will you have
some coffee? One should always appreciate coffee in troubled times.
Humanity is wailing and suffering: let us sip the delectable mocha
slowly; mine will be the egoist's cup, yours whatever you wish; but it
will leave the same bittersweet taste in our mouths."

He took me by the arm and we went into a bar. I am rather fond of
Philbert, who is nicknamed, depending on one's mood, Fil-en-quatre,
Fil-à-l'anglaise, Fil-à-la-patte, for he makes no bones about being a bastard and is agreeably intelligent. He is looking rather well, in spite of
having the pasty look of a night owl who must have carried some rather
nasty diseases; in fact, he gives an almost elegant appearance, in spite
of a certain pimpish air about him. His handshake, cordial, moist, and
flabby is the handshake of a good pal who is "a bit of an s.o.b." His
brown eyes—the eyes of a native of the Belleville quarter—make it
easy for him to pass for Spanish. In private, he tells me that he is a draft
dodger and performs certain vague and lucrative duties in the market
aux Halles at night. The charm of his conversation come from a certain topsy-turvy cynical idealism.

"So you ran out on them, eh, your half-baked revolutionaries? You
were perfectly right, my friend, I would have done the same. It's much
better, I assure you, to work the rackets in Paris, even in these terrible
times, than to set up barricades under the Mediterranean sun. Is Lejeune
still holding up? Would you like a job in our combine: inspecting ice-
boxes? You'd be able to have that ideal relationship that Don Juan never
had: the eternal female and refrigerated beef from La Plata. General
coefficient: the war.

"No! Really? You're leaving for Russia? Been mobilized? You must
have been broke for the last six weeks; or maybe it's your wife who's

turned you into a neurotic . . . For after all, you know very well that one should always be in favor of revolutions—when they happen—try to profit from them, and avoid them like tornadoes. Besides, what could be more comfortable than a decaying world?"

There is, however, something in his mocking way of undressing ideas, like a tiny diamond in a lump of cow dung . . . His normally deceitful look, belying his biting words, hesitates at times, timid, ready to steal away, ready to yield to a private gloom. He probably doesn't feel very well, alone by himself.

"Where are you staying? With Broux? A good man. But a jerk. All those important problems must give him a headache; the more he thinks, the stupider he gets and the prouder he is of himself. A kind of onanist, like all thinkers."

As we are about to separate, Phil adds:

"It's a quiet spot, but watch out anyway. Fugitives cast two shadows: their own and the stool pigeon's."

Suzy, for whom he had been waiting, comes toward us through the street where the sunlight dances. A double ray glimmers under the shade of the brim of her felt bonnet. Our three shadows converge into one, star-shaped shadow.

Suzy, with her pretty gray-gloved hand around Philbert's arm, looks at me and admires him. Her eyes seem to say to me: "Isn't he wonderful, and so intelligent, and so brave, my lover, if you only knew! And there are mysteries in his life . . ." Mysteries like the ones in well-made novels. A fragile, almost sickly bliss radiates from this couple.

"Come over to our house for dinner, tonight," Philbert proposes. "You'll see what kind of housekeeper my baby is. You should spend the night with us. You know, a fugitive ought to sleep out from time to time, just on principle. You never know when will be the right time."

Tempted, I refuse. I have an appointment. Phil inquires: business or pleasure?—and as I hesitate to answer, he makes a hasty guess: "Oh, well then that's sacred. Good luck."

Joy comes at will. I began my day well with this meeting. Was it, later, on, Sam's good mood, in spite of the disastrous news from the camp of La Courtine? Was it the meeting with three comrades in a Charonne café where truck drivers drink at the counter? Marthe had brought some rather poorly written handbills from a Billancourt factory. She told us about her trick of posting them in the washrooms or of slipping them into girl friends' pockets in the locker room. "Let 'em look! Let 'em look!" she said. "Unseen and unknown. There are four of us out of four hundred, but they think we're everywhere." Marthe, her nose aquiline, her mouth large, teeth healthy, round breasts straining the satinette of her bodice, hands masculine but cool as if they had just come out of fresh water; Marthe and her way of walking like a blond mare with cropped hair . . . Next to her, Pellot, of the ditchdiggers, still wanted by the police, low-slung, flourishing mustache, jovial, digging into words and things with the same rhythmic movement of his whole being with which he digs up great shovel loads of earth at the construction yards. "What we should hope for," he was saying, "is a big push from the German side, with a break-through and everything. It'd all go sky high, like in Russia. It'd be splendid!" Was it, finally, these four lines of scrawlish writing from El Chorro: "The party was not a success, but we'll try it again. Gusano sends his best." Grim communiqué on three days of street fighting (seventy dead?).

"Would you like to come for a walk, Broux?"

"No. My legs have already done ten miles today. I'd rather read."

He sat down at the window; his low, stubborn forehead, his large straight nose, and his bushy mustache were silhouetted against the backdrop of a saffron-colored sky. How could I know that we would never see each other again?

"Really feels good, eh?"

The threads of ideas we have pursued together in this room come together in my mind, blowing gently in the breeze of this brisk parting like spider webs shimmering in the wind. With his worn-out lungs, his obstinate self-effacement, his bookish timidity, Broux is nonetheless a strong man; by means of his awareness of how impossible it is to live, he raises himself precisely to a higher possibility of living, to an endurance which is more sure of itself because it believes it has nothing more to lose. From his weakness he was able to create a strength; from his despair, an acquiescence; from his acquiescence, a hope . . . I rapidly descend that staircase which I usually find tiring. Broux's image fades away, absorbed into a saffron-colored sky in which I imagine cranes with great flapping wings, flying. The flight of a bird traced in delicate strokes across a translucent porcelain vase. Fujiyama in the background. Faustin, appears for an instant and crosses a landing with me. Where is he, Faustin, stray, unself-conscious force wandering mindlessly like a spear thrown through dense foliage? Well, what does it matter? I shall follow the street until the *quai*, then the *quai* up to the Pont des Arts.

Two gentlemen are conversing with the concierge in the narrow hallway. On the sidewalk a flash of gold, infinitely delicate, reflection of the nuances of the sky more imagined than seen.

"Pardon me, monsieur," I say.

And I comprehend instantaneously, pinched between the walls and two hulking shapes, that everything—this bright sidewalk only six feet away, the Pont des Arts, Broux's steady voice, the two white-maned portraits, our meetings—is completely finished. All of that was suspended on a shimmering thread: and now it has snapped. And everything comes falling down, down. An animal caught in a trap resists, bites against the steel, struggles for a long while before comprehending. But I understood immediately. The bulkier of the two men, heavy with wine, has a strange high-pitched voice which squeaks out from under his heavy, curved mustache stained around the corners of his mouth.

". . . You're not armed?"

My pockets are already being frisked with deft hands by his companion, a pock-marked man wearing yellow shoes. I have an enormous weight in the pit of my stomach. I close my eyes for a second. All you can ever say to yourself is: "Let's go," as if you were jumping through a trap door blindfolded with your feet tied together. Here I go. Was that all?

I know all about this drudgery of searches and interrogations in advance. These premises, these men, these questions are the same in every country of the world: and afterward you always have the same feeling of coming out completely dressed, but soaked to the skin with dirty water.

"Move on ahead," the pock-marked man in the yellow shoes says to me.

We are alone in a corridor painted chocolate up to eye level, cold as a cellar. Staggering drunkards, unnerved murderers, disconsolate pickpockets, querulous demonstrators with staved-in ribs have followed this route toward the dark bench on which I will sleep.

The pock-marked man slows his step; so do I. I clear my throat. He opens door number 3. A cell like any other. Why is he taking so long to lock me up? He vacillates for a moment. I can see the grease spots on his vest. His face is yellowed, faded. His round straw hat cuts across his forehead. Narrow eyes under wrinkled eyelids, the wide, thin, slightly protuberant mouth of an aging toad. He pulls a copy of *L'Intransigeant* and a packet of Marylands out of his pocket and hands them to me:

"Take these; they'll help you pass the time."

Then I notice his gray and wrinkled hand, which is probably cold. I'm about to yell: "Get the hell out of here, will you, and leave me in peace!" but my glance falls to his flabby feet in their yellow shoes and they seem—I don't know why—pitiful to me. I take the newspaper and the cigarettes without a word. The pock-marked man heaves a sigh.

"If you only knew how sick I am of all this!" he says clumsily.

The pause which follows lasts perhaps a second; but it is singularly heavy and futile.

"Do you know who turned you in?" resumes the pockmarked man. "It was Fil-en-quatre. A bastard."

And he backs away all at once, like a spring unwinding. The door clangs shut; the key turns twice in the lock.

TWENTY-TWO

Dungeon

THE EXAMINING MAGISTRATE, AFTER STUDYING LETTER OF TRANSIT #662-491, told me that he was signing my release. I already feel like a stranger in this cell. I am better able to notice the stench of rancid filth rising from the straw mattress. Somewhere in my skull I can hear the word "freedom" ringing protractedly. Like a stone falling into a deep well, a bottomless well, rebounding from one wall to the other.

Our expectations are rarely fulfilled, almost always interrupted. The door swings open like a blast of wind.

"Get your things together."

I follow the guard with the easy step of a free man. I already begin to look at things through a spectator's eyes. "Halt."

We are standing in front of a metal door from behind which a strange muttering can be heard. The guard, his nose pimply, his neck brick red, opens this door slowly. The door to the outside world, no doubt. I calculate the time it will take to get through the record office. Twenty to thirty minutes. Then the street. Do you know that there is something wondrous in each step you take in the street? . . .

The room is as spacious as the waiting room of a small station, but hardly resembles one with its enormous columns, its Romanesque arches, and this drab impoverished light of a large prison. It could be a Piranesi prison. Prison of all ages, court of miracles, blind alley. Places with no exit are all alike and all unlike any other places. Emaciated figures wander through a semi-transparent fog. An old Jew—long overcoat, filthy bowler, flossy beard, obliterated from front, side, and three-quarters profile by poverty's sores like a postage stamp whose effigy is completely blotted out by greasy ink—is pacing mechanically up and down. Poor wretches out of Goya are squatting toward the rear, in a dark corner; some suspicious-looking beggars seem to be dragging themselves toward me and I suddenly find myself surrounded by them.

They have sly, cunning faces, shapeless jackets, dirty necks, grimy hands. "Where do you come from? Who are you? Vagrant or deportee . . . ?" One of them could be a well-thrashed Sancho Panza; he is biting his nails and staring at me like a beast chewing its cud. His fresh-colored cheeks are covered with a reddish fuzz. Suddenly the swarm of vermin divides and a handsome pale man with a sailor's beard and eyes like burning coals, a kind of pirate, presents himself with outstretched hand. I am unable to catch his guttural name, but the rest is clear:

". . . citizen of the United States. Deserter from the *Oklahoma*, big American ship. Deportee. And you?"

"Me," I say mockingly, "citizen of the world. Free."

The pirate bursts into wild laughter. His laughter seemed to put bats to flight under the eaves.

"O-o-o-boy! We're all free here. Mister Pollack (that's the old Jew who is now passing in front of us, stroking his beard with a diaphanous hand) for the past forty-seven days; Mister Nounés of the Argentine Republic (that's Sancho Panza), a good fellow, the old rascal, for the last fourteen. The others average from five to thirty."

Then Stein, the Alsatian, comes up. A saber wound received in the Taza Pass gave him a harelip which is now half-hidden under a thick stubbly beard. He says:

"Five years in the Foreign Legion. Wounded three times. I've been 'free' like this for six months now. Seventeen days in the big room. Eaten alive by cooties; take a look."

With both violent, hands he tears open the collar of his dirty black shirt and reveals a hairy chest covered with sickly red stripes from the itch.

"Make yourself comfortable," resumes the sailor from the *Oklahoma* quietly. "Come on. There's a very nice spot in my corner."

In the evening they throw the straw mattresses down from a height of several yards, in a cloud of dust, to groups of men thrashing about and swearing. We stretch ourselves out on ours and talk. Jerry Jerry, citizen of the United States, tells me, slowly, with energetic gestures, in satisfactory French mingled with guttural English, the story of his travels through Colorado and Utah before he became a sailor—after a rather unexpected and very unpleasant adventure about which he says nothing but whose memory silences him for a moment.

"Listen to this. Once—*une fois*—at Alamosa near the Rio Grande . . .

He tells of Indian reservations, of rivers between the high cliffs of the Grand Canyon, of the Rocky Mountains, of double-dealing innkeepers,

of the easy money you can make in land speculation, of the joyful bank-
ruptcy of one of his friends; of the insurance business . . . In the opposite
corner, some men are shooting craps. The dice are made of dried-out
bread crumbs. An ill-tempered little Spaniard has just lost his jacket. He
tears it off and throws it angrily into the winner's face. Stein, bare-chested
under his jacket, is patiently pulling the ticks out of his shirt: although
he is six paces away, I can hear the insects cracking under his thumbnail.
The electricity is so poor, the room seems filled with yellowish smoke.

The old Jew is stretched straight out asleep, with his bowler over
his eyes and his hands folded across his chest: the whiteness of those
old hands seems vaguely luminous.

A young rogue resembling Punch gambols up, on tiptoe, toward the
sleeping old man, and gets ready to send his hat flying with a tap. Jerry's
eyes follow the direction of my glance; he turns around as if gathering himself for a spring, his face suddenly tense and hardened. But he
only goes:

"Tsss . . ."

And this slight metallic grating of the teeth has the effect of a knife
held at the end of a muscular arm: it stops the rogue, nonplussed, dead
in his tracks; Punch, thrown into confusion, leaps grotesquely to the
side and collapses like a rag doll at the foot of a wooden partition.

"Poor Mister Pollack," murmurs Jerry, lying on his back, his arms
folded behind his neck. "What kind of a dog's life must he have led? He
detests me, do you know? He detests me: why? I don't know."

We remain awake for a long while, in silence. And I can feel my
neighbor's dark eye boring into me with brutal insistence. We are perhaps the only ones left awake, for the night must be, well advanced. All
time is the same in this yellowish mist, filled with protracted, exhausted
snoring.

Finally Jerry leans over to me and says, very low and right into my
face:

"Who are you?" And he adds: "No point in lying with me. Nothing
to fear."

How do I explain "a revolutionary" to him? While I grope with my
words, his face lights up.

"I get it. Like the IWW [Industrial Workers of the World]. They're
a good bunch, all right. We killed one of 'em in Alabama."

At this recollection a vague grimace, perhaps the beginnings of a crooked smile, twists his even mouth and accentuates the planes of his face.

"You'll never get anywhere," he says. "But you're right anyway. Good night."

Jerry and Stein reign over the big room. Jerry says he can knock out his man with one right to the jaw. Stein explains: "Me, I break in their teeth. I've never been able to do it any other way." They have never struck anyone here. Their law is an unwritten law, but it is just and strong.

Someone is talking in a dream, visited by joy. A stifled laugh rises, stumbles and falls into the mire of our silence.

TWENTY-THREE

Nothing Is Ever Lost

A SOFT RAIN HEIGHTENS THE NUANCES OF THE LANDSCAPES. THE RED-TILED roofs have a sharp freshness. I could almost believe that I've been dreaming the big room and those all-night talks with Jerry, if Nounés the Argentinean weren't snoring quietly on the seat at my left; and if the fat gendarme accompanying us weren't snoozing as well, with his thumbs hooked into his belt, across from me. The Argentinean is dressed in the gabardine of a cardsharp down on his luck. The gray-haired, runny-nosed gendarme looks a little like a great foundered ox. He snorts and sniffles every five minutes; his red fingers, which make you think of half-cooked shellfish, fidget slowly: he half-opens one eye, distractedly checks our presence, and resumes his siesta. Villages with slate roofs follow villages with red-tiled roofs. Some oxen make their way through the rain-soaked grass led by a boy in wooden shoes. A train full of wounded men goes by, beaten by the rain: anemic faces, returned to a sort of plaintive childhood or lighted, one might think, from within by a heatless flame, appear for an instant behind the speeding windows. The November sun, breaking through clouds driven from the ocean by cold winds, suddenly projects extraordinary patches of brightness over the meadows. Here is a road wending its serpentine way between cropped yew trees. The train's pace slackens. Stretch your hand out imperceptibly toward the compartment door, open it sharply, leap straight out, hit the ground somewhere at the base of the embankment, then make a run toward that cluster of golden trees over there under the rainbow. My leg muscles awaken, my hand gets ready, I am on the watch, coiled up beneath a feigned quiescence—dreaming of the gravel path through the meadows . . . Indeed, to walk on the moist earth, under a leaden sky pierced by cataracts of sunlight is well worth the chance of a bullet. But will he shoot, this fat garlic soup eater? Anyway, let him shoot! (I shrugged to myself.)

But he stirs. His chest puffs out, his jaws spread apart for a full thirty seconds in a bulldog yawn; the invisible film of drowsiness has fallen from his eyes.

"Let's go," he says. "We're there."

The moment of sunshine has ended. The rain beats against the windows. I stare at the man's red hands, close to the revolver holster, with an absurd hatred—and I am astonished to discover that I only hate those hands. I'm indifferent to the rest of the man.

We had something to eat in a sub-prefecture wineshop. The Argentinean is getting familiar with our gendarme whom he addresses as "Monsieur Edouard" and for whom he asks my permission to buy a cigar, at my expense.

"As for you, my boy," says Monsieur Edouard to him cordially, "you're no more of an Argentinean than I am . . ."

A little laugh of complicity still fills out our well-thrashed Sancho Panza's face:

Well, what do you expect, after living in Paris for twenty-seven years!"

"Twenty-seven out of twenty-seven, right? Less three in the clink at Loos or Fontevrault, I'd wager," Monsieur Edouard ripostes with verve. "And if you know anything about Buenos Aires, it can only be the brothels . . ."

So much perspicacity vexes my companion, who tries his best not to show it. But I'm beginning to know him. His pitiful wilted collar is spread open around a chubby neck creased by hundreds of tiny wrinkles. His soul is like his flesh: flabby, with a strange capacity for adhering to things, to beings. He is always lying, quietly deceitful, spitefully craven. In the big room, he used to perform occult missions for Stein, who made his living extorting hush money from obscure sources, and shined Jerry's shoes. He carries my bundles, under the pretext that he has nothing to carry himself, that it makes him feel good to carry something, and that I have no right to put on airs with him "just because he has no education." Embarrassed, he is chewing on the wide, flat nails of his chubby hand. And I think I can guess, from an indefinable timbre in his voice, that he has found a way of taking revenge.

"I haven't been to Buenos Aires in a long time, that's true," he concedes. "I used to live part of the time in Levallois, and part of the time at Châlons. Do you know Châlons, Monsieur Edouard? I was back there during the war, when the Front was passing that way . . ."

Monsieur Edouard has the look of a cunning vintner. The uniform goes well with his corpulence. His blotchy face easily loses all trace of joviality. He has the piercing sidewise glance and the disquieting voice, (barely concealing legalized brutality under a self-assured reserve), that are necessary when asking people for their papers. It is in that voice that he carelessly drops these words between two puffs of smoke:

"And what did you happen to be doing in Châlons during the fighting?"

The Argentinean puts on his most innocent air, the air of a complete idiot whose face you'd love to slap but who looks at you with the disarming eyes of a young heifer.

"I stopped to kiss my Aunt Eulalie. But I'll never forget what I saw there, Monsieur Edouard. There was a butcher about a hundred yards from my aunt's place, see? Well just imagine: some poilus—the savages, think of it!—had hung up two gendarmes in uniform, by the chin, in the butcher-shop window, with their hands tied behind their backs and their pants pulled down. Oh! It wasn't a pretty sight to see, you can believe me! There was a fat one . . ."

Is Monsieur Edouard going to burst? The blood rushes to his hardened face. His eyelids narrow over a pointed stare with which he fixes us, each in turn: me, impassible; the Argentinean, paternal. He crushes out his cigar with rage in the ashtray.

The grim, graveled street is lined with white, one-story houses. Led by Monsieur Edouard, we go to our lodging for the night. We won't arrive at the suspects' detention camp at Trécy until tomorrow. The gendarme hurries his step, in silence, with his uniform cap pulled down over his eyes and his heavy jaw protruding, which gives him the profile of a classical Pandarus. The sly Argentinean persists in exasperating him. It is to me that he addresses himself, telling out his entire rosary of dirty and stupid stories all of which take place in Châlons. His mouth is full of that name; he savors it, underlines it, plays on it like a bugle; and, if there's a story about a cuckold, it's always the butcher of Châlons. The gendarme feigns a haughty detachment, but he hears very well. His neck is red as a brick.

We are to sleep in a cellar, a sort of low kennel between a stable in which you can hear the horses snorting and the shed where they keep the fire pumps. A wide stall full of straw fills this nook. The dormer window gives out onto a courtyard: the shafts of a cart are visible there, rising over a dung heap. A barrel stinks of urine; a gardener's watering can is full of delectable water. We soon discover that a man is sleeping under the straw: a sorry railroad worker of whom only a pair of pink feet with widely spaced toes emerge. The Argentinean is indignant over this treatment. "The convicts at St.-Martin-de-Ré are kept better than this! Are we free, yes or no? When I think of my dignity . . ." Happily, he doesn't think of it often. Is he trying to put me on? This kennel is as good as another, and a kennel is just as good as a hole in the mud, a cell in a model prison, or the soft bed of a profiteer or a gendarme! The sun is going down; I hurry over to the dormer window to spread out some newspapers bought on the way; I haven't seen a paper since my arrest. What is this? ". . . it is generally believed that the German agents will be unable to hold power for more than a few weeks . . ." A RADIO-TELEGRAM FROM THE PEOPLE'S COMMISSARS . . . "latest details on the taking of the Winter Palace . . ." "The Soviets' peace offer . . ." A thick slime of words—"treason, infamy, barbarism, bloody anarchy, in the pay of Germany, the dregs and scum of the population," of course!—clings to these dispatches. One might imagine them clipped at random, by a child, out of some big history book—the history of future times? These waves of opprobrium poured over men and events, this bubbling lava is what enlightens me the most. I am better able to see the white pebbles shining on the bottom of the flood through these muddy waves. I am able to see that at last *we* had taken, in the world, cities: prisons—prisons?—general staff headquarters, and what else? God knows. What would we have taken, what would we have done, Dario, if we had taken that city toward which we were stretching out our hands from the other end of Europe? I question myself and I am astonished to find myself so ill-prepared for victory, unable to see beyond it, and yet feeling so clearly that it is we, we (myself as well, even though I am in this kennel) who have taken, conquered, thousands of miles from here, I don't know what . . .

The night is now total: it is raining. A lantern projects a feeble yellowish glow on the courtyard wall opposite. Thanks to the reflection which comes into our kennel, we are able to see each other dimly: black, with ghostly heads pierced by dark gaps. The railroad worker stirs ponderously in the straw, like an animal.

"Good news?" asks the Argentinean. "What's happening out in the world?"

"Let me sleep, Nounés."

I stretch out in the straw. I can hear Nounés stirring; and then I hear him laughing; in the darkness he hands me something: a flat bottle. How in the hell had he been able to get hold of it?

The wine pours its warmth through our veins. This straw is not really disagreeable. I should like to think through the ideas which these newspaper dispatches have dragged out of the limbo where they were dormant in my brain. History is irreversible. This victory is already definitive, as fragile and uncertain as it may be. And then it is the victory of millions upon millions of men. How does one imagine millions of men? The bounds of the imagination are easily reached. The basic theory is very clear: when the peasants have taken over the land, no power in the world will be able to pry it away from them. Streams of blood will only serve to fertilize it. I know the old slogans by heart: Miner, take the mine; peasant, take the land; worker, take the machine. But this is merely an algebra. What is behind these symbols, these words? What has happened? What are we going to do?

Whatever is necessary, no matter what the cost.

I recently reread a forgotten page of Korolenko, relating the following:

On May 19, 1864, a low black scaffold was raised on a seldom-frequented square in Petersburg. The scaffold supported a pillory from which chains ending in large rings were hanging. The sky was gray; a fine rain was soaking through everything; groups of curiosity seekers gathered behind the lines of mounted gendarmes and police. And a thirty-five-year-old man, thin and pale, blond, with a pointed beard and a look of concentration behind a pair of silver-rimmed spectacles was made to climb that scaffold. He was wearing a fur-collared overcoat; at first he remained standing in front of the pillory, his back turned on the public, while an officer wearing a three-cornered hat read out the decree condemning him to public disgrace and to forced labor. The crowd could only hear a feeble murmur of words; horses were snorting, the rain was falling noiselessly, endlessly washing the impoverished faces and things. Then the executioner appeared; he brusquely tore the hat off the man who was now facing the crowd, his large stubborn brows, flaxen hair lying over the right temple, and singularly attentive expression now clearly visible. From the height of a pillory be contemplated the world. They put the chains on him; he crossed his chained arms over his chest. The executioner made him kneel. He wiped his damp glasses with his finger. The executioner broke his use-less sword over his head and dropped the two pieces into the mud on either side of the scaffold. A young woman threw some flowers toward the condemned man: they too fell into the mud at the feet of a colossal gendarme whose horse seemed to be made of bronze. Poor people were murmuring that this educated man, this lord, must indeed be a very great criminal. Siberia would be too good for him! His name was Nikolai Gavrilovich Chernyshevsky: he was without doubt one of the best minds in the country. The youth turned toward him as to a guide. From the depths of his study, he liberated them, taught them to think with the rest of Europe, prepared them for action. He was at once powerful and impotent, like the mind itself. Informers, publicists, forgers, secret agents, factotum senators, the Emperor had conspired to bring him low. Under this interminable rain, attached to that pillory, he was ending his career as a thinker for whom the world was not only to be understood but also to be transformed. His book, written in a cell, was to survive. He lived alone for twenty years in Siberian hamlets.

Every event is the result of an endless chain of causes. And this too, at a distance of a half-century, appears to me as a cause. Chernyshevsky in chains, wiping off his glasses in order to go on seeing the faces of life, listening to the dull rumblings of the crowd under the rain, explains for me the victory of millions of men on the march, besieging palaces, winning over squadrons and fortresses with harangues, burning the lords' manor houses, hanging the hangmen, finally declaring peace on the world and covered with opprobrium by the muzzled, slaughtered, and bamboozled peoples . . . They say that the seeds discovered in the tombs of the Pharaohs germinated. Nothing is ever lost. How many of us in the past, how many of us are there even now, in all the prisons of the world, lulling ourselves to sleep with this certainty? And this force too will not be lost . . .

There is always, in the depths of the soul, in its secret folds, an insidious voice which would like to argue:

"Yes, but the man on the pillory was lost. His intelligence was extinguished like a useless fire set by lightning in the Siberian wilds: it neither guides nor warms anyone. Humanity on the march has endless centuries and lives. Chernyshevsky had only his life.

"Wouldn't he have lost a good deal more had he ended up as an academician?"

TWENTY-FOUR

Little Piece of Europe

THE NEXT DAY WE ARRIVED AT THE DETENTION CAMP FOR SUSPECTS AT TRÉCY. It was a vast abandoned convent, way out in the country, in the middle of beautiful, flat land furrowed with sunken hedge-lined lanes and roads hemmed by poplars stretching toward peaceful blue horizons. Just beyond the archway, the extremely simple, steepleless church, with its peaked blue-slate roof surmounted by a graceful stone Virgin, opened onto a courtyard covered all over with green ivy. The camp administration, occupied several small, low houses with window boxes full of carefully arranged flowerpots. Another gate, guarded by a sentry, gave onto a vast rectangular paved courtyard. On three sides were white buildings; at the end a grill hidden by chestnut trees. From here, the church with its soft slaty hues and that graceful Virgin crowned like a queen overlook dreary barracks where clothes are drying on the window sills. The still-generous November sun has drawn the inhabitants of this closed village out of their lairs: Orientals wearing red fezzes or black toques and long mountain coats are squatting along the chalky wall. An old Albanian is telling the heavy black beads of his perpetual rosary. His bones must be as hard as stones.

Some young men are chasing each other amid peals of laughter farther off among the trees. A buccaneer, high boots, red wool jacket, dented felt hat, rugged face bearded to the eyes, the heavy scrutinizing gaze of a man who buys and sells stolen horses, painted women, forged titles and contraband is walking arm in arm with a tall Serbian officer whose patched tunic has only light patches in the place of insignia. Other more ordinary-looking strollers are pacing up and down under the covered gallery which extends along the side of one of the buildings. Two men are washing under the pump, each in turn pumping for the other: a ruddy chest, a ruffled soapy, tawny-blond Scandinavian's head; a pair of powerful black shoulders of Herculean musculature—but, but, it's

Faustin! Faustin drying himself in a leisurely fashion with a gray towel! He strikes his chest with both fists. The Scandinavian, cupping his hands, throws an unexpected bowl of water right into his face. And now they are boxing joyfully, floundering about in the soapy water, the blond streaming, the black shining. Closed fists thud against resilient bodies. It's good to go at it like that, with all your strength, against a solid chest with a manly heart tireless under the robust carcass of muscle and bone, rolling with the punches, returning the punches; it's good to catch hold of a hundred pounds of force thrown out on the end of your opponent's fist without flinching, when they miss the target, glancing off your ribs. Eh, you bastard! If you had nailed me with that one! It only missed by a hair—and now it's my turn, take that . . . Missed?—No, not quite, take that—you got me—now! Faustin is leading the dance; he pivots on his heels, ducks under a right to the face by the Scandinavian and suddenly staggers, hit hard three or four times, so fast, from all sides, that I can't tell where any more. Nounés stamps his foot with enthusiasm.

"Christ!" growls the Negro. "I've had it!"

"*Tchort!* [the Devil!]" blurts out the other, who turns out to be Russian, not Scandinavian.

We form a circle around them. And Faustin is not Faustin: this fellow is broader, with a larger mouth and a low forehead.

We could be on the main square of a bizarre village where there aren't any women but where strollers from many nations rub elbows around an itinerant boxing match.

And just then I notice, striding across the courtyard, with his long steps, his silky beard, and his crooked half-smile as always, Sam, my old Sam, exactly as he appeared not long ago on the boulevards in quest of a flag for his machine gunners . . .

"So many high-ranking 'comrades' had their eyes on us that it couldn't last," he says.

He leads me through this city isolated from the world by a double ring of barbed wire, a row of sentries, a low wall covered with fragments of broken bottles: not much, this last obstacle, but no one has yet reached it. There, on the ground floor, the Balkans: a whole roomful of anti-Venizelos Greeks, of Macedonians who really can't be classified either as Greeks, Serbs, or Bulgarians and who only want to be themselves; of refugees of the Chetniks who have been holding out in the mountains for years, against all powers. It's only through error, negligence, chance circumstance, or lack of evidence that they haven't put that old man, Kostia the Silent to the sword. He is sitting cross-legged now on his hammock cover telling the black beads of his rosary while two young men argue in low voices in front of him, questioning him in turn with their eyes. Gray whiskers bristle on his granite chin; his nostrils are wide and dark. He knows all the secrets of the Vardar mountains, but he is as silent as a tomb (and several executed traitors are sleeping in that tomb) impenetrably polite, severe, firm, loyal and perfidious. Here's the story they tell: when another Chetnik chieftain sold out to the people in Sofia, Kostia became his friend, pretended to become his accomplice, and during a feast, in the midst of his companions, at the moment of swearing fraternal oaths killed him. How is this known? "Ah, that . . ." The Greeks and Macedonians keep to themselves, in deep silence, idle, meditative, sewing up their ragged clothing, picking their fleas, brewing their coffee, famished and unyielding. Other rooms house Russians, Jews, Alsatians, Belgians, Rumanians, Spaniards, thieves, marauders, adventurers, phony foreign noblemen, probable spies, certain victims, unlucky people, vagabonds, second offenders, undesirables, Germanophiles, simpleminded people, rebels, revolutionaries. There are Jewish tailors and restaurant owners guilty of having elbows on the counter, maintained the integrity of the Bolsheviks; shady interpreters who try to pass themselves off as "political" too, but who in reality used to guide American soldiers to bordellos; convicts coming from penitentiaries who feel *free* because bells no longer direct their mechanical steps in the endless round of dead days; vagrants of uncertain nationality picked up around the camps; Alsatians suspected of illegal trafficking with the enemy or denounced in anonymous letters in villages which have been taken and retaken; businessmen from friendly nations, filthily compromised and strangely protected; deported Belgians with no more territory; Russian sailors known around the ports as troublemakers, defeatists, syndicalists, anarchists, suspected Bolsheviks and Bolshevik suspects . . . There are the rich: the ones who eat as much as they want every day, drink wine at the canteen, dress well, are waited upon, pay for their pleasures; there are the miserable, those fallen into the depths of poverty, like old Antoine, a hobo for the past thirty years, driven by the war from his habitual roads in the Ardennes, who picks up potato peelings, carrot leaves, half-gnawed bones every night out of the garbage heap and makes succulent stews out of them in old "monkey-meat" cans over twig fires—too filthy even to be approached, he leaves a trail of fleas behind wherever he goes.

"Let him croak, the vermin! A public nuisance!" say Blin and Lambert, two gay dogs in sweaters, red-cheeked, inseparable, living together in a comfortable little room above the hole in the wall where the old man sleeps, rolled up in a ball, on a nauseating pile of straw. Blin and Lambert, a pair of gourmets, spend their time fixing chow, reading the papers, playing cards. Half-dressed pinup girls clipped from the pages of *La Vie Parisienne* brighten up their décor, which is that of a pair of sybarites who are very glad to be here where it's warm, and not at the Front, not in prison . . .

"We're not so bad off," they say. "Life isn't very rosy in an occupied country these days. Or in the trenches either! But we get along."

Antoine is going to croak, by God. Out of the four hundred of us who are here, there aren't fifty who can count on getting enough to eat every day. Our group of revolutionaries really has to tighten its belt if we want to hold out. Antoine sells his bread ration (300 grams) in order to buy tobacco. His sole worldly good is a twopenny clay pipe, which has had a charmed life; it's amazing he's been able to keep it all these months. One day a rascally Pole stole it from him; the buccaneer Maerts, bearded to the eyes, hefty under his red wool jacket, drumming his huge strangler's fingers on his counter, had the author of the larceny summoned before him.

"Yanek. You swiped the old fleabag's pipe now. Well, you're gonna give it right back to him *on the double.*"

"Yes, Mista Maerts," says Yanek. "You can count on it."

The old man was wandering around the courtyard with the eyes of a madman. Yanek bounded down the stairs, four at a time, caught up to him on the run and, without a word, stuffed the pipe between his teeth.

Maerts has his good qualities. He eats well. You should see him, in splendid isolation in his "establishment" seated before a hash of lard, potatoes, and green peas with a liter of "red," masticating slowly, moving his whole face and his whole beard, with his two knotty fists square on the table holding the knife and fork as if they were weapons. While he gluts himself, his sly gaze surveys the whole room, follows the clouds through the window, floats around the crowned Virgin rising above the church: superfluous femininity—unsalable! He scrapes the

leftovers of his grub into a basin—gristle, bits of bones, potato eyes—
and goes down into the yard. Old Antoine, who knows the time, is
watching from his usual corner, from which nobody chases him, near
the latrines. Three paces off, Maerts, bending slightly, turns over the
basin, and the grub falls to the earth. Then he steps back and watches
the old man, squatting, devouring these leftovers along with the soil
which clings to the grease, like a dog.

"After all," says Maerts charitably.

And, hands in his pockets, heavy, rugged, beefy, he turns around
suddenly and walks away.

We are in Maerts's cabaret: Room II, on the right as you enter. The establishment makes a nice appearance—the smartest one in the camp. Five
tables, benches with backs. The sign hanging up on the wall bears in
big red letters garnished with flourishes: *A LA BONNE FORTUNE: Café
à toute heure*. The *patrón's* corner is furnished with metal-strapped cof-
fers. A handsome pine trunk which he made himself out of pieces of
packing cases, solid, sealed by a huge padlock, is kept under his well-
made bed for greater security. Some colored posters—BRASSERIE DU LION
DES FLANDRES, CHICORÉE DES TRAPPISTES—finish off creating the atmosphere of a Flemish *estaminet* in this barracks room corner. The huge tin
kettle is singing, heated by an alcohol lamp, enthroned on the counter
between two handwritten signs: *Credit is dead, Help yourself and Heaven
will help you*. A mug of coffee, served with a tenth of a cube of sugar,
costs ten sous (pink cardboard rectangle, oiled by the touch of many
hands: CAMP TRÉCY: 10 centimes). We drink. Maerts, a pencil behind
his ear, meditates over the figures in his ledger. Various assorted objects
hang on nails, lie on shelves made out of planks suspended from hooks
by a system of wires, or are stuffed under the bed in bundles. The entire
room, forty beds, has a good appearance because of this establishment,
illuminated in the evening by the only big oil lamp in the camp. People
do business here, go on binges here, play cards here. Sometimes, after
taps, we can hear the customers of the Bonne Fortune cabaret singing
their heads off in the closed barracks.

Maerts operates a pawnshop. The hunting breeches he wears belong
to the Baron in Room III. He got his beautiful, scarlet jacket, in the end,
for seven francs from the grocer Pâtenôtre, after the latter's attempted
escape . . . The big cavalry coat hanging in the corner with his other

things belonged to his friend Captain Vetsitch, in his debt for twelve francs. There are bundles containing red and white check handkerchiefs—on which the *patrón* lends four sous—foulards, linen. The trunk contains quality shoes, toilet kits, wallets, Russian books. The rings, watches, fountain pens, cigar holders fill a heavy metallic coffer inside the bed, under the pillow, following a custom that goes back to the Middle Ages or earlier. An accordion is lying in a Russian leather hatbox. Canes and umbrellas form a sheaf . . . A miniature—the portrait of a blond child—and a gold medallion containing a lock of hair have been seen in the *patrón*'s hands. He will even give a loan, they say, on photographs of women. Not on those of men "because they don't take them back." I wonder what clever devil, borrowing ten sous from him on the portrait of a gentleman, erased the last traces of naïveté from this pirate.

"The buccaneer," I say, "has the soul of the founder of a financial dynasty. Can you see him, Sam, wearing an overcoat and a soft felt hat in the elevator of a skyscraper?"

Sam considers each of us obliquely:

"But perfectly. And why not? Close-shaven, blue-chinned. Nothing looks more like the desperadoes in the magazines than a businessman who has let his beard go . . . Sometimes it's the same man. Change the décor, add or subtract success. Nothing looks more like a hero than a scoundrel. Sometimes it's the same stuff. Change the décor . . ."

His Uncle Sam profile seems to have dried out; he is nothing but coldness, a twisted smile.

"A nice little piece of Europe," he says, "authentic. Every man . . . a suspect. Free: admire how free we are, from reveille to taps and even later, free behind our barbed wire, under the muzzles of loaded rifles, like citizens of the best-organized republics. Free to live on garbage like Antoine or to get rich like Maerts. And all the nations mixed together, brewed up; equal before the daily slop pail, the lice, and the law. A collection of swine worthy of the greatest capitals, I assure you; and enough innocent victims to make a dozen novelists happy. They are all breathing in the healthy air of the rear . . . And us—incendiaries locked up, for safety's sake, in a powder magazine . . ."

"Sam, the basis of your metaphor is no good. No one gets killed here. It's an oasis!"

"Do you really think no one gets killed here? That would be most extraordinary . . ."

TWENTY-FIVE

Interiors

EACH BARRACKS ROOM HAS ITS OWN STAMP. THE ONE WHERE MAERTS REIGNS, peopled by Belgians, is naked, cold. The beds of these poor wretches who have fallen into slavery under the *patrón* have only the thin furnishings supplied by the administration. Tramps' bundles hang on the walls. A cobbler is patching up some sandals. Someone swears in Flemish, another snores. The little room in the back is reserved for more serious types, dressed in city clothes, abundantly supplied by the canteen. Maerts greets them without any obsequiousness. After all, he's the one who is doing them a favor. A tall, washed-out young man, with drooping mustaches, who wears high collars and striped trousers but who neglects his appearance, flabby, with a four-days' growth of beard, trembles all over, his cheeks suddenly flushed; when the *patrón* gives him the sign:

"Tomorrow, at five o'clock, Monsieur Arthur."

Monsieur Arthur withdraws three green five-franc cardboards from his watch pocket with a delicate, trembling hand. Later he can be seen laughing distractedly, playing a game of piquet, losing good-humoredly. He will go to bed early, in order to dream, turned toward the wall. At five o'clock tomorrow, Floquette, the home guard, his small Mongol's face freckled (a butt hanging on his lower lip), a café waiter in civilian life, on duty at the gate, will signal to him, as well as to fat Pâtenôtre, sweating under his bulky black woolen vest and wearing a weather-beaten, shiny bowler screwed down over his bloodshot face. The two men have ostensibly been summoned to the mailroom. They meet, full of contempt for each other. "That flabby fathead!" thinks Pâtenôtre. "That brute!" says Monsieur Arthur to himself. Floquette winks at them in passing (". . . go to it, my children!") followed by a dreadful clack of the tongue which reverberates through Monsieur Arthur's nerve ends, for a long while after, even down to the tips of his fingers. He is afraid he may stagger; his heart is pounding; he is all

red, this great lanky fellow (a licentiate in law on his visiting cards) like
a bashful kid. The two men pass quickly through the gate, catching a
glimpse of the administration courtyard—walls green with ivy, attractive window boxes filled with flowerpots—and turn left toward the
outbuildings. Here they enter the reassuring semidarkness of a store-
house full of packing cases. Monsieur Arthur, inwardly overcoming a
great weight, gets himself ready to say, "See here, Pâtenôtre, I think
it's my turn today . . ." But just at that instant Pâtenôtre turns around,
very red, his eyes slightly bloodshot, his huge nose like a leech, and brutally hisses into his face, "All right, I'm going in. Keep your eyes peeled,
eh . . . ?" Like an animal diving into a thicket, he ponderously disappears into the shed in the corner. Monsieur Arthur is leaning in the
doorway. Before him are three stretches of red-brick wall, one covered
with ivy: at times Floquette's uniform cap slanting down over his grin-
ning Chinese gargoyle's head comes into view ten paces off. Monsieur
Arthur can hear stirrings from the shed in the corner, a cough, a hoarse
gasp. His heart is beating wildly; a boundless disgust reduces him to a
dishrag. He stares at his hands for a long while: his nails are gray. And
then a long animal agony . . . "Hurry up," mutters Pâtenôtre, who has
finally reappeared, short of breath, buttoning his vest. Monsieur Arthur
takes four steps, like a sleepwalker, toward the corner shed, bathed in
soft shadows, where a blond girl, seated on some old sacks with her
knees spread apart, rises as he enters. "Good day, Monsieur Arthur,"
she says politely. "Good day, Louise," be answers, without her hearing
the trembling in his voice; and he takes hold of her breasts, which are
flabby, for her flesh is lymphatic, milky, and tepid like a thing forsaken.
At this moment, this dishrag of a man, worn out by empty days, suddenly feels erect from his heels to his neck, raised above himself, his
teeth clenched, his chest expanded, like a caricature of some terrible
ancestor, before his passive prey. The girl is as blond as the straw; her
chignon smells of hay. This is the way she earns six extra francs every
time she comes to bring supplies to the camp; for Floquette, who has
already been paid one hundred sous by the customer, makes Louise
give him another forty sous (and the rest when the mood strikes him).
It is he who carries clandestine letters to the post office for the rich;
he who supplies the forbidden booze; he who parleys with visitors. A
thrifty man, he deposits fifty francs in the savings bank every Saturday:
"The war is a gravy train . . ." It's a gravy train for Louise, too, who had
never seen so much money before.

The girl's red-rimmed eyes will awaken Monsieur Arthur in the night, and his soul, crumpled by an awful terror, will be like a rag which has been soaked, wrung out, and flopped down on the flagstones.

In the evening, this barracks room resembles an inn of olden times, in an old port haunted by pirates.

Maerts emerges from time to time in the yellow flame of the lamp, wearing a felt hat which drowns his eyes in shadow—dressed, one might think, in a red doublet. The blue smoke of pipes and cigarettes winds about under the lampshade, like silky thread. Stein, with his blood-red harelip, has the huge wrinkled brow of a disfigured Socrates playing a game of *manille*. His crafty eyes carefully survey the parchment-skin hands of his ageless opponent: a face of thin old leather, crackling around the eyes, a pointed nose, an Adam's apple as big as a child's fist in the middle of a long neck (a knife-proof neck, witness a soft, pink scar like a long flourish) reduced to a bundle of tendons, nerves, and veins. This is Monsieur Oscar, the hatmaker; and the ex-Legionnaire would have won a hundred sous if he had nabbed him with the card in his sleeve and knocked him out amid overturned tables, with a butt in the stomach for a start and a good kick right in the mouth to finish him off (that's his usual manner). There is also the huge livid head, covered with bristles, of a financier in sorry straits; and the carefully trimmed salt and pepper mustache of the Baron who is losing, along with his last effects, the last bit of dignity to which he clings in life. The yellowed and darkened cards are soft to the touch, like greasy rags. Two nobodies, at the next table, are moving pawns across a checkerboard, pawns which are actually buttons off the uniforms of five armies. The rest of the room is little by little invaded by darkness. Interrupted snoring, whispered conferences between beds, quiet swearing; a hobo, tormented by hunger (that bloodsucker in the belly) has glued his forehead to the window and stares out into the night. Escape? No, this is not a harbor, there are the calm orchards; but to reach them it would be necessary to get over that fantastic zone of blinding whiteness under the searchlights, those barbed wires and those invisibly fatal areas, commanded by the muzzles of the rifles posted out there every fifty yards.

Low-ceilinged, the floor unswept, Room III is peopled mostly by Russian Jews. It has its own grimy "café," where you can get credit; the *patrón*, a man with a bizarre yellow mane, wears a blue suit which was once well cut, lapels now shiny with grease spots. A pair of pince-nez—of which one of the lenses is cracked inside the gold frame, causing his melancholy glance to deviate to one side—is perched on his fleshy nose. Goldstein is not, appearances to the contrary, the unhappiest of men. What possessed him to put his two cents in one day, in a crowd on the rue de Rambuteau, maintaining that, after all, the Huns are men like the rest of us and that everyone will have to admit it, sooner or later, when all the bleeding people go home to lick their wounds, like dogs after a frenetic battle? He can't forgive himself for this. The bailiffs auctioned off his shop: I. GOLDSTEIN, *watchmaker.* His wife is barely keeping alive, consumed by cancer. He serves us doses of chicory for one sou; and, after sundown, leaving the Argentinean to watch over the business (this is when the Argentinean pinches sugar and soap from him), passes into the next room, a nice quiet corner inhabited by old Ossovsky, and draws from his marvelous flute ("Ah, what an instrument, my friend!") long, long, heart-rending melodies. "Would you be so kind," suggests Ossovsky sweetly, "as to play the Frug aria?" Sobs, fleeing like ripples, escape from the ebony pipe (and, in the garden, a taciturn soldier, gassed in the Artois, pacing along the barbwire, feels himself overcome by the unknown sadness of the world, shudders, and understands vaguely how poignant things are . . ." Oh, shit—what blues . . .").

Ossovsky lives alone in a monastic cell, entirely white. Meticulously clean, very stiff, with the square, shoulders of an old officer and a faded face encircled by a light silvery beard. His voice is an enveloping smile, for he speaks with great delicacy; his piercing glance dissects things with the sweetness of a well-honed scalpel. Some walnuts spread over the title page of *L'Oeuvre* are drying on the windowsill. Ossovsky rolls a cigarette, murmuring Frug's lines: "Carry my soul into those blue horizons, / where the steppe stretches out to infinity, / wide like a great sadness, / wide like my hopeless pain . . ." and suddenly raises his eyes toward the flute player in an empty half-smile:

"The suffering of Israel."

And it is impossible to say whether he is mocking or serious. He comes from a prison. They say he stole a pearl necklace, seven years ago in a palace in Nice, from a neurotic Brazilian woman.

Squatting on their beds, two tailors are sewing. One, a marionette in a frock coat, says of himself: "Zill is not a man; nothing but a tailor." What does he read, in the evening by the glow of a candle, with his spectacles off and his nose in the book? *The Key to Dreams*. The other, gray tufts at his temples, a collector of anecdotes and gossip with an endless gift of gab, sleeps on three little white cushions, sent from home. Almost every week he makes a tragic scene, to the great delight of the whole room, to his son, the rascally Yanek, played out according to ancient family rites. He is seen pointing a menacing finger at the mocking adolescent: "Your father disowns you, do you understand me? You are no longer my son! Begone, you good-for-nothing!" The biblical fury of this "Begone, you good-for-nothing!" sends all the neighbors guffawing into their pillows. Far into the night, the father and son will be heard insulting each other in whispers. But when, one day, they had to lay the father down in his bed, long and pale like a cadaver, his heart sounding the toxin of agony in his chest, we saw the son trembling in earnest like a dry leaf in the wind.

There is also Professor Alschitz. "Teacher of poise and of Spanish," he says, introducing himself with an exaggerated bow and a curious glance, at once pressing, as if the better to raise your inevitable doubts, and furtive, for he is a visionary who lies even to himself—as well as a sly devil well disposed to swindling you. His slight shoulders are hunched under a decent looking jacket; he has a blue chin, strong features, and great bovine eyes; poise—learned in provincial theaters—and nervous hysteria. He flies into a passion, taps his foot like a spoiled child and, after having talked about his myocarditis or the lesions he has in his right lung or flaring up angrily, dissolves in self-pity and cries shamelessly. At these moments he paces up and down the room, mopping his eyes with his batiste handkerchief. Once a young Russian soldier who was more naïve than should be allowed took him seriously, and the professor won all his linen at cards in eight days. Since we have formed a group, Alschitz pretends to be a "defeatist"; but we are learning little by little that at the beginning of the war he pretended to volunteer for the Legion, and that he was arrested in a Montmartre bar on the eve of his departure for Argentina where he placed housemaids in houses of assignation.

Forty men, mostly Jews, sleep in this room. Some, nameless and faceless, talkative however, grimy, famished, fill the corners with a swarm of voices and gestures, and are forgotten as soon as they are no longer there, as soon as one has turned his back. Two Zionists with the oriental ugliness of pyramid builders and high, red, sugar-loaf skulls shaved like those of fellahs, argue, argue, and argue, tirelessly entangling and untangling the skein of their subtleties. They are, nonetheless, fine fellows.

We assemble here, in the late afternoon, a few from every room. The comrades form a circle around the reader in front of whom the open newspapers are spread out. An embryonic crowd, thirty to fifty silent men, huddle around listening. The reader translates the dispatches: "Congress of the Soviets . . . Trotsky assassinated. . . . The Germans in the Ukraine . . ." At times his voice trembles with emotion. One evening, when he had announced the dissolving of the Constituent Assembly, the group split, leaving two bitter handfuls of men clinging to each other in a violent debate. "They're madmen. They're ruining Russia. They're ruining the revolution. You'll see!"—"Yes, we'll see, we'll see. They're a thousand times right. That's how you have to deal with parliaments: a boot in the tail."—"We can see that our country's blood doesn't cost you anything, snotnose!"—"What? What?"—"A fine invention: socializing poverty! Let's pool all our lice and debts together, eh, comrades? Plekhanov said . . ."—"Your Plekhanov is a fraud. Let him make war to the bloody end safe in his library."—"The revolution should stop at nothing. Socializing poverty is better than exploiting it . . ."

At other times a dreamy group would hang back by the open window. Dmitri, a thin sailor coughing out his lungs, would propose: "'Transvaal?'"

The whole room struck up this hymn, full of allusions, which was often sung in the provincial towns of Russia during the years when the only freedom people were permitted to exalt in the Empire was a South African freedom crushed by the English. "Transvaal, Transvaal, O my country, all ablaze in flames . . ." Singing unites men like shared struggle, suffering, or exaltation. We felt like brothers. Our prisoners' voices floated, supreme, over the darkened orchards of that Normandy countryside, calling up long-silent voices from the depths of a revolutionary past and perhaps reaching out across thousands of miles to choruses of soldiers of a living revolution resting on the banks of wide rivers.

TWENTY-SIX

Us

SUCH WAS THE SLOW-MOTION EXISTENCE OF CONCENTRATION CAMPS: HUNGER doled out with indifference by commissions that probably believed that these people were already much too well off at a time when so many others worth infinitely more were being killed. Each day this collection of suspects, undesirables, and subversives was given a three-hundred-gram slice of bread, soup, and beans; and they had nothing to do but wait for the end of the cataclysm under which empires and cathedrals crumbled. Mail call every morning: newspapers, letters, practical jokes like the following fake answer from a lawyer-deputy which staggered Alschitz for several evenings:

> "Monsieur,
> Your case appears very interesting to me. Your dossier, which I have examined with the permission of Monsieur the Prime Minister, contains documents on which full light must be shed. Please let me know, with the greatest possible accuracy, your whereabouts on the night of the 17th to the 18th of August 1914; between seven and nine in the evening . . ."

The professor of poise and Spanish searched desperately through his past, at a distance of years. "I think," he said at last, "that I was in Nancy . . ."—"In Nancy!" exclaimed Sam. "In the east! Oh, my poor friend!"

Long walks in the yard, to kill the time. Rare were those, in this forced leisure, who still knew the value of time, who read, who sketched, who studied. Equally rare the obstinate ones who refused to let themselves go. Shaving every day, washing thoroughly at the pump, then deep-breathing exercises, brushing your clothes, polishing your shoes, were, however, sure signs of victory over demoralization. This self-discipline kept a man upright, full of simple confidence, among the flabby.

The regulations weren't hard. It was only isolation from the outside world, idleness, hunger, captivity without any reason or definite limit, the loaded rifles aimed at our windows. From reveille to taps we were free. And the days floated by as empty as in a prison, but filled with a distracting hum of talk, of laughter, of walks, of unimportant tasks, of card games or checkers. Maerts was getting richer. Faustin II washed the gentlemen's laundry. The Argentinean ran unseemly errands from one room to another and mingled with the orderlies. Alschitz gave lessons (six sous a visit). Ossovsky, that saintly old thief, read by his window; old Kostia told his black beads, Antoine wandered along the walls, staggering a little, face turned toward the ground, as if drunk—drunk perhaps from hunger; the others, four hundred others, in the end just like these, four hundred prisoners, imagined they were killing the time that was slowly killing them . . . The sick lived face to face with their disease, like Krafft; with his wrinkled cheeks—in whose garret room we used to gather— who would turn aside in order to spit into his handkerchief and then count up the threads of blood in his sputum. Stool pigeons wrote down things overhead among the groups in childishly scrawled penciled notes, and in the evening Richard, the gendarme, would pass under our windows inside the stockade and pick up the wads of paper weighted with pebbles. There were two old men, completely white, one Alsatian, the other Belgian, both equally broken, walking with the aid of the same crutches, nourished on the same scraps, smoking the same butts, rooming together under the stairway of the unused infirmary, who hated each other with a deadly hatred. We used to go to listen to them at the pharmacy, for they slept under the neighboring loft. Jean, the male nurse, made them retire an hour before taps and locked them in. You could hear them grumbling, moaning, stirring up the straw in their mattresses, undressing slowly. Powerless oaths fell about them like flaccid globs of spit. Then each curled up on his mattress, they would resume their old quarrel, repeated each day, and their voices alternated, so similar that it took a practiced ear to distinguish between them, coming together in a single litany of invective. "Filthy carrion, eh, filthy carrion, species of dirty camel, camel—God's name if you're not a misery . . ." they continued insulting each other in this manner until grogginess overcame them; then they would fall asleep, openmouthed, with the greenish faces of the asphyxiated, and their breath continued to mingle.

The infirmary was deserted, since the sick preferred to remain in the barracks. The male nurse Jean lived alone in a suite of empty rooms. He had a quiet corner smelling of carbolic, a window (barred) looking out on the garden, and as much ether, cocaine, and morphine as he wanted. This chubby lad, pale and fat-cheeked, with round eyes like bubbles of Japanese porcelain ready to leap out of their sockets, constantly drugged himself. "I'm a happy man," he used to say. "I'm the dispenser of dreams, the warden of the keys to Paradise, Saint Jean of the Charitable Syringe. Let all the good fellows looking for a good time come unto me." And, cordially, putting a brotherly arm around his visitor, he would blow a breathful of ether in his face: "A little drink, or an injection? An injection, old boy, there's nothing like it . . . And now listen . . ."

And if you listened he would tell you endlessly about his loves with Stéphanie: Stéphanie, a cute kid with green eyes, as spiteful and as affectionate as a cat; Stéphanie, who was "under my skin, in my blood"; Stéphanie who cheated on him ("Believe me, I'll kill her some day!"); Stéphanie who still wrote him a four-page letter every day full of profound double meanings, read between the lines, reread, learned by heart from one evening to the next; Stéphanie, exasperating and ravishing bitch: "Ah, if only you could see her arms, her neck . . .

"Ah, her letters. Oh, baby, when I think of you I almost want to forget you, to tear you out of here, yes, tear you out . . ."

His tone would suddenly become excruciating. He would open the poison drawer, always kept locked, and pull out a packet of bizarre, crosshatched letters, written over, you might think, several times.

Sam crushed him one evening.

"Tell me, Jean," he asked him quietly, "does it really amuse you to write yourself letters from Stéphanie every day? You end up believing in them, eh?"

Jean seemed to emerge from a dream or to awaken; a clear, white glimmer passed over his pasty face. And went out. He seemed to grow larger, harder, heavier; perhaps stunned; perhaps on the point of charging forward like a brute beast. He walked ponderously up to my comrade and whispered:

"Get out."

Sam turned his back on him, out of bravado, drummed his fingers on the table for a moment, and left. Never again did Jean talk to us of Stéphanie . . .

We stayed alive. The days passed by. The weeks, the months, the seasons, the battles, the revolution, the war passed by. Life passed by.

We formed a world apart within this city. It sufficed for one of us to call the others together with that magic word "Comrades," and we would feel united, brothers without even needing to say it, sure of understanding each other even in our misunderstandings. We had a quiet little room with four cots, the walls papered with maps, a table loaded with books. There were always, a few of us there, poring over the endlessly annotated, commented, summarized texts. There Saint-Just, Robespierre, Jacques Roux, Baboeuf, Blanqui, Bakunin were spoken of as if they had just come down to take a stroll under the trees. Robespierre's error, "decapitating the Parisian masses themselves when he struck at the *enragés* of the Commune," exasperated our old Fomine, who would thunder—his white mustache bristling, his eyebrows and mane in battle array, leonine despite his provincial's frock coat—that the Incorruptible One had doomed the Revolution by cutting off too many heads. "As long as he guillotined to the right, he was correct; the day he began guillotining to the left, he was ruined. That's my opinion." It was the opinion of a fine old man, astonishingly young, always ready to fly off the handle, susceptible, irritated by trifles—his face abruptly screwed up like a bulldog's at these moments— but devoured by a need for activity, for solidarity, for struggle, for passionate affirmation. Expelled from England, expelled from France long ago—"Under another name, they don't know anything about it!"— interned at the age of sixty. The misfortune of Blanqui, a prisoner during the Commune, the head of the revolution cut off and preserved in the Château du Taureau at the very moment when the Parisian proletariat lacked a real leader, still troubled us as the worst kind of ill luck. Krafft, the chemist, member of the Russian Social Democratic Workers' Party (Bolsheviks), a sickly, tidy little man, sharp profile, thin lips, would explain in his extremely gentle voice—a copy of Karl Marx's *Civil War in France* covered with penciled notes in hand—that a firm offensive by the Communards against Versailles could probably have changed the course of history . . .

This past is not all we have: we also have the world and the future. Three syndicalist sailors, Wobblies, have arrived, two from the United States, one from Australia; if they can't delve profoundly into history, they still have some great stories to tell. Dmitri, a Little Russian who had been an athlete, now lanky, hollow-chested, wrinkled on the neck and face, almost succeeded in causing the incredibly ill-nourished crew of an English steamer to mutiny. A commonplace incident of a howl of wormy soup thrown into the face of the first mate earned him long days in irons, tormented by the cold, in the brig where the water was sometimes up to his knees; then, passing through the Red Sea in the deadly furnace heat. The result is that he is dying, his lungs consumed. But he would still like to see the Don again. "There perhaps . . ." But he has hardly proffered these words when a doubt of living (already a certainty of death) pierces through him and he bravely shrugs his shoulders. After all, here or there, a grave is a grave. His two pals from America, Karl and Gregor (in whose bunks leaflets were discovered during a search aboard the *Theodore Roosevelt*) were happier men: calm Vikings, joyful boxers in the morning at the pump, mending their clothes in the afternoons, waiting serenely. Admirable in appearance: that golden, flaxen beard—Karl; and that other massive, almost square head, the head of a Reiter practicing physical culture, bending over the needle, the thread, the cloth—Gregor. Gregor, the elder, can still remember the days when, as a boy, he used to take long walks through the forests of the Düna, alone, carrying messages to the Brothers of the Forest in the depths of their hidden glades. "I once met Yann the Great," he said, "Yann the Great who was shot down at Wenden . . ."

Sonnenschein adds a note of tender comedy to our group. He is short, with a conical forehead, bald around the temples, a rather sharp Semitic profile, thick Assyrian lips, and tiny intelligent eyes which see everything with an ironic indulgence. His mind was shaped in a rabbinical school somewhere in Poland. He was a Zionist before becoming a socialist. He has a humorous way of arguing. His eyes are illuminated by a sharp glimmer of laughter. "Listen to a story," he says . . . And it's always a Jewish story, slightly facetious, embellished with savory details, but of great wisdom. In order to explain to us that each task must be accomplished in its own time, he told us the definitive aphorism of Schmoul the tailor, whose neighbor had come to order a pair of pants. "When will you finish sewing it, Schmoul?"—"In two weeks, Itzek, my friend."—"Two weeks, to sew a pair of pants? When God himself made the world in six days?" Schmoul withdrew the pins he was holding in his mouth, considered his bearded interlocutor, the room, and the universe that could be seen through the window and said: "Yes, but what a world. Itzek! And what a pair of pants it will be!"

When there are six of us around a table, we have the experience of all the continents, all the oceans, all the pain and the revolt of men: the Labor parties of New South Wales, the vain apostleship of Theodor Herzl, the Mooney trial, the struggles of the Magón brothers in California, Pancho Villa, Zapata, syndicalism, anarchism, Malatesta's exemplary life, the individualism and the death of those bandits who wanted to be "new men," Hervéism, social democracy, the work of Lenin—as yet unknown to the world—all the prisons.

We used to come together almost every day, sometimes after the reading of the papers, sometimes in regular meetings of the group. And at times stormy division appeared in our debates, ready to become sources of hate among fraternal enemies. Old Fomine looked upon the revolution as the explosion and the disorderly growth of popular forces. The soundest ideas would quite naturally come to the fore amid the thousands of interconnected conflicts; the example of the best men would— through success, the exaltation of their souls and their own passion— impose itself on the masses, torn between their own higher aspirations and the dead weight of the past, of the lies, of the backward-looking egoism (for enlightened egoism understands that the good of the individual is found in solidarity) . . . When he had finished talking, Krafft took the floor and sprinkled his short, colorless sentences, spoken in a tone of insignificance, over that ardent voice still ringing in our ears: it was like a thin stream of ice water being poured over a glowing hearth . . . This old-fashioned romanticism would only be good for leading the revolution to disaster; happily the proletariat had already passed through that stage some time ago. It was based on utopian socialism and not on scientific socialism. Henceforth there is a technique of revolution, which demands organization, discipline, watchwords, order. Persuasion before the conquest of power, yes: the competition between false ideologies and the correct political line, the latter winning over the masses because it best expresses their true aspirations (hence its correctness). Of course. But after the conquest of power, Jacobin centralization, systematic resistance to the reactionary tendencies among the workers themselves, a merciless struggle against confused, reactionary, or romantic ideologies that have become pernicious . . .

A tense silence fell little by little around Krafft, whose feeble hand was making authoritarian gestures. And Fomine exploded in a voice snarling with sarcasm, stunning laughter, impetuosity:

"Ah! No! After all! If you want to imagine you are carrying the truth in your right-hand vest pocket, sharp and clear like a white pebble, that's your business. But if, from that, you want to close my mouth by calling me a reactionary, a romantic, a utopian, a petit-bourgeois or whatever you like, then no! I won't stand for it. Nobody will stand for it. In two words: Are you for freedom of the press, yes or no?"

"Under a bourgeois regime, before the conquest of power, yes, because it is necessary to the proletariat. Afterward, that notion becomes superfluous. We control the press. We are free. The unhealthy and reactionary tendencies of the working class have no right to what you call—using an old liberal word, not really revolutionary—freedom."

A hubbub of exclamations drowned out his voice. "But who is to judge?"—"The organized proletariat."—"That is to say the party, your party."—"The only party of the proletariat."

"Then," cried Fomine, "you'll have to throw me into prison, do you understand? You'll have to mass-produce prisons! And then—then—I'd really like to see that!"

"I don't know," retorted Krafft, without raising his voice, "if it will be necessary to build new prisons, for prisons are destined to disappear, but we'll certainly need the old ones for the enemies of the revolution as well as for bunglers. Besides, they'll be quite well off there. Much better than here, you can believe me . . . The only choice we have is between victory and destruction. Fantasy and poetry are beside the point. Look, it's entirely possible that three-quarters of the workers themselves will turn against us at the first serious difficulties. Aren't we well aware that they, too, are permeated with the old ideas, the old instincts of the bourgeoisie? that they have only *its* newspapers to read? Ought we, out of a respect for some high principles inculcated by the enemy, to leave him alone so that they can help to hang us and then take up the yoke again?"

Krafft remained alone. Shrugs, Karl's broad smile in his sunny beard, and one of Sonnenschein's good stories calmed everyone down. Krafft, overcome by sheer weight of numbers, considered us calmly, with a nuance of irony in his eyes.

The news from Russia filled us all with a boundless confidence.

TWENTY-SEVEN

Flight

HAVING STRETCHED OUT IN THE YARD, IN THE SUN, UNDER HIS BLANKET, OLD Antoine fell asleep. At soup call at four o'clock he didn't get up and nobody paid any attention to him. The shade crept over the sleeper. Strollers bent over him; a group formed. They were looking at his fleas. The blanket was covered with wide milky spots with moving edges. After a long moment, someone wondered why those thousands of parasites were fleeing the man, already as cold as a stone.

"'E's dead."

Nobody was willing to touch the hunched-up corpse. The male nurse Jean promised God-knows-what to two miserable devils who finally dragged him off without lifting him, stiff as a wax doll.

"Our crew is ready," Sam announced to us that day.

They had been preparing their escape for long days—three of them: Sam, a tall, sad boy called Markus (a Russian Jew in his twenties), and the Rumanian. Markus had been my bunkmate for a while. Captivity oppressed him to an inexplicable degree. He was covered with invisible chains; they wore out his muscles, they drove him to despair. His young worker's hands had become soft, thin, pale: "Ladylike hands, wouldn't you say?" he would ask, full of scorn and humiliation. His spirits rose abruptly once his decision had been made. "What the hell, I'll take the chance!" he told us, exalted. We considered the barbwire fence under the window and, near his sentry box, the sleepy sentry, recognizable by his red neck and his elephantine hindquarters: it was Vignaud, a socialist solider who never spared the Bolsheviks his disapproval. "Do you think Vignaud would shoot?" questioned Sonnenschein. "And how!" said Sam. "I think so too," said Sonnenschein, "but he would miss his man . . ."—"Without doing it on purpose, the fat-ass bastard!" Vignaud noticed us and gave us a friendly wave of the hand . . . The Rumanian who was supposed to leave with our two comrades rather worried us. Certainly suspected of espionage, he was truly elegant, ageless, his hair carefully pomaded, his eyelids wrinkled; a jaded habitué of nightclubs, an expert poker player, deceitful and polite, who trimmed his nails carefully every morning. He needed resolute companions for this daring attempt; his contribution to the group was a wad of banknotes artistically sewn into the lining of his clothes.

Their plan was simple. Wait for one of those stormy evenings when the rain forces the sentries to huddle in their shelters while the white glare of the searchlights fights against the rain squalls, and the noises of the downpour fill the garden. Then they would climb down, with the help of knotted blankets, from a second-story window conveniently hidden by the shade of an apple tree. Like shadows fleeting through the darts of rain, they would cross over the most dangerous zone, one after the other. The scaling of the barbwire seemed relatively easy near certain fence posts, the sentries' attention being focused principally on the lighted space between the buildings and the barbwire. They could count, with luck, on getting over the obstacle and plunging into the night. They would travel by night and hide during the day.

As well as the secret was kept, something must have leaked out, for Maerts made it known to us that he was inviting two members of the group for coffee. I went there with Sam. The buccaneer flashed a dark, enigmatic look at us from under his felt hat.

"You can have confidence in Maerts," he said, talking of himself in the third person. "The whole camp knows that. So let's be frank! You're preparing a break, eh?"

"Some people prepare them and some people only dream of them," said Sam, leaving matters undetermined.

We were drinking the coffee in little sips, without hurrying, like sly old foxes talking over a business deal. But what were we selling there?

"It will succeed," declared Maerts at last, "if I want it to. That will only cost you a hundred francs."

To have him against us could be dangerous. To fall in with him could be worse. Discussing it would be tantamount to admitting it.

"You're wasting your drinks, Monsieur Maerts; you shouldn't let people take you in like that . . ."

We felt it was proper to remain a little longer out of politeness.

We exchanged firm handshakes with the scoundrel. He couldn't know anything very precise. His suspicions must have fallen on our group. Maybe the gendarme Richard had even commissioned him to test us out?

The gendarme Richard, having made his rounds, entered Adjutant Soupe's office. Boredom held these two men together like a thick layer of glue and made them as impermeable to each other as two stones cemented into the same wall. The adjutant was thinness itself, the gendarme roundness. One was known as the Beanpole and the other the Billiard Ball. The Beanpole lived surrounded by bills of lading, pots of geraniums, letters from a little village in the Oise where he had a bit of property, and newspapers snitched from the internees' mail. The Billiard Ball guarded his camp with the diligence of a man who knows his craft, without zeal however and without malice. "Billiard Ball's a round fellow," they used to say. The Billiard Ball wiped his tar-black mustache with the back of his hand and unfolded some little rolled-up bits of paper he had taken from his pockets.

"Well, well! The Rumanian is informing against the tavernkeeper: trafficking in money."

"That's all the same to me!" replied M. Soupe, stuffing his nose with snuff. "Is that all?"

"No. The tavernkeeper is informing against the Rumanian: attempted escape."

That was more serious. The Beanpole put down his newspaper; his head, reduced to the proportions of a hairy skull, and his eyes, like mollusks on the half-shell, now strangely animated came out of the zone of indifference. The Billiard Ball knew all about it anyway. The Russian group was running the show, probably in order to send someone to Paris.

"Who is supposed to be leaving?"

"A chubby lad, worker from Billancourt. Not dangerous. If it were up to me," said the round fellow, "I'd let him run. The other: one Potapenko, known as Sam. Pass me his dossier."

They learned nothing disturbing from the dossier.

"It's the Rumanian I'm gunning for," said the Billiard Ball. "That one mustn't get through. In God's name, no! Not for anything in the world! Ever since they shot Duval he's been shitting in his pants, and I can understand why. As for me, I'd give orders, and clear ones. What do you say?"

M. Soupe always gave his approval, as long as trouble was avoided—
"Oh, of course. Do your best"—so that the round one led the lanky
one by the nose.

There was only one window, sheltered by an apple tree, from which the
descent into the garden would be easy. There was only one sentry box
from which it could easily be watched. On nights when the weather
looked like it might be stormy, M. Richard placed on this spot the man
he had chosen for his good eyesight, his sharp hearing, and above all
because he had quite a few little things to be forgiven for: the home-
guard Floquette.

"Listen carefully," the Billiard Ball explained to him: "Three of them
are leaving. The first, I don't care about. They can always catch up with
him on the road. Same for the third. The second has 'spy' written all over
him. On no condition should he be allowed to pass. You can fill his ribs
full of lead without a second thought. They won't give you the Military
Medal for that, of course. But you will get a hundred sous out of it."

From then on Floquette walked slowly, his loaded rifle on its sling,
under that window which opened over the road to death. We would
observe the sky with a sailor's solicitude. The splendor of the fiery
sunsets tormented us, for they announced peaceful nights full of constellations, nights of absolute captivity, nights without possible flight,
without possible death. Every evening three faces turned toward the
future: Markus, erect once again, a frank smile traced on the corners of
his mouth, a spark of joy—perhaps of power being born—in his eyes;
Sam, his mouth twisted, seemed to mock his own fate; and, at a distance from them, at another window so as not to he seen together, the
pasty-faced Rumanian, devoured by anxiety, afraid of staying, afraid of
fleeing, afraid of opening a newspaper and horribly afraid each time
a uniform came into the yard. Wasn't his life hanging on a thread as
thin as that shiny spider's web among the branches? His letters, trans-
mitted by a neutral embassy, were probably known to the authorities.
Everything depended on the silence of a man who had been waiting
for three months in a light-blue cell for them to fling open the door
suddenly in the middle of the night and say to him: "Take courage . . ."
Would he keep quiet? He was keeping quiet. Why was he keeping
quiet? Why? "If, it were me, I would talk . . ." This thought wormed its
way into every nook of his coward's soul. "He" could still make some

last-minute revelations, gain a week of stay of execution by turning in the man who was here, anxious, chewing on his well-manicured nails and saying to himself: "I would do it myself . . ." So, treacherous, he felt himself betrayed.

Markus was telling us how he had been knocked out one May Day in the Place de la République. When he named the streets, the squares of Paris, they were no longer names but realities. He would go to see the comrades at the Committee for Social Defense. This accepted mission lifted his revived spirits even more. His face smiling, enraptured, in the semidarkness, he at last confessed his secret to us: "Laura, I can't live without her!" And, as if this were somehow unworthy of a revolutionary, he quickly spoke of something else. Laura would write to us on his behalf, in a prearranged language. "Here is her writing . . ."— her illegible handwriting.

Sam, who was the strongest, besides being chosen by the group, would go over first. The Rumanian would follow, then Markus, so that the Rumanian could be helped, if necessary, in the scaling of the barbwire.

TWENTY-EIGHT

Blood

THE NEWSPAPERS INFORMED US OF LENIN'S ASSASSINATION. THIS TIME THE news seemed authentic. No one had been more marked for such an end than Lenin. We assembled early, in a near-empty barracks room, more numerous than usual. Our impotence, our sense of futility, of time running out while things were being accomplished, were turning, at long last, into cold rage. We walked about, furious, hands in our pockets, brooding over our anger like animals in a zoo, like men in jail. In vain Krafft would tell us, "All revolutionaries have known times like these, these captivities, these insipid moments; this is how men are tempered, how their power is born, how they learn to be hard and to see clearly; we are under an iron heel: but we are alive and stronger than those who judge and hold us, and growing even stronger. There comes a time when they can do nothing more but kill us; and then it is too late, for our blood might be more useful spilled than in our veins . . ." Krafft was right, but a kind of choking fury grew in us, causing us at times to reject that truism, as if we wanted to despair, for despair meant respite, renunciation.

"We are ready."

Ready for what? Perhaps to fight. Perhaps to die any kind of absurd or necessary death—here, by chance. Or elsewhere, because it must be so, doing rigorously, pitilessly what must be done. Perhaps to live without weariness, without turning sour—relentlessly. Perhaps to harness ourselves for years, for life, to thankless tasks, to dark struggles, to the obstinate destruction of things, to the obstinate gathering of the forces whose coming we would not see. Ready. This feeling came to us all at once, born out of a hatred so vast that it could not be expressed even in thought. From the depths of the outcasts' pit we condemned the world, the war, the law, the powerful, the rich, the liars, the corrupt, the idiots.

Fomine opened the meeting, his head lowered.

"Seems that it's true they've killed Lenin. The revolution has responded with a reign of terror. Six hundred bourgeois have been shot in Petrograd. The cost, in blood, of a few skirmishes in the Somme after which both headquarters write 'all quiet.' I endorse the reign of terror, comrades. Let us not grieve over Lenin's blood. He did his job. The revolution must finally stand up straight, sword unsheathed, and strike."

He became impassioned. From the back of the room, Belgians and Macedonians were staring at this tall, white-maned old man who recalled historic massacres, heads cut off in '93, red streams of the Château-d'Eau barracks in '70, and who sang the praises of terror.

Everybody wanted to speak. Words brought relief. Sonnenschein stood up, his pince-nez in his hand, his eyes misty, and said: "I endorse the terror . . ." The rest was lost in a hubbub of confused voices. Dmitri, coughing out his lungs, Karl and Gregor as solid as oaks, Krafft, the only one who seemed really calm, Markus, beaming, and even the puppet Alschitz, all cried out: "Terror, terror!"

A driving rain was beating against the windows. Sam remained silent, a little to one side. Old Fomine's eye found him in his corner.

"And you, Sam," cried Fomine, "speak out if you are against, if you have doubts! We are locked up, we are in chains, we are nothing, but we are voting for terror. For or against?"

Sam answered in a hollow voice.

"For."

And got up, bidding us farewell, with his eyes. Furtively, Markus shook hands with people, murmuring: "What luck!"

They slipped away, followed by Sonnenschein, who had been picked because of his innocuous appearance, to help them at the last minute. We prolonged the meeting. Evening had come very quickly under bursting clouds. The flaming tongues of the candles rose up in front of old Fomine, causing huge shadows to dance around us, and illuminating hands and faces frozen in an attitude of violence. We sang the "Farewell to the Dead" as at revolutionary funerals in Russia. That powerful lament, transforming masculine grief into solemn affirmation, drawing an act of faith from a farewell and an oath from tears, elevated the souls of thirty men, a few of whom were mediocre and the majority no different from most men. They were all sincere. They sang:

"Our path is the same as yours,
Like you, the prisons will destroy us . . ."

when a rifle shot tore through the rainstorm, the night, our song, sub-
merging us all suddenly in a glacial silence; only the rain, the faraway
howl of a watchdog could be heard; then a harsh voice:

"Halt there!"

And again the silence exploded on all sides in a clatter of rifle
fire which made our hearts leap, choked off the cries in our throats,
resounded in our skulls like madly clanging bells. And again the silence
descended immediately over the light drumming of the rain. The flaming tongues of the candles had not moved. Their raw light showed
three heads immobile, singularly inexpressive: Fomine; Gregor, huge,
his heavy jaw resting on powerful and clean hands; Krafft, exhausted,
thin-lipped, his eyes slightly compressed . . . For a second everyone could
cling to the wild idea that nothing had happened. But a formless moan,
a sob, the death rattle of a murdered man sent us dashing to the windows, fists clenched, yelling:

"Murderers! Murderers!"

During the night our prison wore a halo of white light. The squalls
of the rainstorm fought against the emptiness. A group of shadows disappeared at the edge of our field of vision. Our useless clamor was lost
in this whiteness and this night, this silence and this emptiness.

As the sentry watched, Sam had crossed the danger zone in three bounds.
He had managed successfully to climb over the barbwire fence, near a
stake. Markus and the Rumanian waited for him to get through: the huge
room was dark and empty behind them; Sonnenschein was guarding the
door. The night came in through the window, cold, damp, full of anguish.

"Your turn, Kagan," said Markus, smiling to his companion. "Sam
slipped through like a letter through the mail . . . If you have trouble
at the stake, wait for me."

The Rumanian made out clearly only the ominous words: "at the
stake." He leaned out and stared for a long time into the darkness.
The sentry was not visible, hidden in his sentry box; but the barrel of
his rifle shone out and perhaps the Rumanian sensed the furious eyes
of the watchman over the spiraled tube of steel: Floquette, with his
Mongol's head, hunched in on himself, all ears so as not to miss the
second escapee, the spy.

"Don't dawdle like that," urged Markus. "Go ahead. Give me your
arm . . ."

The Rumanian drew back sharply.

"No. I'm staying. I've changed my mind. Good luck."

His arms were trembling, his lips black on a face of gray canvas. Markus shrugged his shoulders, threw his leg over the windowsill, and let himself slide down the knotted blankets. The first gunshot crackled. Markus saw a flame obstructing his path. The searchlights were blinding him; he hadn't expected such a brilliant light, made more intense by the huge din of the explosion; he plunged ahead into the night directly in front of him, seized the fence, and began to climb—a splendid target hanging on barbwire. Coldly, Floquette fired on him at fifteen yards, cursing him under his breath: "Guzzle your Heinie gold, go on guzzle it, you bastard, you spy." They dragged him, bleeding into the mud, up to the infirmary. Billiard Ball ran up, pushing through the outraged group intent upon the dying man, and turned his flashlight on that young face, ravaged by his final suffering.

"Hell!" exclaimed the gendarme, "it's not him!"

"Quick, in God's name, the male nurse . . . Pick him up, you brutes!"

The Rumanian shivered in his bed, hideously happy, in every fiber of his being, that someone else had been killed in his place, but transfixed by the inescapable and devastating thought that now there was no escape possible and that the man who would be shot tomorrow would talk, would certainly talk . . .

TWENTY-NINE

Epidemic

SAM WAS RECAPTURED THE NEXT DAY AFTER COVERING FIFTEEN MILES OVER muddy roads.

Billiard Ball appeared in the large courtyard, his shoulders slumped, sullen and broken-hearted. To a group of Belgians who were standing around him he said: "It was a disaster. I would gladly have let him run, the poor lad . . ." A few men, their heads bowed, were staring fixedly at the holster of his revolver. The male nurse Jean passed by, trailing an odor of chloroform behind him. "They gave him six injections," he whispered, his eyes wide open, his stare vacant. He never sobered up any more. We were overwhelmed by this murder, which we could reconstruct to the last detail; we were overcome by the feeling of complete powerlessness. Nothing had yet been changed in Room III which Markus had occupied. His wicker trunk was there, his magazines, his toothbrush. The Rumanian was playing checkers in the Bonne Fortune cabaret with Monsieur Arthur. Both had the same flabby hands, long and white.

We deliberated. We would have liked an uprising. But we felt it to be impossible, futile; we were afraid: afraid of being cowardly, afraid of throwing ourselves into an adventure out of fear of being cowardly, afraid of our own impotence. Our repressed fury changed to disgust. We paced about as if in a cage weighing all the possibilities. What possible revolt against the thirty armed men who were guarding us with good rifles, starved as we were, without even a real knife? But just to let silence cover that pool of blood? What if we tried to protest, to demand an investigation? But a protest against whom? An investigation by whom? The Greeks had let us know that they would support us if we acted. We counted how many we were, eighteen trustworthy men, around ten more who would join us as long as *we* held out—twenty-eight—another ten hardy fellows who would join us. Thirty-eight out of four hundred. Fifty Greeks who could hold out for a good while. The rest more than doubtful, capable of supporting us in the beginning and giving in at the next moment.

A tall blond fellow, wearing a blue and white striped sailor's jersey, came to tell the Committee:

"Don't give in. I'll kill Floquette."

He had his plan. And a weapon: an iron bar, pointed at the end, patiently sharpened into a stiletto, which he had been carrying around for a long time, inside his pants' leg.

When we were alone together, he told me:

"I've been wanting to kill somebody for a long time now."

"Why, Ivan?"

With a circular gesture he pointed to the black and gray corridor where we were standing, the old worn-out planks under our feet, the wide-open window through which—at the foot of the church and a somber building—you could see men who looked like larvae dragging themselves around the yard: bent old men leaning on their canes, an idiot—always half-naked, always shivering, even in the sunlight—and some Greeks moving slowly in their dirty caftans.

"For this, for *everything*."

I asked:

"But what can *they* do about it?"

And I remembered—as I looked at his bowed head, hard shell of bone ready to plunge straight ahead, even against a wall, with its load of gray matter devastated by thought—I remembered the dazzled bull in the arena, that human ring, who feels himself the plaything of strange powers and tormenting insects dancing around him, golden, scarlet, vermilion, emerald green, and who wants, yearns with all his strength, the dark strength of a powerful beast bearing a prodigious load of vital ardor, to knock them down with his muzzle, to disembowel them with his horns, to crush them under his hooves, these dancing insects spinning all around him—men.

I explained to him that his primitive weapon, whose quadrangular point and metallic shimmer he was inspecting, would not accomplish anything; that his rebellion was just, but not well thought out; that Floquette, guilty or innocent, was in any case negligible; that we had to lock up everything inside ourselves, to forget nothing, to wait, know how to wait for years and to resist, because the time to change everything, to be the stronger, would come . . .

And, shaking his head, stubborn as an Andalusian bull, he began to smile vaguely.

However, the next day or the day after, an agitated hand rang the bell like a tocsin. Anxious soldiers appeared at the grill. Stormy groups milled around the yard protesting *because the beans were inedible.* We spoke of Markus in our harangues. There was hunger and there was blood. There was time and there was war.

And there was death.

It came without fanfare, simply, faceless, without terror, and it curbed the rebellion, which was ready to rise up, as a great wind curbs the sheaves of grain (—but the grain stands up again . . .).

A few Greeks feverish, had begun to cough, to moan. Little Nikos was delirious. We improvised a new infirmary in an empty room on the ground floor, known as the "schoolroom" which was used for our meetings . . . The bars on the windows, shaped like inverted hooks, projected crude fleurs-de-lis on the background of the green foliage in the garden. Nikos spent his last night there, alone, as in a bare chapel. He had the extremely red cheeks, the damp forehead, the intense stare of one who now can only look inwards. Jean was supposed to sit, up with him, but he fell asleep, drunk with ether, before a senseless letter from Stéphanie. When he awoke, at dawn, Nikos was frozen. His greenish body was marbled with gray spots, like the shadow of a panther skin. We had to place three living men beside him. Three men who looked as he had yesterday, who would be tomorrow what he was already today. The three were Greeks too, lined up together according to their age; one beardless, twenty years old; the other hirsute, forty; the third, a gray-bearded patriarch. The last alone had remained conscious—serious, still authoritarian, talking quietly to his bearers.

"What did he say?"

"He said to write to his sons that they shouldn't sell the house; to give his wool blanket to old Kostia—and also: 'Let the Devil take them, those sons of bitches!'"

That very day the Belgians were attacked. The new infirmary had five beds, six, seven in the evening (and Nikos' speckled corpse was still there, exuding a stale odor; for there were no coffins ready in the village; Monsieur Soupe, farsighted, but not farsighted enough, ordered a dozen of them—for which he received a commission of twenty-four francs). Sonnenschein and Faustin, two volunteers, watched over them in the glow of a kerosene lamp. The Jew had taken up a book; but the murmurs of the delirious, their calls, the white light cut off by stooped shadows which came through the bars from the outside, the smell of urine, of defecation and death, the tense silence of the dead created an atmosphere from which one could not hope to escape. Sonnenschein stood in the doorway in order to breathe in the cool night air, his arms folded, wiping his pince-nez from time to time—in his gestures and attitudes like the man on the pillory who stood out in my memory. He forced himself to think, calmly, like a wise man, about life, death, matter, spirit, eternity. Faustin II's tall dark body slipped noiselessly between the cots. A division of the labor had occurred of itself between the two men. The Negro, sure of his strength and conscious of the vulnerability of his ignorance, took upon himself the hard task of turning over the moaners on their damp cots, of taking them to urinate, of giving them something to drink, of keeping them covered at every moment, of forcibly restraining the delirious when they arose, going off with uncanny energy on God-knows-what voyages. Sonnenschein would explain, point things out, help . . . "What should I do?" Faustin asked him when a heavy-set man tied down to his cot tossed about ponderously and moaned loudly. Faustin seemed to have no fear of the corpses, who were like men asleep, yet immediately recognizable by the stiff way they were laid out, by an indefinable look of being broken-down or of hardness, which reduced them to objects; Faustin had all the gravity of a child performing a painful duty and desirous above all of pleasing the teacher. "Nothing to be done," answered Sonnenschein, underlining their common impotence with a gesture of his two open hands. And the Negro, smiling with all of his powerful teeth: commented, "Strong will live, weak will die."

The old patriarch fought on for two days and a night, keeping or recovering by moments his cruel clear-headedness. He only knew a few words of French mixed with slang. Each time he woke up he would raise his head and look around him, counting the living and the dead. He called Sonnenschein over with his eyes; and Sonnenschein, troubled by that clear look—as if he ought to be ashamed, himself, of letting his fellow creatures die and of surviving them, angry at himself for not knowing in what language to address this old man—would ask:

"*Comment ça va? Wie geht's? Nié loutché?*"

The patriarch's bloodshot eyes would move slowly and direct an unswerving glance, like an invisible ray, toward a form stretched out

nearby; his lips, at the same time gray and violet-tinged stirred, pro-
nouncing only one word:

"Croaked?"

Sonnenschein lacked the courage to lie—a lie would doubtless have
exasperated this solid old man, as would cheating on a bargain, or a pre-
caution unworthy of him in danger. But in order to comply with a desire
for dignity in death which he believed he sensed in him, Sonnenschein
would go over to the designated remains, close the dead man's eyelids
with his fingertips, and join his hands across his stomach. The patriarch followed all these movements with a serious attention in which
Sonnenschein discerned approbation. He alone out of eight was alive
on the third day. They didn't know what to do with him. The doctor
did not appear.

Before falling into a coma, the patriarch painfully stirred his great
arms, which made one think of the rugged branches of a felled tree.
Sonnenschein thought he understood his wish, went over, and gently,
but not without difficulty, raised his hands with their shapeless nails
like the worn claws of an old tiger—hands which had firmly held the
swing-plow, the ax, the knife, the woman's shoulder, the child's frail
body, the friend's hand . . . The Jew thought obscurely of those things
as he joined them over the huge tortured chest in which the heart made
a dull sound as of shovels of earth filling into a faraway grave.

"Good," said the old man.

It was still night. The twinkling stars emitted an extraordinary calm.
All at once to himself, Sonnenschein said that life is marvelous. He took
a few steps in the darkness, stumbling over some sharp stones, and pronounced aloud: "Marvelous." He looked at the stars, and, between them,
making his eyes blink, the tiny luminous points that were still more
stars. And he thought wordlessly of those countless worlds, of those
great fires gravitating through space, following necessary courses, of the
continents, of the races, of the cities, of the flowers, of the machines,
of the animals in the warm grass, the teeming water, the jungle, the
cold steppe, of the children who were laughing, at that moment, on
beaches in the sun, on the other side of the earth; a mother giving
suck to her greedy child, somewhere, perhaps in California, perhaps
in Malaysia, bronzed or copper-colored madonna . . . madonna with
half-closed eyes, with pointed breasts . . . white madonna . . . "But they
exist, they exist," thought Sonnenschein with astonished joy. "There is
no death," he said, surprised by his own words, without the presence

of cold corpses, behind him in the nauseating room, seeming to contradict the inexpressible affirmation with which he was brimming.

"Sonnenschein!"

Faustin II joined him. "Sonnenschein," he asked, "do you know
how to row?"—"No."—"It's good to row," said the Negro. He leaned
over, his neck bent, working imaginary oars with his Herculean arms.
"Like this. The night so. There are reeds, the river is terrible, you know,
calm and terrible, treacherous like a sleeping serpent . . ."—"What river,"
thought Sonnenschein, but without asking. He murmured:

"Yes, it's good to row, Faustin. You'll take up the oars again, Faustin,
on the peaceful and treacherous river."

THIRTY

The Armistice

UPON WAKING, PEOPLE WOULD WONDER WHO HAD DIED DURING THE NIGHT. We used to call the infirmary *the Morgue*. A sick man even said, feeling very low: "All right, I'm cooked. Take me off to the Morgue." They took him. He was an Alsatian or a Belgian, worker or peasant, one lad among many others about whom nothing in particular was known. The disease, obliterating his youth, depersonalized him even more. His greatest preoccupation during his last day was to prevent anyone from stealing his nickel-plated watch, attached to his wrist by a copper band. Consumed by fever, he would raise his arms: trying to join them behind his neck in order to hide the watch. We went to see him, Sonnenschein and I: he came out of his bewildered despair in order to wave good-by to us with his hand over his head: Farewell, farewell . . . The pain of death could be read clearly on that damp and dried-out face, as if ossified, streaked with purple, livid at the temples where the eyes, drowned in a haze, had an atrocious fixity. He was only one dead man among many others.

Almost all of us had been infected, but our group held out victoriously against the epidemic. From the beginning we had noticed that the disease only killed off the most miserable, the famished, the lice-infested. The Greeks, reduced for the most part to living off the administrative pittance, and whose hygiene was poor, had been the first to be touched. The Belgians and the Alsatians had been decimated. We Russians held out thanks to our solidarity. Our emergency fund provided just about enough extra provisions for even the least fortunate among us to keep the flame of life glowing, if only as an ember. We allowed no one to be carried off to the Morgue, while the others cleared their rooms of the feverish at the first opportunity. We went to bed, one after the other, teeth chattering, while the convalescents and those who had been spared watched over the sick. We continued to struggle, to think. To a comrade rolled up in his covers, his burning head buried in a pillow covered by an old dishrag, we had to bring the news of the day—dispatches from the front: the Château-Thierry "pocket," the last big push of the Central Powers against Paris; dispatches from Russia: terror, exploits of the Czechoslovaks, "barbarism of the Chinese and Lett praetorians forming the People's Commissars' guard," denial of the rumor of Trotsky's assassination, Lenin's recovery, nationalization of heavy industry—and the sick man would chuckle, think things over, want to argue: and this signaled the victory of life within him . . .

I'll never forget the joy of a young lad who had really thought he was a goner for a while; he kept silent, but his eyes cried out his anguish. Every time we approached him, he would follow our movements with a sort of dread and a terrible cough would wrack his body. We finally understood that he was afraid we had come to tell him that it was necessary to move him to the infirmary. "As for me," said Sonnenschein in an offhand way, standing in front of his bed, "I don't let anybody go down there." A morning came when the sick man felt saved. I could see it in his eyes as soon as I had crossed the threshold of Room II. He was lying in the back, only his head emerging from under the covers; but he greeted me from afar with such a spring like smile that I myself was refreshed, like a thirsty man who has just tossed off a big glass of spring water. What life-giving spring water flowed from him to me, from him to everyone! For several days he was radiant with his joy of living, too great to be expressed, and which he held in, besides, out of a kind of modesty; and this gave him the confused air of young lovers whose secret is discovered, who blush, betray themselves, smile, recover themselves . . . He had taken up but little place among us until then, but he became dear and close to us because of his happiness and the good that his happiness did us. The group was no longer complete without him. A new ardor made his limbs more supple. I don't know what quality of nimbleness and frolicsomeness in the movements of this young man whom I had known and ignored as taciturn made me think of the delightful spontaneity, of young kittens . . . He would laugh gladly, and even when he wasn't laughing, his eyes still laughed.

People continued to die around us, a little more slowly since the more helpless were now sleeping in the little Trécy cemetery behind a low church with a pointed spire; some of them with white wooden crosses, like those which were planted in such numbers at the Front, the others, more numerous, under a common mound. The life of the

camp continued unchanged above the Morgue and those graves. Is it
not as simple to die as to live?

Men had been killed during those days, somewhere, in commonplace
trenches over which hope passed, like a putrefying breeze. They were
the last dead of the war; and we thought about them, I don't know
why, with an even more indignant sadness. The Armistice exploded
above us like a dazzling rocket, tracing a meteoric curve through the
sky of our gray life. In the yard, radiant soldiers carrying newspapers
mingled together with groups which would suddenly come together
and then fly apart in an explosion of shouts: men began to run up and
down the stairways, pursuing each other, pursued by their joy. Armistice,
peace, the end of the nightmare, the end of captivity? We shared in
that great joy, we too were carried away. The minutes which passed
were henceforth no longer those of immense fratricide. But we were
full of second thoughts:

"It's a crushing victory," said Krafft.

"Therefore: no revolution. Order, triumph, trophies, parades, the
survivors' pride guaranteeing that the sufferings and the deaths would
be forgotten, apotheosis of the generals."

"Here, yes," resumed Fomine . . . "And for the moment. But over
there it's already the revolution, the true victory of the vanquished,
born in defeat."

Yes. Over there and here. Wherever it may be, this victory of the
vanquished, lighting its torches now in Kiel, in Berlin, in Vienna, in
Budapest, in the flames of red flags; proclaimed by Liebknecht, come
out of prison to harangue the crowds from the Emperor's balcony ("...
he took to his heels, the Kaiser, like a rabbit")—this victory is ours! What
leaps it is making, from the Neva, from the Volga, to the Vistula, to the
Rhine, to the Escaut! Will the old armies, heavy with their old, deadly
victories, be able to stop it? We concluded, in turn, that it was impossible and that it was probable.

The Morgue had its contingent of half-dead men. They heard the
Armistice being acclaimed. An excited group burst through the door
of their cold and nauseating room. They were able to glimpse the
upturned faces, the open arms calling to them; they could hear the vigorous voices calling to them:

"The grip can't hold us any more! This time it's peace! Get up!"

"Get up!" shouted another enthusiast before they dragged him off and the door was closed again over the tumultuous apparition, reflected without astonishment in the glassy eyes of the dying men.

One of them, benumbed by a feverish somnolence, would question me every time I went to see him. The effort he had to make in order to speak and understand dilated his pupils. "What's happening?" he finally articulated. I leaned over to his ear and I said forcefully, but too loud not to trouble the silence of the room, "The Armistice!" But he couldn't understand and would ask, an hour later, with the same effort: "What's happening?" And I answered him, as best as I could, like a man trying to make himself understood through walls—but already there was nothing left for him.

The Baron was dying in a deserted room, on the second floor, along with another moribund. They had not been sent to the Morgue on account of their lucidity. The room was illuminated by bay windows full of a milky sky. These two men had dysentery or intestinal typhus. A horrible stench thickened the air around them. They were in the throes of death amid defecation, light, and calm.

We had seen the Baron go down slowly among us, step by step, on the invisible stairway to that level which was even more piteous than the grave in which his remains would soon be laid out. We had known him elegant, dressed in a gray hunting costume, his calves molded by leather leggings. He smoked a handsome meerschaum pipe: and his eyes, gray like his mustache, leveled a distant but good-natured glance at people. Months passed without letters, without hope, without money. Somewhere in Flanders a patriotic notary was looking after his estate and cheating him. He borrowed from Maerts in order to amble in the Bonne Fortune cabaret. We saw him wash his own linen, swap his hunting jacket for an old soldier's tunic, and take his seat, his mustache drooping and his eye humiliated, next to Lamblin who would say to him, familiarly: "Willya 'ave a coffee, Baron." He would borrow thirty centimes from people without returning them. "A moocher," they said. His badly patched shoes became broken-down clodhoppers. He was a poor wretch. The Flemish used to call him *Barontje*. He had a yellow complexion, cheeks covered with an ashy brush, a lifeless gaze. He sold his bread to buy cigarettes. Now his tall body, thin and hairy, is being slowly drained of its blood, its strength, of everything. A pile of shapeless old clothes rests on a stool at his bedside. Faustin II, who had been taking care of him, has fallen sick as well. "There's nothing left to do," says Jean, the male nurse. "Let him be." His cot, caked with defecations, is like a dung heap. He moans feebly, falls asleep, is delirious at moments, falls back into a torpor full of dreams . . . It is then he calls Charlie, his handsome intelligent setter, stuffs his pipe, and sets off on the Campine road, walking stick in hand, greeted by the people he passes; the road turns, lined with alder trees; cows watch this peaceful man go by; the animals belong to Jef van Daele, a sly chap who knows everything about breeds and prices, really a character out of Brueghel, that fat Jef, and a joker, but what a shot with a bow and arrow . . . He enters the Cabaret du Coq, but that's not old Mother Mietje bringing him his gin at his usual seat near the window through which he can see the gray waters of the Nethe—it's Maerts, a huge Maerts, whose bearded head, covered by a little dented hat, grows larger, puffs up, blocks the window, is about to crash through the ceiling and knock down the poster-covered walls. "You didn't expect to find me here, eh Monsieur le Baron?" mocks that formidable disembodied head. "Ah! Bastard!" cries the Baron, and he strikes with all his strength, strikes that monstrous, fantastic head which bounces back flabbily under his blows without ceasing its mocking laughter . . .

That head is shouting. What is it shouting? "*Vive la paix! Vive la France!*" What peace? The room is white, invaded by sky. "This one's croaking, that's for sure . . ." From the second floor, through the glass door, the noisy progress of a wild farandole can be seen. The door opens and there stand Maerts, Lamblin, Arthur, Jean, and others; they enter, arm in arm, joyous, but repressing a shudder . . .

"Baron," says Maerts, "gotta get better! There's peace!"

"Get better, my poor fellow," says Jean, his eyes humid, in the tone of voice in which he would have said, "better die."

The Baron follows their more and more muddled group with his eyes. He was understood irrevocably: he no longer can feel his feet, which had been cold. His stomach is a stone. Tears gather in the corner of his eyes and roll down into his mustache.

THIRTY-ONE

Hostages

OUR FATE, HOWEVER, WAS BEING DECIDED THOUSANDS OF LEAGUES FROM there. Moscow was sleeping the tense and heavy sleep of cities where famine, fear, energy, and the unknown are at work. In a large apartment in the Hotel Metropole, furnished with Louis XVI consoles, glass-front cupboards for porcelains—now stuffed with files—and gilded chairs loaded down with papers, in which the disorder reigning was that of an old and slightly eccentric scholar, an old emigré, grizzled and hunch-backed, with the delicate gestures of a numismatist, was wearily moving papers around on his mahogany Empire desk ornamented at the corners by gilded lions' heads. There were newspapers brought by courier from the borders, all of which had become battlefields, some of them marked with checks in red pencil, American books, tracts published in Paris by the Committee for the Third International, copies of a review from Geneva, decrees reproduced by typewriter, sealed envelopes bearing the stamp of the Central Committee and sheets of notepaper carrying only a few words followed by initials: "Reject the Swedish proposal," or "Please have some canned foods given to Mr. Hastings." And rough drafts of diplomatic notes on the backs of sheets from desk calendars . . . This particular paper had almost got lost between a glass of tea, the erotic correspondence (devoid of interest) seized on the person of a spy, and a stack of papers to be filed. If it had been lost, would not our fates have been lost too for a few days, enough for the rebellion or the epidemic? The old emigré read it with his habitual attention, the attention of an extremely conscientious functionary, interrupting his reading for a sip of detestable KINGDOM OF DENMARK tea (followed by an involuntary grimace: that lowest grade tea in hard tablets sent by the Kouznetzov brothers from Central Asia . . .). Since it was six in the morning and this man was fighting against such great fatigue that his eyelids drooped irresistibly, heavy with sleep, his mind was no longer able to master the words entirely. He thought: "Elsinore . . . 'Something is rotten in the state of Denmark . . .' Who said that?" And, his eyes completely shut, remembered: "Marcellus, in the first act." *Red Cross.* What's this business all about? Another intercession for some executed bankers? This probability added weight to his fatigue. As if he could do anything about it! There was nothing to do, after all, but send an evasive answer . . . "The projected exchange of hostages could take place on the Finnish border . . ." Suddenly the man felt completely awake. Two lists of names were annexed to the letter. Generals, colonels, captains, ah! that little lieutenant who so stupidly let himself get arrested in that Yaroslav bridge business . . . and that general who was seen trembling right after the attempted assassination, when everyone still thought Lenin was dying, that general who said that "personally he had nothing to do with it . . ." Personally, by God! What a mess on this desk where a paper of such importance had been lost for two days. (". . . I need a good secretary, but where can I find one?" Eyelids heavy.) Lets look at the other list. *Civilian Internees:* Potapenko, mechanic; Krafft, chemist; Fomine, commercial traveler; Levine, tailor, and his family, seven persons; Sonnenschein . . . Not a single recognizable name: no doubt, as usual, fifty per cent scoundrels and adventurers. That will give us a little more: a drop in the ocean . . . This business must be expedited rapidly. Let's get rid of these generals whose precious skins are difficult to preserve in periods of plebeian terrorism . . .

Thus the exchange of hostages was decided, signed two days later. The city lay under a blue haze, brightened slightly by a layer of snow covering all things. The façade and the white columns a the Grand Theater looked out on a huge deserted square where the night lay over the whiteness, twinkling in places, without smothering it. A little black stone lay encrusted there in a dead flowerbed; one might have thought it the tip of a grotesque rock flowering there above the earth in the middle of the city. It was in fact a block of granite, the color of old blood, of rust and coral, bearing these words:

This
is the first stone
of the monument to be raised
to
KARL MARX
leader and guide of the proletariat

All of us did not leave. This sudden denouement disconcerted Fomine, who had been living in Paris for thirty years and who, for twelve years, had made a nook for himself in Fontenay-aux-Roses, peopled with voices and works dedicated to the revolution. The Revolution of '89 gave his study its atmosphere. An autograph of Collot d'Herbois, under glass, hung alongside The Incorruptible's profile, engraved, on the occasion of the Festivals of Reason, by a sycophant artist; a precious copy of Baboeuf's *Tribune of the People*, dating from the good period—not the one when the Egalitarian was a Thermidorian but the one when he was repenting for having been one—was placed under beveled glass in one of the corners of the worktable. Memoirs of that period, along with Taine and Jaurès, filled a whole glassed-in cupboard; Marx and the Russians held another; Kropotkin and Sorel, the anarchists and syndicalists, a third. "All the explosives which will blow up the modern world are stored within these three panels," Fomine would sometimes say. These three libraries looked out through a large bay window over the garden, between the thickets and the lilacs. The old man used to return there after his errands in Paris, disgusted by the world, pleased by his successful deals, despising himself a little for having pulled them off successfully, but looking forward with pleasure to the profits he had made (he had two ways of announcing that he was an insurance salesman: one full of dignity and spirit, with the squaring of the shoulders and the brow of a businessman confident of overcoming all objections—and the other, toneless, without any pride, in front of certain comrades). Back in his "lair" he recovered his real face, that of an exile who will never give in; his real step (muffled by slippers), that of a leader of men whose time is past or has not yet arrived; his real thoughts, the thoughts of a saboteur—and his confidence in the future. He trusted serenely in history, that abstract divinity which leads peoples, prosperous or impoverished, from catastrophes to revolutions; in good books; in correct theories; in comrades, whoever they might be, his hand forever open with welcome or aid, not in the least a dupe of their pettinesses, their stupidities and dishonesties, but certain that everything is settled in the long run and that the future makes its way, making use of petty rascals and thoroughgoing scoundrels, idiots and men of intelligence, cowards and brave men, errors and truth, all at the same time. They would come to ask him for articles (signed, out of prudence, with pseudonyms), addresses, advice, money. The Armistice signed, he had expectations of going back to his "old lady" with whom, for a third of a century, he had been living "in free union," so that the whole neighborhood believed they were legally married. If the revolution should need his head one day, all right, on Sansom-Deibler's machine or in any other way[10]—"it's still good for taking, my head!"—he was ready at any moment ("after all it's not my library that would weigh in *that* balance!")—but to speak the truth, though he didn't say so, he no longer felt strong enough to leave his lair forever and to plunge into the unknown at an age when Bakunin himself was retiring. In order to justify himself in front of us he searched for contradictory reasons; he would be more useful by staying. We voted our approval, for everyone does his task in his place, as long as he really wants to. Sam murmured with an equivocal smile: "You will be the repository of our illusions."

That question settled, Fomine considered us with a new sadness. Suddenly he felt himself old, bothered again by a rheumatic ache in the knee; he was on the point of sending his library, Fontenay-aux-Roses and the rest, to the Devil. "Well, too bad," he said to himself. "My old lady can leave too . . ." But the thought that the two of them would be plunging into the great storm of clubs, "days" in the squares, red flags, firing squads—he, all white and suffering from his knee; she, hunched, enslaved for such a long time under the drudgeries of housework—was even worse than the pain of watching us leave.

Krafft, without any explanation, announced that he was staying too. "Take me along!" demanded Faustin II.

He had been coughing for several days. His handsome vigor had suddenly left him. Slightly stooped, his shoulder blades sticking out under an old lightweight spring overcoat which was too short and too tight and which he couldn't even button, he went up and down the stairways leaning on the banister; his hands, whose fingers were terminated by nails that were almost white, seemed to have faded. He hardly laughed any more: and when he did laugh, his softened lips parted over anemic gums which were tinted with the nasty bluish pink of disease. He was still holding up, however, The announcement of our departure caused him a strange sorrow, which he only realized himself while watching us pack our bags, when the corners of the room were empty and when it became clear to him, with inexorable clarity, that twenty men whom

---

10 Family of French executioners, 1740–1840, *père et fils*. Killed Louis XVI and Marie Antoinette.

he knew well, with whom he had looked after the sick, taken the dying to the Morgue, survived, would no longer be there in a few hours.

He sat down on the partition next to Sonnenschein, who was leaving him his blankets, remained there without speaking, his hands clasped on his knees, his jaw hanging, like an old man. "Don't worry about it," Sonnenschein said to him. "The war is over. Soon you'll be free."

He replied only after a long moment of silence.

". . . I don't need much."

And he stared at us with a discouraged smile, as vulnerable as a child. How like that other Faustin he seemed to me at that moment: his unknown double, that soldier who was doubtless long buried in some lousy corner of Champagne! It was really the same expression as that of a man who has a mistake to be forgiven for—but what mistake he didn't know himself?—and would like to lie, perhaps to lie to himself, but feels that it's useless.

"Farewell, Faustin."

We set off one evening, over dark roads, twenty men flanked by gendarmes and home guards. We went along with such a lively step that we dragged our escort behind, striking the hard earth with our hobnailed boots. The whole camp had given out a shout when they saw us go. We were leaving its misery surrounded by barbwire; we were entering the night, going toward a distant conflagration. The camp cheered us; clusters of hands stretched out toward us, the bad, the vile and the unclean along with the others. Now we were a troop on the march, projected toward a goal thousands of miles distant, but one already strong with an immense élan, for the whole past was but an élan, and the very earth, stuffed with dead men, seemed to rebound under our feet like a springboard . . .

Some policemen in plain clothes took charge of us in a small railroad station. We felt singularly free and proud, still captives, but from now on following our own road: that road toward the great victory of our people . . . We traveled in second-class coaches. Our thinness and our shabby belongings contrasted with the luxury of the blue compartments and the well-dressed bulk of the gentlemen—more suspicious than we—who guarded the doors at stops while chatting agreeably with us. Dust of the vanquished that we were, leftovers from struggles without glory—for it is the masters who give out the glory—here it was that we answered for the very precious existence of generals destined for all times to judge us; here it was that they answered for us, hostages themselves, before the revolution, our victory.

"What do you say about it, Sam?"

"I say that it's beginning too well. I hardly believe it."

"I say it's about time!" murmured Dmitri, standing at the coach window, so thin that we wondered whether he would last out the voyage.

The train passed through a town at the Front. Gutted houses opened their dead insides, papered with bright wallpaper, to the wind. Blackened timbers lay all about a station whose metal roof supports were twisted and ripped apart. We stopped for a moment in a sort of dismal suburb: the white wooden crosses filled the landscape.

Overworked women pushed through the blue mobs at the stations under the December rains. Houses leaning over, sometimes crushed in, their windows cut out like dark wounds, watched peace being born in boundless fatigue. Red Cross ladies, blond, powdered, elegant, and attractive, appeared, placed there like tall sheaves of brilliant flowers at the doors of neat barracks. "Devotion in lace," said Sam. In a dark city, beneath the spire of a cathedral, there were mutilated houses held up by beams as if on crutches; a dark cabaret, brimming with exhausted Britons, and Dmitri, whom we had brought there searching for a hot supper, talking to them in English; and suddenly their handshakes, the enthusiasm in their eyes, a whole circle of anxious faces around us saying, "Us too! us too!" with a profound accent of menace and of hope. "A whole camp mutinied near Calais," a skinny Tommy whispered to us, like a miner out of the mine, on the sly so as not to be noticed by the embarrassed gentleman who accompanied us . . .

Some poor bastards of Bavarian peasants floundering about in the mud, under a rain as sad as their days—and so many of ours—were watching the trains go by from behind barbwire; in order to greet them we waved a red handkerchief which provoked a confused commotion among them.

And then the sea.

THIRTY-TWO

"As in Water, the Face of a Man . . ."

THE GREEK STEAMER *ANDROS*, SAILING UNDER FRENCH REGISTRY, WAS CAR-
rying seventeen hundred Russian wounded and convalescents in its
hold and steerage: a whole starving mob, like ourselves guarded by tall
Senegalese, savage shepherds of this peaceful flock. We occupied comfortable first- and second-class cabins: Other groups had joined ours and,
since the exchange was arranged by head, children were counted as hostages too. A few gangs of undesirables, collected off the slum streets of
Paris and Toulon, delighted by the clean whiteness of the cabins and
the good food, were living a waking dream there. The North Sea was
tinted with gray silk and silvery reflections; heavy white clouds scuttled
ceaselessly by. Derelict hulks were often sighted. A destroyer, slicing
through the waves in front of us, shelled a mine, a black object which
you could see, through field glasses, floating like a cork; a tall geyser of
splashing water, a fantastic palm tree surging out of the waves and then
immediately engulfed, erased that floating death. The hazes in the evening glowed red, splendid as in the first days of the earth. Children and
childlike young women leaned over the bulwarks with us before these
flaming horizons. Streams of gold on the surface of the sea ran right
up to us. In the end, the pale blues came inexorably over the sky, soon
dotted by the winking points of the constellations. At times the long
brilliant shafts of searchlights would glide through the night in even
flight. We watched the land appear and disappear; outlined so lightly
on the horizon that they hardly seemed to exist: Denmark, Sweden,
islands. Even the cold seemed tonic and purifying.

I loved to follow the sober curve of the seagulls' flight around the ship.
The extended shapes—gliding, piercing—of the white birds had, in their
capricious yet precise flight, an almost perfect harmony. I thought of

the beauty of a law fulfilled with simplicity. I should have wished for a fate similar to that sinuous yet direct curve of white flight above the foam, in the vast pale light. To accomplish one's task among those who are moving ahead, to accomplish it simply, without weakening or souring, as difficult as it might be. And with our eyes open: refusing to lie to others, refusing to lie to oneself.

We were nearing our goal. The prow of the *Andros* was slicing through new oceans with powerful ease. The waves, now milky, now oily, mirrored the white Baltic skies.

We were approaching the revolution with each turn of the ship's screws. I was seized by a certain anxiety, as at the end of any long wait, as on the eve of any great accomplishment. It would no longer be books, theories, dreams, newspaper clippings, reminiscences from history, the inexpressed, the inexpressible; it would be reality. Men similar to all men, things, struggles. Struggles against ourselves and among ourselves. Were we not to be overrun, after the conquest, by the sly, the adaptable, the false companions? That crowd would come to us because we were the power. To be the power: what a weakness! The dregs that were in us, a little in each of us, would ferment. How does one contain in oneself the old man ready to take over?

At least hall of us, even on this ship, saw in the victory only an adventure doubled by a conquest; they were arriving, their souls greedy to *take*, to become masters in their turn, to eat their fill, to open for their children a life which, in the end, they envisioned according to old examples. They would fight for that against all comers and even against each other. They had just been arguing, with a sharpness ill-masked by comradeliness, over two trunks of warm clothing. Professor Alschitz, arching his narrow shoulders, was saying: "In Odessa? But my dear friend, I will immediately be elected to the Soviet." A swarthy old man was already preparing a denunciation against his bunkmate. And we had good reason to be keeping on eye on *him*.

Weren't we running the risk of being conquered by our own conquest, of being ourselves overcome by the evils we were fighting against? What was to become of our comrades' solidarity? How were we to find ourselves, to recognize each other in the crowd of newcomers, false enthusiasts, masqueraders of the day after the victory? Would we not be too overburdened with functions and tasks, sometimes terrible ones, even to dream of it? Would I have the right, who, according to history, judged the terror to be necessary, to push aside the hand which offered me the weapon and to answer the man who says to me, *"Go, and strike; I am spent"*—to answer him abjectly, "No, I want to keep my hands clean, go ahead and dirty your own, comrade; I'm squeamish about my soul, you see, in these times when that is really the question! and I'll leave all the dirty jobs to you . . . ?" We would have to be hard on ourselves, in order to be hard on others, since we were at last the power. It would be necessary to stop at nothing, or all would be lost. Would we be strong enough? Would we be worthy of you, Revolution? Would we be able to consent to the inevitable sacrifice of the best among us? Are we sufficiently tempered? The prisons, the poverty, the concentration camps from which we have come, the epidemics, the vanquished rebellions, the strikes, the trials, the death of our brothers, all of this has become a providential preparation. But other men, of another stamp, one which might not please us, would they not soon be stronger than we, better adapted to the realistic work to be done? Would we know how to recognize, in reality, the unexpected face of justice, would we know how to distinguish the necessary from the arbitrary, compromise from treason? Things never turn out the way one dreams about them. We must not be imprisoned by dreams or by theories. But then what guides remain?

Sam joined me on the deck, taciturn. His usual half-smile had disappeared. His hollow-checked profile seemed sharper than usual.

"I'm thinking about Pittsburgh," he said. "I had set up a bicycle repair shop which brought in a hundred dollars a week. I wavered. To leave? Not to leave? It was all right, Pittsburgh. But Europe: war and revolution. Chaos. I could no longer live back there. The restaurants, the people, the policemen, The Star-Spangled Banner, my own Uncle Sam's face in the mirror, disgusted me. O.K. Now here we are practically in the eye of the hurricane. We're about to arrive in the middle of chaos."

He became his usual mocking self again.

"I'm wondering whether I'm not an idiot?"

"An idiot, no. But perhaps you would have done better to stay in Pittsburgh."

We need whole men, cast in a solid block, in work, in suffering, in rebellion; men born for this victory; men made for holding a rifle in the Red Guards as firmly as they hold their tools, able to carry out the tasks of organized revolt with the expert attention of sailors rapidly tightening a knot; men like Karl and Gregor, a calm spark of joy in their eyes, who pass by on their morning walk around the deck, thinking about the day's weather, greeting the black sentry keeping watch on the spar deck with a smile.

The sentry returns their greeting with his eyes. Sheathed in sheep-skin, a thick leather belt tightened around his waist, a flattened nose, eyes black under the gay helmet, strap across his chin—he is a warrior of former times, a slave trained for murder, placed here, on the thresh-old of our freedom, to call us back to an inexorable law . . . whom we disarm with a fraternal smile.

Last night an incident took place. Out of fraud or negligence, the authorities who drew up the lists of hostages had placed on them, despite us, some commonplace adventurers, happy to declare them-selves "politicos" and to go looking for profitable fishing in the troubled waters of a revolution. There are a dozen of them among the forty of us. They play cards in the smoking room. They intervene cautiously in our conferences. They despise us somewhat, fear us obscurely, hate us certainly. Two of them had had a fight over a missing card. They were on their feet, swearing at each other—one had a puffed eye, the other a bloody lip—from opposite sides of the polished oak table on which the square of green felt had slipped, forming a diamond. The ship was pitching slightly; they were bobbing about, ready to let their fists fly, shoulders hunched, necks drawn in, foreheads low, of pimps getting ready for a knife fight. Karl and Gregor entered. "Enough!" said Karl in a commanding voice. "Watch what you are getting mixed up in!" said one of the men, over, his shoulder, without ceasing to stare at his oppo-nent. But he didn't even have to touch him. Never had Gregor's square face been more massive; he repeated tranquilly:

"Enough, Davidsohn, if you don't want to get a bullet through the head when we arrive. We don't fool around with your kind."

The brawl quieted down under our threats. Happily, no one, no out-sider, had seen it. Our Committee met a little later on the deck. Gregor spoke, punctuating his words with a short gesture, sharp and heavy, of his clenched fist. He was saying simple and terrible things, as if he were chopping down an old rotten tree, which had become an obstacle, with solid ax blows. Even his sentences had the dull echo of blows struck into worm-eaten wood. "What to do with that riffraff? What do they have in common with the proletariat? What do they want from the revolu-tion? I say we must show them a fist of iron. I say that the terror must not only strike down the bourgeoisie, but also hit the scoundrels, the rotten apples, the filth carriers, that whole vermin which will infect us with its syphilis if we don't treat it with the hot iron . . . We don't have the time to weigh each piece of slime and then sweep it quietly off to the sewers. You besmudge the revolution? You cheat at cards and sell women while we fight for expropriation? And then you come and lie in our faces, rotten bastard? No speeches. We are purifiers . . .

As we approached our goal a kind of transformation came over Karl and Gregor: our common transformation, but sharper, I don't know why. It is stiffening inside. They have always held themselves straight, whatever the circumstances; but a new assurance reinforces their footsteps, they cast a commanding gaze over men and things, they already see themselves, confusedly, as organizers, fighters, masters . . . One feels they are ready to unleash a force tamed and turned around, the discipline of the great American warships which they underwent for a long time, and to which they owe their martial step, their cleanliness, the methodical use of their days.

Gregor is here. We watch the foam bubbling along the sides of the ship. We have been talking about trifles. We have laughed. We notice chunks of ice floating on the crests of waves: the frozen seas and lands are near . . . Suddenly he looks into my eyes as if opening his soul to me.

"So, we are arriving. So, it's true. It's real. Can you believe it?"

"I believe it."

The lieutenant, dressed in horizon blue, who is passing behind us on the deck, cannot understand why we suddenly take each other by the shoulders, like men who find each other at last after having looked for each other for a long time and whose lightheartedness is such that they would like to fight joyfully . . .

The *Andros* has entered a snowstorm. The siren wails every quarter of an hour. We are passing through old mine fields in this white fog. Heavy floating blocks of ice strike the ship's hull with a dull noise. Sonnenschein, hunched as always, his pince-nez askew, takes my arm in the stark white second-class corridor. His happiness is expressed in wringing his hands without reason and in a dull desire to laugh—a low, mischievous laugh. "Listen to a good story," he says. I suspect that he actually makes them up himself; this one, however, ends with a proverb of Solomon which he pronounces with a kind of somewhat confused gravity: "As in water face answereth to face, / So the heart of man to man."

"Isn't that so?"

A long whistle pierces through the storm over the sea; the *Andros* comes to a halt. We look at each other, smiling for an instant, in the sudden silence, and we enter the Levines' cabin.

There are seven of them, including four children and a very young woman, the most solemn of the children. The father's voice, energetic and talkative, fills the narrow cabin, which is full of shining brass work and has doubtless never yet seen such passengers—immigrants suddenly come up from steerage. The mother, soft, white, a little heavy, watches over her brood with an imperious love. Her life consists in nourishing—first with her body, then with her breasts, then with her housewife's hands—these greedy lives that have come out of her without her knowing why, that have martyred her on hospital beds in Buenos Aires, that have made her happy, anxious, cruel. The father speaks a polyglot enriched by the slang of the docks. A good animal warmth emanates from them and attracts us—the homeless, familyless, used to cold beds. "My children," says Levine, "will grow up free. Famine? I've known it all my life." Like most eloquent phrases pronounced with sincerity by people who don't know how to tone down their involuntary cleverness, this one rings a little false. For his whole life this man has been battling like a primitive in foreign cities so that his kids should have warm bellies in the evening, covered by blankets bought on credit. He has been knavish and valiant, ardent and clever, lucky and unlucky, never forgetting however that it is necessary to struggle, as well as one can, against the rich—the rich whom you admire, envy, detest—to organize unions, to support strikes, to send money to distant prisons, to hide contraband . . . He tells us about a pitiful, jobless day spent searching for bread for his brood in a large, opulent port city. Was he lucky, that day, mistaking one streetcar for another and ending up in the harbor just in time for the arrival of an American freighter? Thus his life took a new track, thirteen years ago . . . The young woman, still only a solemn child, with narrow hips and breasts barely suggested under her blue jersey, listens distractedly. Her features are barely sketched in; the slight carmine of her lips is going to disappear or become more pronounced; her brow is half-hidden under a cloud of hair; she has a direct glance, timid and luminous; large eyes the color—sometimes green, sometimes blue, sometimes gray—of the sea we are crossing. "The greatest happiness," she told us one day, "is to have children."

THIRTY-THREE

The Essential Thing

OUR FOOTSTEPS SINK INTO THE SOFT SNOW. WE ARE ENTERING A NEW NIGHT, biting with cold, transparent as if under a totally black crystal dome. Our convoy moves ahead by groups, loaded down with packages, tripping over invisible obstacles under the snow. Children are crying, terrified by such deep darkness, their fingers frostbitten. We are being escorted by gaunt shadows. They move about lightly at the dividing line between reality and the bottomless darkness which begins at either edge of the road under the dense blackness of tall pines. I know that they are blond Finns, dressed in long overcoats, armed with the short carbines of border guards. Their eyes, in which the image of cold lakes is reflected, have been watching over us for two days with an impassable hostility. They are mute. They move forward, opening up the night. They halt. The darkness slowly engulfs them. We are still moving ahead into a sort of glacial no man's land . . . A motionless shape emerges suddenly from the night, so close when we notice it that we can touch it. It is a soldier, standing stock-still, leaning with both hands on his rifle, covered with earth, wearing an astrakan hat, bearded up to his glowing wolf-like eyes—an emaciated *muzhik*. The red star incrusted in the fur above his forehead glows black like a fantastic wound on an animal skin. We greet him in a low voice, with an exalted, but curiously heavy heart. "Greetings, brother!" Our brother, this soldier, stares at us severely . . . Brothers? brothers? Are we really brothers? What man is not a threat to another man? Karl plants himself in front of him and his resonant voice, dispelling all unreality, cuts through the night. The no man's land has been crossed.

"Greetings, comrade. What's the news?"
"Nothing . . . Hunger . . . Nothing."
What is nothing? Hunger?
"Do you have any bread?"

We have some. Take, Comrade. Bread, that is the essential thing.

Lanterns ran up and down the tracks. A dark shape counted us without seeming to see, us as we moved by. We might have thought we were in a hostile desert. The locomotive whistled. The coaches were dark and frozen, but inside them we found straw on the long lateral bunks, a good cast-iron stove and piles of cordwood. The fire sparkled; the glow of candles surrounded us, in this encampment on wheels, with a primitive intimacy.

We passed slowly through a strange, black and white lunar landscape. Not a single light. The train rolled through this frozen desert until dawn, which rose over the crystalline, iridescent snows, as pure as on mountaintops. Little wooden houses appeared, grouped around the blue bulbs of a church. Fields of snow were stretched out to either side, piled up in oddly shaped drifts: we perceived at last that it was a deserted station. The sky had a blue, near-white, unutterable purity. The first houses of the city appeared in absolute silence, immobile, peaceful. Our hearts were more and more constricted. Not a soul. Not a noise. Not a tuft of smoke. This implacable splendor of the snow, the polar limpidity of the sky. The dead houses were terrifying.

Ah!

A thin line of smoke rose above a chimney. And all at once, a marvelous apparition, a golden-haired young woman, wearing a red kerchief on her head, doming out of a gray hovel with a hatchet in her hand, began to chop wood, some hundred yards off. We listened avidly to that rhythmic sound, we admired the virile curve of her bare arms. Dmitri, whose last strength was waning, forced a smile.

"We are out of the darkness at last," he said.

The train came to a halt. We had spent the day rolling through the deserts of the outlying railroad yards. The *Internationale* broke out in a din of brasses. A long red banner, running across the fronts of the wooden shelters, cried out: "WELCOME TO THE CAPTIVES OF IMPERIALISM!" The snow-covered wooden platform seemed deserted, however. We saw only about thirty people huddling under a wide calico banner (THE REIGN OF THE WORKERS WILL LAST FOREVER!), the band, and a few men dressed in black leather and carrying heavy Mausers in wooden holsters at their waists. The brasses fell silent; a tall devil sheathed in a reversed sheepskin, but wearing a light English cap on his head, jumped up on a bench. He had a resounding voice, made for dominating crowds, which flowed over our little group and carried off into the distance in the vast empty station. He began to speak all at once, without looking at us, his eyes circled by little silver-rimmed glasses, his chin black, his mouth enormous. While he was talking, we noticed the motionless musicians, a dozen yellowed faces, bony noses, beards like burnt grass—faces lined with deep fatigue. They were wearing old, unmatched uniforms, all equally gray, and various forms of headgear: huge white fur bonnets, astrakan hats, the flat caps of the old army. The trombone player had put on a pair of magnificent green gloves. Others had red hands, stiffened by the cold. Some wore old gloves, of leather or cloth and full of holes. They were of every age, from eighteen to sixty. An old man who might once have been fat, now flabby with hanging cheeks, stared stupidly at us next to a skinny kid, blowing on his fingers. By their indifferent expressions, their undernourished looks, the incongruousness of their dress, high boots, Belgian uniform leggings, civilian trousers falling over down-at-heel rubbers—by their hunched shoulders, their weary and detached attitudes—they expressed only hunger and fatigue. They were freezing. Never could the idea come to anyone to rush toward them with outstretched hand saying *Brothers!* for they belonged entirely to a world where words, feelings, fine sentiments shed their prestige immediately on contact with primordial realities. One could only have talked to them about a fire in front of which you could warm up; about shoes to be mended, about flannels to keep your empty stomach warm, about hot soup with which to fill it. I stared intensely at these silent men, standing there in such great distress. I thanked them for teaching me already about true fraternity, which is neither in sentiments nor in words, but in shared pain and shared bread. If I had no bread to share with them, I must keep silent and take my place at their side: and we would go off somewhere to fight or to fall together, and would thus be brothers, without saying so and perhaps without even loving each other. Loving each other, what for? It is necessary to stay alive. At that instant the Agitator's words came through to me. Endlessly he was repeating the same gesture of hammering a nail into hard wood with sharp blows. He was giving all the capitals of the world to the Revolution: Berlin, Stockholm, London, Paris, Rome, Calcutta. He cried: "Liebknecht!" and

"... we have taken Revel! We have taken Riga! We have taken Ufa! We have taken Minsk! We will take Vilna! We will conquer famine, typhus, lice, imperialism! We will not stop, neither on the Vistula nor on the Rhine! Long live ..."

He stopped short and disappeared into the group, now revivified by the explosion of the brasses. The Agitator, without looking back at us, crossed the deserted rooms with broad strides. He had to be at the Baltic factory at five o'clock to give a report on the international situation at the workers' conference where the Mensheviks were cooking something up. And we had nothing to teach him. He was suffering from a stomach virus; his boots were leaky.

Who is that other fellow?

Why it's Fleischmann! Of course!

He has hardly changed, only his clothing: black leather, worn out at the elbows and pockets, the jacket pockets stuffed full, as in Paris. He is still wearing his striped trousers, he has the same look of a preoccupied old night bird ...

"Greetings. How are you? A letter for you sent through the Danish Red Cross. I've been here six months already. I've just come back from the Front. We took Riga. I hope it holds! Where is Potapenko!"

"Here I am," said Sam, appearing. "Hello."

Fleischmann shakes hands with him perfunctorily, staring at the others—He takes a stack of lodging papers out of his pocket. There. There. "Potapenko, you come with me; I have a car. Let's go."

"See you later," Sam told us.

THIRTY-FOUR

Balance Due

THE AUTO, AN OLD FORD WITH A GRAY CANVAS TOP AND ISINGLASS WINDOWS had probably not been washed since an apprentice drove it to the Soviet of the Second District saying: "The boss has run out. I am nationalizing the machine. I place it in the service of the revolution." (Which was, by the way, a good way of not having to leave for the Front.) Fleischmann opened the door for Sam. There was already someone in the car.

"What, Fleischmann, you're not coming?"

"No. I'll meet you later. This comrade will drive you."

The door slams; he moves off, in such a hurry that he doesn't say good-by. The auto rolls over the snow with a clanging of hardware and wild backfires.

"So what kind of gas do you use?" Sam asks his neighbor, to break the ice.

"Whatever kind we have," grumbles the other man.

All Sam can see of him is a long, regular profile and a clear complexion. Probably a Lett. The isinglass sheets jumble the streets together, all alike under the snow with their closed store fronts and shop windows full of spidery bullet holes. The machine bounces, pants, and pitches through the ruts of hardened snow. Sam, overcome by the cold, wishes he could shake off this fogginess. Carelessly, but with a secret anxiety, he asks his companion:

"Where are we going?"

"Here we are."

Through the half-open door, the Lett holds out his pass. A triangular bayonet scratches against the isinglass. The Ford turns into a narrow little courtyard where there is nothing but a broken-down truck, covered with snow.

"To the rear, on the right," says the Lett.

Sam moves ahead, with the man behind him, strangely troubled. A typewriter is crackling somewhere. The narrow corridors, intersected by sharp corners, are deserted, badly illuminated by feeble electric lights. They form a labyrinth; you go down one flight of stairs only to climb another. A woman with her hair cut short on the back of her neck passes by very rapidly, carrying some blue files. Finally a rather large waiting room opens up, poorly lighted by an electric bulb covered with flyspecks, hanging, shadeless, from a huge chandelier. Some worn blotters, covered with those mechanical drawings that preoccupied people put on paper with such childish attention, are lying about on tables. Sam collapses into a green leather couch, whose arms are supported by naiads carved in oak. The broken springs squeak; the leather is cracked. Opposite, a double door.

"Well?" Sam hesitantly asks at last of the Lett, who, sitting crosswise on a fluted chair of gilded wood, has pulled a crust of black bread out of his pocket and is getting ready to have supper.

"Wait," says the Lett in a low voice.

Sam comes rapidly to his feet.

"Come on now. What is this? Am I under arrest?"

"Not so loud," says the Lett. "I don't know anything about it."

Sam flops down on the couch again. The fogginess, the silence, the presence of this man whose regular chewing is all he can hear, the dilapidation of this ruined former salon, slowly fill him with a foreboding.

Finally one of the leaves of the door at the rear opens, and someone calls:

"Potapenko."

Sam enters like an automaton powered by a spring. An enormous fear possesses him, he feels an indistinct anxiety in his chest, his stomach, his bones, and a tightness in his skull. Through a sort of foggy glass he can see three austere faces turned toward him: a dry old woman with grizzled hair gathered in a bun, an ageless man with a bulldog face who seems to be struggling with great effort against sleep, a big tall fellow with ruffled hair perched on the window sill in a cloud of smoke. The latter is the only one in uniform: bristling with braids, a huge red and gold insignia plastered across the right-hand pocket of his tunic. The tired bulldog, having puffed his sagging cheeks full of air, interrogates:

"How much a month did they pay you for your services, *Le Matois*?"

Potapenko, feeling the triple stare fixed on him, does not flinch, in spite of the shudder which passes from the small of his back to his throat. Behind these men, on a mahogany console, a gilded Empire clock marks the time: 11:20. *Cupid and Psyche* . . . Above, a portrait of Lenin. Potapenko takes a deep breath.

"I don't understand."

"We don't have any time to waste," resumes the bulldog, unmoved; and his eyelids droop shut, in spite of himself (he hasn't slept for twenty hours). "Embassy Secretary Droujin used to send you eighty rubles a month from Washington. On June 27, 1913, Police Captain Kügel, on mission; raised your salary to one hundred rubles a month. Here is the note written in his hand: 'A good, conscientious agent who knows emigré circles extremely well . . .' You thanked him by letter on July 4. Here is your letter." (His eyes are now entirely closed, he feels his head ready to fall down over agent *Le Matois'* blue dossier.) "Do you have any statement to make to us?"

Everything staggers around the dumb struck man standing there. This little room seems to be pitching like a cabin aboard the *Andros.* Everything is finished. He nods *No.*

"Why did you return?" asks the woman with the smoothed-back hair whom you might mistake for an old governess in a great house.

He answers in a whisper, surprised by his own answer because it comes from deep within him:

"I couldn't live otherwise."

"Is that all?"

"That's all."

"Go."

All at once Sam feels curiously lightheaded. He recovers his slightly twisted, ironical smile. He makes a sign to the tousled-haired smoker, a Georgian or Turkistani with a ravenous profile: "A cigarette?" The colorful box bears a woman's name: *Ira.* Diminutive: *Irotchka* . . . She would be a tall, auburn-haired girl . . .

Sam is gone. The bulldog places a blank form on the table in front of him: "Your opinion, Arkadi: on the debit side?"—"On the debit side."—"Yours, Maria Pavlovna?"

". . . Naturally." Four lines in an uneven handwriting, signed forcefully, run across the form. "What's next, Arkadi?"—"That business at the Whal factory . . ."

Sam found the waiting room empty. The other door open . . . Open! The narrow corridor is empty. He moves forward, on tiptoe, tense all over, unthinking, raised up by a senseless hope . . ." Where are you going?" Where has he come from, that damned Lett? The magic thread snaps . . .

"To the bathroom."

"In the corner on the right."

This boxlike room smells of urine. The electricity fills it with a feeble light. Having pulled the cord, Sam feels himself sinking. His elbow against the wall, his face in the hollow of his arm, he bites into the cloth to keep from sobbing. No more salvation, no more hope, no more anything. Ira. *Irotchka*. No one. No one will know that this sharp-featured man is there, like a terrified child, in complete collapse . . .

The Lett has heard nothing. Sam reappears, aged, thinned in four minutes, but straight, hard. As he is about to retrace his steps, the Lett says:

"Don't bother. Pass this way."

"Where are we going?"

The Lett answers with terrible solicitude:

"Please be patient a few moments longer."

These stifling corridors are like the galleries of an underground city. A door, at the bottom of a stairway, and then the good feeling of the cold fresh air right on one's face, the soft crackling of the snow, glimmering with silver flakes, under the feet. It is a little courtyard between tall buildings with black windows, like a mineshaft, but crudely illuminated by an electric bulb. Some stars shine high above. Sam, as if he knew this road which no one ever travels twice, moves toward a high rectangular pile of logs covered with snow. The trampled snow has taken on a brown tinge here; it gives off a stale odor. Some birch chips glisten on the edge of the bark, sliced off with an ax. The ax . . . Here they use a Nagan revolver, made in Seraing. Sam closes his eyes, shuddering. Someone comes up behind him. It must be 11:30.

THIRTY-FIVE

The Laws Are Burning

THE CENTRAL OFFICE OF PRISONERS OF WAR AND REFUGEES WOULD ONLY AGREE to lodge us, in its barracks where typhus was raging, for a few days, for Circular 3499 of the Council of Peoples' Commissars of the Northern Commune had just limited its prerogatives. They advised us to address ourselves, to simplify the formalities, to the Secretariat of the Executive Committee of the Soviet. This Secretariat directed us—Sonnenschein and myself, who had taken charge of securing housing for the families as rapidly as possible—to the Repatriation Service of the Commissariat for Social Aid. From this Commissariat we obtained an imperative directive (two signatures and a seal on paper with a rubber-stamped letterhead, and crosswise, in huge letters, underlined in blue pencil: *"URGENT!"* . . .) to the Housing Subsection of the Soviet for the Second District. This Soviet had just moved out of a building where the firewood had been used up and into another one where there was still some left; their offices occupied several luxurious apartments which looked as if they had been visited by a tornado the day before. Not only had the Housing Subsection got lost in the process of moving, but its leader (who, according to one version, had gone off to the front in the latest draft call, known as the Five Hundreds, or according to another, been arrested while returning from the country with a sack of flour in spite of the prohibition on transporting foodstuffs individually) had disappeared several days ago. Night was falling and we were dead with fatigue when a typist—seated before her machine smoking, in a delicious pink boudoir, between rolls of carpeting stamped with the seal of the Extraordinary Commission and rifles stacked against an Empire commode—dissipated our last hopes.

"It's always like that with *them*," she said.

Slowly, with an inexperienced finger, on the reverse side of a bill of lading of the firm V.I. Kozmine-Kataev and Son, Wholesale Grain Dealers, she typed the words "Housing Order." And, in a nasty voice:

"That's how it is. I type out orders and there is no housing. The whole city is empty and sacked and there is no housing! Do you think that this can go on much longer?"

We had already visited a half-dozen institutions, covered miles through the snow, stomachs empty, through silent streets where the rare passers-by dragged their feet, some carrying sacks, others their meager dinners in little greasy pots. Already, in a few hours, we had learned more about the revolution than in many long meditations. And it had appeared to us under aspects very different from those suggested by our imagination, shaped by legend and by history, which is very close to legend. We had been thinking of the squares transformed into tumultuous forums, of the excited clubs of '92; of the blossoming of many little journals, each crying out its own solution, its system, its fantasy; of the great "days" of the Soviets, like Conventions. In the language, in the slogans posted everywhere, in the only two newspapers published, among the men, we discovered one enormous uniformity of a single way of thinking, imperious, almost despotic, but supreme, terribly true, made flesh and blood at each moment through action. We found not the passionate mobs going forward under new flags to struggles begun anew each day in tragic and fruitful confusions, but a sort of vast administration, an army, a machine in which the most burning energies and the clearest intelligences were cold) integrated and which performed its task inexorably. And that task was to strain ceaselessly; for commonplace, often invisible achievements, with forces which, each day, seemed to be the last; to live and to persevere day after day; it was also to make an exhausted country, on the point of falling back into inertia, rise, above itself; it was, finally to resist and to conquer everywhere, at every moment, transcending all logic.

We had glimpsed that vast city—not at all dead, but savagely turned in on itself, in the terrible cold, the silence, the hate, the will to live, the will to conquer; that city divided by broad rectilinear perspectives at the end of which you could see the dull, frozen glint of golden spires that made you think of elegant swords . . . We were beginning to understand the faces of its empty white streets, lined with closed or shattered shop windows.

The silence of the houses, the emptiness of the straight avenues no longer distressed us. We knew that within all those glacial houses, in the depths of their souls, they were burning bushes of anger, of fury, of perfidy; that the ground was mined everywhere under our feet; that people were waiting—unatonable vengeances slowly ripening in brains debilitated by famine and terror—for the uprising brought on by hunger or the onslaught of the Finns, implacable wolf hunters who would massacre us like wolves; that the workers' quarters were being slowly drained of their living strength by the Army, the supply services, the State; that the dregs were rising and overflowing around the men of energy and truth: a swarm of adventurers, profiteers, speculators; the slow conquest of the factories by those without faith or devotion; that there were only enough foodstuffs for three days, not enough munitions for more than twenty-four hours of combat if the Finnish invasion took place, only enough combustibles—some wood cut last week—for five days on the Moscow railway . . .

We had stopped for a moment in the middle of these white splendors, in front of the granite-banked Neva, a river of ice on which human ants were moving back and forth on yellowing paths. Behind us rose the Marble Palace, as dead as the Theban tombs, all in stern, sharp outlines, all in flat, polished surfaces of a light, dusk like gray. "Men," said Gregor, "move across that hard ice never thinking of the deep river rolling along beneath. The revolution lives on a layer of ice too, and we do not know what dark ocean lies beneath, ready to engulf us tomorrow." Engulf us, eh? What of it! As if it were we who really mattered . . . But no, on the contrary, it is we who matter, we who must obstinately persist in living, in holding out despite everything, in doing at last what we have so much wanted to do . . . The times when it was necessary for us to know how to accept prison, exile, poverty, and—the best, the strongest of us—death itself are in the past. From now on we must persist obstinately in living and only consent to everything for that! We were looking at a tall gold spire atop a church dome, surmounted by a lantern of delicately sculpted filigree, which rose over the old stone-colored bastions of the fortress, lying low across the opposite bank. We repeated to ourselves: "This is Peter and Paul." Those who, in these bastions, had waited ten years, fifteen years, twenty years, until madness, until death, for the days which we were living; those who had been led along the battlements to the scaffold, those who had been allowed to die of hunger or to disappear there—but where was the Alexis ravelin? our eyes searched into the distance for the emplacement of its dungeons—had thus been right! Now it was our turn to be right, whatever the thickness of the ice might be! "Yes, but it's much more difficult," the youngest among us said naively. We burst into laughter.

Amid a great clatter of clanking metal, a filthy streetcar—on whose windows the frost had traced a luxuriant flowering of delicate ferns—so overcrowded that you couldn't even move—so that an odor of grease, of sweat, of stale cloth and wet leather suffocated you—brought us, Sonnenschein and myself, back toward the Smolny Institute, the seat of government. The dreary façade was already disappearing into the fog. The narrow muzzles of cannon, placed between the columns of the peristyle, pointed their blind menace into the cold night. At the foot of a white staircase down which a double file of young ladies wearing the wide, brilliant collarettes of daughters of the nobility had only lately trod, stood a soldier wearing a banker's fur cape, the velvet collar raised, filing slips of pink paper on the blade of his bayonet. In the commander's absence, a young lad armed with a revolver was writing out these passes in a room on the ground floor. At his worktable, surrounded by telephones, alone in a huge room from whose windows you could see the icy river and the boundless solitudes, we discovered a man wearing an old unbuttoned uniform tunic who told us, between two phone calls:

"Ah so! You've begun to run the rounds of the offices! I sympathize with you. You will discover that they are no good for anything yet. Nests for saboteurs, scoundrels, thieves, incompetents, do-nothings, idiots, and little young ladies with powdered noses. We'll put them in order in time, if they don't hang us on the way."

He stamped a huge red seal on a piece of notepaper covered by a few lines of writing.

"Take this and run over to Social Aid before they close. Take the Secretariat's car. I'll tell the commander."

We were obliged to abandon that worn-out luxury car—its flower holders stuffed with cigarette butts—along the way, for its motor stopped dead every five minutes after a pitiful series of explosions. The chauffeur disappeared into a nearby house, looking for a telephone from which to ask for reinforcements from the central garage, which was called, in order to emphasize its importance, the Auto Combat Service. After a few minutes wait, the huge red seal opened the oak doors for us, guarded by an old footman in livery. For twenty-seven years he had been attached to this corner of the universe, that is to say to this corner of the corridor at the top of a marble stairway, and he was still there, full of a distressed scorn, already ministering to the seventh revolutionary institution in fourteen months. There, by an accident which seemed to us to touch upon the marvelous, we found a suite of impeccably kept offices functioning noiselessly under the direction of a woman with close-cropped gray hair. Her cold blue eyes fixed us with a sharp stare (already, I thought, the habit of making judgments; already the necessity, among us who call each other "comrades," far a great deal of mistrust; already the second thought that we may be lying . . .) "Where do you come from? Who are you? What do you want?" Then her face changed, as the water brightens when the clouds have passed, revealing the vast shining circles which cavort on its surface.

"Heavens, where are we going to lodge your families? Four, you say? Would you like the Grand Duchesses' rooms in the Winter Palace? You'd never be able to heat them. Besides, you would find nothing to burn there but the furniture, which would be too bad even though it is in very bad taste . . . I think I still have the apartment of a Counselor of the Empire . . ."

The Levines moved in there two hours later. It was on the second floor of a tall gray house, a series of twelve rooms abandoned to the cold, the darkness, the strange desolation of places where life has suddenly come to a halt. The grand salon seemed to have been turned topsy-turvy in a brawl. The grand piano, covered with a layer of dust, had been pushed out into the middle of the floor. The naiad coming out of her bath, attributed to Bryulov, which had smiled down for twenty years on several generations of ladies, was hanging crooked . . . A cooking pot full of mold was standing on the marble windowsill. In the open drawers of a little mahogany secretary you could see a jumble of photographs of children and schoolboys, seashells from the Lido, cards postmarked Wiesbaden, a whole pile of those dusty nothings to which our memories cling: favors, ribbons, sachets, trinkets, calendars, old-fashioned jewelry. And fragments of letters: ". . . met Mama on the Promenade des Anglais . . ." In Counselor of the Empire Benedick Illarionovitch Stavski's study, behind the master's straight-back armchair bearing a carved monogram, the back wall was entirely covered by a glassed-in bookcase in which the massive volumes of the COLLECTION OF THE LAWS OF THE EMPIRE, boxed in green cardboard, were lined up. One could easily imagine the late master, as he appeared on a photograph which had been used to pick up sweepings in the next room standing behind that table: narrow forehead, stern monocled eye; an intelligent, egotistical industrialist, resembling a Roman senator; and a little girl bursting into that austere study clapping her hands: "Papa, little Papa, it's the revolution! If you knew how happy everyone is in the streets. I saw some soldiers with red ribbons, how pretty it is!"

I arrived there in the middle of the night. Darkness reigned over the city. Not a light anywhere. It was a necropolis buried under snow; but at times you could make out the uncertain glow of a night light in some window where people were awake. On a square, in front of the Opera, I stumbled against the carcass of a horse lying at the foot of an unrecognizable monument between two banks of hardened snow. Far off in the distance a gunshot reverberated for a long time in a silence as deep as the darkness. Perhaps a sailor, guarding a woodpile, shooting suddenly, without knowing why, at the shadows or at the shadow of an enemy. There were no stars. The emptiness seemed to stretch out over the city and, slowly, irresistibly, in a frozen dizziness, to draw it in: the dark stones and the snow, blending together, seemed about to vanish . . .

An old woman wearing pince-nez, and a peevish man, whose features I could not make out but whom the old woman called "Doctor," were on guard at the threshold of the house. They struck a light in order to stare at me. The Levines had gathered in the smallest of the rooms, probably a nursery, furnished with two iron bedsteads with gilded balls on which only the mattresses remained . . . (one of them appeared to be stained with blood). This candle-lit room was like a corner in steerage on an immigrant ship. The children had fallen asleep on the baggage, rolled up in blankets. The mother was resting in a low armchair. The young woman, like a solemn child, with large limpid eyes which seemed by turns distended by fear and then victorious over the fleeting shadows, was dreaming before the open stove, the reddish glow of which illuminated from below her graceful hands, her thin neck, and her fine features. Old Levine's footsteps echoed on the floor of the grand salon, plunged in darkness. He entered, his arms loaded with heavy green-covered books which he dropped softly next to the stove. Silent laughter illuminated his ruddy face.

"The laws are burning!" he said.

The friendly warmth in front of which the young woman was stretching out her hands came from the flames devouring Tome XXVII of the *COLLECTION OF THE LAWS OF THE EMPIRE*. For fun, I pulled out a half-burned page, edged with incandescent lace. The flames revealed these words forming a chapter heading: CONCERNING LANDED PROPERTY . . . and, farther down: ". . . *the rights of collateral heirs* . . ."

It was only then, after thirty harassing hours, that I remembered the letter I had received the previous day. I had carried it through this unknown city, hereafter ours, without doing more than glancing at it very superficially, so absorbed had I been by the at times forbidding novelty of things. (Besides, I wasn't expecting news from anyone, not having left any particular ties behind me.) The letter was postmarked Spain. With the laws burning, I sat down on a stool near the stove, in that comforting warmth and that sudden peace, in which only the even breathing of the children was audible. Dario, El Chorro, José, Joaquin, Comrades, how I remembered you all at once! How I remembered the city which we had not been able to take, our hope, our will, our power, our real power, since I was about to go to sleep at last in a conquered city where everything was booty taken in the height of battle—everything, even this moment, this shelter, this warmth which allow me to think of you. All at once it seemed to me that Dario was about to walk in, to shrug his invisible burden off his shoulders, to say, in that joyful tone of voice reserved for glad evenings spent together, "Brrr! What cold, my friends!" then to turn toward me, his palms open, his eyes full of mischief, "Well, old man, what was I telling you? You see that we *can* take cities! and it's not over yet, and we will take the world!" I unfolded the letter. It was in El Chorro's uneven but forceful script. "Gusano sends his regards. He's sure you haven't forgotten him, for people only forget whole men, he says . . ." No, I haven't forgotten you, Gusano—a more complete man in what is left of your mutilated flesh than many of those who pity you because they still have all four of their slaves' or Pharisees' limbs. Perhaps I hesitated to read on. I skimmed over those four pages of writing once more, at a glance, and I stumbled upon one line, no different from all the others in the forest of symbols, which said:

". . . ever since they killed our Dario . . ."

Leningrad, 1929–30

Translator's Acknowledgments

Of the many people who were helpful in making this publication possible, I would like to thank the following:

Raya Dunayevskaya, a genuine American Marxist-Humanist, who first introduced me to the works of Victor Serge;

The Columbia University Libraries which supported me financially in gathering rare and out-of-print works by Victor Serge;

Peter Sedgwick, the British translator of Serge's *Memoirs of a Revolutionary*, who unselfishly helped and encouraged me;

Vladimir Kibalchich, Victor Serge's son, a good comrade and a fine artist;

Eugene Eoyang, a book editor who likes good books;

Daniel Aaron, Daniel Bell, Erich Fromm, Robert Herbert, Irving Howe, Dwight Macdonald, Henry L. Roberts, I.F. Stone, and Bertram D. Wolfe, who were kind enough to write letters supporting the publication in English of Serge's early novels;

Professor Jean-Albert Bédé of Columbia University, who encouraged and guided my research, both for my doctoral dissertation on Serge and on this book;

My wife Julie, who worked with me at every stage of translating.

Victor Serge: Writer and Revolutionary

Serge (pseudonym for Victor Lvovich Kibalchich, 1890–1947) was born 'by chance' in Brussels, Belgium, the son of an unmarried couple of anti-Czarist Russian refugees wandering Europe "in search of good libraries and cheap lodgings." Home-schooled by these penniless, idealistic exiled scholars, young Victor imbibed the heady revolutionary traditions of the Russian intelligentsia while growing up poor on the streets of Brussels. His father had been close to the terrorist People's Will Party and proudly bore the name of one of the assassins of Czar Alexander II, N.I. Kibalchich, who was hanged in 1881 and whose portrait adorned his parents' 'makeshift lodgings.'[1]

They were so poor that at age eleven he watched horrified as his younger brother died of malnutrition, while he survived on pilfered sugar soaked in coffee that little Raoul refused to eat. "Throughout the rest of my life," he recalled, "it has been my fate always to find, in the undernourished urchins of the squares of Paris, Berlin and Moscow, the same condemned faces of my tribe."

At age fourteen Victor is a militant Socialist Young Guard, and at fifteen a member of a rebel gang of Brussels apprentices writing and printing their own radical anarchist sheet The Rebel (pseudonym Le Rétif: 'The Maverick').[2] At eighteen he is starving in Paris, devouring the contents of the Sainte-Geneviève library, editing l'anarchie, lecturing on individualism and translating Russian novels to survive. At twenty-one Kibalchich is sentenced to five years in a French penitentiary for refusing to rat on his Brussels buddies who, impatient of waiting for Utopia, terrorized Paris as the "tragic gang" of anarchist bank-robbers.

---

1   See Richard Greeman, "History and Myth: Victor Serge's Russian Heritage," The Massachusetts Review 53, nos. 1, 2, and 3 (2012).
2   See the anthology of Serge's anarchist writings, trans. Mitch Abidor, Anarchists Never Surrender (Oakland: PM Press, 2015).

The experience of five years in the harsh French prison system (a regime of total silence, collective work, solitary confinement) tempered his soul. Ten years later, when he became a writer, his first novel, *Men in Prison*, was an attempt to rid himself of that suffering and to testify for all those prisoners whose voices are stifled in that "machine for grinding up men."[3]

Released from prison in 1917, Victor is expelled from France and comes back to life in Barcelona, where he works as a printer, participates in a revolutionary uprising, and publishes his first article, signed "Victor Serge." The title: "The Fall of a Czar."

Soon Serge attempts to reach revolutionary Russia via Paris, where he is arrested a 'Bolshevik suspect' and held for over a year as in a typhus-infested concentration camp. It is his first contact with Bolshevism. After four bloody years the First World War finally comes to an end in November 1918. Exchanged for a French officer held by the Soviets, he arrives in St. Petersburg (then called Petrograd, later Leningrad) in January 1919. He would fictionalize these experiences of class struggle in Spain, detention in wartime France, and arrival in Red Russia in his second novel, *Birth of Our Power* (1931). This odyssey from Barcelona to Petrograd completes his evolution from 'Maverick,' the anarcho-individualist rebel, to 'Victor Serge' the revolutionary.

Victor joins in the defense of the frozen, starving Red capital, besieged by Western-backed White armies, and chronicles the siege in the French left-wing press.[4] Petrograd under siege would be the subject of Serge's third novel, *Conquered City* (1931).[5] Twenty-odd years later, he would draw on his memories of the 1919 siege to describe the Germans' World War II siege of Leningrad in *Unforgiving Years*.[6]

Despite misgivings about Communist authoritarianism, he joins the Party in May 1919, at the very moment when the Revolution seems about to go under. Serge is drawn to the Bolsheviks' heroic energy and participates in the creation of Press Service the Communist International (or Comintern) from its inception. By the spring of 1921, however, Serge's loyalties are severely torn when anarchist and dissident Communist sailors rebel and seize the island fortress of Cronstadt. Serge joins in

3   Serge, *Men in Prison*, trans. Richard Greeman (Oakland: PM Press, 2014).
4   See Victor Serge, *Revolution in Danger: Writings on Russia, 1919–1921*, trans. Ian Birchall (London: Redwords, 1997).
5   Serge, *Conquered City*, trans. Richard Greeman (New York: NYRB, 2011).
6   Serge, *Unforgiving Years*, trans. Richard Greeman (New York: NYRB, 2008).

the thwarted attempt by Emma Goldman to mediate the conflict and then looks on in horror as the rebels and volunteer Communists massacre each other in a fratricidal combat across the melting ice floes.[7]

After withdrawing briefly from politics, Serge accepts a Comintern assignment in Germany where the promise of a new revolution poses a last hope for saving the isolated Soviets from smothering under increasing bureaucratic dictatorship in Russia. In Berlin Serge serves the Comintern both as journalist and under various identities as a militant or 'agent' (in those days there was little distinction). Serge's Berlin articles (signed 'R. Albert') report on galloping inflation, mass unemployment, mutilated veterans begging, strikes, and abortive *putsches* were later collected as *Witness to the German Revolution*.[8] This experience introduced him into the world of secret agents he explores in his last novel, *Unforgiving Years*, while his familiarity with the desperation of the German people living through the post–World War I crisis helped him recreate the atmosphere of Berlin at the end of World War II in the third movement of that novel.

In March 1923, the German Communists are outlawed after the fiasco of their aborted Hamburg *putsch*, and Serge flees with his family to Vienna, where he works for the Comintern and dialogues with Georg Lukacs and Antonio Gramsci. In 1925, despairing of a renewal of revolution in the West, Serge makes the insanely idealistic decision to return to Russia and join in the last-ditch antibureaucratic fight against Stalin as a member of the doomed Left Opposition led by Trotsky. Expelled from the Party in 1928, Serge turns to full-time writing after a near-death experience. In quick succession he publishes three novels and a well-documented history of *Year One of the Russian Revolution* in Paris before being arrested and deported to the Ural in 1933.

In a letter smuggled out of Russia and published after his arrest, Serge defends democratic freedom as essential to workers' socialism and describes Stalinist Communism as 'totalitarian.' After months of interrogation in the notorious Lubianka prison, Serge is deported to the Ural, where he is joined by his teenaged son, the future artist Vlady.[9] Serge's wife Liuba Russakova, driven insane by the Stalinist terror, is confined

---

7   Cronstadt later became a bone of contention between Serge and Trotsky in exile.
8   Translated by Ian Birchall (London, Redwords, 1997)
9   I was privileged to know Vlady from 1963 until his death in 2004, and he is the source of much of my information about his father. Please see http://www.vlady.org.

to an asylum. In 1936, protests by French trade-unionists and writers (including André Gide and Romain Rolland) lead to Serge's release from Russia, but the two novels he completed in captivity ("the only ones I had time to polish") are seized by the GPU at the Polish border.[10]

From precarious exile in Brussels and later in Paris, Serge struggles to support his wife and their two children while writing furiously to unmask the 'big lie' of the Moscow show trials and Stalin's murderous intrigues in Republican Spain. His scrupulously documented eyewitness books and articles are greeted with silence by complacent intellectuals hypnotized by the 'antifascism' of Communist-manipulated popular fronts. Serge is obliged to fall back on his old prison-trade of proofreader and find work in the print-shops of socialist papers that boycott his articles. Meanwhile, Serge and his comrades are living in a "labyrinth of pure madness" as Stalin's agents kidnap and murder Trotsky's supporters in the middle of opulent, indifferent Paris. "The Secret Agent," the first section of Serge's posthumous novel, *Unforgiving Years*, is an eerie evocation of a doomed world capital paralyzed before the looming threat of war.

By 1939, Serge is on the verge of literary success with a novel about deported oppositionists in Stalin's Gulag: *Midnight in the Century*.[11] At the outbreak of the war, however, his books—considered subversive—are withdrawn from publication. When Paris falls to the Nazis, Serge, penniless, joins the exodus on foot—accompanied by his young companion Laurette Séjourné and his son Vlady. They survive a Luftwaffe strafing attack on the Loire and eventually find refuge in a Marseille villa rented by Varian Fry of the American Refugee Committee and shared with André Breton and his family. Aided by Dwight Macdonald in New York and by exiled comrades of the Spanish POUM settled in Mexico, Serge and Vlady board the last refugee ship out of Vichy France and end up in Mexico City in 1941, a year after Trotsky's assassination. Here Serge finds himself politically isolated—cut off from Europe by the war, unable to publish, boycotted, slandered, and physically attacked by Stalinist agents.

Nonetheless, it is in Mexico that Serge completes his most enduring work: *Memoirs of a Revolutionary, The Case of Comrade Tulayev*, and

---

10 The manuscripts have never been recovered, despite diligent searches of recently opened Soviet archives. See Richard Greeman, "The Victor Serge Affair and the French Literary Left," *Revolutionary History* 5, no. 3 (Autumn 1994).

11 Trans. by Richard Greeman (NYRB Classics, 2014).

Unforgiving Years, which he finishes in 1946.[12] He also studies psycho-
analysis, writes a manuscript on pre-Columbian archaeology and meditates on consciousness and death. He explores the meaning of the war
not only in theoretical and political 'theses' but also terms of dreams,
earthquakes, volcanoes, and luxuriant vegetation. In 1947 his heart gives
out, stressed by the altitude and exhausted by years of prison and pri-
vation. Penniless and stateless as usual, Serge is buried in a pauper's
grave. In his posthumously published *Memoirs of a Revolutionary* he
reflects: "Of this hard childhood, this troubled adolescence, all those
terrible years, I regret nothing as far as I am myself concerned. . . . Any
regret I have is for energies wasted in struggles which were bound to
be fruitless. These struggles have taught me that, in any man, the best
and the worst live side by side, and sometimes mingle—and that what
is worst comes through the corruption of what is best."

Serge's books have had almost as hard a life as their author. At the
end of World War II, when Serge began *Unforgiving Years*, he was painfully aware of writing "exclusively for the desk drawer"—in which his
classic *Memoirs* and *Comrade Tulayev* were already languishing, unpublished. Little hope in postwar Paris, what with paper shortages and the
influence of the Communists in publishing. No luck either in New York
and London, even with the help of Dwight Macdonald and George
Orwell. With at least one Stalinist and two conservatives in every publishing house, "I'm at the point where I wonder if my very name will
not be an obstacle to the novel's publication."

Although *Tulayev* and the *Memoirs* eventually did achieve the status
of 'classics' (albeit neglected classics), for a variety of reasons Serge the
novelist has remained marginalized. Yet he is arguably as important a
novelist in the political genre as Malraux, Orwell, Silone, Koestler, and
Solzhenitsyn. Nonetheless, Serge's radical socialist politics continue to
disturb the consensus, while his prestige as a revolutionary participant-
witness, oft-quoted by historians and political scientists, has tended to
obscure his status as a literary artist. For example, political scientist
Susan Weissman's recent book on Serge takes the position that "writing,
for Serge, was something to do only when one was unable to fight."[13]

---

12 All three have been published in English translation by NYRB Classics.
13 Susan Weissman, *Victor Serge: A Political Biography* (New York: Verso, 2013), pre-
    viously published as *The Course Is Set on Hope* (New York: Verso, 2002), 67. The
    book's main argument is that "Serge's critique of Stalinism was the core of his

Another reason for Serge's neglect is his nationality, or lack thereof. As a stateless Russian who wrote in French, he apparently fell through the cracks between academic departments organized around national notions of French or Russian Literature. As a result, as yet no PhD theses on Serge have been written in any French university, nor will you find "Serge, Victor" listed in French biographical dictionaries and literary manuals.[14]

To be sure, although he wrote in French, Serge is best situated in the Russian intelligentsia traditions of his expatriate parents. He inherited his father's scientific culture—physics, geology, sociology—while his literary culture came from his mother, who taught him to read from cheap editions of Shakespeare, Hugo, Dostoyevsky, and Korolenko and whose family was apparently connected with Maxim Gorky.[15] By his concept of the writer's mission, Serge saw himself "in the line of the Russian writers" who wrote about life in prison (Dostoyevsky's *House of the Dead*) and *The Lower Depths* (Gorky). And although he borrowed freely from cosmopolitan and modernist influences like Joyce, Dos Passos, and the French Unanimists, Serge developed as a writer within the Soviet literary 'renaissance' of the relatively free NEP period.

Indeed, during the 1920s, Serge was the principal transmission belt between the literary worlds of Soviet Russia and France. Through his translations and regular articles on Soviet culture in the revue *Clarté* he introduced French readers to the postrevolutionary poetry of Alexander Blok, Andrei Biely, Sergei Yesenin, Ossip Mandelstam, Boris Pasternak, and Vladimir Mayakovsky as well as to fiction writers like Alexis Tolstoy, Babel, Zamiatine, Lebidinsky, Gladkov, Ivanov, Fedin, and Boris Pilnyak—his colleagues in the Soviet Writers Union.[16]

By the mid-1930s, all of Serge's colleagues had been reduced to silence (suicide, censorship, the camps). "No PEN-club," wrote Serge in

---

life and work" (p.6), and she gives short shrift to his anarchist years, his poetry, and his fiction, which she finds 'useful' in understanding Stalinism.

14　Serge is better known in U.S. and British departments, with two PhD theses: my own (Columbia) and Bill Marshall's (Oxford), later published as *Victor Serge: The Uses of Dissent* (New York: Berg, 1992).

15　Serge went to see Gorky as soon as he arrived in Russia in 1919, but declined an offer to join the staff of Gorky's newspaper. During the Civil War, Serge depended on Gorky's relationship with Lenin to intercede to save anarchist comrades from being shot by the Cheka.

16　See Victor Serge, *Collected Writings on Literature and Revolution*, trans. Al Richardson (London: Francis Boutle, 2004) exile, "even those that held banquets for them, asked the least question about their cases. No literary review, to my knowledge, commented on their mysterious end." Of that great generation of Soviet writers, only Serge—because he wrote in French and was rescued from the Gulag by his reputation in France—managed to survive. Only Serge had the freedom to further develop the revolutionary innovations of Soviet literature and to submit the world of Stalinism to the critical lens of fiction in novels like *Midnight in the Century, The Case of Comrade Tulayev*, and *Unforgiving Years*. As one Russian scholar put it: "Although written in French, Serge's novels are perhaps the nearest we have to what Soviet literature of the 30s might have been."[17]

French novelist François Maspero, whose leftist publishing house revived Serge's books (all but forgotten in postwar France) in the wake of the May 1968 near-revolution, remarks: "There exists a sort of secret international, perpetuating itself from one generation to the next, of admirers who read, reread [Serge's] books and know a lot about him." As Adam Hochschild notes in his foreword to Serge's *Memoirs*, 'It is rare when a writer inspires instant brotherhood among strangers.' As Serge's translator, it is my great pleasure (and revolutionary duty!) to welcome you into the growing 'English-language section' of this Invisible International.

---

17   Neil Cornwell, review of *Midnight in the Century, Irish Slavonic Studies* 4 (1983).

Victor Serge: Biographical Note

Victor Serge was born into the revolutionary movement as some people are said to be born "to the manor." His parents were part of the emigration of Russian *intelligenti* which streamed into Western Europe during the dark decade of repression that followed the assassination of Czar Alexander II by the terrorist arm of the populist "Narodnik" party on March 1, 1881. He was born Victor Lvovich Kibalchich (Serge was a pseudonym) in Brussels on December 30, 1890, a child of want, exile, and revolt.

Serge's earliest memories were of adult conversations dealing with "trials, executions, escapes and Siberian highways, with great ideas incessantly argued over, and with the latest books about these ideas." Idealism and readiness for sacrifice were the values that reigned in his parents' milieu. "On the walls of our humble and makeshift lodgings," he recalled in his *Memoirs of a Revolutionary*, "there were always the portraits of men who had been hanged." Serge's father had barely escaped hanging for his part in the 1881 attack on the Czar, and one of Russia's most famous martyrs was Serge's relative on his father's side, Nikolai Kibalchich, the genial chemist who fashioned the bombs that were used against Alexander II.

Serge's birthright was a tradition of rebellion and sacrifice in the face of Czarist autocracy and repression, a tradition begun by the Decembrists in 1825, passed on through Chernyshevsky, Herzen, Bakunin, and the generation of students who had gone "to the people" in the 1870s, to culminate in the terrorism of 1881, a tradition that combined the most intellectualized idealism with danger and desperate deeds.

Growing up in comfortable, complacent Brussels, but in a household where extreme poverty caused the death of his younger brother and where the atmosphere was charged with revolutionary fervor, Serge, even as a child, became obsessed with the idea that he was living in a "world without possible escape," and determined that the only acceptable career would be that of the professional revolutionary. Since his father, an impoverished scholar, despised public education—he called it "stupid bourgeois instruction for the poor"—Serge never went to school. He learned to read in his father's library of revolutionary books and learned about life in the slum streets of Brussels. As an adolescent he worked as a photographer's apprentice. He was active in the Socialist *Jeunes-Guardes* but still found it "impossible to live" in a city where even the "revolutionaries" believed in gradual reform. In 1908, after a short stay in a Utopian colony in the Ardennes, he heeded the call of Paris, "the Paris of Salvat, of the Commune, of the CGT, of little journals printed with burning zeal; the Paris where Lenin edited *Iskra* from time to time and spoke at emigré meetings in little co-operative houses."

Disgusted with the watered-down Marxist and reformist-socialist doctrines of the day which promised "revolution for the year 2000" but neglected the impossible here-and-now, Serge and his young comrades in Paris were drawn to theories of anarchist-individualism, the personal rebellion and "conscious egotism" of Nietzsche and Stirner: "Anarchism swept us away completely because it both demanded everything of us and offered everything to us." The revolution was to be personal, total, immediate. But in Paris, just as in Brussels, it was "impossible to live." There, poverty and hunger were the daily "impossibilities," and many of the young individualists were soon converted to the theory (and practice) of "individual expropriation" based on Proudhon's idea that "legal" property is merely "theft." Driven by want, disease, and desperation, and inspired by half-digested revolutionary ideas, many of Serge's young comrades banded together and embarked on what was probably the most bloody and tragic series of bank robberies in modern times. Known as the "Bonnot Gang" and the "Tragic Bandits," they terrorized Paris for almost a year; all of them met violent ends— in gun battles, by suicide, and on the guillotine. Serge, then editor of *l'anarchie*, was repelled by the slaughter and revolted by the excesses to which their idealistic theories had led. But he refused to break with his comrades and turn informer; after a sensational trial, the French state rewarded his silence with a five-year prison sentence as an "accomplice."

Of his term in prison (1912–17), Serge wrote: "It burdened me with an experience so heavy, so intolerable to endure, that long afterward, when I resumed writing, my first book [*Men in Prison*, a novel] amounted to an effort to free myself from this inward nightmare, as well as the performance of a duty toward all those who will never so free themselves." Released from prison at the height of World War I and banned from France, Serge made his way to Barcelona, a city "at peace," busily turning out weapons for both sides in the great conflict. It was there that he abandoned individualism, and began to agitate in the ranks of the syndicalists. In Barcelona, he wrote his first article signed "Victor Serge," and Barcelona on the eve of insurrection (twenty years before the great Spanish Revolution and Civil War) is the setting for the first half of *Birth of Our Power.*

Involved as he was in Spain, it was the Russian Revolution, which had just erupted at the other end of Europe, that was for Serge "my" revolution, the end of that "world without possible escape." He left Barcelona and attempted to join the Russian Army in France in order to be repatriated to the homeland, as it were. But he succeeded only in getting himself thrown into a French concentration camp as a "Bolshevik suspect." After the Armistice, he was sent to Russia as a hostage in exchange for some French officers interned by the Soviets. He arrived in Red Petrograd (the setting for the final chapters of *Birth of Our Power* and for *Conquered City*) in January 1919, at the height of the Civil War and famine. It was here that the evolution from Victor Kibalchich, homeless exile and anarchist-individualist, to Victor Serge, spokesman for Soviet power, was completed.

Serge's libertarian sympathies made him, from the start, wary of the authoritarian nature of Bolshevik rule. But, as a revolutionary, only one course was open to him: he threw himself, body and soul, into the work of defending and building the Soviet Republic. During the Civil War, he served as a machine gunner in a special defense battalion, collaborated closely with Zinoviev the founding congresses of the Communist International, became a Commissar in charge of the czarist secret police archives (under Krassin), and eventually a member of the Russian Communist Party. At the same time, however, he openly criticized Bolshevik authoritarianism, frequented anarchist, Left-Menshevik, and Left-Socialist circles, and interceded in favor of many prisoners of the Cheka (predecessor of the GPU and the NKVD). At this time, too, Serge was translating into French the works of Lenin, Trotsky, and Zinoviev. Among poets and writers, he was friendly with Yessenin, Mayakovsky, Pilnyak, Pasternak, Panait Istrati, and Maxim Gorky (a distant relative on his mother's side).

By 1923, he was a confirmed member of the Left (Trotskyist) Opposition; at that date it was still possible to be simultaneously "loyal" and an "oppositionist" in Soviet Russia. But his presence in Russia was troublesome; he was made editor of the *International Communist Bulletin* and sent off to Germany and the Balkans to agitate, a task which he performed with perfect loyalty and discipline.

When Serge returned to Moscow in 1926 to take part in the inner-Party struggle against Stalin, however, the political climate was greatly changed. A little over a year later, he was expelled from the Party and held in prison for several weeks; his relatives, including many who had no political affiliations, were also made to suffer. It was during this period (1928–33) that, relieved of all official functions and systematically deprived of any means of earning a living because of the Stalinist "blacklist," Serge turned to serious writing. Already known in France for his pamphlets and political articles, he soon attracted a larger audience there as an historian (*Year One of the Russian Revolution*, 1930) and novelist (*Men in Prison*, 1930; *Birth of Our Power*, 1931; *Conquered City*, 1932).

Surely no writer has ever produced under more difficult conditions, and the vivid tension and rapid episodic style of his works may well have been dictated in part by his personal situation. "I knew that I would never have time to polish my works properly. Their value would not depend on that. Others, less involved in struggle, would perfect a style; but what I had to tell, *they* could not tell. To each his own task. I had to struggle bitterly for my family's daily bread [Serge had married soon after arriving in Russia] in a society where all doors were closed to me, and where people were often afraid to shake my hand in the street. I asked myself every day, without any particular feeling, but engrossed by the problems of rent, my wife's health, my son's education, whether I would be arrested in the night. For my books I adopted an appropriate form: I had to construct them in detached fragments which could each be finished separately and sent abroad posthaste; which could, if absolutely necessary, be published as they were, incomplete; and it would be difficult for me to compose in any other form."

Serge was arrested again in 1933, and this time sent to Orenburg where he was joined by his young son, Vlady. He might well have perished there, like so many other Soviet writers, during the period of the great purges, had it not been for his reputation in the West. A group of young Parisian intellectuals campaigned openly for his freedom, and his plight was brought to the attention of pro-Soviet luminaries like

Romain Rolland, André Gide, and Audré Malraux, some of whom may have interceded in his favor with Stalin. In 1936 he was removed from Orenburg, but he was also deprived of Soviet citizenship, relieved of his manuscripts (both actions in violation of Soviet law), and expelled from the Soviet Union. His return to Europe was heralded by a vicious slander campaign in the Communist press.

Serge settled first in Brussels, then in Paris, where he continued to battle for the ideals of Soviet democracy and against the rising tides of Stalinism and fascism. His next novel, *S'il est minuit dans le siècle*, 1939, told the story of the heroic resistance of the Oppositionists and Old Bolsheviks in Stalin's concentration camps, and he analyzed the Stalinist counterrevolution in books like *From Lenin to Stalin*, 1937, and *Destiny of a Revolution*, 1937. Serge was one of the few to recognize the outrage of the Moscow frame-up trials (which deceived a whole generation of Leftist intellectuals and even the U.S. Ambassador in Moscow) and to raise a voice against them.

Revolution had again broken out in Spain, and long before his contemporary and admirer, George Orwell (cf. *Homage to Catalonia*), Serge saw through Stalin's machinations there. While the workers and farmers were dying valiantly for the Spanish Republic, the Communists were quietly "eliminating" their political rivals in the rear. In spite of Serge's efforts, by the end of 1937, the Stalinists had murdered Serge's comrade Andrès Nin, the leader of the Spanish POUM (independent Marxist party) and jailed and killed countless others. "We are building a common front against fascism. How can we block its path with so many concentration camps behind us?" he wrote to André Gide (with whom he was later associated) on the eve of the latter's voyage to Russia.

World War II soon put an end to the limited possibilities for action that had remained open to Serge and his friends. As if reluctant to admit the catastrophe he hid long predicted and fought against, Serge was one of the last to leave Paris before the advancing Nazis in 1940, although he was clearly marked for death by the Gestapo. Arriving penniless in Marseille, with the Gestapo at his heels, he fought for months to get a visa while the great "democracies" closed their doors to him. At the last moment, he found refuge for himself and his family in Mexico.

Isolated as he now was from the European socialist movement that had been his life, forced to be an impotent witness to the debacle of Europe under Hitler, menaced by NKVD assassins (who had recently murdered his friend Trotsky, also in Mexico), deprived of a journalistic platform by his Stalinist opponents, Serge might well have been thoroughly demoralized by his years in Mexico. But he continued to write, though without hope of publication, and produced some of his finest works (*The Case of Comrade Tulayev* and *Memoirs of a Revolutionary*) "for the desk drawer." At the end of the war, in spite of failing health and financial difficulties, he made plans to return to France. But his many projects for new books and new struggles were cut short by his death on November 17, 1947.

Even at the lowest ebb of his fortunes (in 1943), Serge had found the courage to write: "I have undergone a little over ten years of various forms of captivity, agitated in seven countries, and written twenty books. I own nothing. On several occasions a press with a vast circulation has hurled filth at me because I spoke the truth. Behind us lies a victorious revolution gone astray, several abortive attempts at revolution, and massacres in so great number as to inspire a certain dizziness. And to think that it is not over yet. Let me be done with this digression; those were the only roads possible for us. I have more confidence in mankind and in the future than ever before."

The Writer as Witness
Serge's dedication to absolute political honesty and clear-sightedness (*probité* and *lucidité*) as the only bases for building a genuine revolutionary movement had its corollary in his devotion to artistic truth.

The noun "witness" is a rough English equivalent of the Greek *martus*, from which our word "martyr" is also derived. The idea of being a witness to one's faith implies not only testifying to a creed, but also participation and active suffering, freely accepted, in the name of something larger than one's personal ego. It also implies a privileged situation. Poets and other creative artists have long claimed this kind of status for themselves. Whether they chose to suffer in the name of the forward march of Humanity (Hugo and the social romantics) or for the purity of Art and the Ideal (Baudelaire and the symbolists), they have regularly assumed that the greater the risk and the deeper the plunge into the mysteries of existence, the richer will be the prize with which the artist returns and which he offers up to an often uncomprehending humanity.

Victor Serge was such a martyr-witness. He felt that "artistic detachment" was not a means of being objective about reality, but only a fashionable means of avoiding a confrontation with it. And he plunged headlong into a maelstrom of social destruction and revolutionary upheaval. His commitment to revolution was made long before Communist state power made it easy and at times profitable for writers to become *engagé*, and it continued long after many of them had returned to their ivory towers proclaiming that their new-found god had failed. At the time of his death, Serge was one of the only survivors of three revolutionary generations. He had occupied a unique position, a position from which he, perhaps better than any other writer, was able to render both the heroism and the tragedy of a whole age of revolution.

For Serge, "He who speaks, he who writes is above all one who speaks on behalf of all those who have no voice"; he wrote out of a bond of solidarity with the men whose often tragic destinies fill the pages of his works—the heroes and the victims, the brave and the cowardly, the anarchists, Bolsheviks, bandits, madmen, poets, beggars, and the common workers. He defined the need to write as a need "first of all to capture, to fix, to understand, to interpret, to recreate life; to liberate, through exteriorization, the confused forces one feels fermenting within oneself and by means of which the individual plunges into the collective unconscious. In the work itself, this comes across as Testimony and Message . . ." He goes on to say, "Writing becomes a search for poly-personality, a means of living several destinies, of penetration into others, of communicating with them. The writer becomes conscious of the world he brings to life, he is its consciousness and he thus escapes from the ordinary limits of the self, something which is at once intoxicating and enriched with lucidity" (*Carnets*, Paris, 1952).

This attitude made it possible for Serge fully to appreciate the experiences of his turbulent life and to distill them into the concrete characterizations in his fiction. His life as an activist was unique in that he managed to be in virtually every revolutionary storm center during the first part of this century. But his experiences were nonetheless typical for a man of his times; individually, they recapitulated the experiences of millions of men caught up in the struggles of European society.

In the solitude of his Mexican exile, after a chance meeting with Trotsky's widow, Natalia Sedova, Serge wrote sadly in his diary: "[We are] the sole survivors of the Russian Revolution here and perhaps anywhere in the world . . . There is nobody left who know what the Russian Revolution was really like, what the Bolsheviks were really like—and men judge without knowing, with bitterness and a basic rigidity." That ineffable quality, "what things were really like"—the aspect, tone

of voice, emotional context of a human event, personal or historical—
that is what the novelist's ear and eye can catch and what makes of his
social or historical fiction a truer record of living reality than the historian's data or the theoretician's rational frames.

Richard Greeman
New York, 1966

Serge in English

FICTION

Men in Prison (*Les hommes dans la prison*, 1930). Translated and introduced by Richard Greeman. Garden City, NY: Doubleday & Co., 1969; London: Victor Gollancz Ltd., 1970; Middlesex: Penguin Books Ltd., 1972; London and New York: Writers and Readers, 1977; Oakland: PM Press, 2014. A searing personal experience transformed into a literary creation of general import.

Birth of Our Power (*Naissance de notre force*, 1931). Translated by Richard Greeman. Garden City, NY: Doubleday & Co., 1967; London: Victor Gollancz Ltd., 1968; Middlesex: Penguin Books Ltd., 1970; London and New York: Writers and Readers, 1977; Oakland: PM Press, 2015. From Barcelona to Petersburg, the conflagration of World War I ignites the spark of revolution, and poses a new problem for the revolutionaries' power.

Conquered City (*Ville conquise*, 1932). Translated and introduced by Richard Greeman. New York: NYRB Classics, 2009. Idealistic revolutionaries cope with the poison of power as the Red Terror and the White struggle for control of Petrograd during the Civil War.

Midnight in the Century (*S'il est minuit dans le siècle*, 1939). Translated and introduced by Richard Greeman. London and New York: Writers and Readers, 1981; New York, NYRB Classics, 2014. On the eve of the great Purges, convicted anti-Stalin oppositionists in deportation attempt to survive, resist the GPU, debate political solutions, ponder their fates, and fall in love.

The Long Dusk (*Les derniers temps*, 1946). Translated by Ralph Manheim. New York: Dial Press, 1946. The fall of Paris (1940), the exodus of the refugees to the Free Zone, the beginnings of the French Resistance.

The Case of Comrade Tulayev (*L'Affaire Toulaèv*, 1951). Translated by Willard Trask. Introduction by Susan Sontag. New York: NYRB Classics, 2007. A panorama of the USSR (and Republican Spain) during the Purges, with a cast of sharply etched characters from provincial policemen to Old Bolsheviks and the Chief himself.

Unforgiving Years (*Les années sans pardon*, posthumous, 1973). Translated and introduced by Richard Greeman. New York: NYRB Classics, 2010. Tormented Russian revolutionaries in Paris on the eve of World War I, Leningrad under siege, the last days of Berlin, and Mexico.

POETRY

Resistance: Poems by Victor Serge (*Résistance*, 1938). Translated by James Brook. Introduction by Richard Greeman. San Francisco: City Lights, 1972. Most of these poems were composed in deportation in Orenburg (1933–36), confiscated by the GPU, and reconstructed from memory in France.

PM Press plans to publish James Brook's new translation of Serge's complete poetry in 2016.

NONFICTION

Revolution in Danger: Writings from Russia 1919–1921. Translated by Ian Birchall. London: Redwords, 1997; Chicago: Haymarket Books, 2011. Serge's early reports from Russia were designed to win over his French anarchist comrades to the cause of the Soviets.

Witness to the German Revolution (1923). Translated by Ian Birchall. London: Redwords, 1997; Chicago: Haymarket Books, 2011. A collection of the articles Serge wrote in Berlin in 1923 under the pseudonym R. Albert.

What Every Militant Should Know about Repression (*Les Coulisses d'une Sûreté Générale: Ce que tout révolutionnaire doit savoir sur la répression*, 1925). Popular pamphlet reprinted in a dozen languages. Serge unmasks the secrets he discovered working in the archives the Czarist Secret Police, then explains how police provocateurs operate everywhere and gives practical advice on security to activists.

The Chinese Revolution (1927–1928), Online at http://www.marxists.org/archive/serge/1927/china/index.html.

Year One of the Russian Revolution (*L'an 1 de la révolution russe*, 1930) Translated by Peter Sedgwick. London: Pluto Press; Chicago, Haymarket Books. Written soon after Stalin's takeover in Russia, this history presents the Left Opposition's take on the October Revolution and early Bolshevism.

From Lenin to Stalin (*De Lénine à Staline*, 1937). Translated by Ralph Manheim. New York: Monad and Pathfinder Press, 1973. A brilliant, short primer, on the Russian Revolution and its degeneration, with close-ups of Lenin and Trotsky.

Russia Twenty Years After (*Destin d'une Revolution*, 1937). Translated by Max Shactman (Includes "Thirty Years After the Russian Revolution," 1947). Atlantic Highlands, NJ: Humanities Press, 1996. Descriptive panorama and analysis of bureaucratic tyranny and chaos in Russia under Stalin's Five-Year Plans, based on statistics and economic, sociological, and political analysis.

The Life and Death of Leon Trotsky (*Vie et Mort de Léon Trotski*, 1951), by Victor Serge and Natalia Sedova Trotsky. Translated by Arnold Pomerans. London: Wildwood, 1975; Chicago: Haymarket Books, forthcoming. Still the most concise, authentic, and well-written one-volume Trotsky biography, based on the two authors' intimate knowledge of the man and his times and on Trotsky's personal archives (before they were sealed up in Harvard).

Memoirs of a Revolutionary (*Mémoires d'un révolutionnaire*, 1901–1941) Paris: Éditions du Seuil, 1951. Translated by Peter Sedwick. New York: NYRB Classics, 2012. Originally titled "Souvenirs of Vanished Worlds," Serge's *Memoirs* are an eyewitness chronicle of the revolutionary movements Belgium, France, Spain, Russia, and Germany studded with brilliant portraits of the people he knew. This is the first complete English translation and comes with a glossary.

The Serge-Trotsky Papers: Correspondence and Other Writings between Victor Serge and Leon Trotsky. D. Cotterill, ed. London, Pluto Press, 1994. Includes their personal letters and polemical articles as well as essays on Serge and Trotsky by various authors.

Collected Writings on Literature and Revolution. Translated and edited by Al Richardson. London: Francis Boutle, 2004. Includes Serge's reports on Soviet Cultural life in the 1920s (published in Paris in *Clarté*), studies of writers like Blok, Mayakovsky, Essenin, and Pilniak as well as his highly original contributions to the debate on "proletarian literature" in the 1930s.

Anarchists Never Surrender: Essays, Polemics, and Correspondence on Anarchism, 1908–1938. Oakland: PM Press, 2015. An original anthology of Serge's writing on anarchism translated, edited, and introduced by Mitchell Abidor. Foreword by Richard Greeman.

Notebooks, 1936–1947. Sketches and meditations on subjects ranging from the Stalinist terror, Gide, Giraudoux, and Trotsky to Mexican earthquakes, popular wrestling matches, and death. NYRB Classics plans to publish this in 2016. Translation by Mitch Abidor and Richard Greeman. Intro by Claudio Albertani.

UNTRANSLATED BOOKS IN FRENCH:
Le tropique et le nord. Montpellier: Maspero 1972; Paris: La Découverte, 2003. Four short stories: *Mer blanche* (1931), *L'Impasse St. Barnabé* (1936), *La folie d'Iouriev* [*L'Hôpital de Léningrad*, 1953] and *Le Séisme* [*San Juan Parangarcutiro*]

Retour à l'Ouest: Chroniques, juin 1936–mai 1940. Preface by Richard Greeman. Marseille: Agone, 2010. From the euphoria of Pop Front France in June 1936 to the defeat of the Spanish Republic, Serge's weekly columns for a trade union–owned independent daily in Belgium provide a lucid panorama of this confused and confusing period.

MANUSCRIPTS:

The Victor Serge Papers (1936–1947), Beinecke Library, Yale University. Twenty-seven boxes of correspondence, documents, and manuscripts (mostly unpublished) on a wide variety of subjects from politics to Mexican anthropology. Catalog online:

http://drs.library.yale.edu:8083/fedoragsearch/rest?filter=&oper ation=solrQuery&query=Victor+Serge+Papers.

The Life of Victor Serge

1890   Victor Lvovich Kibalchich (Victor Serge) born on December 30 in Brussels to a family of sympathizers with Narodnik terrorism who had fled from Russia after the assassination of Alexander II.

1908   Photographer's apprentice and member of the socialist *Jeunes-Gardes*. Spends a short period in an anarchist 'utopian' community in the Ardennes. Leaves for Paris.

1910–1911   Becomes editor of the French anarchist-individualist magazine, *l'anarchie*. Writes and agitates.

1912   Serge is implicated in the trial of the anarchist outlaws known as the Bonnot Gang. Despite arrest, he refuses to turn informer and is sentenced to five years in a *maison centrale*. Three of his co-defendants were guillotined.

1917–1918   Serge is released from prison and banned from France. Goes to Barcelona where he participates in the syndicalist uprising. Writes his first article signed Victor Serge. Leaves Barcelona to join the Russian army in France. Is detained for over a year in a French concentration camp as a Bolshevik suspect.

1919   Arrives in Red Petrograd at the height of the Civil War. Gets to work organizing the administration of the Communist International under Zinoviev.

1920–1922   Participates in Comintern Congresses. Edits various international journals. Exposes Tsarist secret-police archives and fights in the defense of the city.

1923–1926   Serves Comintern as a secret agent and editor of *Imprekor* in Berlin and Vienna. Returns to the Soviet Union to take part in the last stand of the left opposition.

1927	Series of articles on the Chinese Revolution in which he criticizes Stalin's complacence towards the Kuomintang and draws attention to the importance of Mao Zedong.
1928	Expelled from Communist Party and relieved of all official functions.
1928–1933	Barred from all other work, Serge takes up writing. He sends his manuscripts to France, since publication in the Soviet Union is impossible. Apart from many articles, he produces *Year One of the Russian Revolution*, 1930; *Men in Prison*, 1930; *Birth of Our Power*, 1931; and *Conquered City*, 1932.
1933	Serge is arrested and deported to Orenburg in Central Asia, where he is joined by his young son, Vlady.
1935	Oppositionists raise the 'Case of Victor Serge' at the Congress for the Defense of Culture in Paris. Paris intellectuals campaign for his freedom.
1936	Serge is released from Orenburg and simultaneously deprived of Soviet citizenship. His manuscripts are confiscated and his is expelled from the USSR. He settles first in Brussels, then in Paris. His return to Europe is accompanied by a slander campaign in the Communist press.
1937	*From Lenin to Stalin* and *Destiny of a Revolution* appear in which Serge analyses the Stalinist counter-revolution. He is elected a councilor to the Spanish POUM (Independent Marxist Party) and campaigns against the Moscow trials.
1940	Serge leaves Paris just as the Nazis advance. In Marseilles, he struggles for months to obtain a visa. Finally finds refuge in Mexico.
1940–1947	Serge lives in isolation and poverty. Writes *The Case of Comrade Tulayev* and *Memoirs of a Revolutionary* for his "desk drawer," since publication was impossible.
1947	November 17: Serge dies and is buried as a "Spanish Republican" in the French section of the Mexico City cemetery.

Victor Serge (1890–1947) was born to Russian anti-Tsarist exiles living in Brussels. As a young anarchist firebrand, he was sentenced to five years in a French penitentiary in 1912. In 1919, Serge joined the Bolsheviks. An outspoken critic of Stalin, he was expelled from the Party and arrested in 1929. Nonetheless, he managed to complete three novels (*Men in Prison, Birth of Our Power,* and *Conquered City*) and a history (*Year One of the Russian Revolution*), published in Paris. Arrested again in Russia and deported to Central Asia in 1933, he was allowed to leave the USSR in 1936 after international protests by militants and prominent writers such as André Gide and Romain Rolland. Hounded by Stalinist agents, Serge lived in precarious exile in Brussels, Paris, Vichy France, and Mexico City, where he died in 1947.

Richard Greeman has translated and written the introductions for five of Victor Serge's novels. Cofounder of the Praxis Center and Victor Serge Library in Moscow, Greeman is the author of *Beware of Vegetarian Sharks: Radical Rants and Internationalist Essays.*

ABOUT PM PRESS

PM Press was founded at the end of 2007
by a small collection of folks with decades of
publishing, media, and organizing experience.
PM Press co-conspirators have published and
distributed hundreds of books, pamphlets,
CDs, and DVDs. Members of PM have founded enduring book fairs,
spearheaded victorious tenant organizing campaigns, and worked closely
with bookstores, academic conferences, and even rock bands to deliver
political and challenging ideas to all walks of life. We're old enough to
know what we're doing and young enough to know what's at stake.

We seek to create radical and stimulating fiction and non-fiction books,
pamphlets, T-shirts, visual and audio materials to entertain, educate
and inspire you. We aim to distribute these through every available
channel with every available technology—whether that means you are
seeing anarchist classics at our bookfair stalls; reading our latest vegan
cookbook at the café; downloading geeky fiction e-books; or digging new
music and timely videos from our website.

PM Press is always on the lookout for talented and skilled volunteers,
artists, activists and writers to work with. If you have a great idea for a
project or can contribute in some way, please get in touch.

PM Press
PO Box 23912
Oakland, CA 94623
www.pmpress.org

FRIENDS OF PM PRESS

These are indisputably momentous times—the financial system is melting down globally and the Empire is stumbling. Now more than ever there is a vital need for radical ideas.

In the seven years since its founding—and on a mere shoestring—PM Press has risen to the formidable challenge of publishing and distributing knowledge and entertainment for the struggles ahead. With over 250 releases to date, we have published an impressive and stimulating array of literature, art, music, politics, and culture. Using every available medium, we've succeeded in connecting those hungry for ideas and information to those putting them into practice.

Friends of PM allows you to directly help impact, amplify, and revitalize the discourse and actions of radical writers, filmmakers, and artists. It provides us with a stable foundation from which we can build upon our early successes and provides a much-needed subsidy for the materials that can't necessarily pay their own way. You can help make that happen—and receive every new title automatically delivered to your door once a month—by joining as a Friend of PM Press. And, we'll throw in a free T-shirt when you sign up.

Here are your options:

- **$30 a month** Get all books and pamphlets plus 50% discount on all webstore purchases

- **$40 a month** Get all PM Press releases (including CDs and DVDs) plus 50% discount on all webstore purchases

- **$100 a month** Superstar—Everything plus PM merchandise, free downloads, and 50% discount on all webstore purchases

For those who can't afford $30 or more a month, we're introducing **Sustainer Rates** at $15, $10 and $5. Sustainers get a free PM Press T-shirt and a 50% discount on all purchases from our website.

Your Visa or Mastercard will be billed once a month, until you tell us to stop. Or until our efforts succeed in bringing the revolution around. Or the financial meltdown of Capital makes plastic redundant. Whichever comes first.

Also from SPECTRE CLASSICS from PM Press

Men in Prison

Victor Serge
Introduction and Translation by
Richard Greeman

ISBN: 978-1-60486-736-7
$18.95   232 pages

"Everything in this book is fictional and
everything is true," wrote Victor Serge in the
epigraph to *Men in Prison*. "I have attempted,
through literary creation, to bring out the
general meaning and human content of a
personal experience."

The author of *Men in Prison* served five years in French penitentiaries
(1912–1917) for the crime of "criminal association"—in fact for his
courageous refusal to testify against his old comrades, the infamous
"Tragic Bandits" of French anarchism. "While I was still in prison," Serge
later recalled, "fighting off tuberculosis, insanity, depression, the spiritual
poverty of the men, the brutality of the regulations, I already saw one
kind of justification of that infernal voyage in the possibility of describing
it. Among the thousands who suffer and are crushed in prison—and how
few men really know that prison!—I was perhaps the only one who could
try one day to tell all . . . There is no novelist's hero in this novel, unless
that terrible machine, prison, is its real hero. It is not about 'me,' about a
few men, but about men, all men crushed in that dark corner of society."

Ironically, Serge returned to writing upon his release from a GPU prison
in Soviet Russia, where he was arrested as an anti-Stalinist subversive
in 1928. He completed *Men in Prison* (and two other novels) in "semi-
captivity" before he was rearrested and deported to the Gulag in 1933.
Serge's classic prison novel has been compared to Dostoyevsky's *House
of the Dead*, Koestler's *Spanish Testament*, Genet's *Miracle of the Rose*,
and Solzhenitsyn's *One Day in the Life of Ivan Denisovitch* both for its
authenticity and its artistic achievement.

This edition features a substantial new introduction by translator Richard
Greeman, situating the work in Serge's life and times.

"No purer book about the hell of prison has ever been written."
—Martin Seymour-Smith, *Scotsman*

"There is nothing in any line or word of this fine novel which doesn't ring true."
—*Publishers Weekly*

Anarchists Never Surrender: Essays, Polemics, and Correspondence on Anarchism, 1908-1938

Victor Serge

ISBN: 978-1-62963-031-1
$20.00   304 pages

Anarchists Never Surrender provides a complete picture of Victor Serge's relationship to anarchist action and doctrine. The volume contains writings going back to his teenage years in Brussels, when he was already developing a doctrine of individualist anarchism. The heart of the anthology is the key articles written during his subsequent period in Paris, when he was a writer and then an editor of the newspaper *l'anarchie*. In these articles we see the continuing development of his thought, including most crucially his point of view concerning the futility of mass action and in support of the doctrine of illegalism. All of this led, of course, to his involvement with the Bonnot Gang.

His thought slowly but most definitely evolved during the period of his imprisonment for his association with Bonnot and his comrades. The anthology includes both his correspondence with his comrade Émile Armand and articles written immediately after his release from prison, among them the key letters that signify the beginning of his break with his individualist past and that point the way to his later engagement alongside the Bolsheviks. It also includes an essential article on Nietzschean thought. This collection also includes articles that Serge wrote after he had left anarchism behind, analyzing both the history and the state of anarchism and the ways in which he hoped anarchism would leaven the harshness and dictatorial tendencies of Bolshevism.

Anarchists Never Surrender anthologizes a variety of Serge texts nowhere previously available and fleshes out the portrait of this brilliant writer and thinker, who has reached new heights of popularity and interest.

"Serge is not merely a political writer; he is also a novelist, a wonderfully lyrical writer... He is a writer young rebels desperately need whether they know it or not... He does not tell us what we should feel; instead, he makes us feel it."
—Stanley Reynolds, *New Statesman*

"I can't think of anyone else who has written about the revolutionary movement in this century with Serge's combination of moral insight and intellectual richness."
—Dwight Macdonald

Also from SPECTRE CLASSICS from PM Press

William Morris: Romantic to Revolutionary

E. P. Thompson

ISBN: 978-1-60486-243-0

$32.95   880 pages

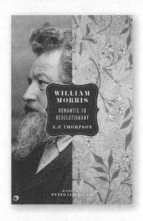

William Morris—the great 19th-century craftsman, architect, designer, poet and writer—remains a monumental figure whose influence resonates powerfully today. As an intellectual (and author of the seminal utopian *News from Nowhere*), his concern with artistic and human values led him to cross what he called the "river of fire" and become a committed socialist—committed not to some theoretical formula but to the day-by-day struggle of working women and men in Britain and to the evolution of his ideas about art, about work and about how life should be lived. Many of his ideas accorded none too well with the reforming tendencies dominant in the Labour movement, nor with those of "orthodox" Marxism, which has looked elsewhere for inspiration. Both sides have been inclined to venerate Morris rather than to pay attention to what he said. Originally written less than a decade before his groundbreaking *The Making of the English Working Class*, E. P. Thompson brought to this biography his now trademark historical mastery, passion, wit, and essential sympathy. It remains unsurpassed as the definitive work on this remarkable figure, by the major British historian of the 20th century.

"Two impressive figures, William Morris as subject and E. P. Thompson as author, are conjoined in this immense biographical-historical-critical study, and both of them have gained in stature since the first edition of the book was published... The book that was ignored in 1955 has meanwhile become something of an underground classic—almost impossible to locate in second-hand bookstores, pored over in libraries, required reading for anyone interested in Morris and, increasingly, for anyone interested in one of the most important of contemporary British historians... Thompson has the distinguishing characteristic of a great historian: he has transformed the nature of the past, it will never look the same again; and whoever works in the area of his concerns in the future must come to terms with what Thompson has written. So too with his study of William Morris."
—Peter Stansky, *The New York Times Book Review*

"An absorbing biographical study... A glittering quarry of marvelous quotes from Morris and others, many taken from heretofore inaccessible or unpublished sources."
—Walter Arnold, *Saturday Review*

Also from ■SPECTRE▶ from PM Press

Catastrophism: The Apocalyptic Politics of Collapse and Rebirth

Sasha Lilley, David McNally, Eddie Yuen, and James Davis, with a foreword by Doug Henwood

ISBN: 978-1-60486-589-9
$16.00   192 pages

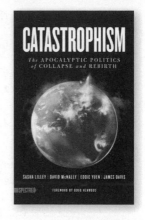

We live in catastrophic times. The world is reeling from the deepest economic crisis since the Great Depression, with the threat of further meltdowns ever-looming. Global warming and myriad dire ecological disasters worsen—with little if any action to halt them—their effects rippling across the planet in the shape of almost biblical floods, fires, droughts, and hurricanes. Governments warn that no alternative exists than to take the bitter medicine they prescribe—or risk devastating financial or social collapse. The right, whether religious or secular, views the present as catastrophic and wants to turn the clock back. The left fears for the worst, but hopes some good will emerge from the rubble. Visions of the apocalypse and predictions of impending doom abound. Across the political spectrum, a culture of fear reigns.

Catastrophism explores the politics of apocalypse—on the left and right, in the environmental movement, and from capital and the state—and examines why the lens of catastrophe can distort our understanding of the dynamics at the heart of these numerous disasters—and fatally impede our ability to transform the world. Lilley, McNally, Yuen, and Davis probe the reasons why catastrophic thinking is so prevalent, and challenge the belief that it is only out of the ashes that a better society may be born. The authors argue that those who care about social justice and the environment should eschew the Pandora's box of fear—even as it relates to indisputably apocalyptic climate change. Far from calling people to arms, they suggest, catastrophic fear often results in passivity and paralysis—and, at worst, reactionary politics.

"This groundbreaking book examines a deep current—on both the left and right—of apocalyptical thought and action. The authors explore the origins, uses, and consequences of the idea that collapse might usher in a better world. Catastrophism is a crucial guide to understanding our tumultuous times, while steering us away from the pitfalls of the past."
—Barbara Epstein, author of *Political Protest and Cultural Revolution: Nonviolent Direct Action in the 1970s and 1980s*

Also from ■SPECTRE▶ from PM Press

Stop, Thief!
The Commons, Enclosures, and Resistance

Peter Linebaugh

ISBN: 978-1-60486-747-3

$21.95   304 pages

In this majestic tour de force, celebrated historian Peter Linebaugh takes aim at the thieves of land, the polluters of the seas, the ravagers of the forests, the despoilers of rivers, and the removers of mountaintops. Scarcely a society has existed on the face of the earth that has not had commoning at its heart. "Neither the state nor the market," say the planetary commoners. These essays kindle the embers of memory to ignite our future commons.

From Thomas Paine to the Luddites, from Karl Marx—who concluded his great study of capitalism with the enclosure of commons—to the practical dreamer William Morris—who made communism into a verb and advocated communizing industry and agriculture—to the 20th-century communist historian E.P. Thompson, Linebaugh brings to life the vital commonist tradition. He traces the red thread from the great revolt of commoners in 1381 to the enclosures of Ireland, and the American commons, where European immigrants who had been expelled from their commons met the immense commons of the native peoples and the underground African-American urban commons. Illuminating these struggles in this indispensable collection, Linebaugh reignites the ancient cry, "STOP, THIEF!"

"There is not a more important historian living today. Period."
—Robin D.G. Kelley, author of *Freedom Dreams: The Black Radical Imagination*

"E.P. Thompson, you may rest now. Linebaugh restores the dignity of the despised luddites with a poetic grace worthy of the master... [A] commonist manifesto for the 21st century."
—Mike Davis, author of *Planet of Slums*

"Peter Linebaugh's great act of historical imagination... takes the cliché of 'globalization' and makes it live. The local and the global are once again shown to be inseparable—as they are, at present, for the machine-breakers of the new world crisis."
—T.J. Clark, author of *Farewell to an Idea*

Also from ■SPECTRE▶ from PM Press

Capital and Its Discontents: Conversations with Radical Thinkers in a Time of Tumult

Sasha Lilley

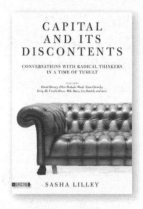

ISBN: 978-1-60486-334-5
$20.00   320 pages

Capitalism is stumbling, empire is faltering, and the planet is thawing. Yet many people are still grasping to understand these multiple crises and to find a way forward to a just future. Into the breach come the essential insights of *Capital and Its Discontents*, which cut through the gristle to get to the heart of the matter about the nature of capitalism and imperialism, capitalism's vulnerabilities at this conjuncture—and what can we do to hasten its demise. Through a series of incisive conversations with some of the most eminent thinkers and political economists on the Left—including David Harvey, Ellen Meiksins Wood, Mike Davis, Leo Panitch, Tariq Ali, and Noam Chomsky—*Capital and Its Discontents* illuminates the dynamic contradictions undergirding capitalism and the potential for its dethroning. At a moment when capitalism as a system is more reviled than ever, here is an indispensable toolbox of ideas for action by some of the most brilliant thinkers of our times.

"These conversations illuminate the current world situation in ways that are very useful for those hoping to orient themselves and find a way forward to effective individual and collective action. Highly recommended."
—Kim Stanley Robinson, *New York Times* bestselling author of the *Mars Trilogy* and *The Years of Rice and Salt*

"In this fine set of interviews, an A-list of radical political economists demonstrate why their skills are indispensable to understanding today's multiple economic and ecological crises."
—Raj Patel, author of *Stuffed and Starved* and *The Value of Nothing*

"This is an extremely important book. It is the most detailed, comprehensive, and best study yet published on the most recent capitalist crisis and its discontents. Sasha Lilley sets each interview in its context, writing with style, scholarship, and wit about ideas and philosophies."
—Andrej Grubačić, radical sociologist and social critic, co-author of *Wobblies and Zapatistas*

Also from ■SPECTRE▶ from PM Press

Global Slump: The Economics and Politics of Crisis and Resistance

David McNally

ISBN: 978-1-60486-332-1

$15.95   176 pages

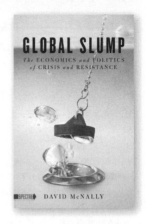

Global Slump analyzes the world financial meltdown as the first systemic crisis of the neoliberal stage of capitalism. It argues that— far from having ended—the crisis has ushered in a whole period of worldwide economic and political turbulence. In developing an account of the crisis as rooted in fundamental features of capitalism, *Global Slump* challenges the view that its source lies in financial deregulation. It offers an original account of the "financialization" of the world economy and explores the connections between international financial markets and new forms of debt and dispossession, particularly in the Global South. The book shows that, while averting a complete meltdown, the massive intervention by central banks laid the basis for recurring crises for poor and working class people. It traces new patterns of social resistance for building an anti-capitalist opposition to the damage that neoliberal capitalism is inflicting on the lives of millions.

"In this book, McNally confirms—once again—his standing as one of the world's leading Marxist scholars of capitalism. For a scholarly, in depth analysis of our current crisis that never loses sight of its political implications (for them and for us), expressed in a language that leaves no reader behind, there is simply no better place to go."
—Bertell Ollman, professor, Department of Politics, NYU, and author of *Dance of the Dialectic: Steps in Marx's Method*

"David McNally's tremendously timely book is packed with significant theoretical and practical insights, and offers actually-existing examples of what is to be done. Global Slump *urgently details how changes in the capitalist space-economy over the past 25 years, especially in the forms that money takes, have expanded wide-scale vulnerabilities for all kinds of people, and how people fight back. In a word, the problem isn't neo-liberalism—it's capitalism."*
—Ruth Wilson Gilmore, University of Southern California and author, *Golden Gulag: Prisons, Surplus, Crisis, and Opposition in Globalizing California*

Also from ■SPECTRE▶ from PM Press

In and Out of Crisis: The Global Financial Meltdown and Left Alternatives

Greg Albo, Sam Gindin, Leo Panitch

ISBN: 978-1-60486-212-6
$13.95   144 pages

While many around the globe are increasingly wondering if another world is indeed possible, few are mapping out potential avenues—and flagging wrong turns—en route to a post-capitalist future. In this groundbreaking analysis of the meltdown, renowned radical political economists Albo, Gindin, and Panitch lay bare the roots of the crisis, which they locate in the dynamic expansion of capital on a global scale over the last quarter century—and in the inner logic of capitalism itself.

With an unparalleled understanding of the inner workings of capitalism, the authors of *In and Out of Crisis* provocatively challenge the call by much of the Left for a return to a largely mythical Golden Age of economic regulation as a check on finance capital unbound. They deftly illuminate how the era of neoliberal free markets has been, in practice, undergirded by state intervention on a massive scale. In conclusion, the authors argue that it's time to start thinking about genuinely transformative alternatives to capitalism—and how to build the collective capacity to get us there. *In and Out of Crisis* stands to be the enduring critique of the crisis and an indispensable springboard for a renewed Left.

"Once again, Panitch, Gindin, and Albo show that they have few rivals and no betters in analyzing the relations between politics and economics, between globalization and American power, between theory and quotidian reality, and between crisis and political possibility. At once sobering and inspiring, this is one of the few pieces of writing that I've seen that's essential to understanding—to paraphrase a term from accounting—the sources and uses of crisis. Splendid and essential."
—Doug Henwood, *Left Business Observer*, author of *After the New Economy* and *Wall Street*

"Mired in political despair? Planning your escape to a more humane continent? Baffled by the economy? Convinced that the Left is out of ideas? Pull yourself together and read this book, in which Albo, Gindin, and Panitch, some of the world's sharpest living political economists, explain the current financial crisis—and how we might begin to make a better world."
—Liza Featherstone, author of *Students Against Sweatshops* and *Selling Women Short: The Landmark Battle for Workers' Rights at Wal-Mart*

Portugal: The Impossible Revolution?

Phil Mailer, with an afterword
by Maurice Brinton

ISBN: 978-1-60486-336-9
$24.95   288 pages

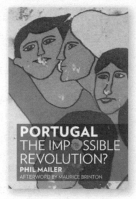

After the military coup in Portugal on April
25, 1974, the overthrow of almost fifty years
of Fascist rule, and the end of three colonial
wars, there followed eighteen months of
intense, democratic social transformation which challenged every aspect
of Portuguese society. What started as a military coup turned into a
profound attempt at social change from the bottom up and became
headlines on a daily basis in the world media. This was due to the
intensity of the struggle as well as the fact that in 1974–75 the moribund,
right-wing Francoist regime was still in power in neighboring Spain and
there was huge uncertainty as to how these struggles might affect Spain
and Europe at large.

This is the story of what happened in Portugal between April 25, 1974,
and November 25, 1975, as seen and felt by a deeply committed
participant. It depicts the hopes, the tremendous enthusiasm, the
boundless energy, the total commitment, the released power, even the
revolutionary innocence of thousands of ordinary people taking a hand in
the remolding of their lives. And it does so against the background of an
economic and social reality which placed limits on what could be done.

*"An evocative, bitterly partisan diary of the Portuguese revolution, written from a
radical-utopian perspective. The enemy is any type of organization or presumption
of leadership. The book affords a good view of the mood of the time, of the
multiplicity of leftist factions, and of the social problems that bedeviled the
revolution."*
—Fritz Stern, *Foreign Affairs*

*"Mailer portrays history with the enthusiasm of a cheerleader, the 'home team' in
this case being libertarian communism. Official documents, position papers and
the pronouncements of the protagonists of this drama are mostly relegated to the
appendices. The text itself recounts the activities of a host of worker, tenant, soldier
and student committees as well as the author's personal experiences."*
—Ian Wallace, *Library Journal*

The CNT in the Spanish Revolution Vols. 1–3

José Peirats
with an introduction by Chris Ealham

Vol. 1 **ISBN: 978-1-60486-207-2**
$28.00   432 pages

Vol. 2 **ISBN: 978-1-60486-208-9**
$22.95   312 pages

Vol. 3 **ISBN: 978-1-60486-209-6**
$22.95   296 pages

The CNT in the Spanish Revolution is the history
of one of the most original and audacious, and
arguably also the most far-reaching, of all the
twentieth-century revolutions. It is the history
of the giddy years of political change and hope
in 1930s Spain, when the so-called 'Generation
of '36', Peirats' own generation, rose up against
the oppressive structures of Spanish society.
It is also a history of a revolution that failed,
crushed in the jaws of its enemies on both the
reformist left and the reactionary right. José
Peirats' account is effectively the official CNT
history of the war, passionate, partisan but,
above all, intelligent. Its huge sweeping canvas
covers all areas of the anarchist experience—
the spontaneous militias, the revolutionary
collectives, the moral dilemmas occasioned
by the clash of revolutionary ideals and the
stark reality of the war effort against Franco
and his German Nazi and Italian Fascist allies.
This new edition is carefully indexed in a way
that converts the work into a usable tool for
historians and makes it much easier for the
general reader to dip in with greater purpose
and pleasure.

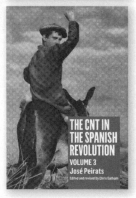

"José Peirats' The CNT in the Spanish Revolution *is a landmark in the
historiography of the Spanish Civil War . . . Originally published in Toulouse in the
early 1950s, it was a rarity anxiously searched for by historians and others who
gleefully pillaged its wealth of documentation. Even its republication in Paris in 1971
by the exiled Spanish publishing house, Ruedo Ibérico, though welcome, still left
the book in the territory of specialists. For that reason alone, the present project to
publish the entire work in English is to be applauded."*
—Professor Paul Preston, London School of Economics

Vida

Marge Piercy

ISBN: 978-1-60486-487-8

$20.00   416 pages

Originally published in 1979, *Vida* is Marge
Piercy's classic bookend to the Sixties.
Vida is full of the pleasures and pains, the
experiments, disasters, and victories of an
extraordinary band of people. At the center
of the novel stands Vida Asch. She has lived
underground for almost a decade. Back in the
'60s she was a political star of the exuberant antiwar movement—a red-
haired beauty photographed for the pages of *Life* magazine—charismatic,
passionate, and totally sure she would prevail. Now, a decade later,
Vida is on the run, her star-quality replaced by stubborn courage. She
comes briefly to rest in a safe house on Cape Cod. To her surprise and
annoyance, she finds another person in the house, a fugitive, Joel, ten
years younger than she, a kid who dropped into the underground out
of the army. As they spend the next days together, Vida finds herself
warming toward a man for the first time in years, knowing all too well the
dangers.

As counterpoint to the underground '70s, Marge Piercy tells the
extraordinary tale of the optimistic '60s, the thousands of people
who were members of SAW (Students Against the War) and of the
handful who formed a fierce group called the Little Red Wagon. Piercy's
characters make vivid and comprehensible the desperation, the courage,
and the blind rage of a time when "action" could appear to some to be a
more rational choice than the vote.

A new introduction by Marge Piercy situates the book, and the author, in
the times from which they emerged.

*"Real people inhabit its pages and real suspense carries the story along… 'Vida' of
course means life and she personifies it."*
—Chicago Tribune

*"A fully controlled, tightly structured dramatic narrative of such artful intensity that
it leads the reader on at almost every page."*
—New York Times Book Review

*"Marge Piercy tells us exactly how it was in the lofts of the Left as the 1960s
turned into the '70s. This is the way everybody sounded. This is the way everybody
behaved. Vida bears witness."*
—New York Times

Cazzarola!: Anarchy, Romani, Love, Italy (A Novel)

Norman Nawrocki

ISBN: 978-1-60486-315-4
$18.00   300 pages

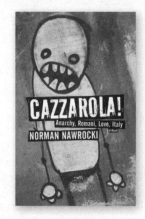

Cazzarola! is a gripping, epic, political, historical, and romantic novel spanning 130 years in the life of the Discordias, a fictional family of Italian anarchists. It details the family's heroic, multigenerational resistance to fascism in Italy and their ongoing involvement in the anarchist movement. From early 20th-century factory strikes and occupations, armed anarchist militias, and attempts on Mussolini's life, to postwar student and labor protest, and confronting the newest wave of contemporary neofascist violence sweeping Europe, the Discordias navigate the decades of political, economic, and social turmoil. Against this historical backdrop, Antonio falls in love with Cinka, a proud but poverty-stricken Romani refugee from the "unwanted people," without a country or home, forced to flee again and again searching for peace. Theirs becomes a life-changing and forbidden relationship. Both are forced to reevaluate their lives and contend with cultural taboos, xenophobia, and the violent persecution of Romani refugees in Italy today.

"Might just be one of my favourite books of all time. I have never read a more delicate portrayal of a Romani woman in my life… I highly recommend to Roma and non-Roma alike. With the rise of neo-Nazi and neofascist groups throughout Europe, this book is definitely timely and a must read. It's a history lesson and a lesson about racism, love, and fighting for what you believe in at all cost."
—Qristina Zavacková Cummings, Romani journalist/activist

"In Romani culture, when enjoying music we don't say, 'Did you hear that?' We say, 'Did you feel that?' I didn't just read Cazzarola! *I felt it. As a Romani woman who has lived in Italy, this very relatable novel often echoed the pages of my own life. Bravo, Ta Aves Baxtalo!"*
—Julia Lovell, Romani activist and filmmaker

*"*Cazzarola! *is a powerful, blunt, epic scream against social injustice."*
—David Lester, author of *The Listener*

"A brilliant title for a brilliant story of love and rage, which the author shares with his characters in every page. Cazzarola! *reads like a film, a sort of Bertolucci's* Novecento *recast in contemporary Italy. Nawrocki skillfully manages to interweave scenes of everyday Italian life and fine psychological analysis in a grandiose historical fresco."*
—Davide Turcato, historian of Italian anarchism, editor of *The Complete Works of Errico Malatesta*